Oddly ★ Normal

WRITTEN & ILLUSTRATED
by OTIS FRAMPTON

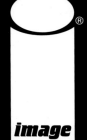

IMAGE COMICS, INC.
Robert Kirkman—Chief Operating Officer
Erik Larsen—Chief Financial Officer
Todd McFarlane—President
Marc Silvestri—Chief Executive Officer
Jim Valentino—Vice-President

Eric Stephenson—Publisher
Corey Murphy—Director of Sales
Jeff Boison—Director of Publishing Planning & Book Trade Sales
Chris Ross—Director of Digital Sales
Kat Salazar—Director of PR & Marketing
Branwyn Bigglestone—Controller
Susan Korpela—Accounts Manager
Drew Gill—Art Director
Brett Warnock—Production Manager
Meredith Wallace—Print Manager
Briah Skelly—Publicist
Aly Hoffman— Conventions & Events Coordinator
Sasha Head—Sales & Marketing Production Designer
David Brothers—Branding Manager
Melissa Gifford—Content Manager
Erika Schnatz—Production Artist
Ryan Brewer—Production Artist
Shanna Matuszak—Production Artist
Tricia Ramos—Production Artist
Vincent Kukua—Production Artist
Jeff Stang—Direct Market Sales Representative
Emilio Bautista—Digital Sales Associate
Leanna Caunter—Accounting Assistant
Chloe Ramos-Peterson—Library Market Sales Representative
IMAGECOMICS.COM

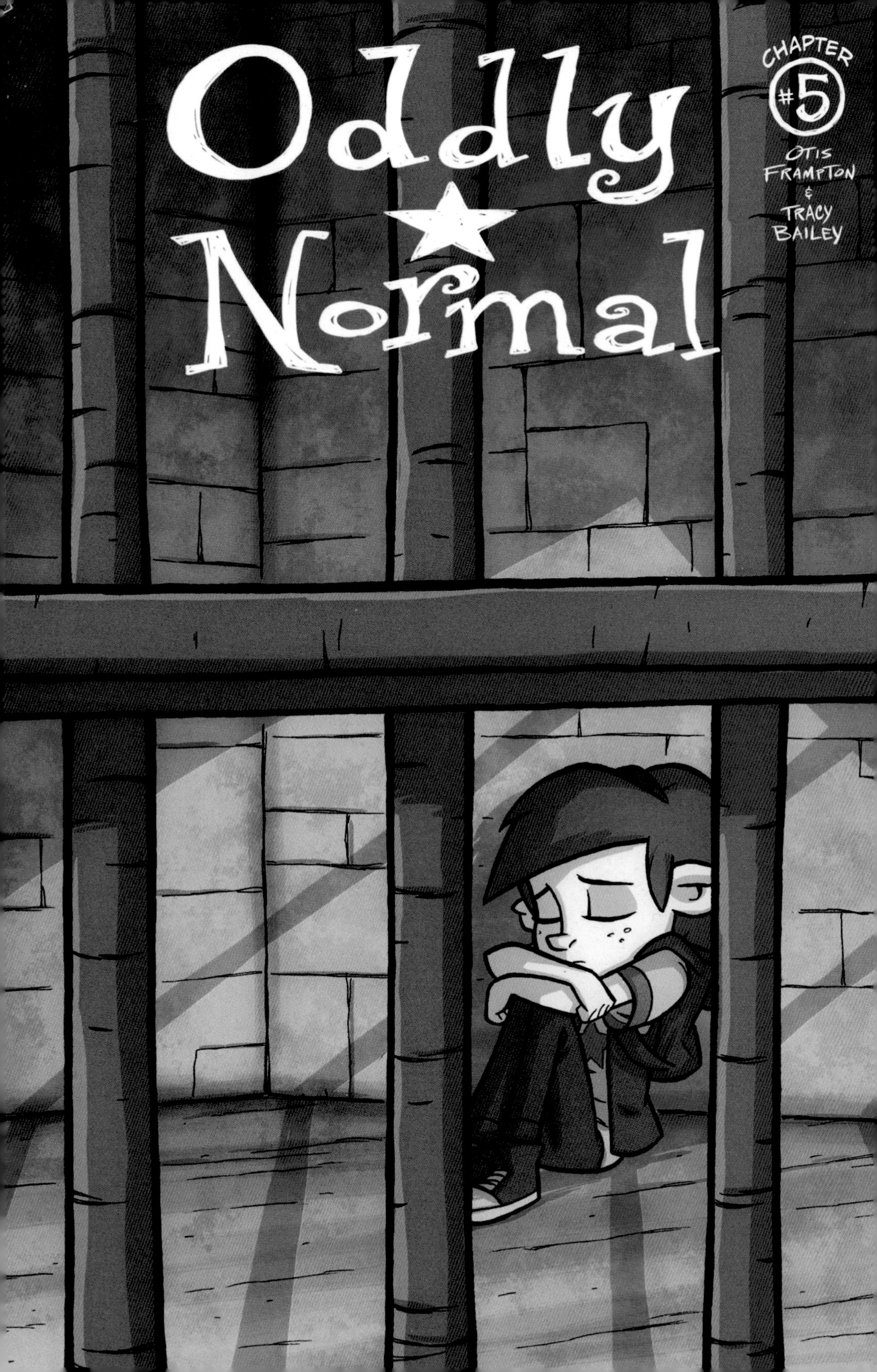

Oddly ★ Normal
CHAPTER #5
OTIS FRAMPTON & TRACY BAILEY

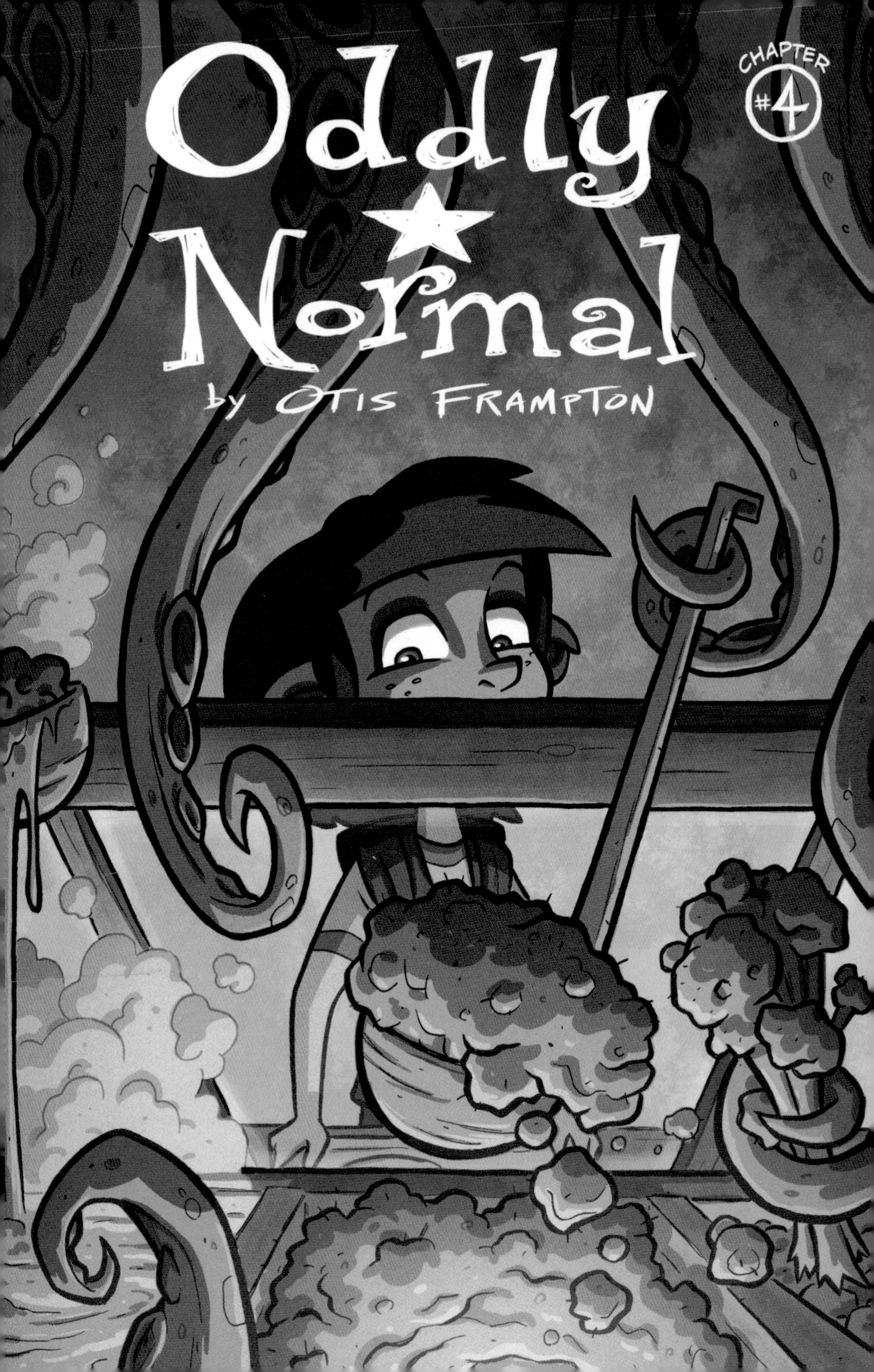
Oddly Normal
by OTIS FRAMPTON
CHAPTER #4

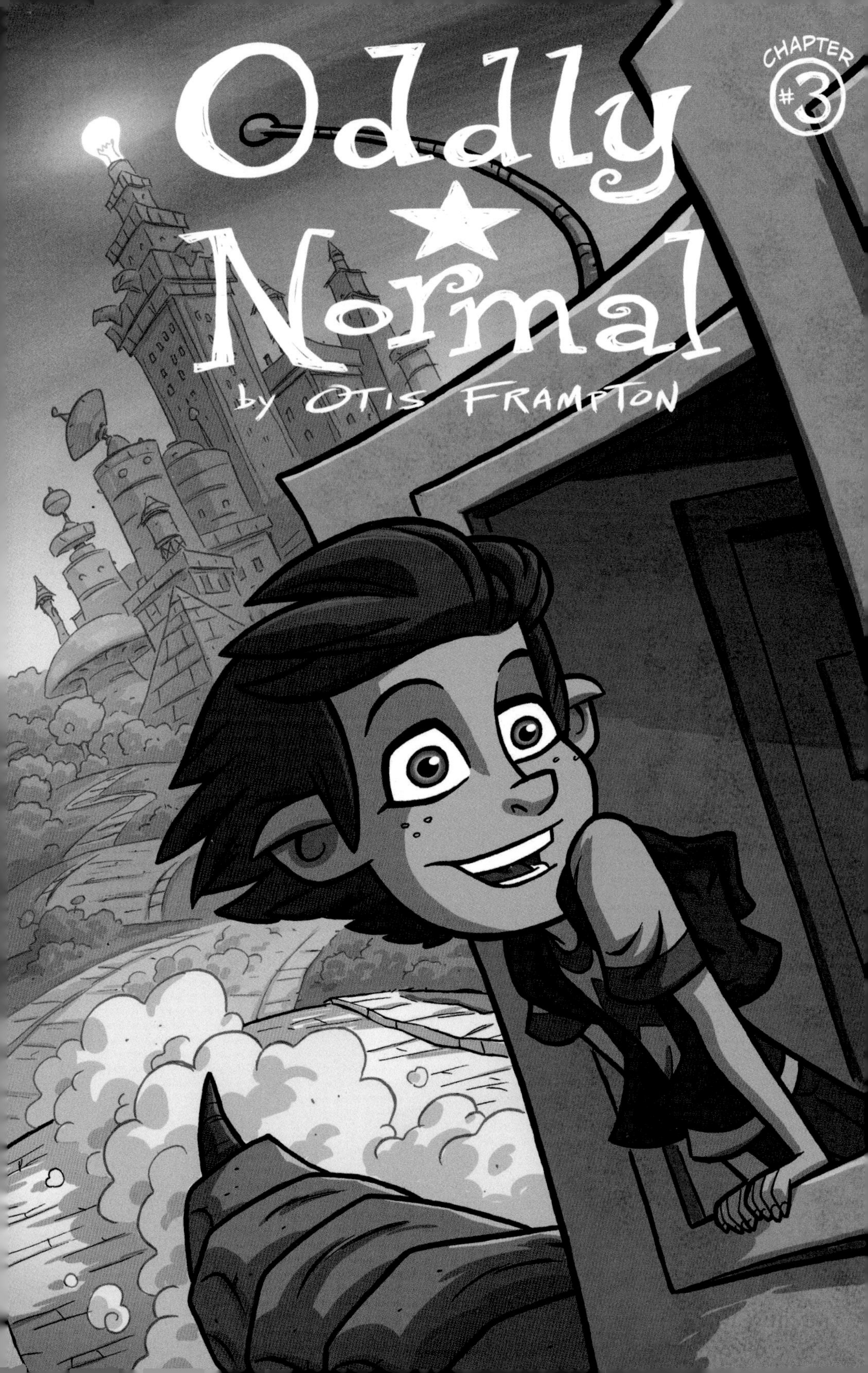
Oddly ★ Normal
by OTIS FRAMPTON
CHAPTER #3

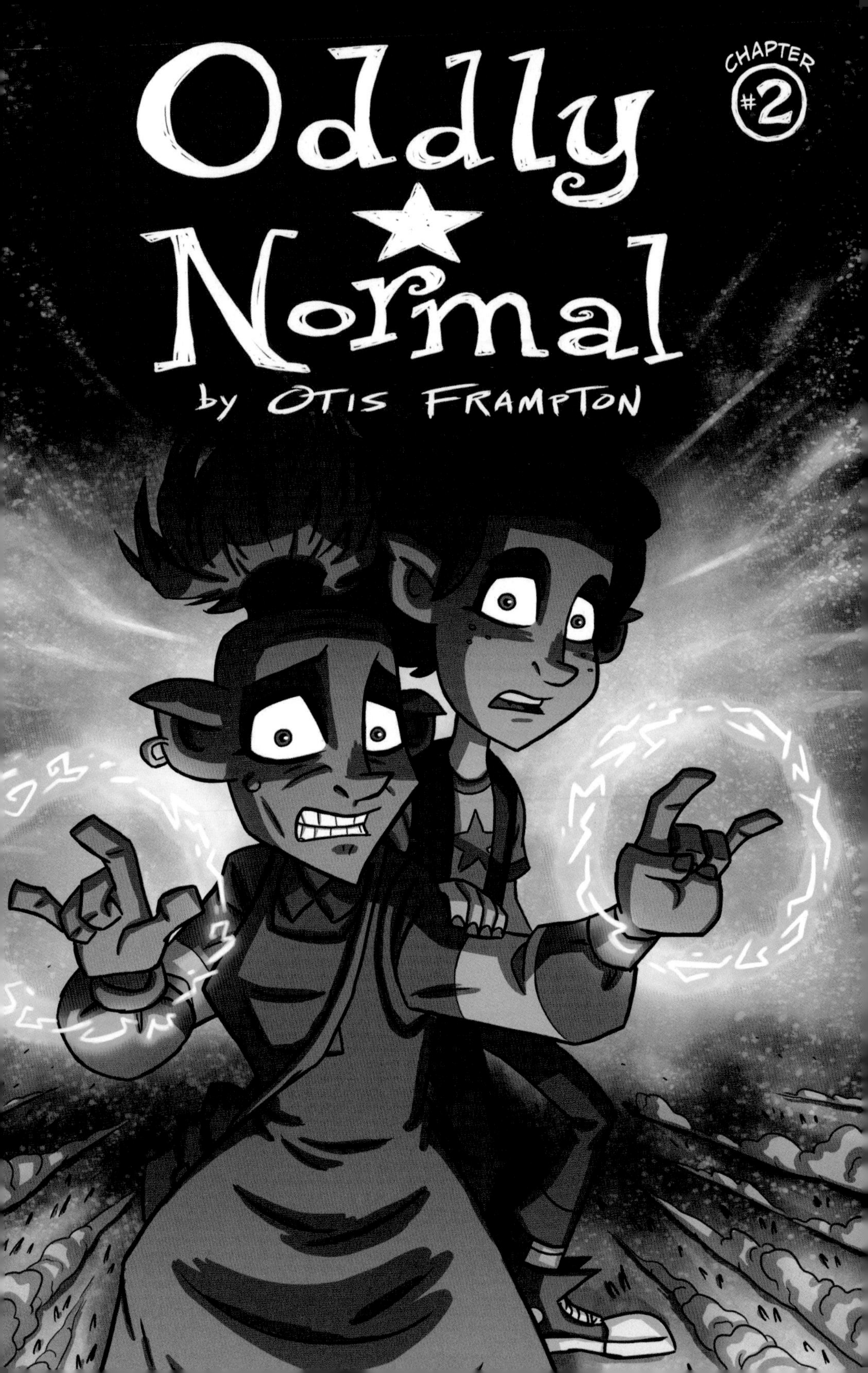
Oddly ★ Normal
CHAPTER #2
by OTIS FRAMPTON

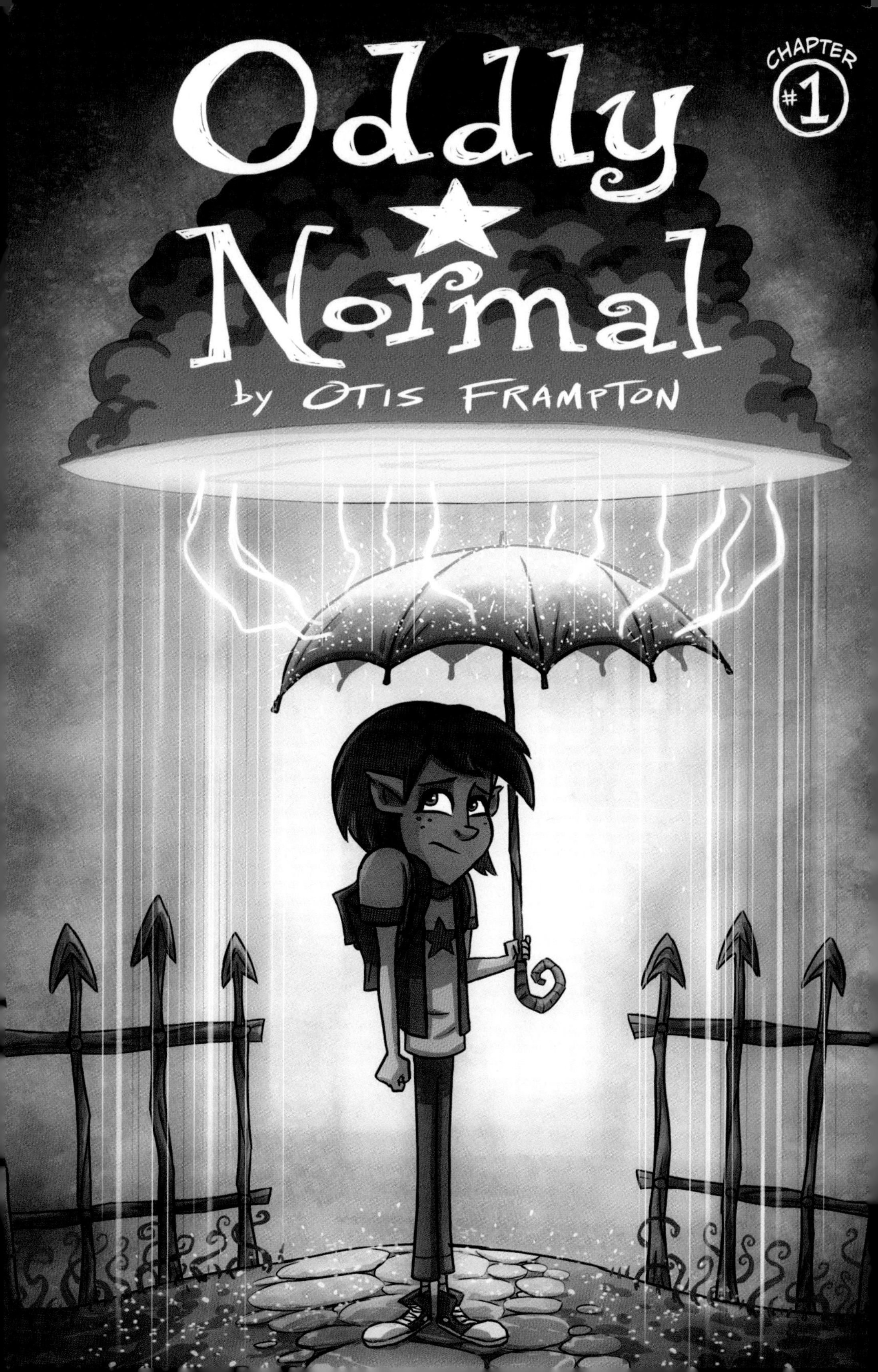
CHAPTER #1
Oddly Normal
by OTIS FRAMPTON

ABOUT THE AUTHOR

Otis Frampton is a comic book writer/artist, freelance illustrator and animator. He is the creator of the webcomic and animated series "ABCDEFGeek." He is also one of the artists on the popular animated web series "How It Should Have Ended."

You can visit Otis on the web at: www.otisframpton.com

Oddly ★ Normal

BOOK ①

WRITTEN, ILLUSTRATED & LETTERED BY
OTIS FRAMPTON

CHAPTERS 1-4 COLORED BY
OTIS FRAMPTON

CHAPTER 5 COLORED BY
OTIS FRAMPTON & TRACY BAILEY

COLOR FLATS BY
DANIEL MEAD, TRACY BAILEY,
OTIS FRAMPTON AND THOMAS BOATWRIGHT

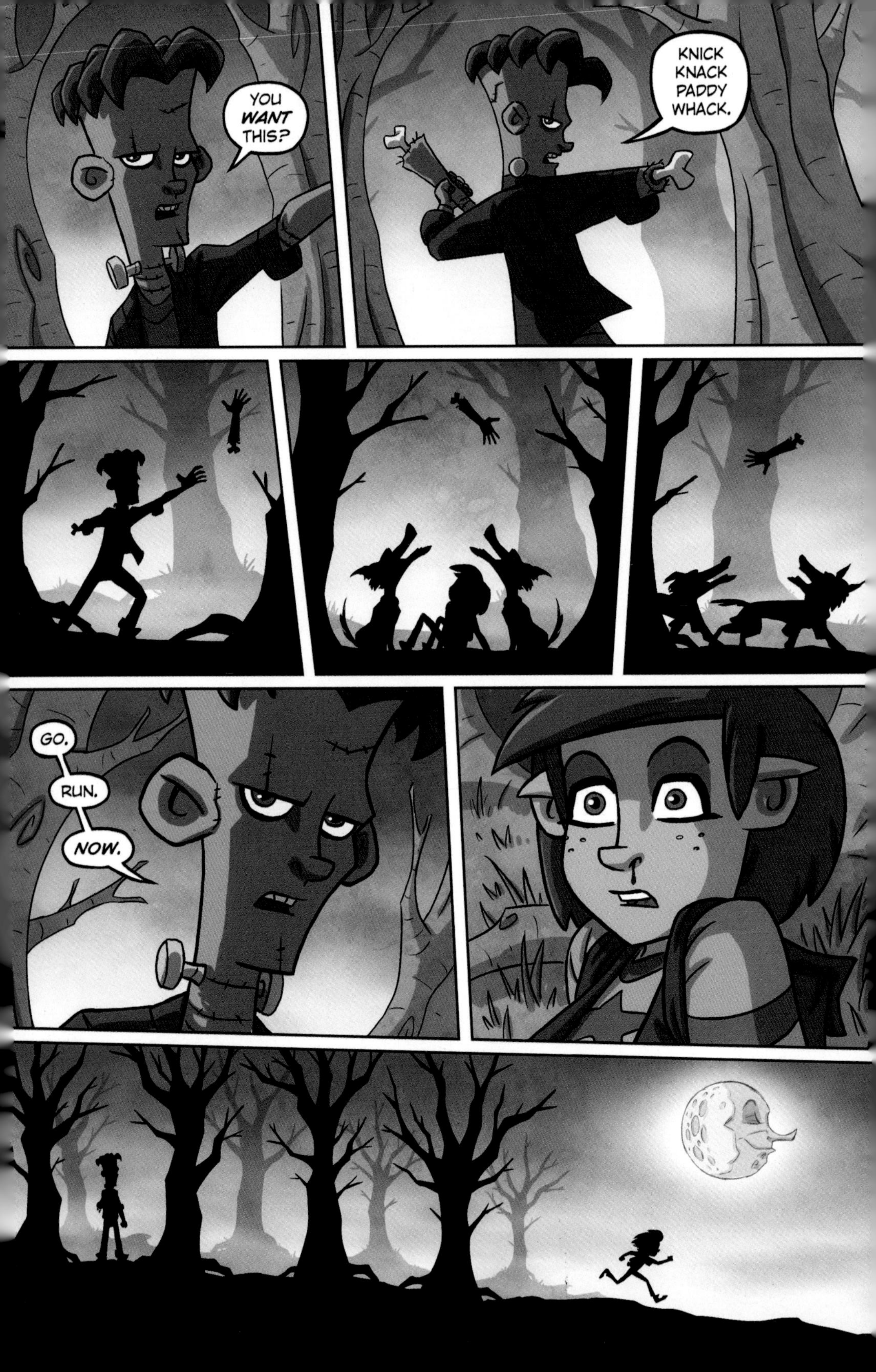
YOU WANT THIS?
KNICK KNACK PADDY WHACK.
GO.
RUN.
NOW.

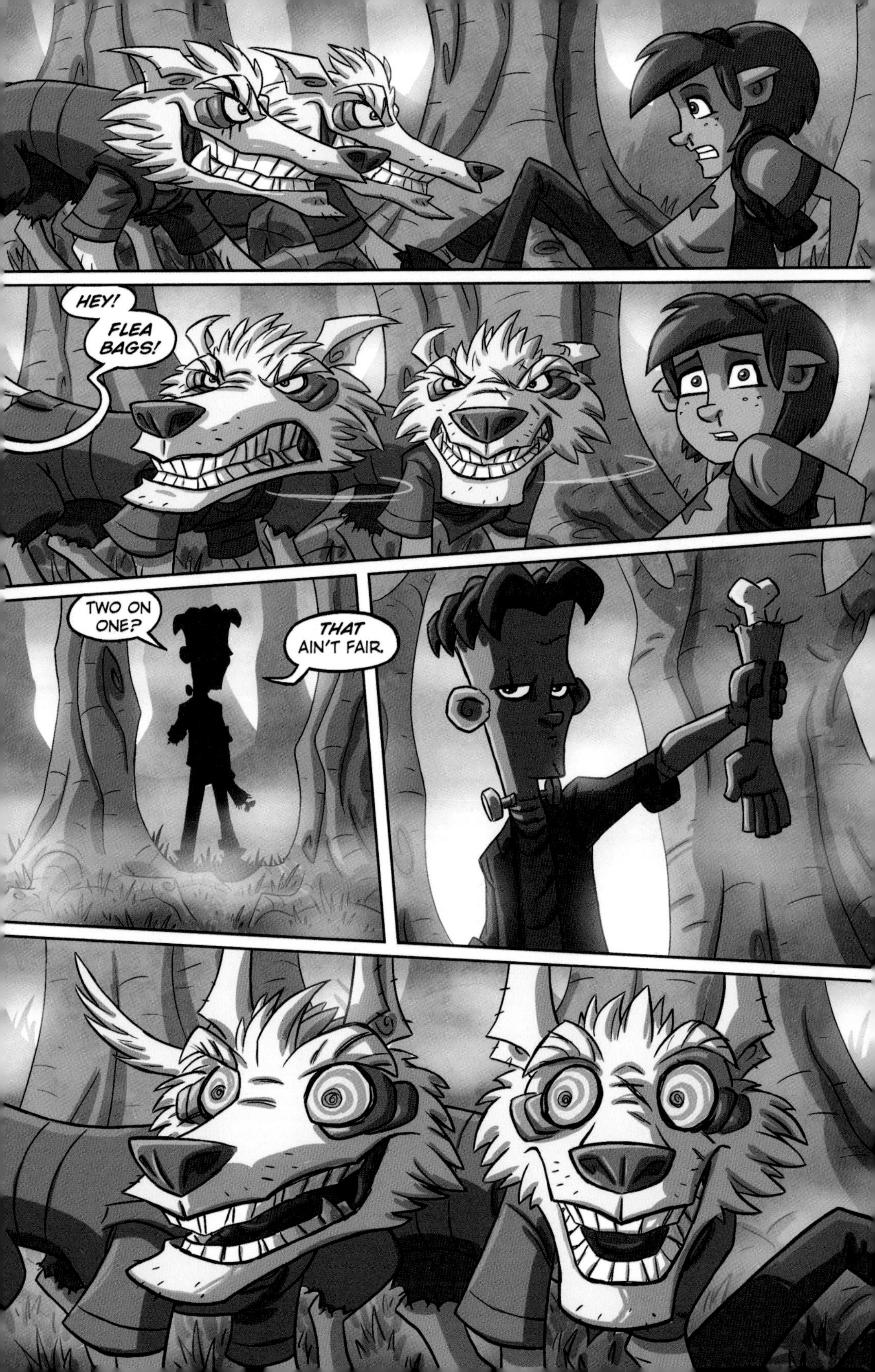
HEY! FLEA BAGS!
TWO ON ONE?
THAT AIN'T FAIR.

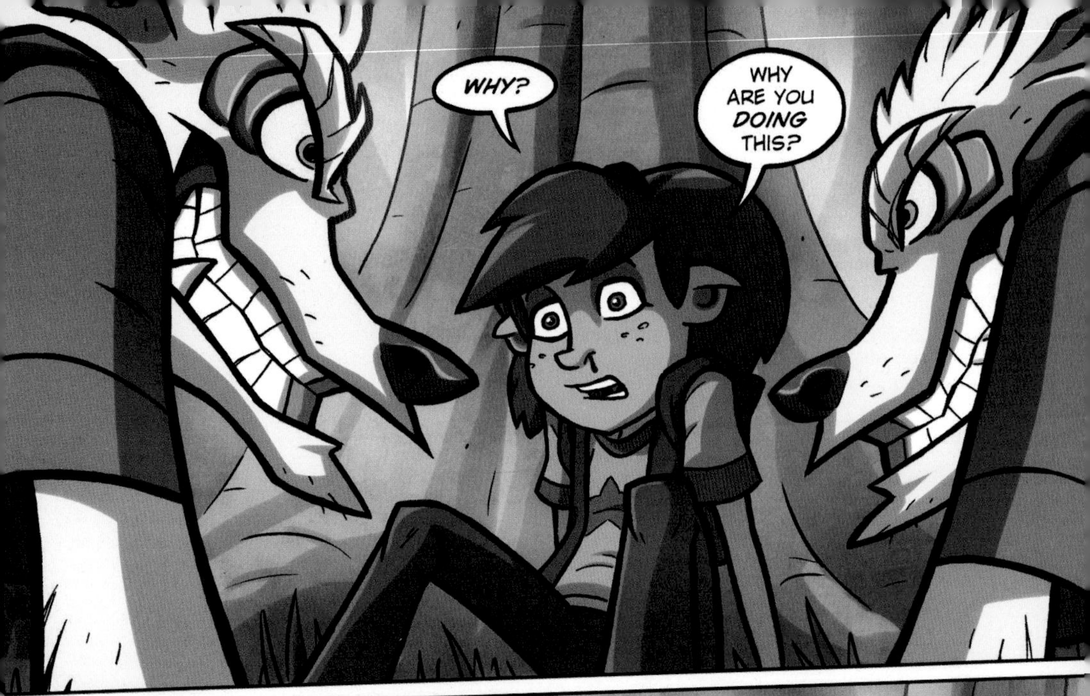
WHY?
WHY ARE YOU *DOING* THIS?

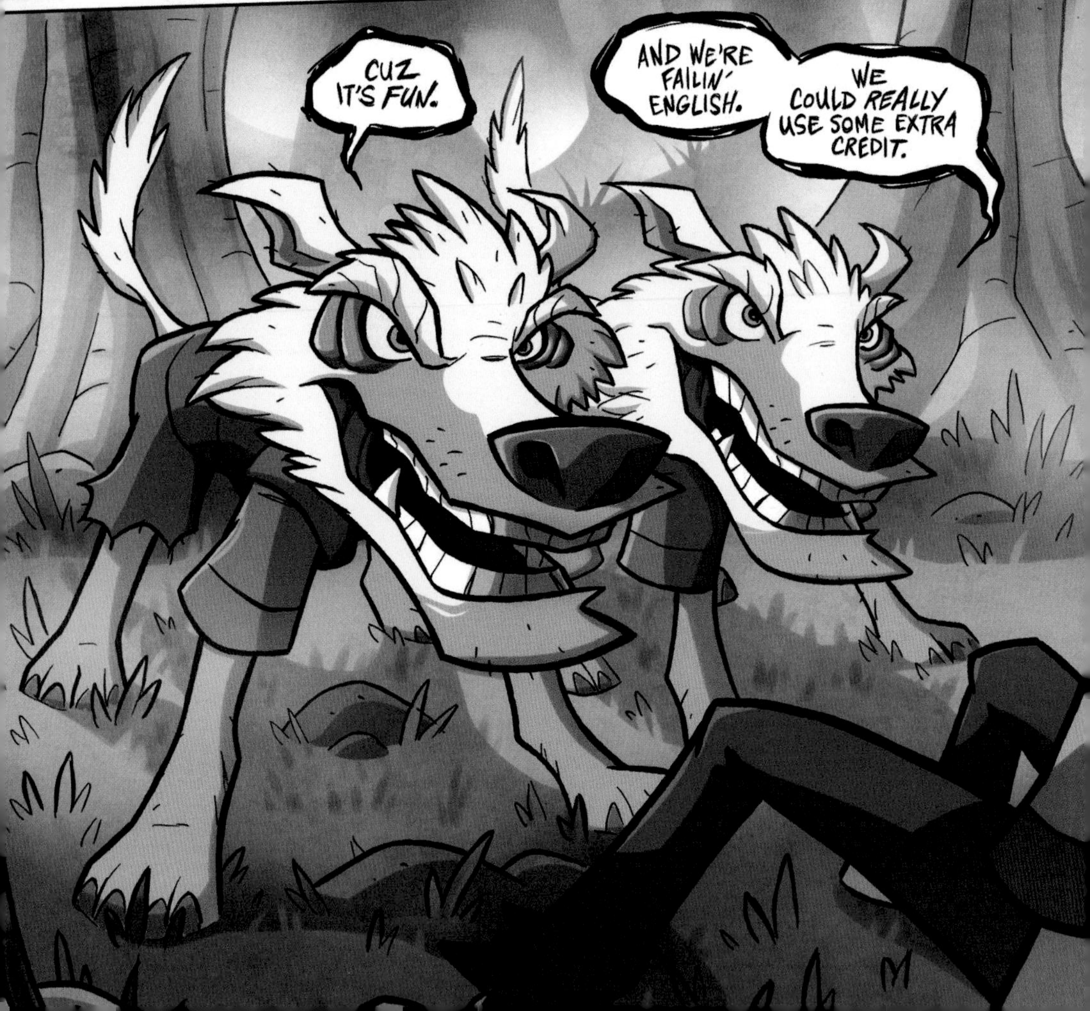
CUZ IT'S *FUN*.
AND WE'RE FAILIN' ENGLISH.
WE COULD *REALLY* USE SOME EXTRA CREDIT.

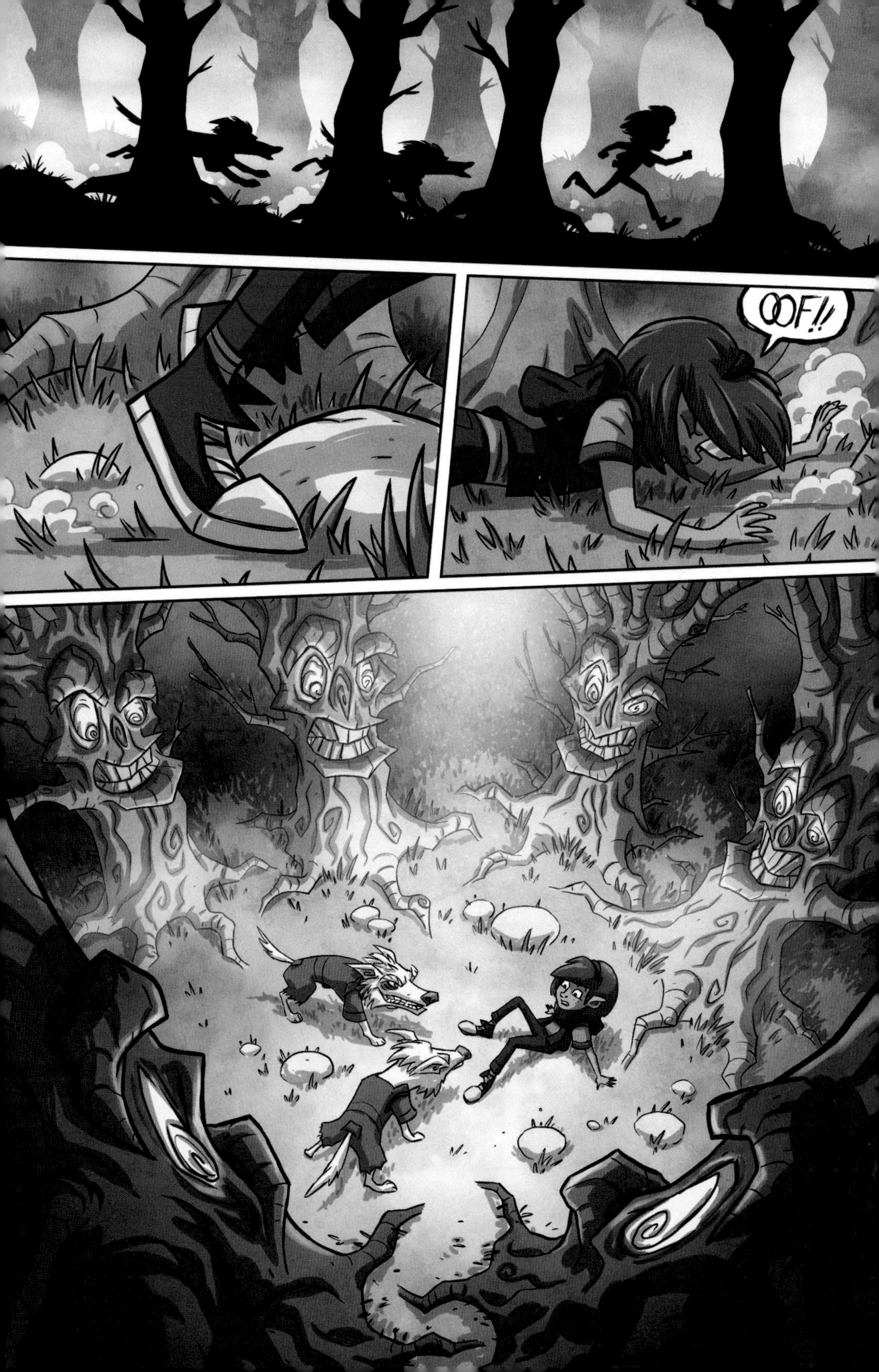
OOF!!

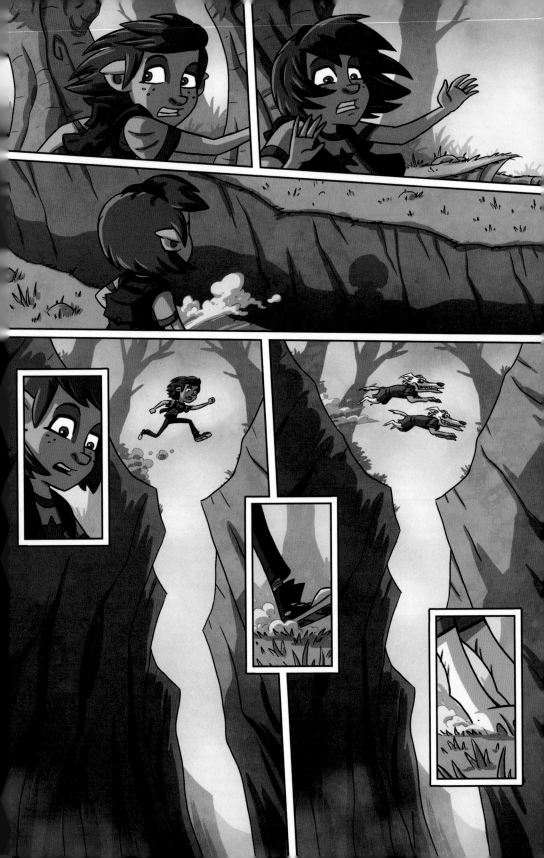

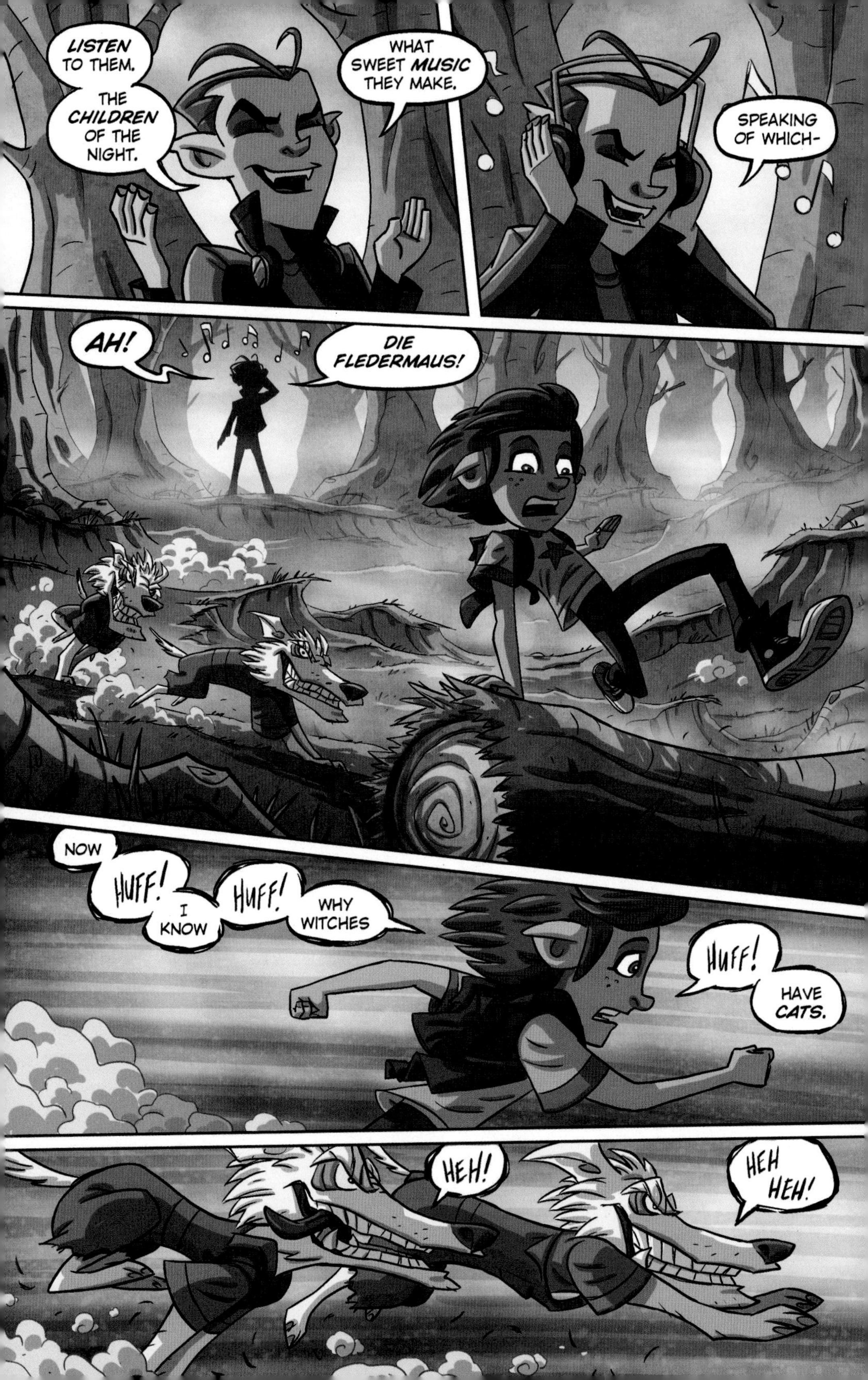
LISTEN TO THEM.
THE CHILDREN OF THE NIGHT.
WHAT SWEET MUSIC THEY MAKE.
SPEAKING OF WHICH-
AH!
DIE FLEDERMAUS!
NOW
HUFF!
I KNOW
HUFF!
WHY WITCHES
HUFF!
HAVE CATS.
HEH!
HEH HEH!

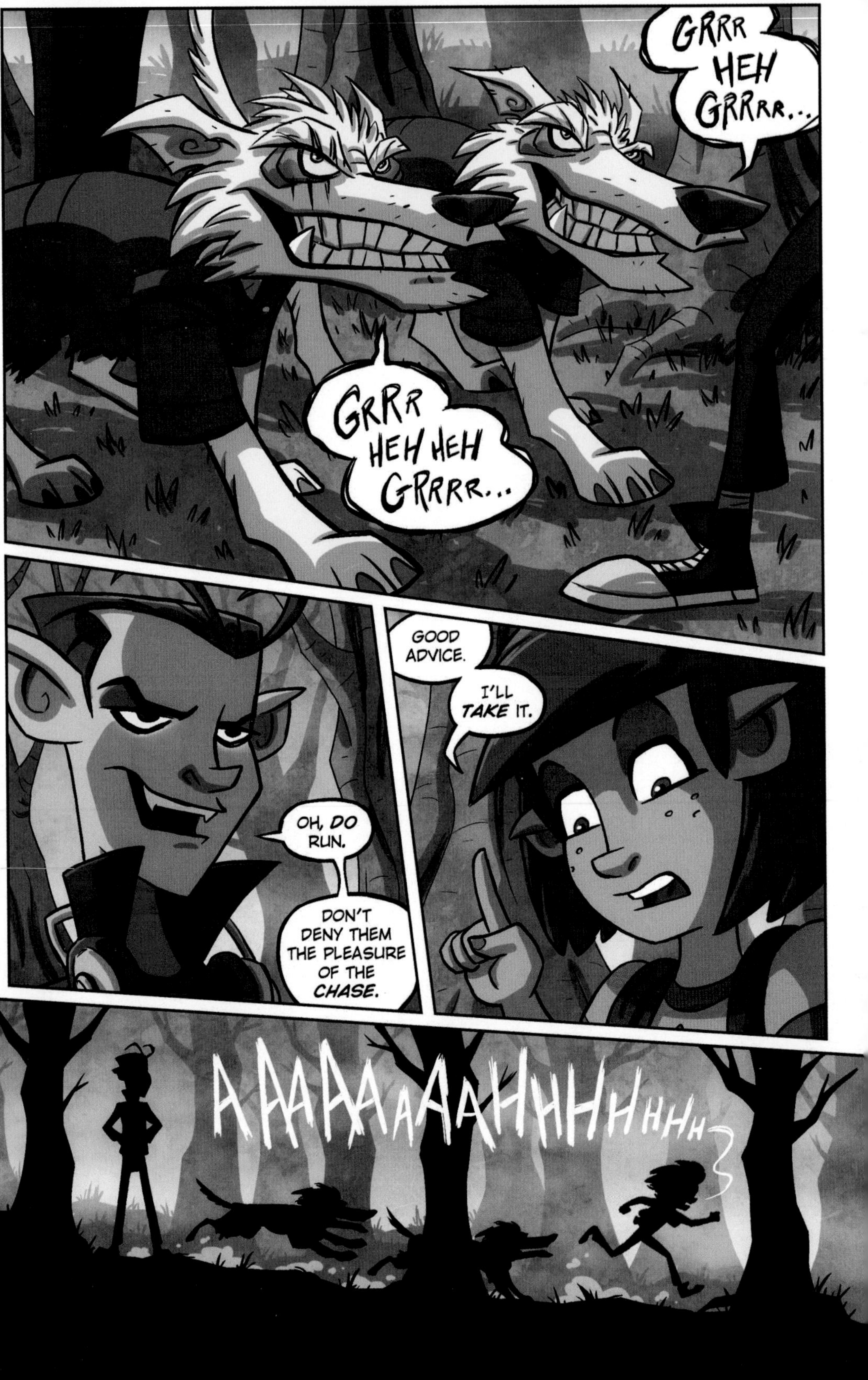
GRRR HEH GRRRR...
GRRR HEH HEH GRRRR...
OH, *DO* RUN.
DON'T DENY THEM THE PLEASURE OF THE *CHASE*.
GOOD ADVICE.
I'LL *TAKE* IT.
AAAAAAAAHHHHHHHH

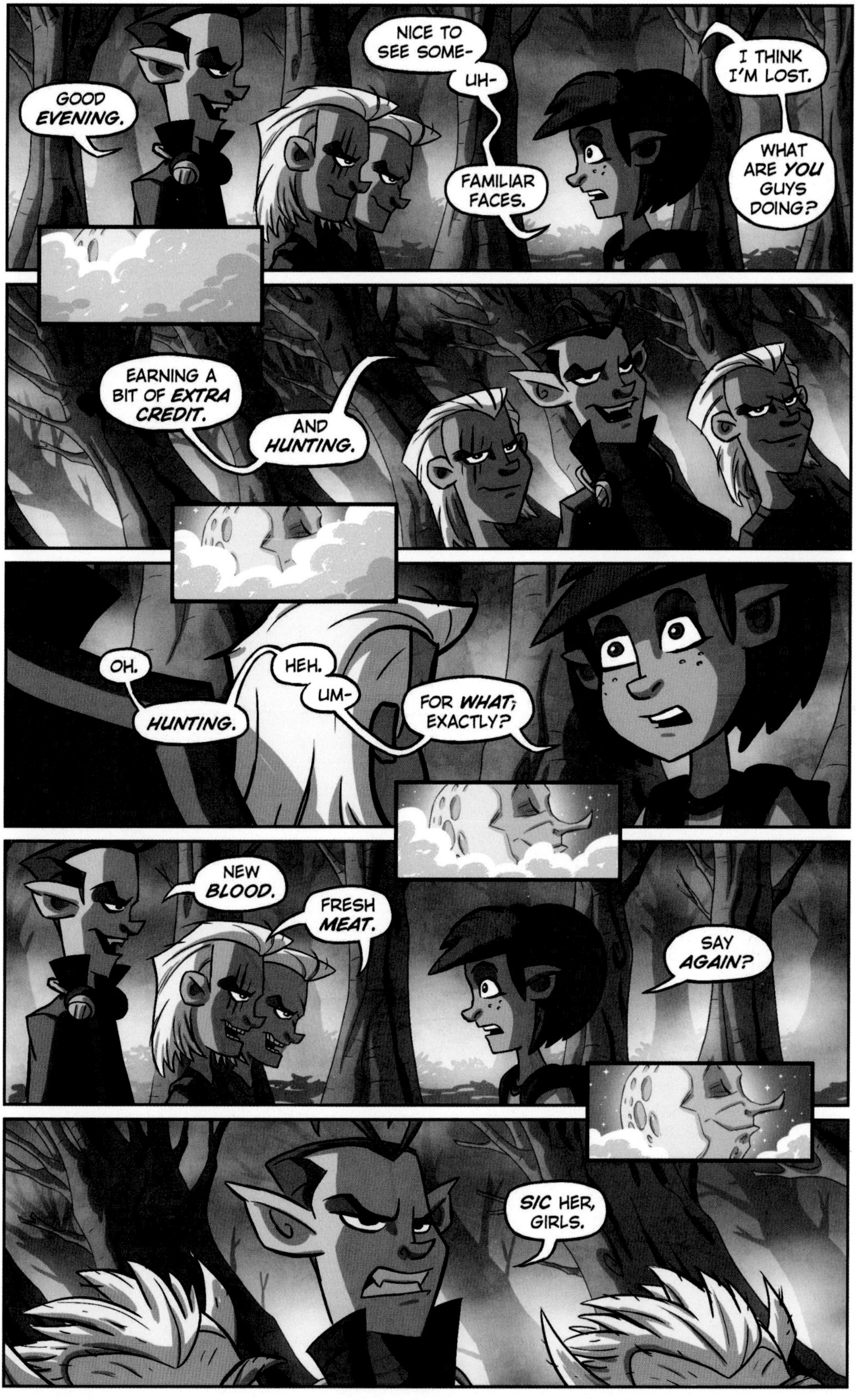
GOOD EVENING.
NICE TO SEE SOME-
UH-
FAMILIAR FACES.
I THINK I'M LOST.
WHAT ARE YOU GUYS DOING?
EARNING A BIT OF EXTRA CREDIT.
AND HUNTING.
OH.
HUNTING.
HEH.
UM-
FOR WHAT, EXACTLY?
NEW BLOOD.
FRESH MEAT.
SAY AGAIN?
SIC HER, GIRLS.

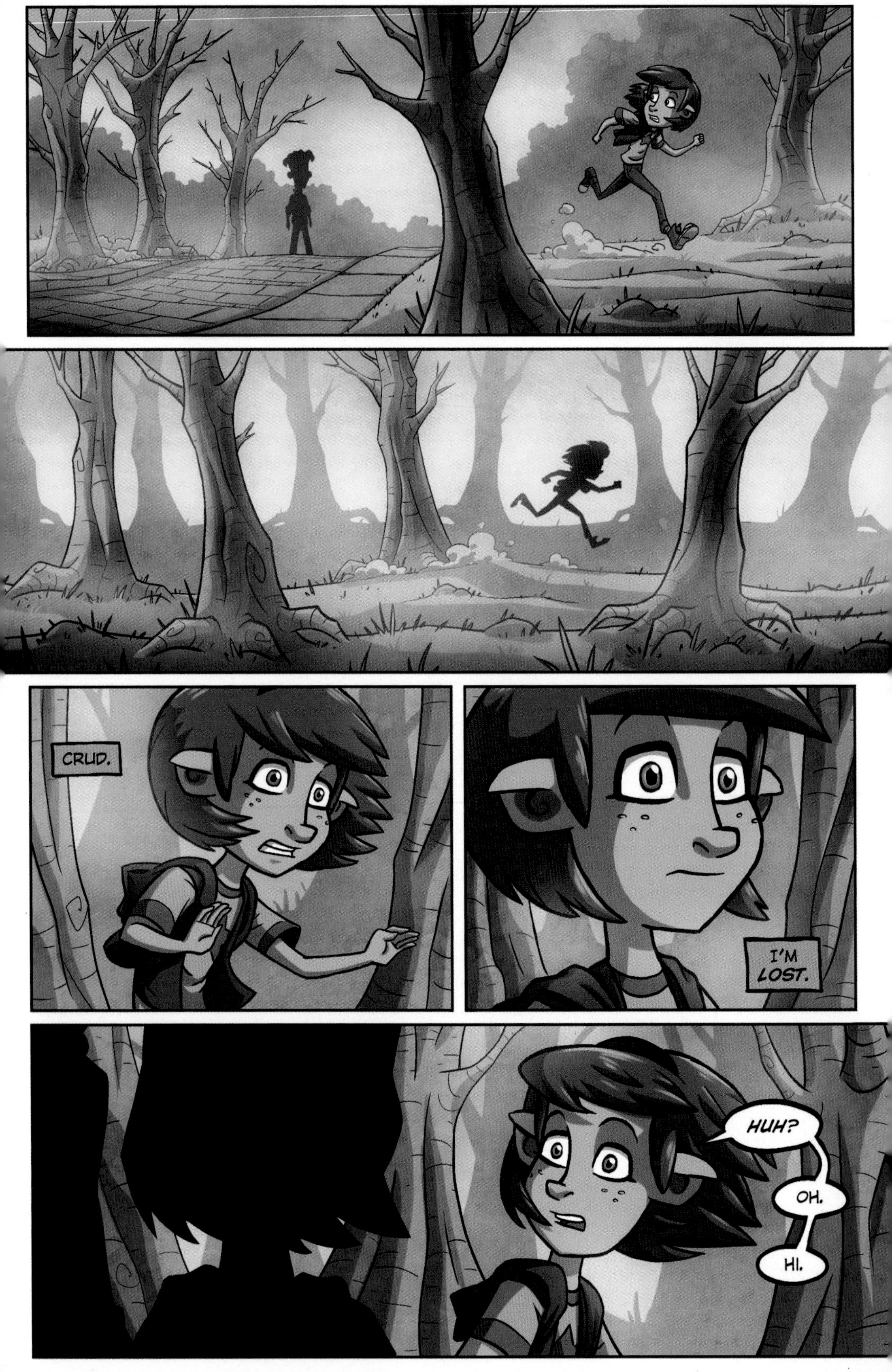
CRUD.
I'M LOST.
HUH?
OH.
HI.

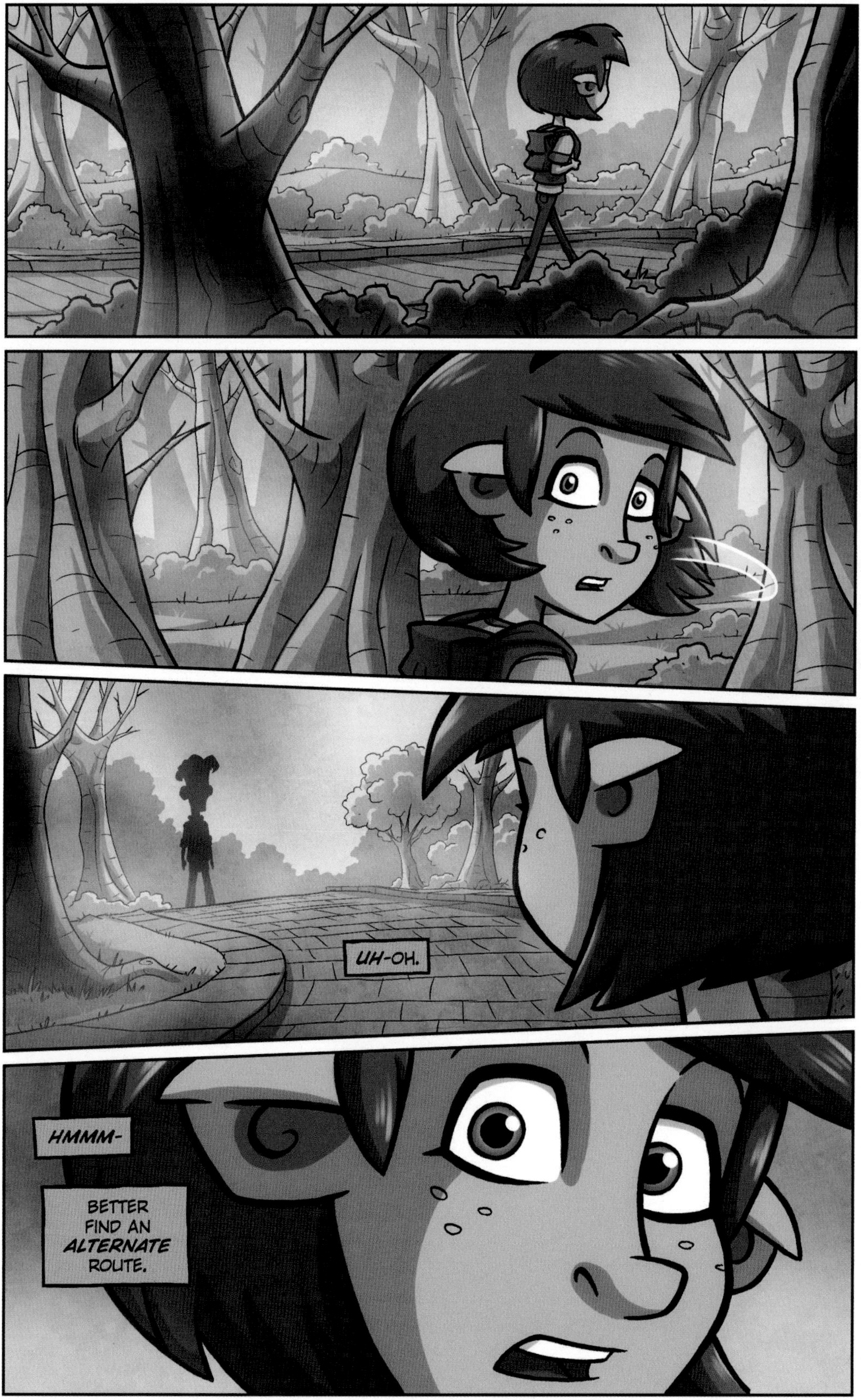
UH-OH.
HMMM-
BETTER FIND AN ALTERNATE ROUTE.

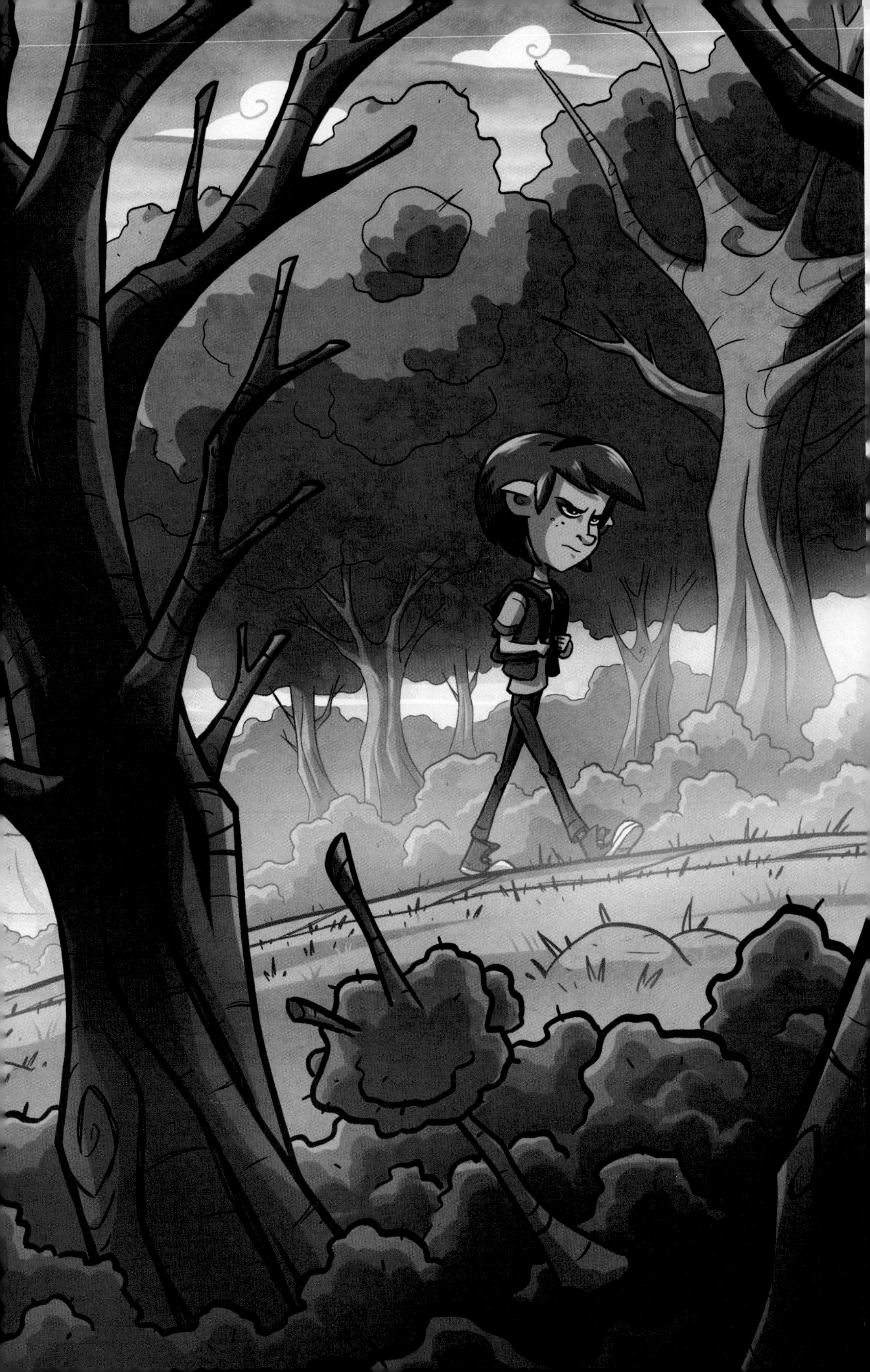

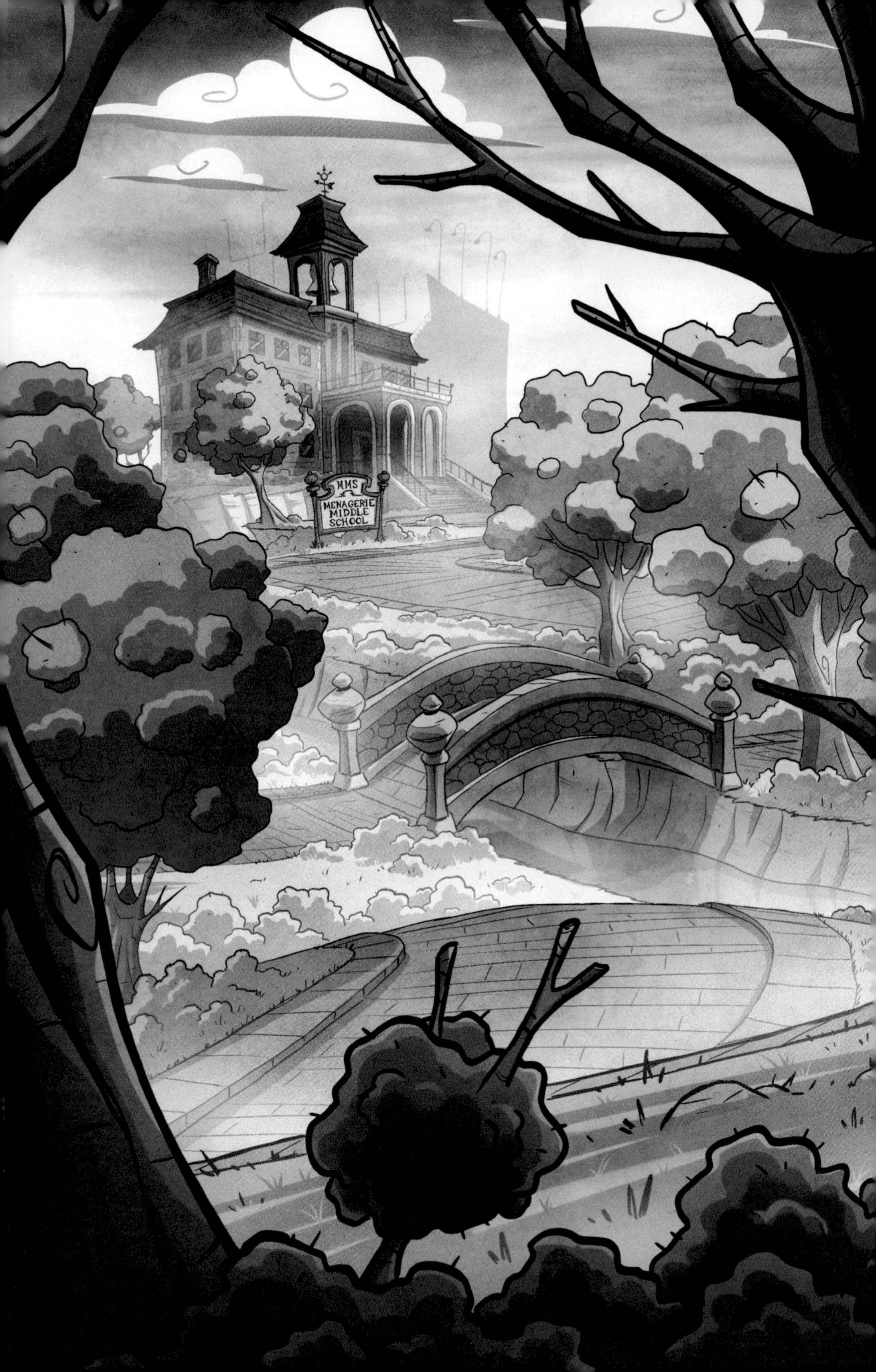
MMS
MENAGERIE MIDDLE SCHOOL

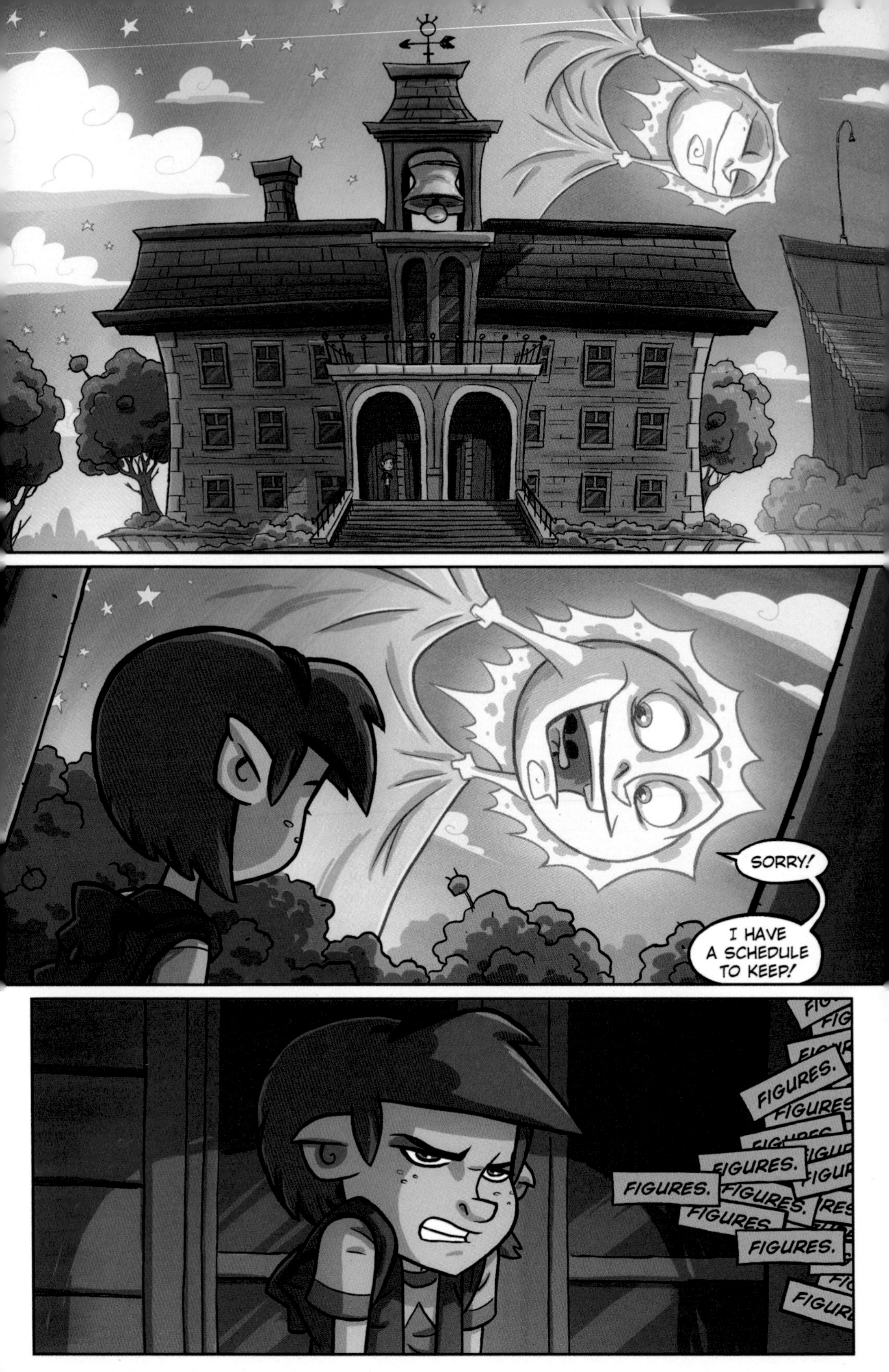
SORRY!
I HAVE A SCHEDULE TO KEEP!
FIGURES.
FIGURES.
FIGURES.
FIGURES.
FIGURES.

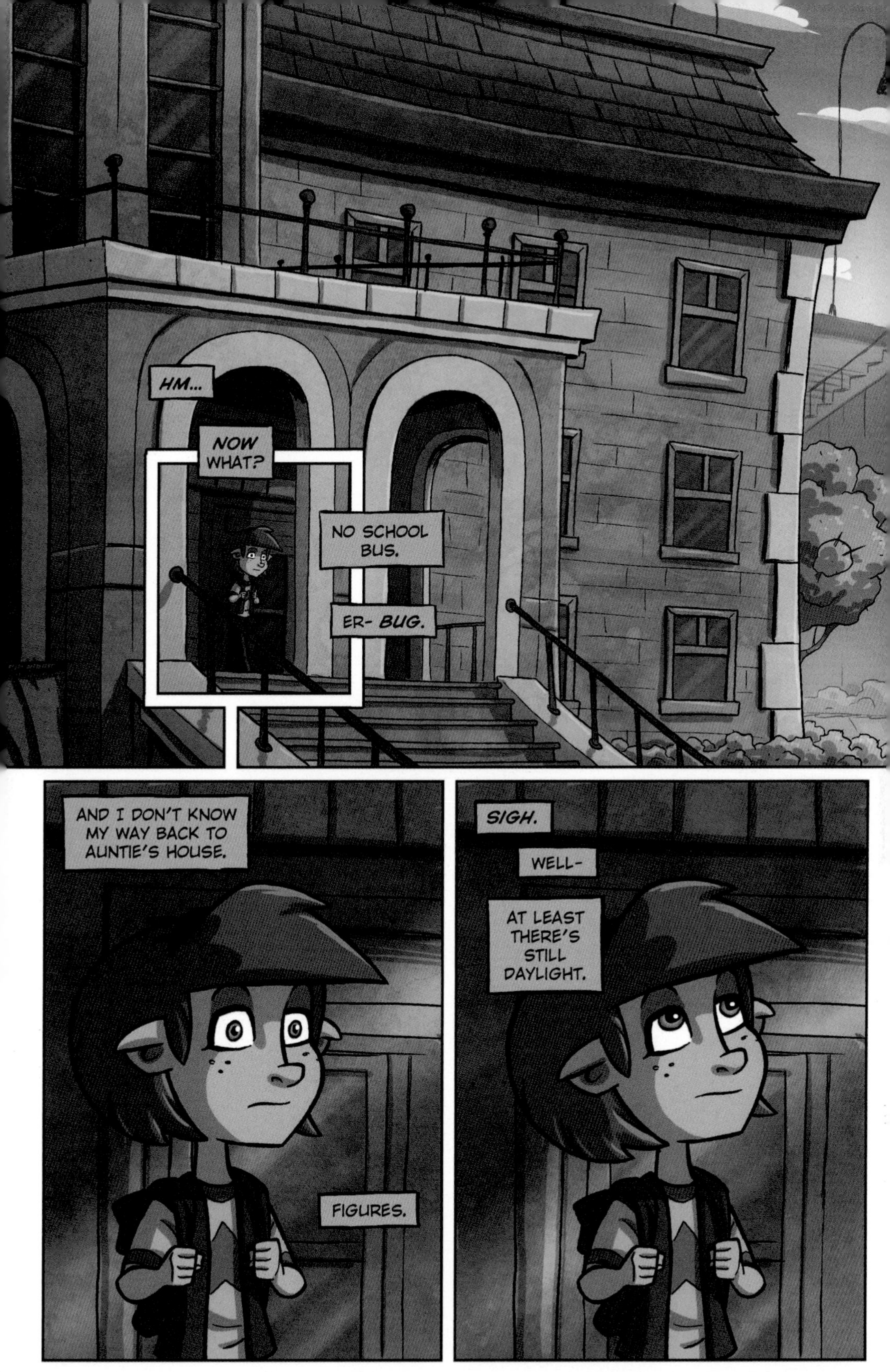
HM...
NOW WHAT?
NO SCHOOL BUS.
ER- BUG.
AND I DON'T KNOW MY WAY BACK TO AUNTIE'S HOUSE.
FIGURES.
SIGH.
WELL-
AT LEAST THERE'S STILL DAYLIGHT.

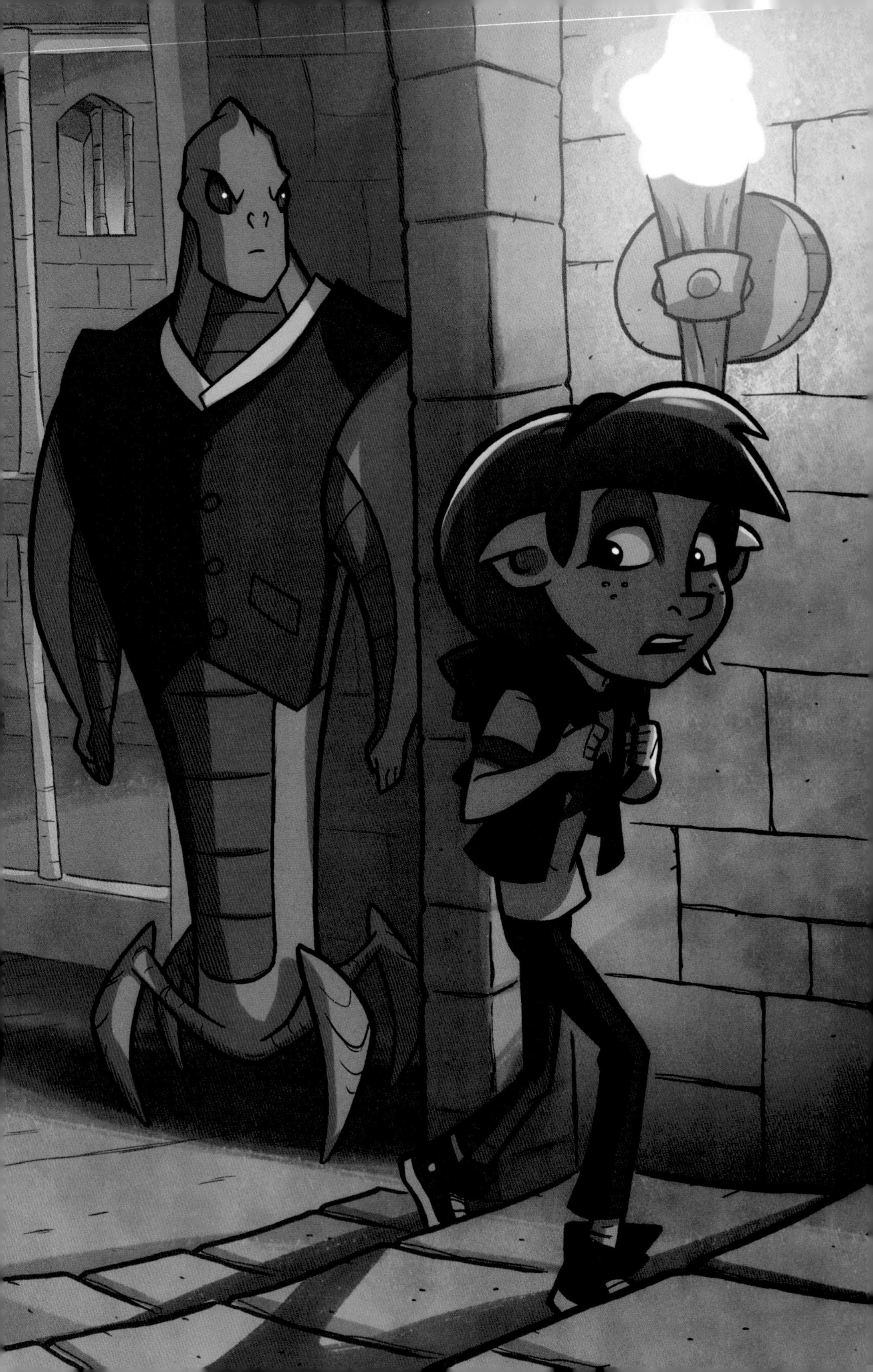

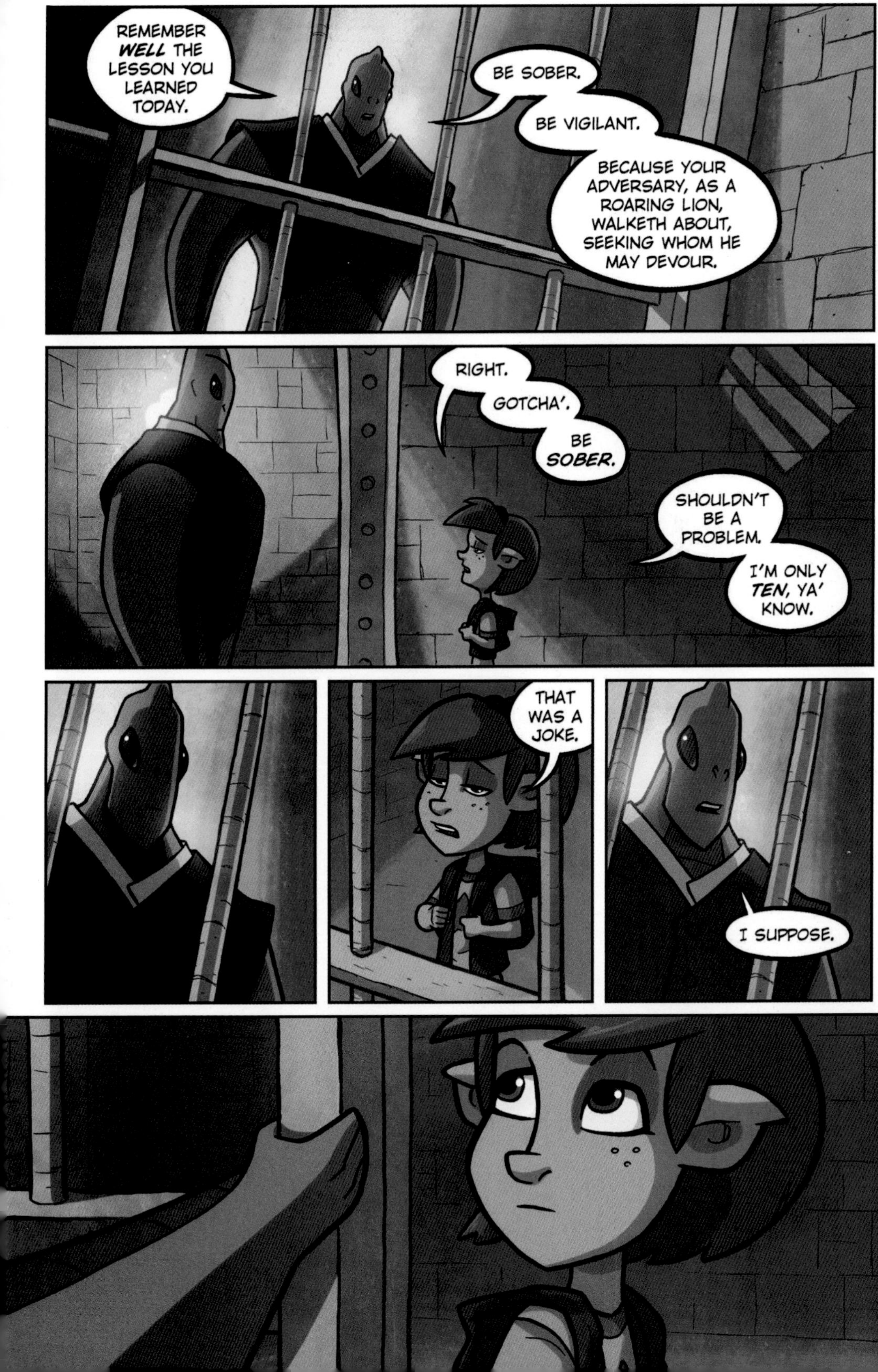
REMEMBER WELL THE LESSON YOU LEARNED TODAY.
BE SOBER.
BE VIGILANT.
BECAUSE YOUR ADVERSARY, AS A ROARING LION, WALKETH ABOUT, SEEKING WHOM HE MAY DEVOUR.
RIGHT.
GOTCHA'.
BE SOBER.
SHOULDN'T BE A PROBLEM.
I'M ONLY TEN, YA' KNOW.
THAT WAS A JOKE.
I SUPPOSE.

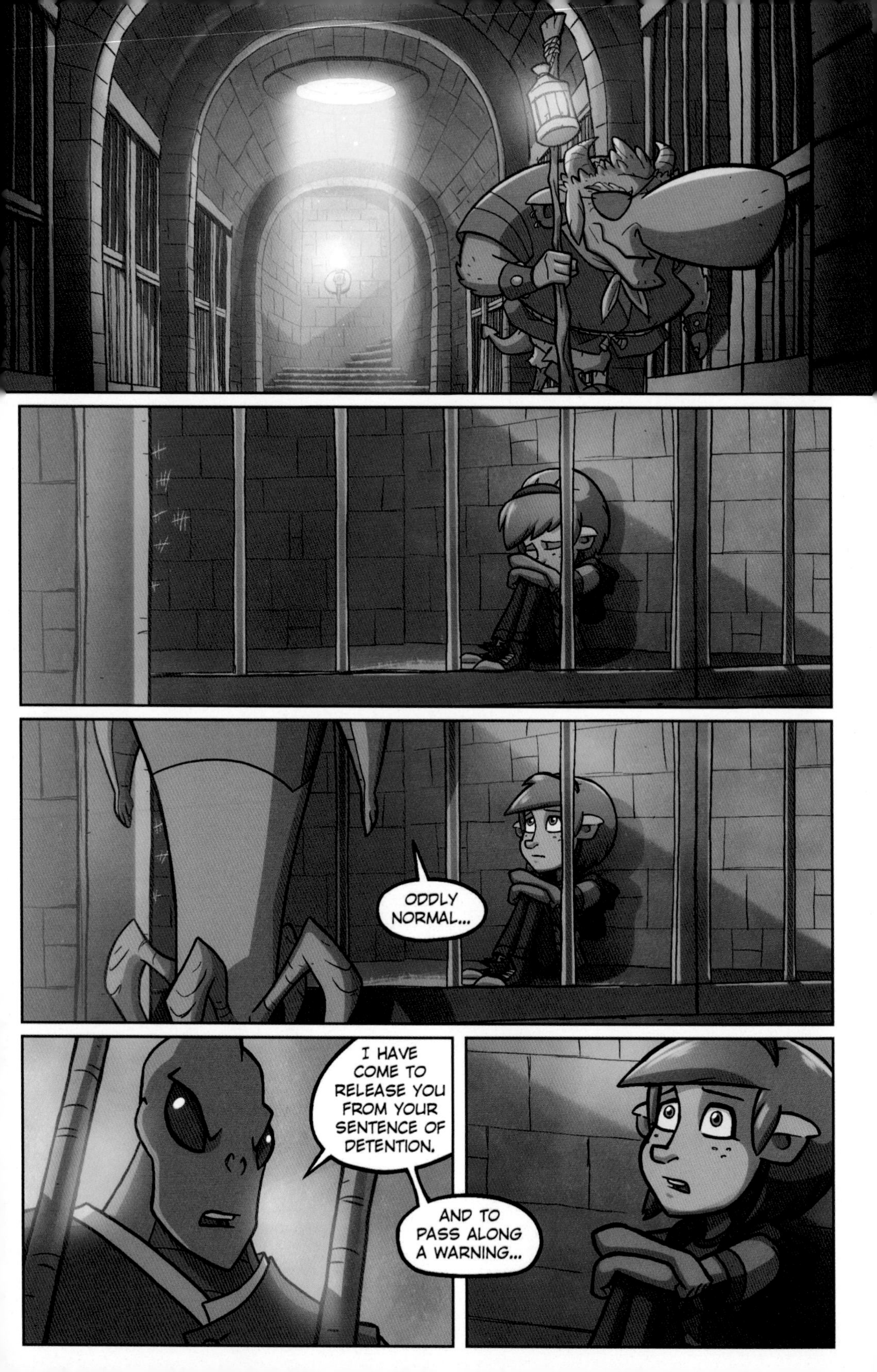
ODDLY NORMAL...
I HAVE COME TO RELEASE YOU FROM YOUR SENTENCE OF DETENTION.
AND TO PASS ALONG A WARNING...

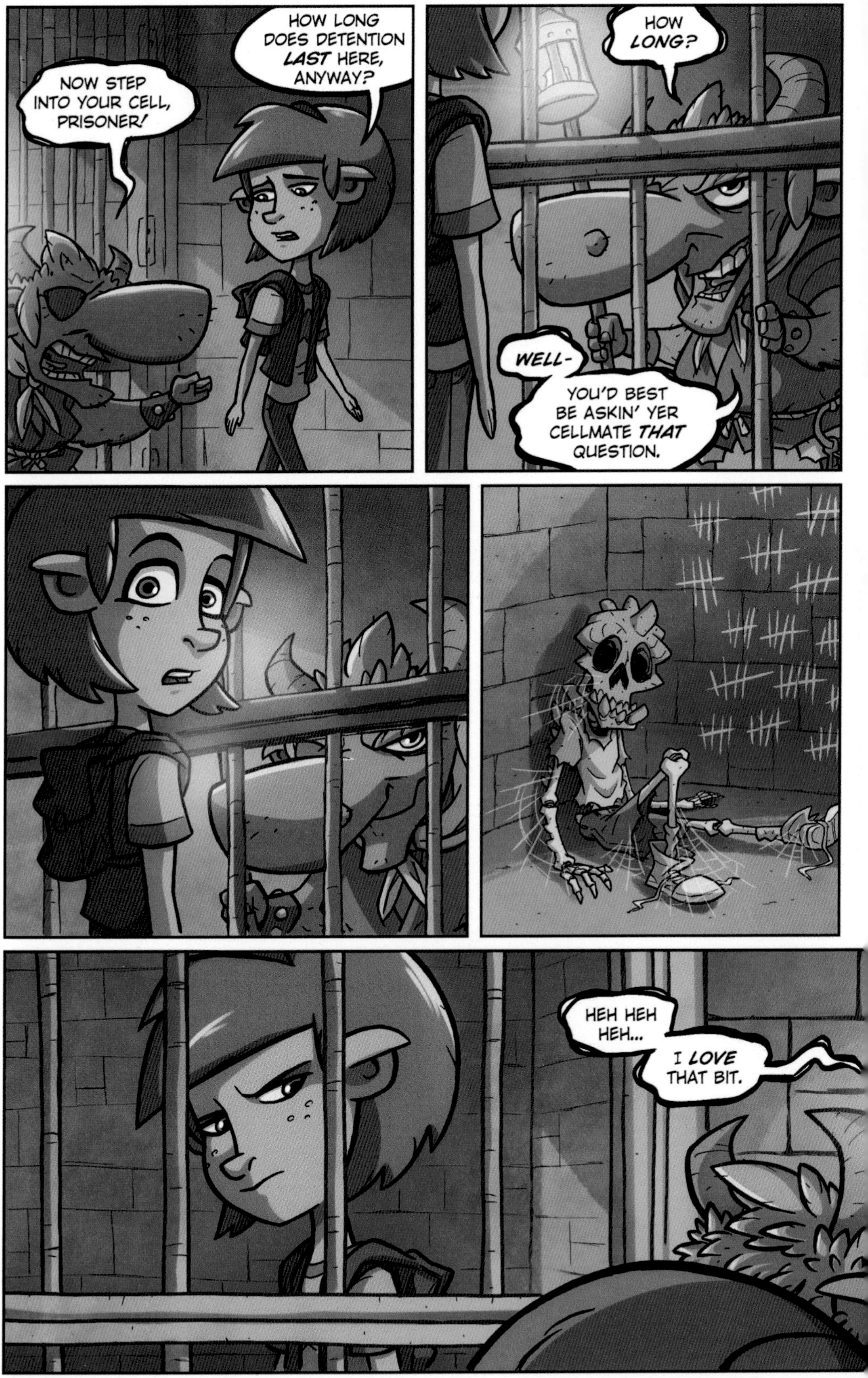
NOW STEP INTO YOUR CELL, PRISONER!
HOW LONG DOES DETENTION LAST HERE, ANYWAY?
HOW LONG?
WELL-
YOU'D BEST BE ASKIN' YER CELLMATE THAT QUESTION.
HEH HEH HEH...
I LOVE THAT BIT.

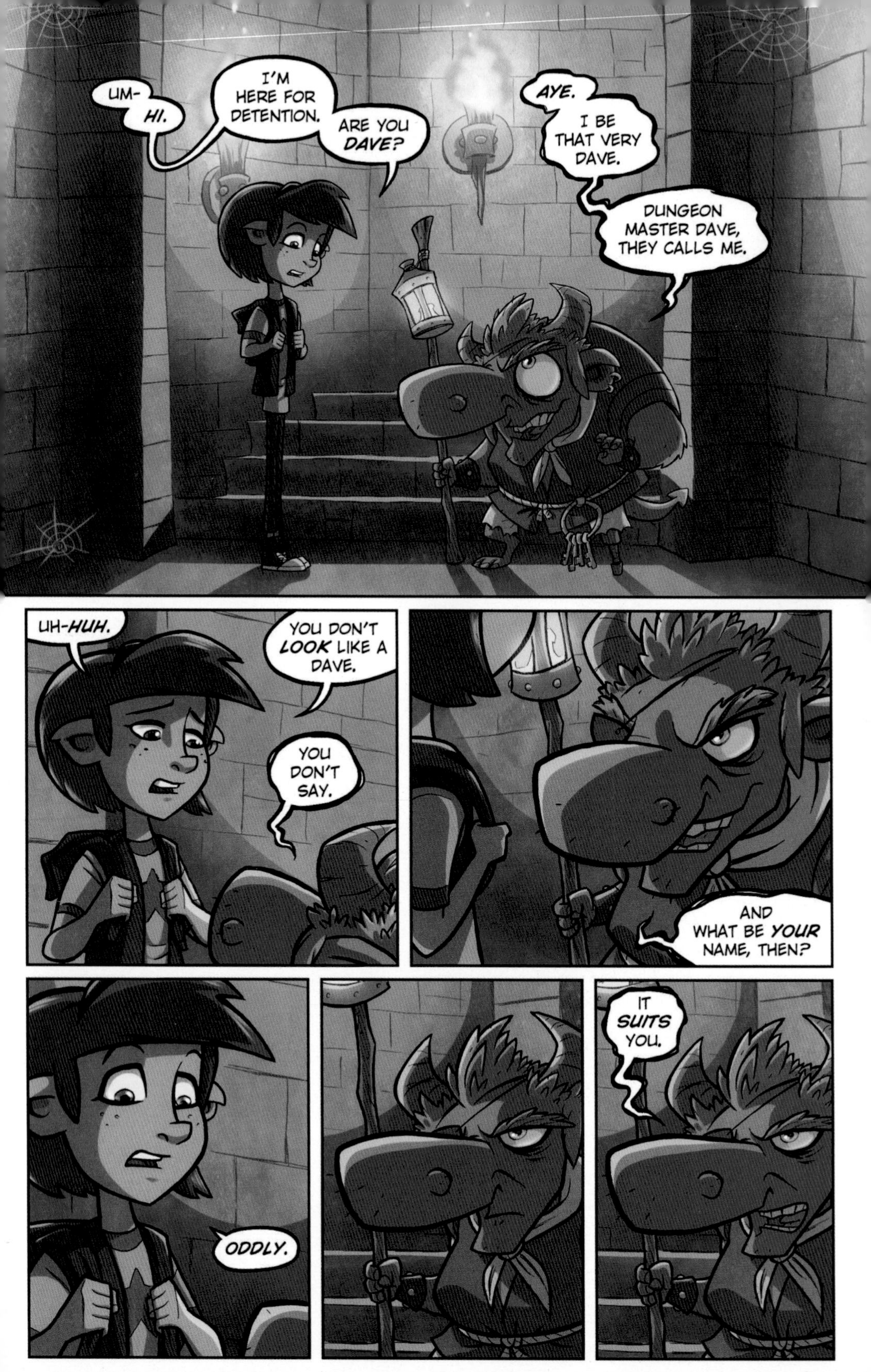
UM- HI.
I'M HERE FOR DETENTION.
ARE YOU DAVE?
AYE.
I BE THAT VERY DAVE.
DUNGEON MASTER DAVE, THEY CALLS ME.
UH-HUH.
YOU DON'T LOOK LIKE A DAVE.
YOU DON'T SAY.
AND WHAT BE YOUR NAME, THEN?
ODDLY.
IT SUITS YOU.

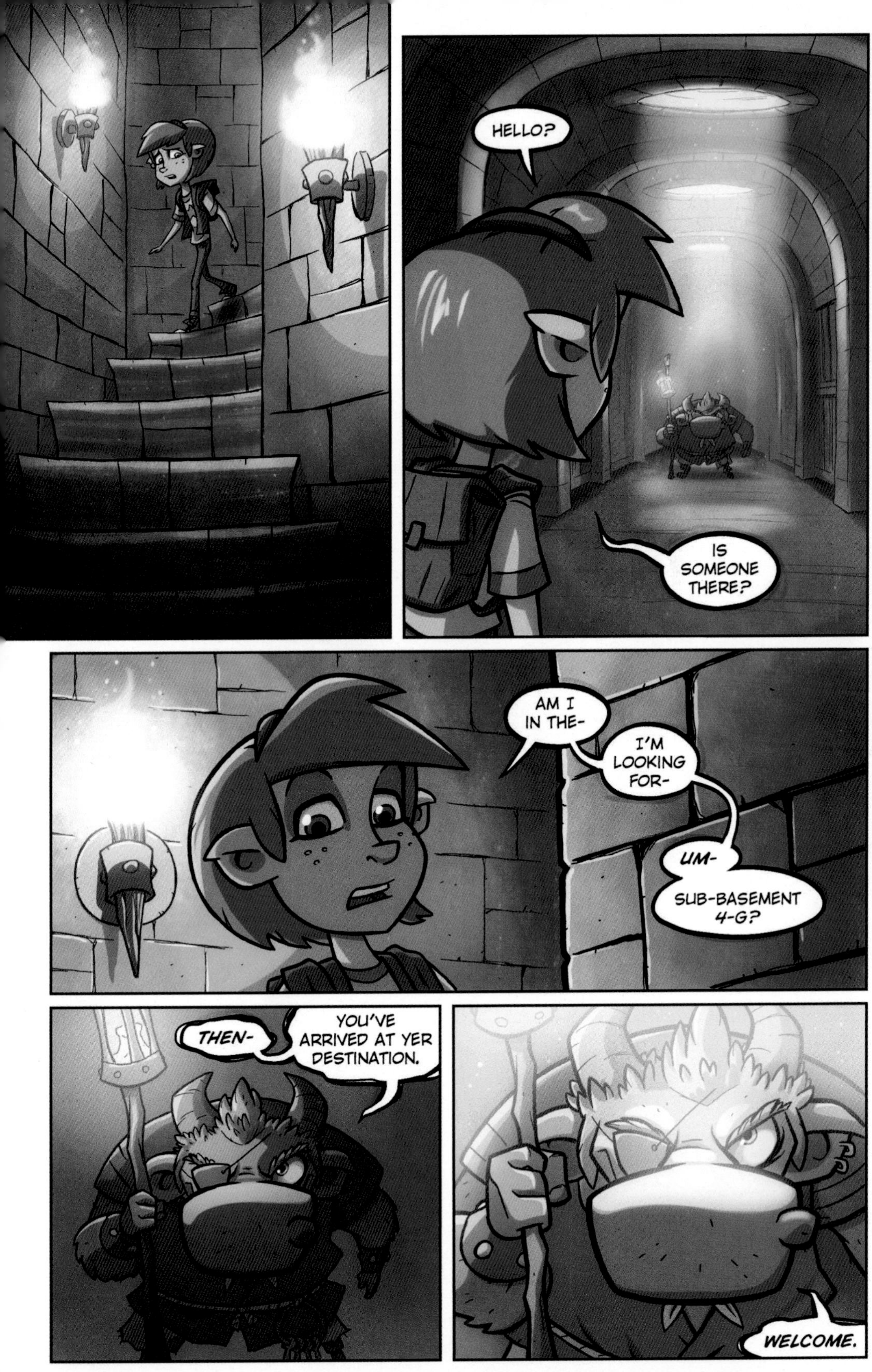
HELLO?
IS SOMEONE THERE?
AM I IN THE-
I'M LOOKING FOR-
UM-
SUB-BASEMENT 4-G?
THEN-
YOU'VE ARRIVED AT YER DESTINATION.
WELCOME.

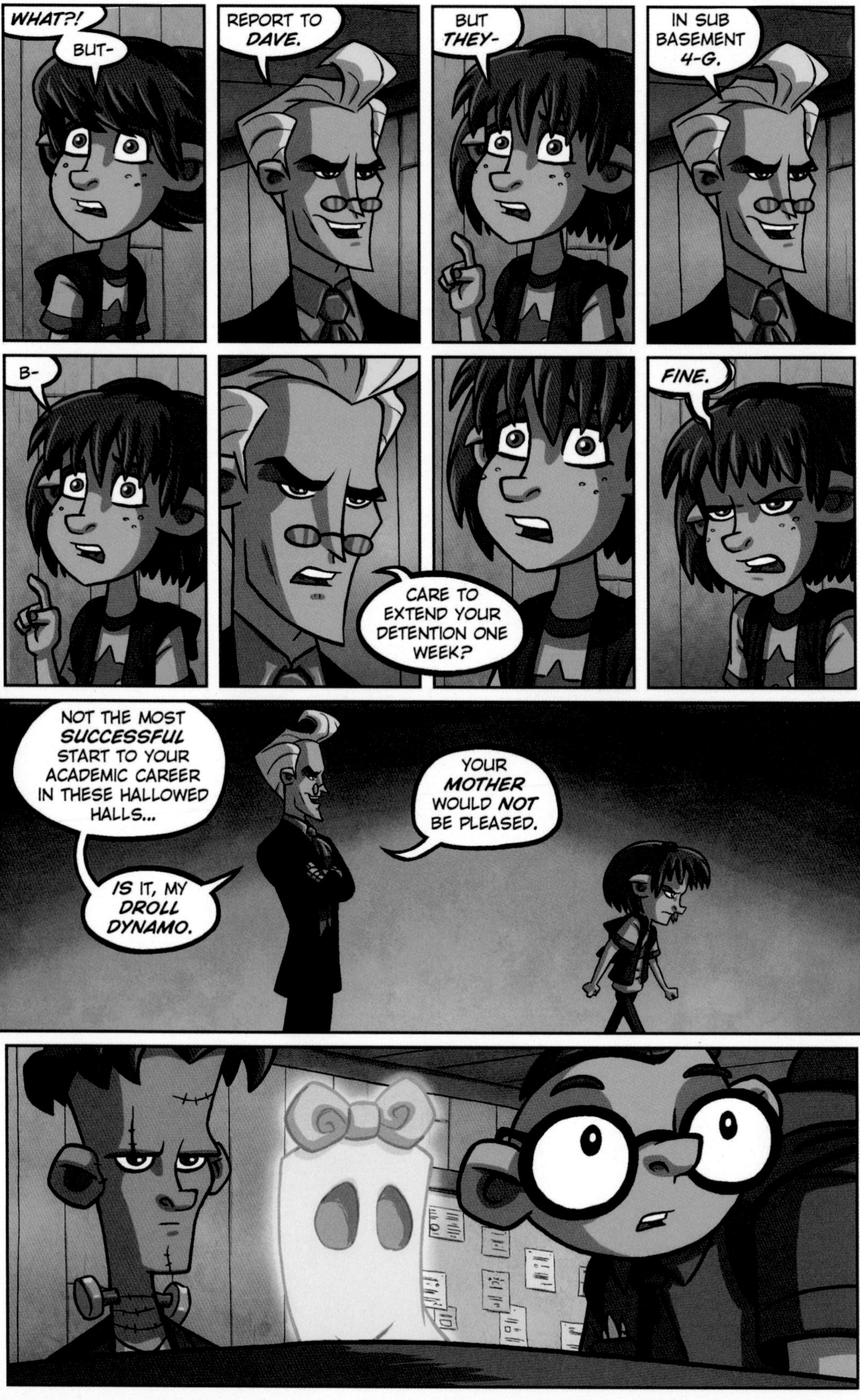
WHAT?!
BUT-
REPORT TO DAVE.
BUT THEY-
IN SUB BASEMENT 4-G.
B-
CARE TO EXTEND YOUR DETENTION ONE WEEK?
FINE.
NOT THE MOST SUCCESSFUL START TO YOUR ACADEMIC CAREER IN THESE HALLOWED HALLS...
IS IT, MY DROLL DYNAMO.
YOUR MOTHER WOULD NOT BE PLEASED.

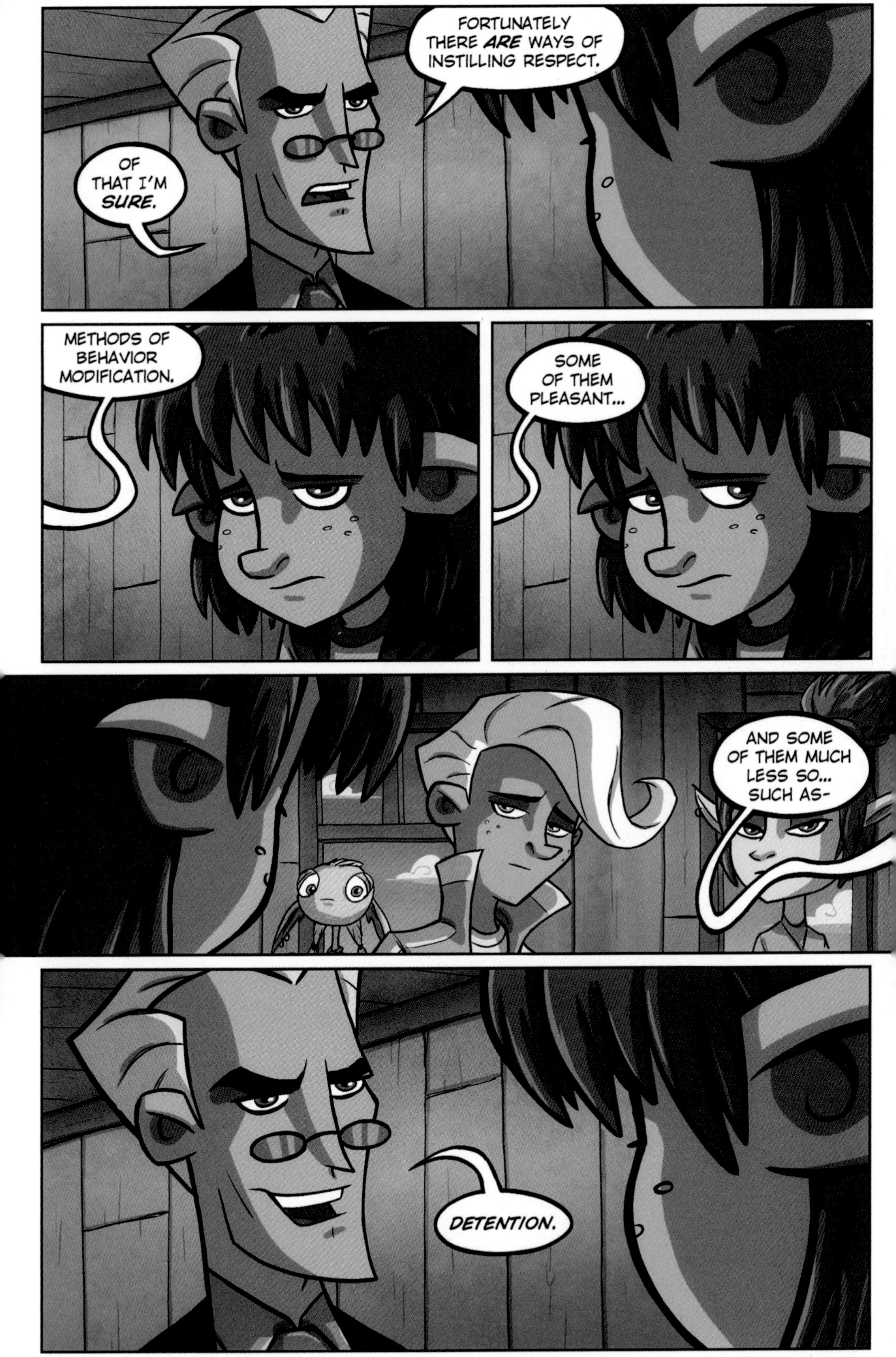
FORTUNATELY THERE *ARE* WAYS OF INSTILLING RESPECT.
OF THAT I'M *SURE.*
METHODS OF BEHAVIOR MODIFICATION.
SOME OF THEM PLEASANT...
AND SOME OF THEM MUCH LESS SO... SUCH AS-
DETENTION.

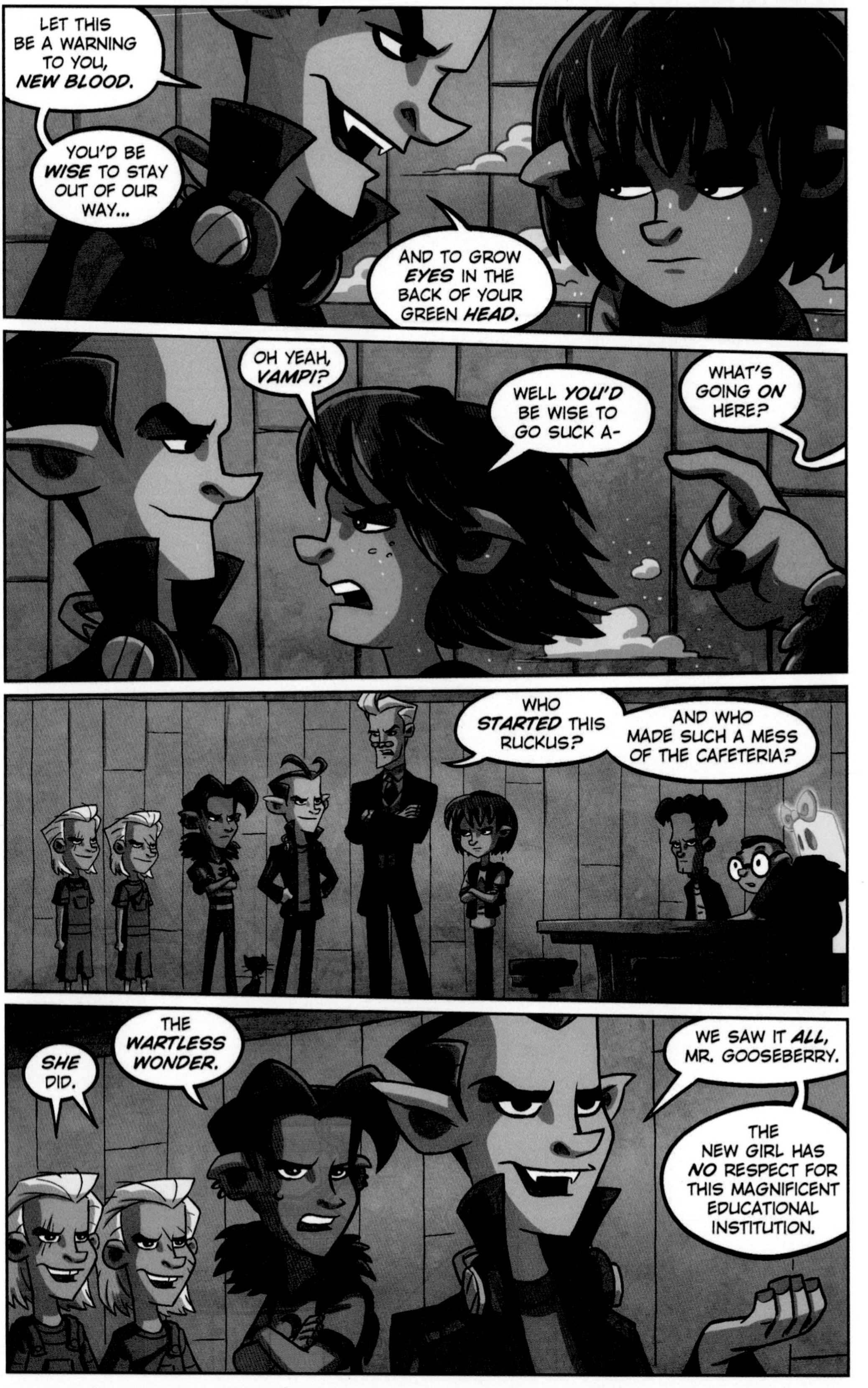
LET THIS BE A WARNING TO YOU, NEW BLOOD.
YOU'D BE WISE TO STAY OUT OF OUR WAY...
AND TO GROW EYES IN THE BACK OF YOUR GREEN HEAD.
OH YEAH, VAMPI?
WELL YOU'D BE WISE TO GO SUCK A-
WHAT'S GOING ON HERE?
WHO STARTED THIS RUCKUS?
AND WHO MADE SUCH A MESS OF THE CAFETERIA?
SHE DID.
THE WARTLESS WONDER.
WE SAW IT ALL, MR. GOOSEBERRY.
THE NEW GIRL HAS NO RESPECT FOR THIS MAGNIFICENT EDUCATIONAL INSTITUTION.

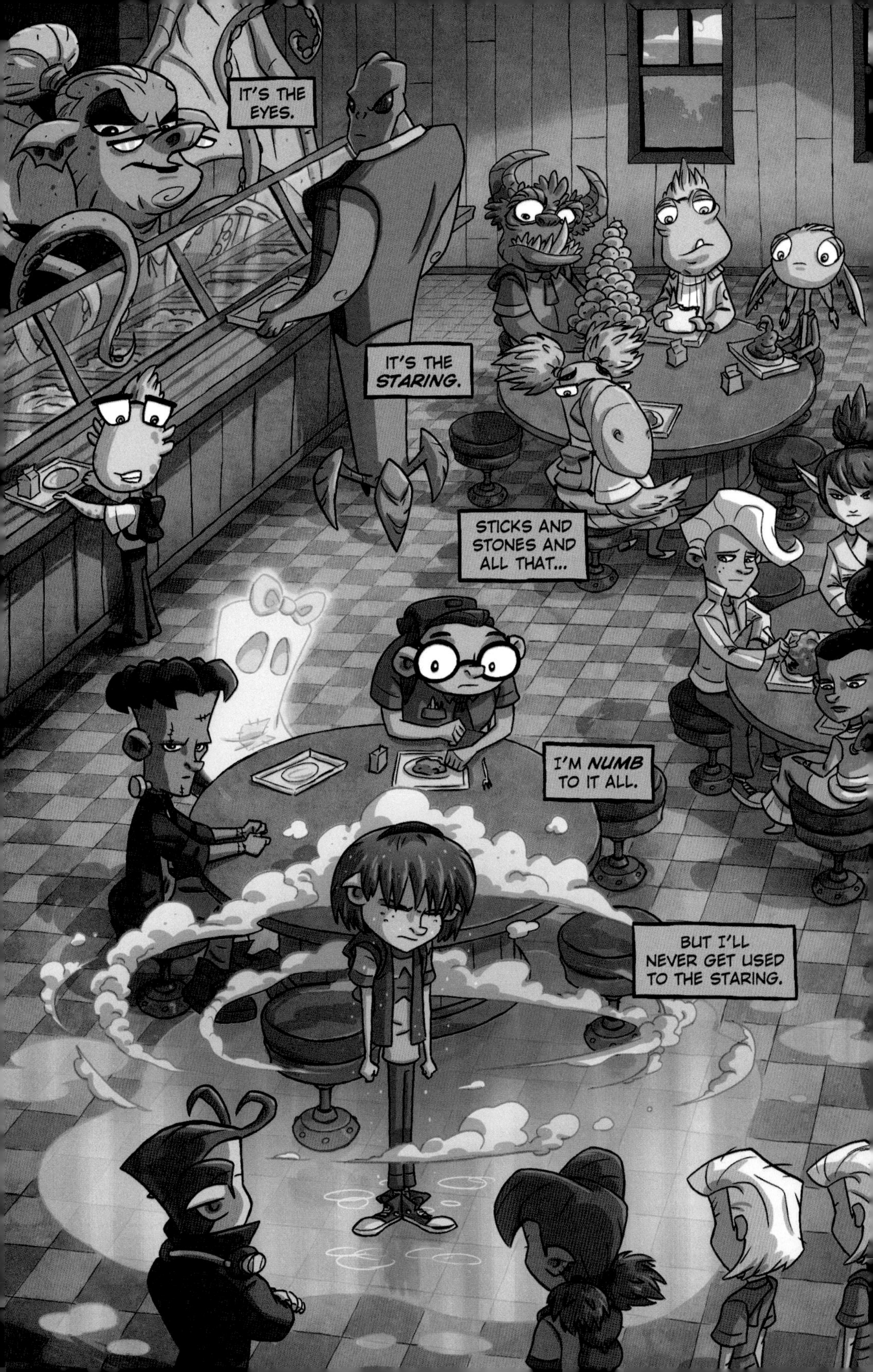
IT'S THE EYES.
IT'S THE *STARING*.
STICKS AND STONES AND ALL THAT...
I'M *NUMB* TO IT ALL.
BUT I'LL NEVER GET USED TO THE STARING.

Chapter 5

Sticks, Stones, Words & Bones

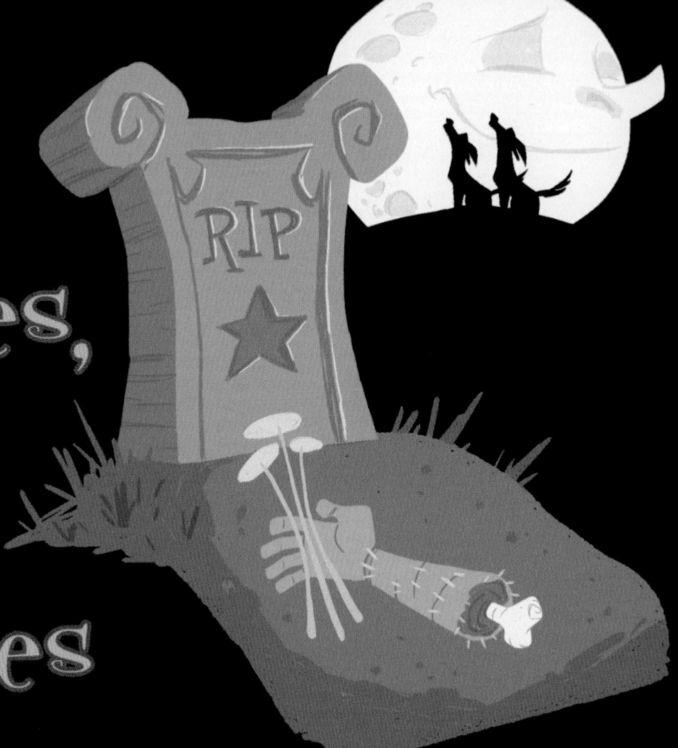
RIP

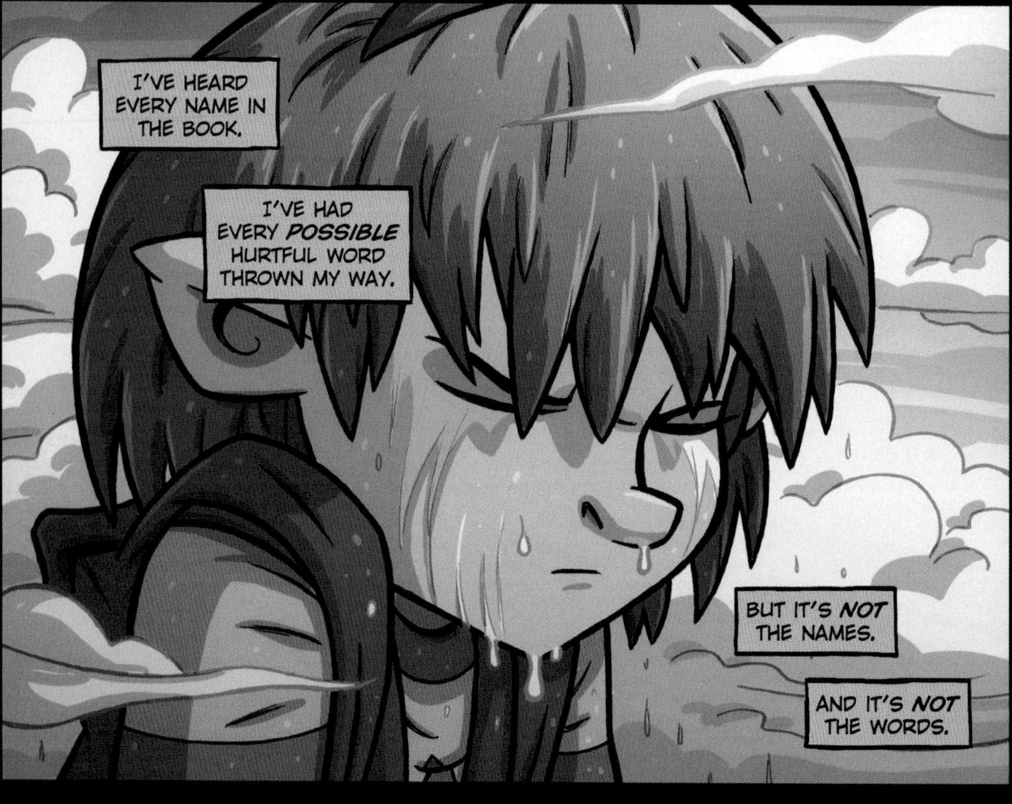
I'VE HEARD EVERY NAME IN THE BOOK.
I'VE HAD EVERY *POSSIBLE* HURTFUL WORD THROWN MY WAY.
BUT IT'S *NOT* THE NAMES.
AND IT'S *NOT* THE WORDS.

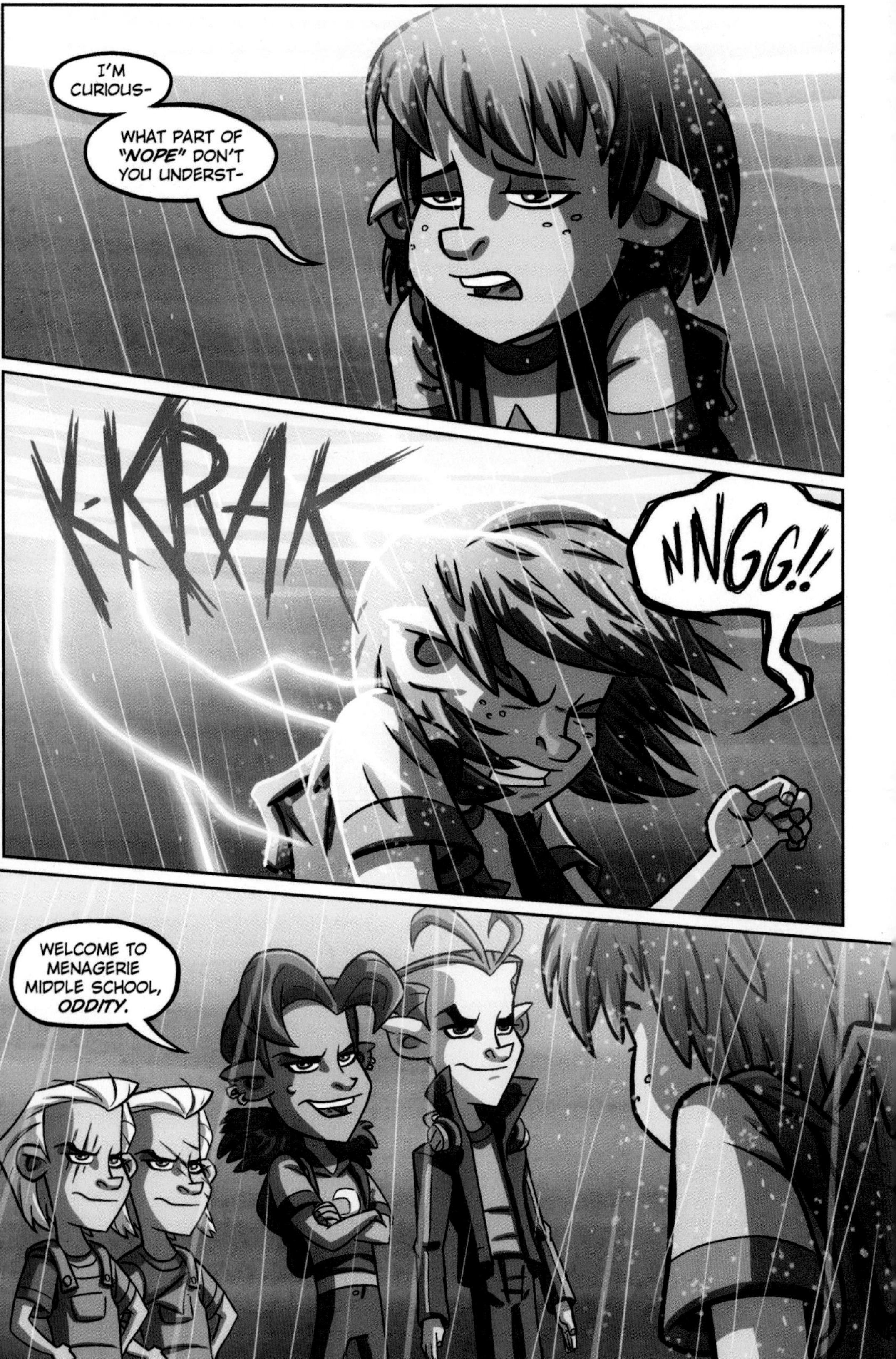
I'M CURIOUS-
WHAT PART OF "NOPE" DON'T YOU UNDERST-
K-KRAK
NNGG!!
WELCOME TO MENAGERIE MIDDLE SCHOOL, ODDITY.

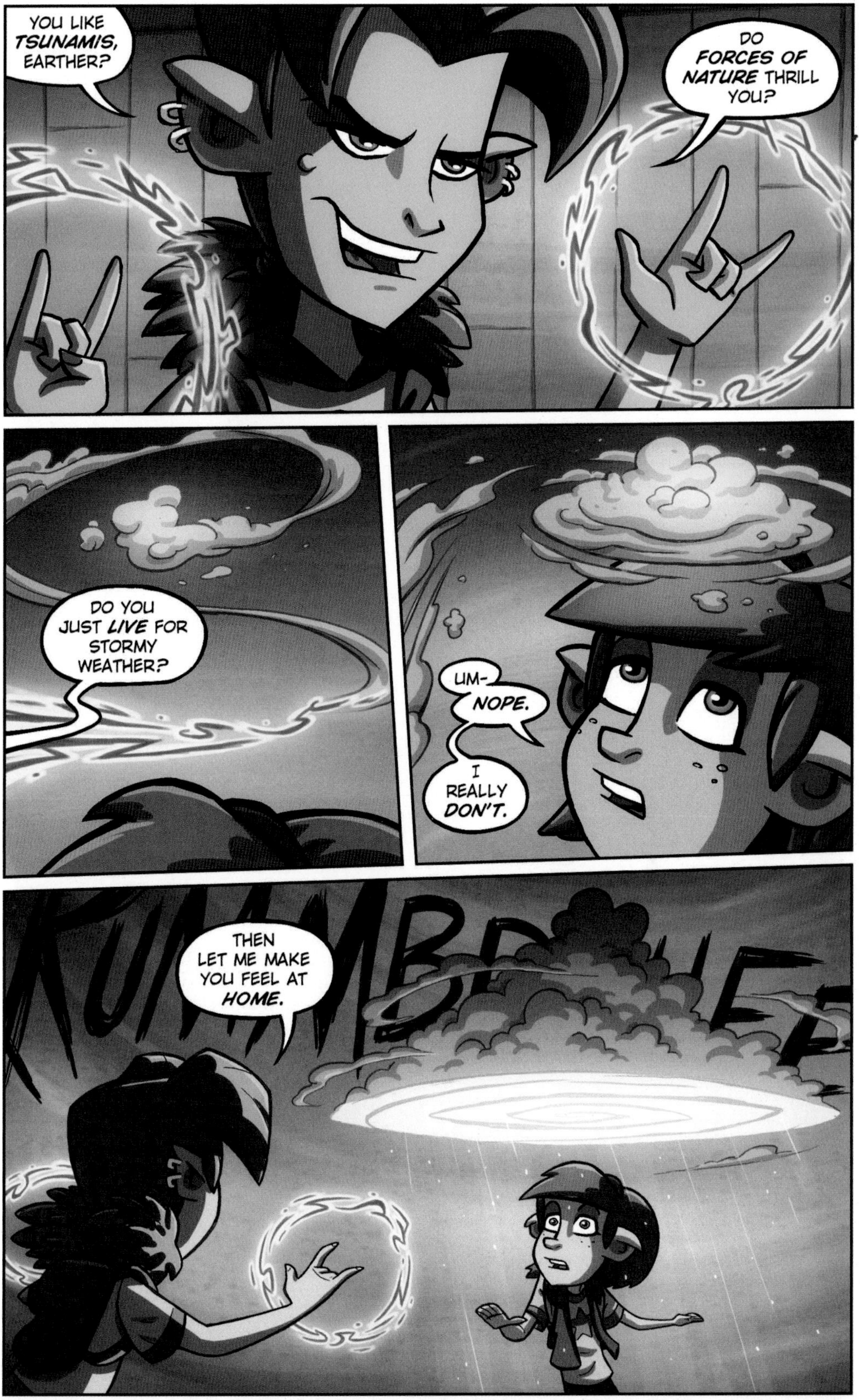
YOU LIKE TSUNAMIS, EARTHER?
DO FORCES OF NATURE THRILL YOU?
DO YOU JUST LIVE FOR STORMY WEATHER?
UM- NOPE.
I REALLY DON'T.
THEN LET ME MAKE YOU FEEL AT HOME.

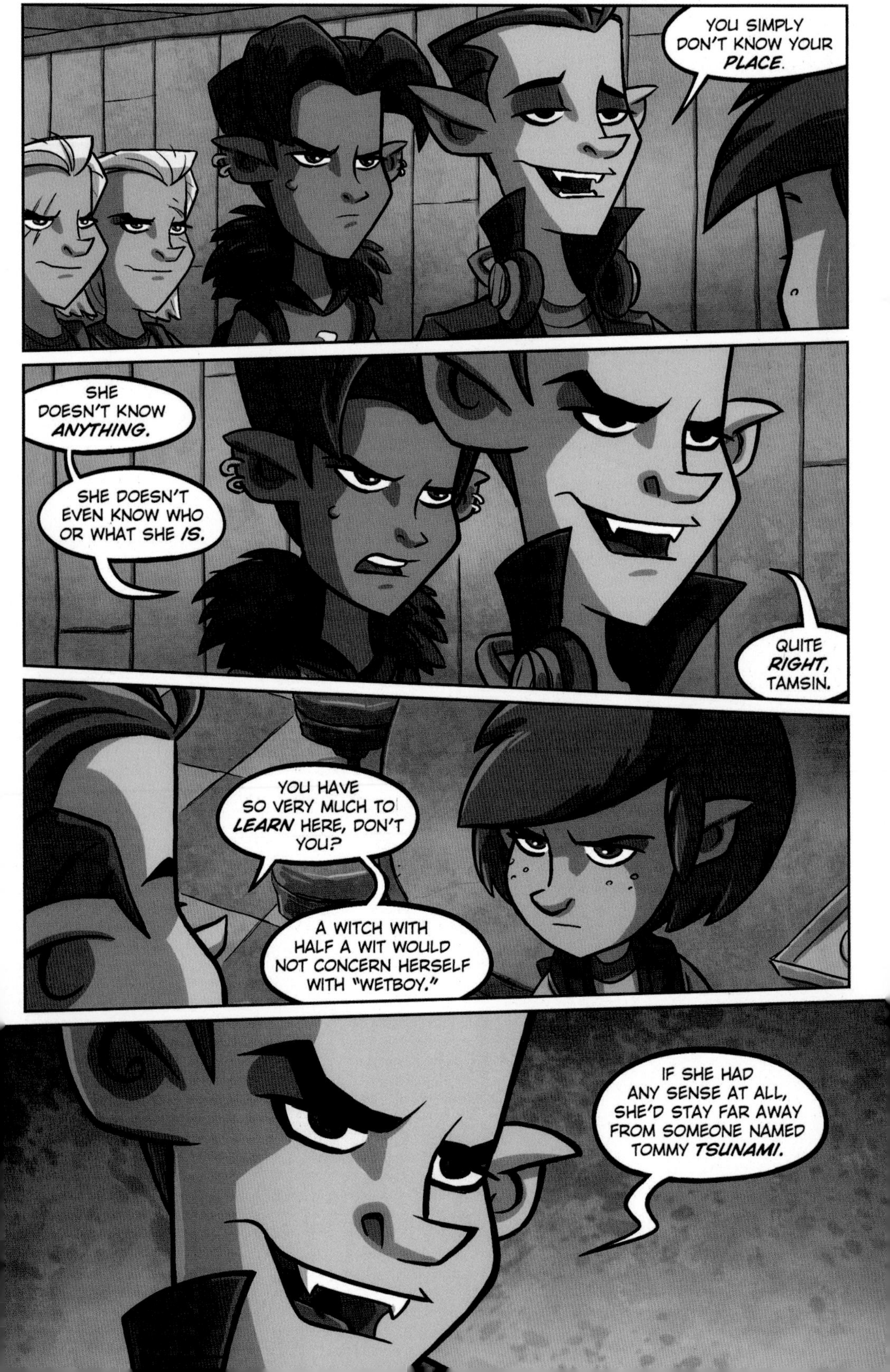
YOU SIMPLY DON'T KNOW YOUR *PLACE*.
SHE DOESN'T KNOW *ANYTHING*.
SHE DOESN'T EVEN KNOW WHO OR WHAT SHE *IS*.
QUITE *RIGHT*, TAMSIN.
YOU HAVE SO VERY MUCH TO *LEARN* HERE, DON'T YOU?
A WITCH WITH HALF A WIT WOULD NOT CONCERN HERSELF WITH "WETBOY."
IF SHE HAD ANY SENSE AT ALL, SHE'D STAY FAR AWAY FROM SOMEONE NAMED TOMMY *TSUNAMI*.

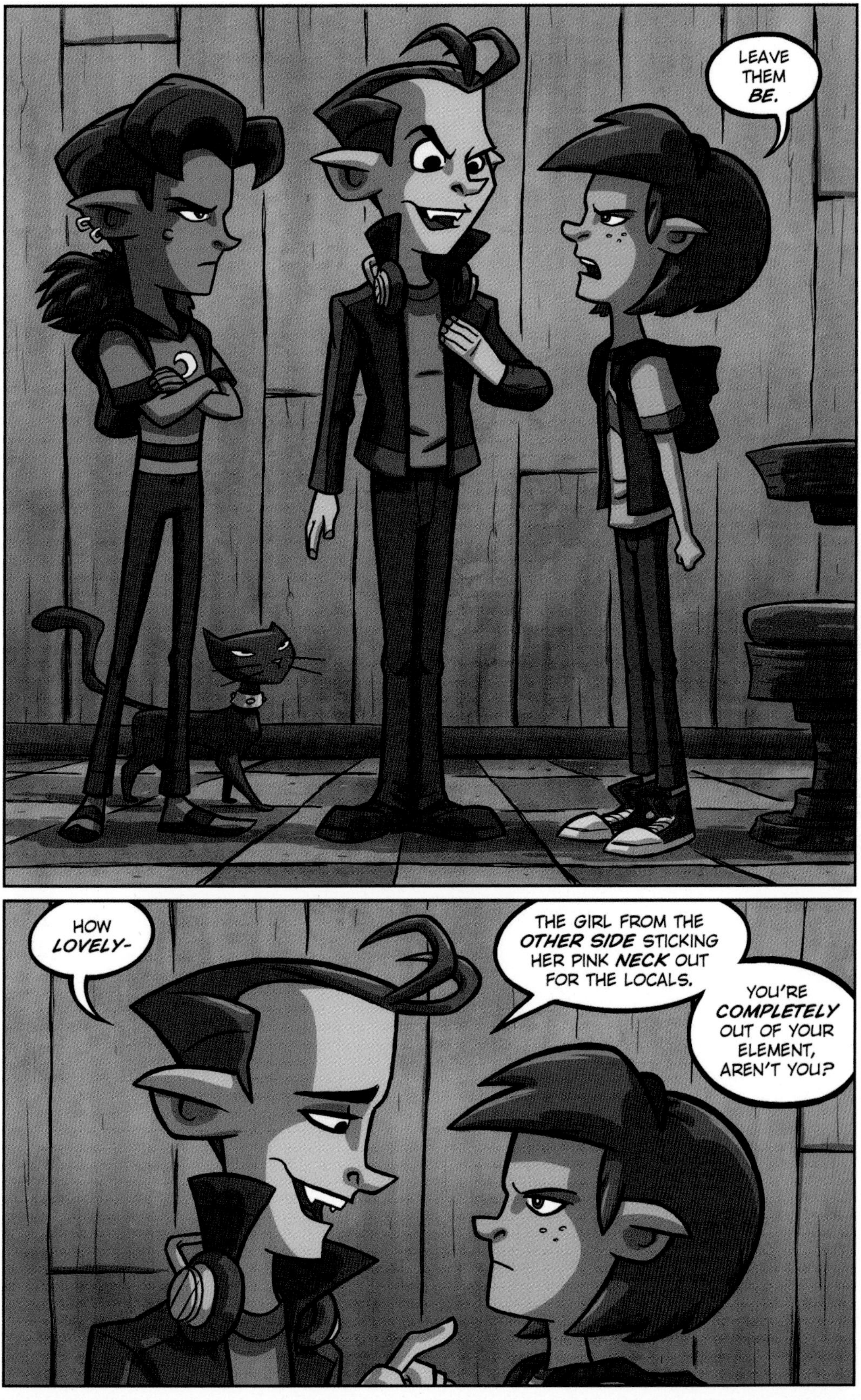
LEAVE THEM ***BE.***
HOW ***LOVELY-***
THE GIRL FROM THE ***OTHER SIDE*** STICKING HER PINK ***NECK*** OUT FOR THE LOCALS.
YOU'RE ***COMPLETELY*** OUT OF YOUR ELEMENT, AREN'T YOU?

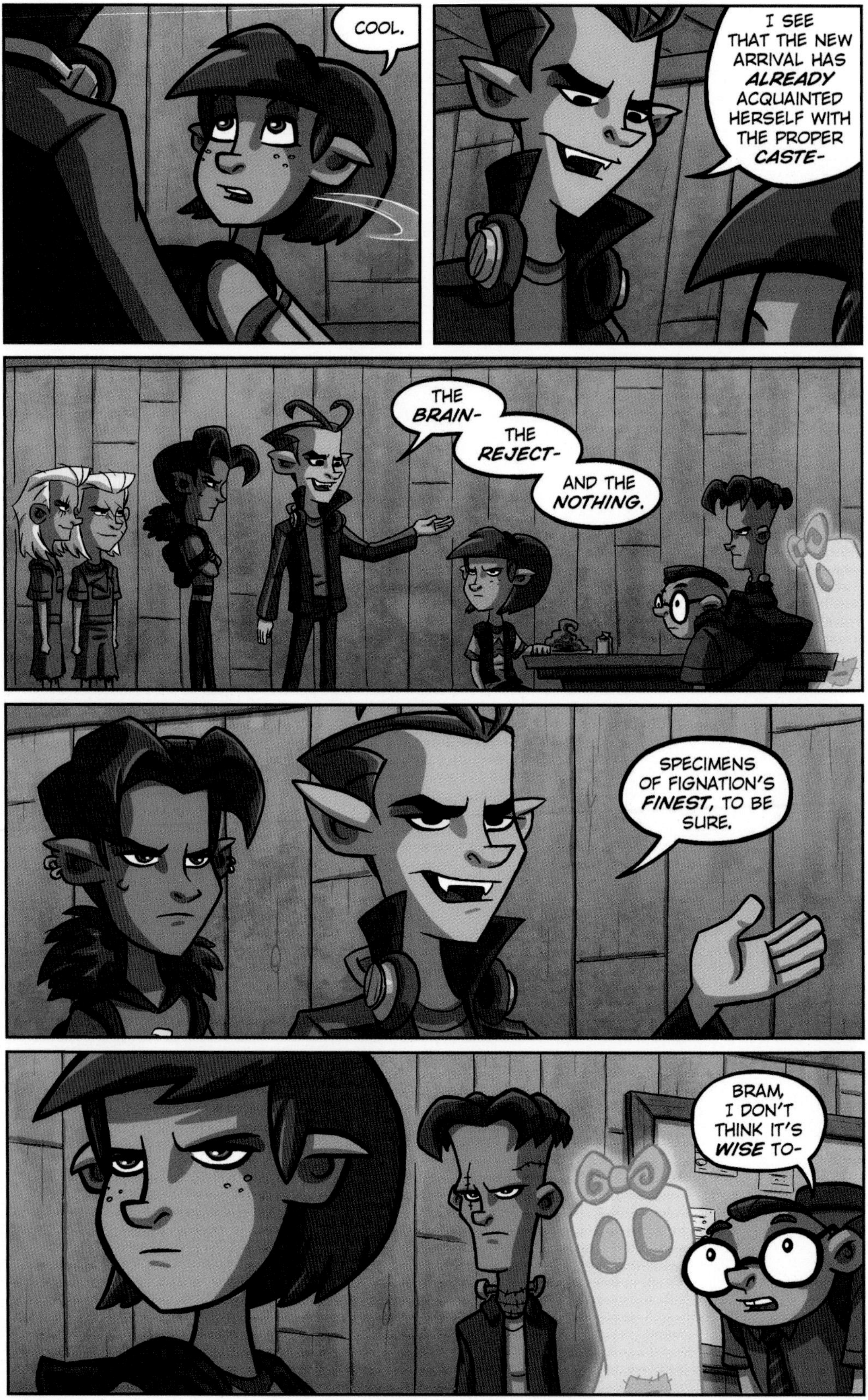
COOL.
I SEE THAT THE NEW ARRIVAL HAS ALREADY ACQUAINTED HERSELF WITH THE PROPER CASTE-
THE BRAIN-
THE REJECT-
AND THE NOTHING.
SPECIMENS OF FIGNATION'S FINEST, TO BE SURE.
BRAM, I DON'T THINK IT'S WISE TO-

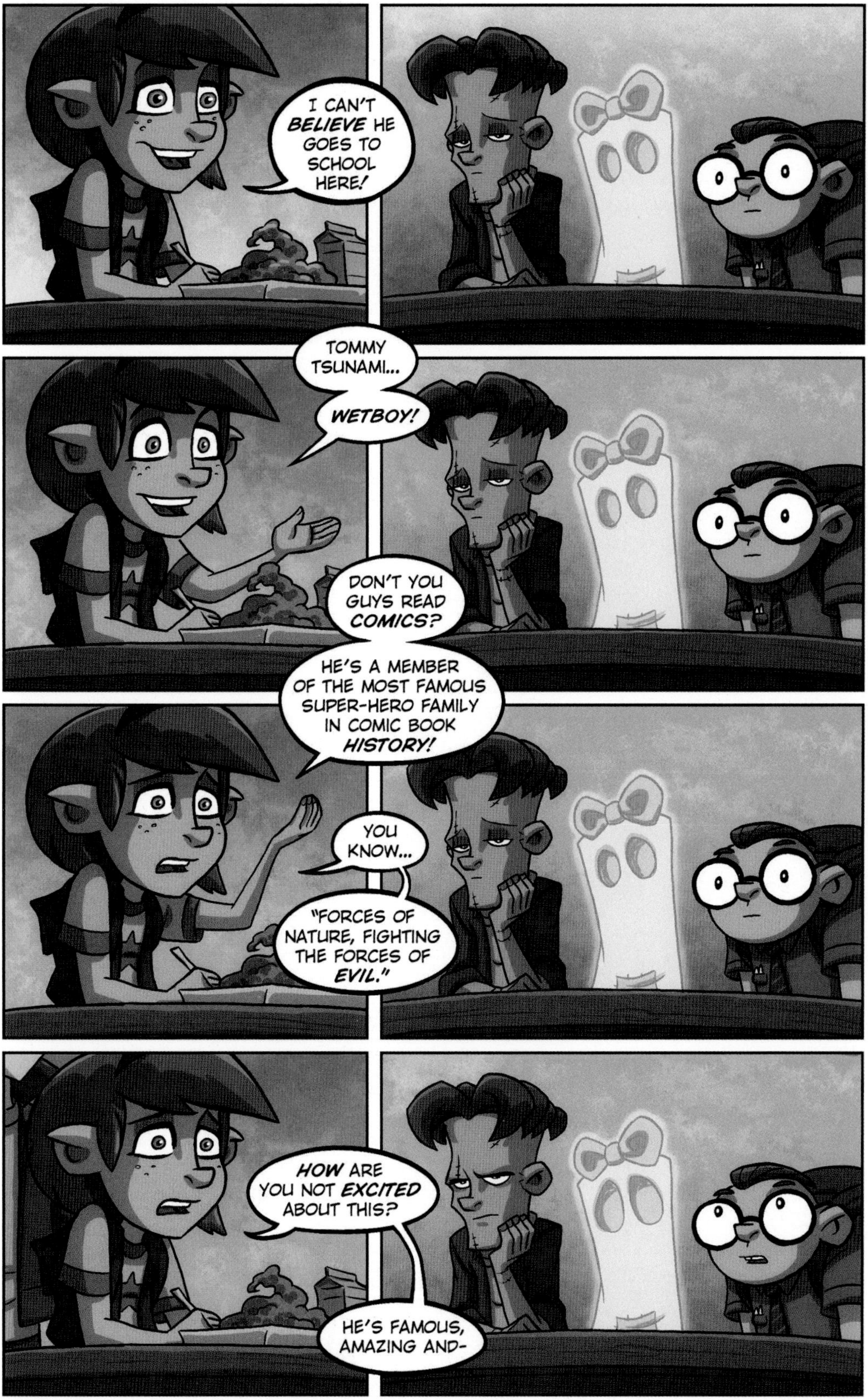
I CAN'T *BELIEVE* HE GOES TO SCHOOL HERE!
TOMMY TSUNAMI...
WETBOY!
DON'T YOU GUYS READ *COMICS?*
HE'S A MEMBER OF THE MOST FAMOUS SUPER-HERO FAMILY IN COMIC BOOK *HISTORY!*
YOU KNOW...
"FORCES OF NATURE, FIGHTING THE FORCES OF *EVIL.*"
HOW ARE YOU NOT *EXCITED* ABOUT THIS?
HE'S FAMOUS, AMAZING AND-

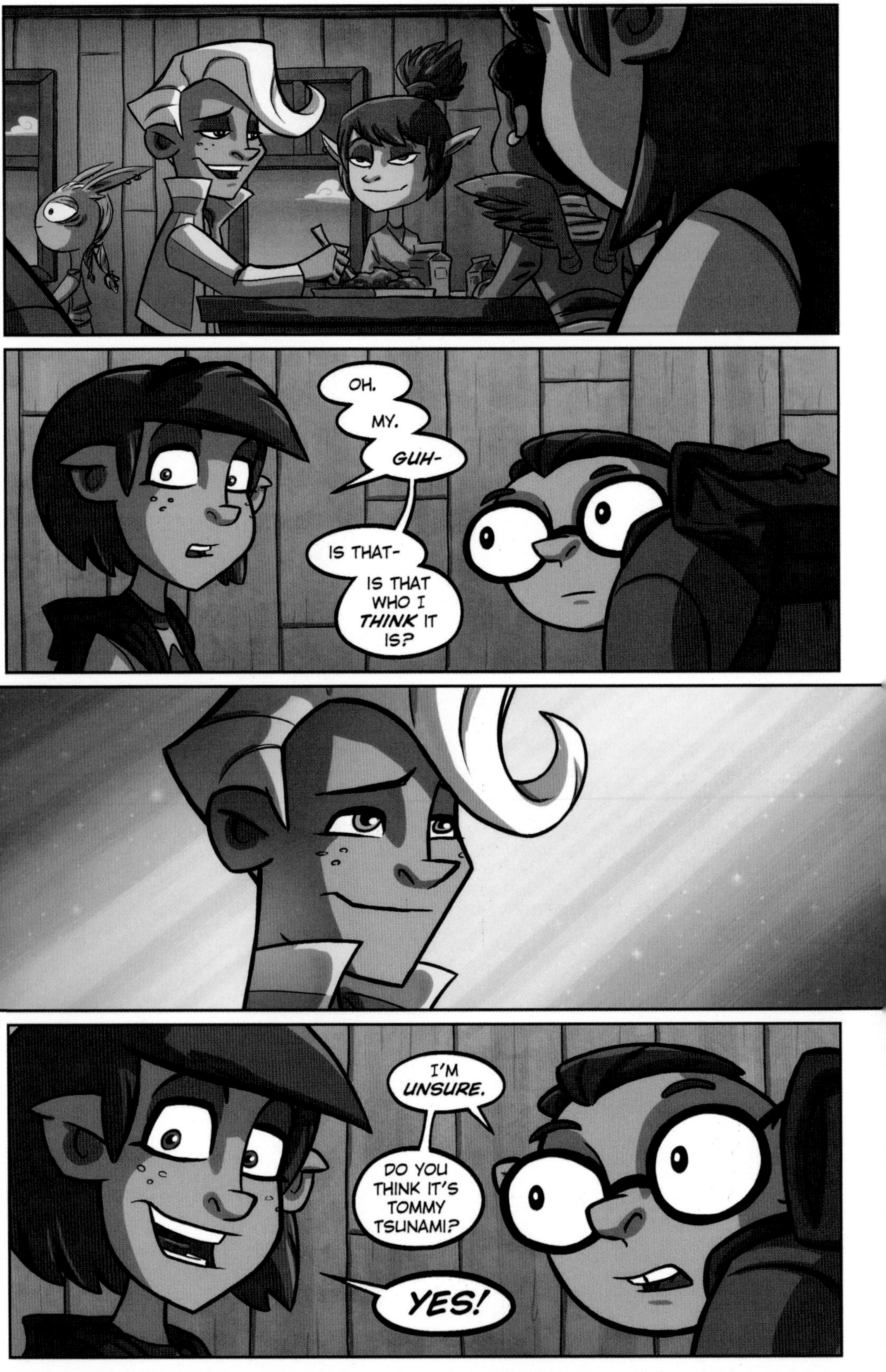
OH.
MY.
GUH-
IS THAT-
IS THAT WHO I *THINK* IT IS?
I'M *UNSURE.*
DO YOU THINK IT'S TOMMY TSUNAMI?
YES!

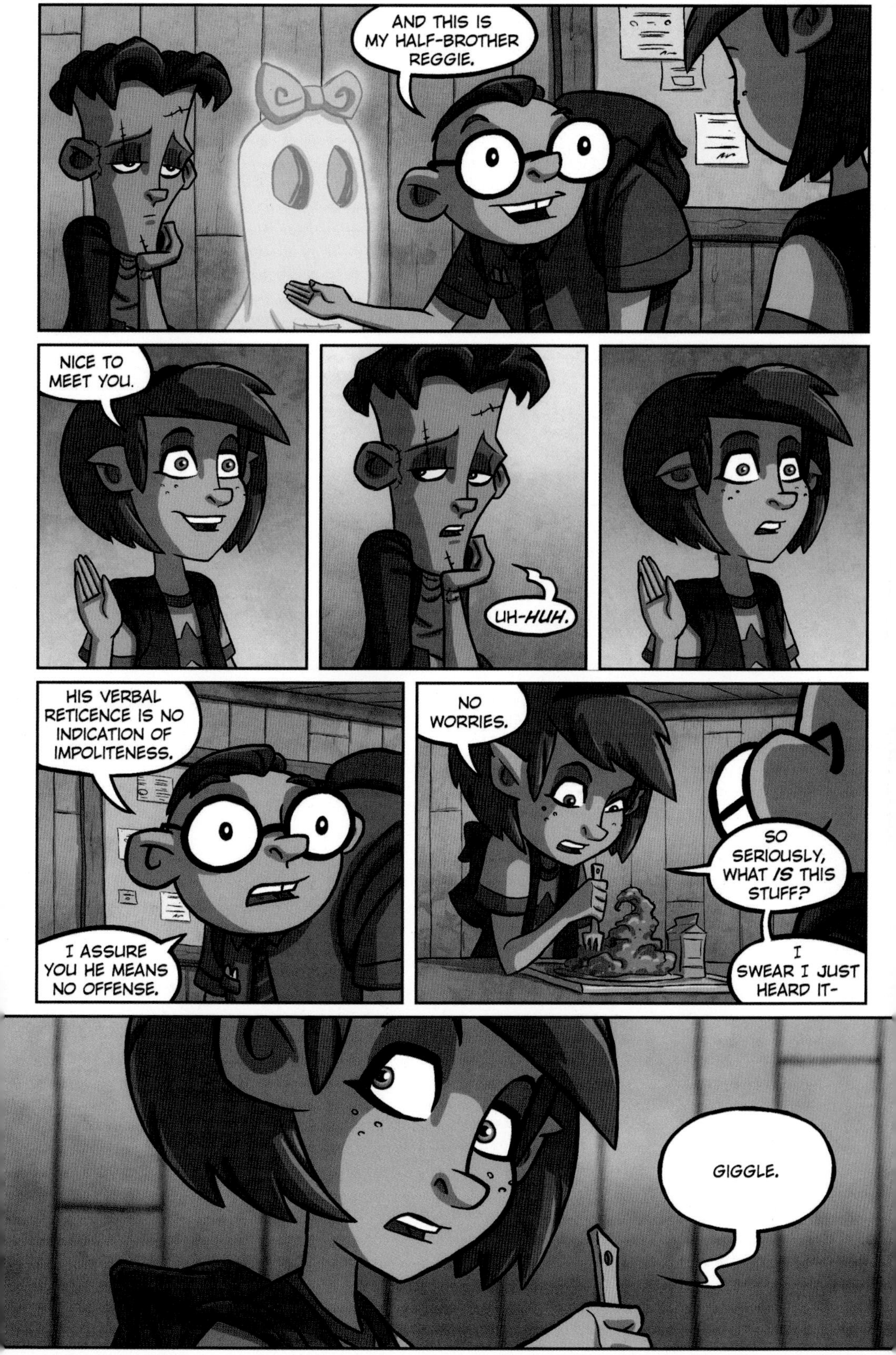

AND THIS IS MY HALF-BROTHER REGGIE.
NICE TO MEET YOU.
UH-*HUH.*
HIS VERBAL RETICENCE IS NO INDICATION OF IMPOLITENESS.
I ASSURE YOU HE MEANS NO OFFENSE.
NO WORRIES.
SO SERIOUSLY, WHAT *IS* THIS STUFF?
I SWEAR I JUST HEARD IT-
GIGGLE.

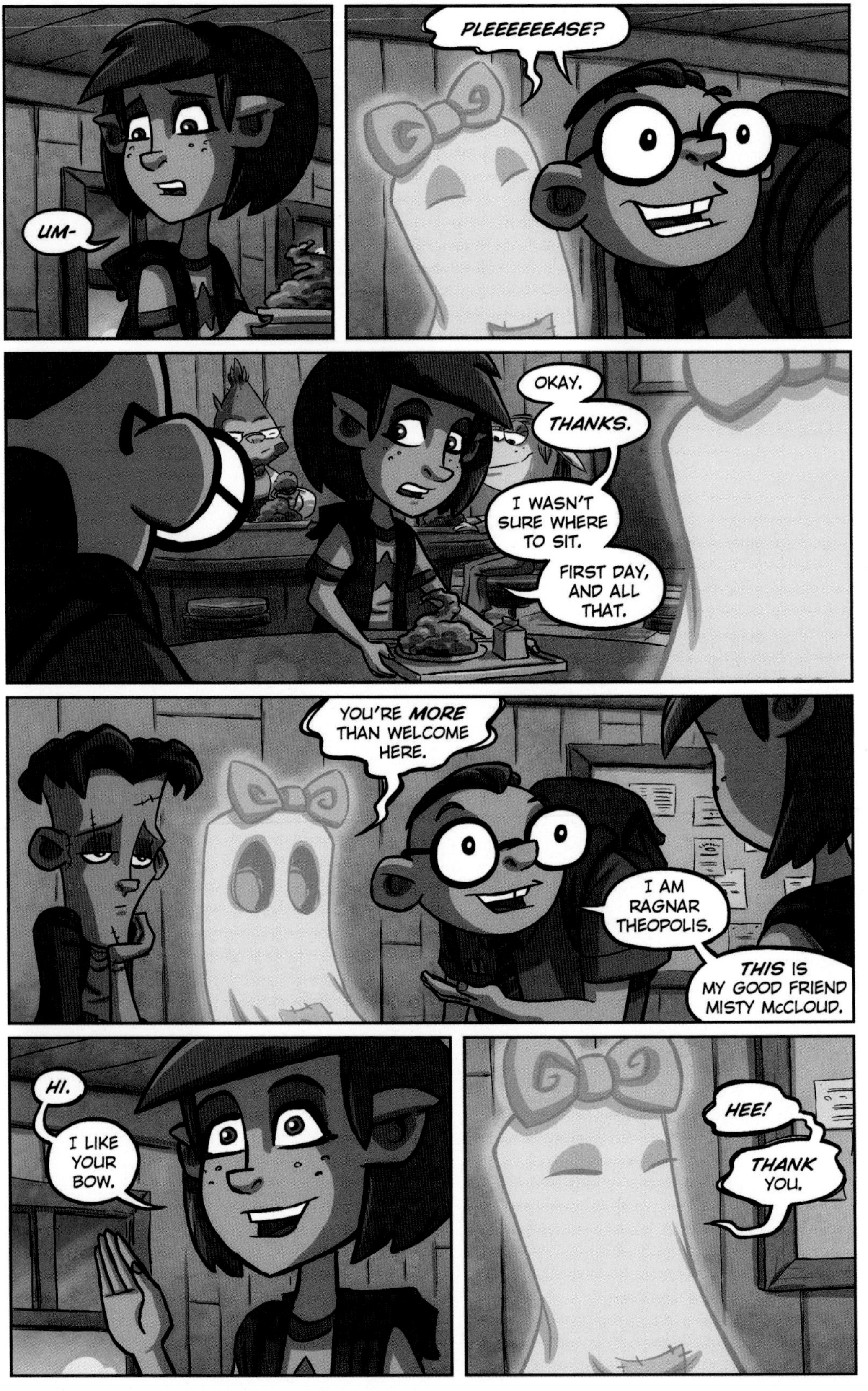
UM-
PLEEEEEEASE?
OKAY.
THANKS.
I WASN'T SURE WHERE TO SIT.
FIRST DAY, AND ALL THAT.
YOU'RE MORE THAN WELCOME HERE.
I AM RAGNAR THEOPOLIS.
THIS IS MY GOOD FRIEND MISTY McCLOUD.
HI.
I LIKE YOUR BOW.
HEE!
THANK YOU.

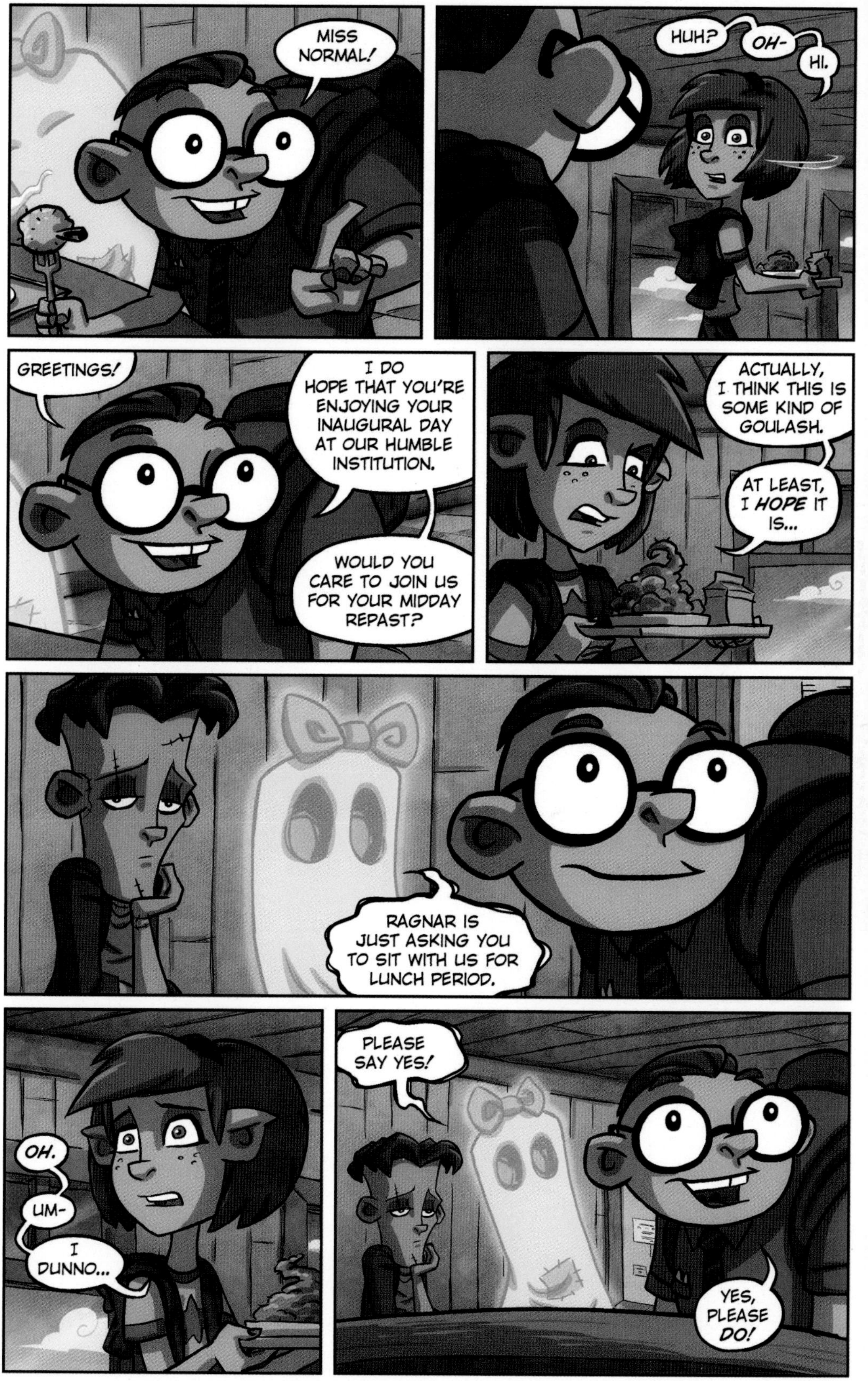
MISS NORMAL!
HUH?
OH-
HI.
GREETINGS!
I DO HOPE THAT YOU'RE ENJOYING YOUR INAUGURAL DAY AT OUR HUMBLE INSTITUTION.
WOULD YOU CARE TO JOIN US FOR YOUR MIDDAY REPAST?
ACTUALLY, I THINK THIS IS SOME KIND OF GOULASH.
AT LEAST, I *HOPE* IT IS...
RAGNAR IS JUST ASKING YOU TO SIT WITH US FOR LUNCH PERIOD.
OH.
UM-
I DUNNO...
PLEASE SAY YES!
YES, PLEASE *DO!*

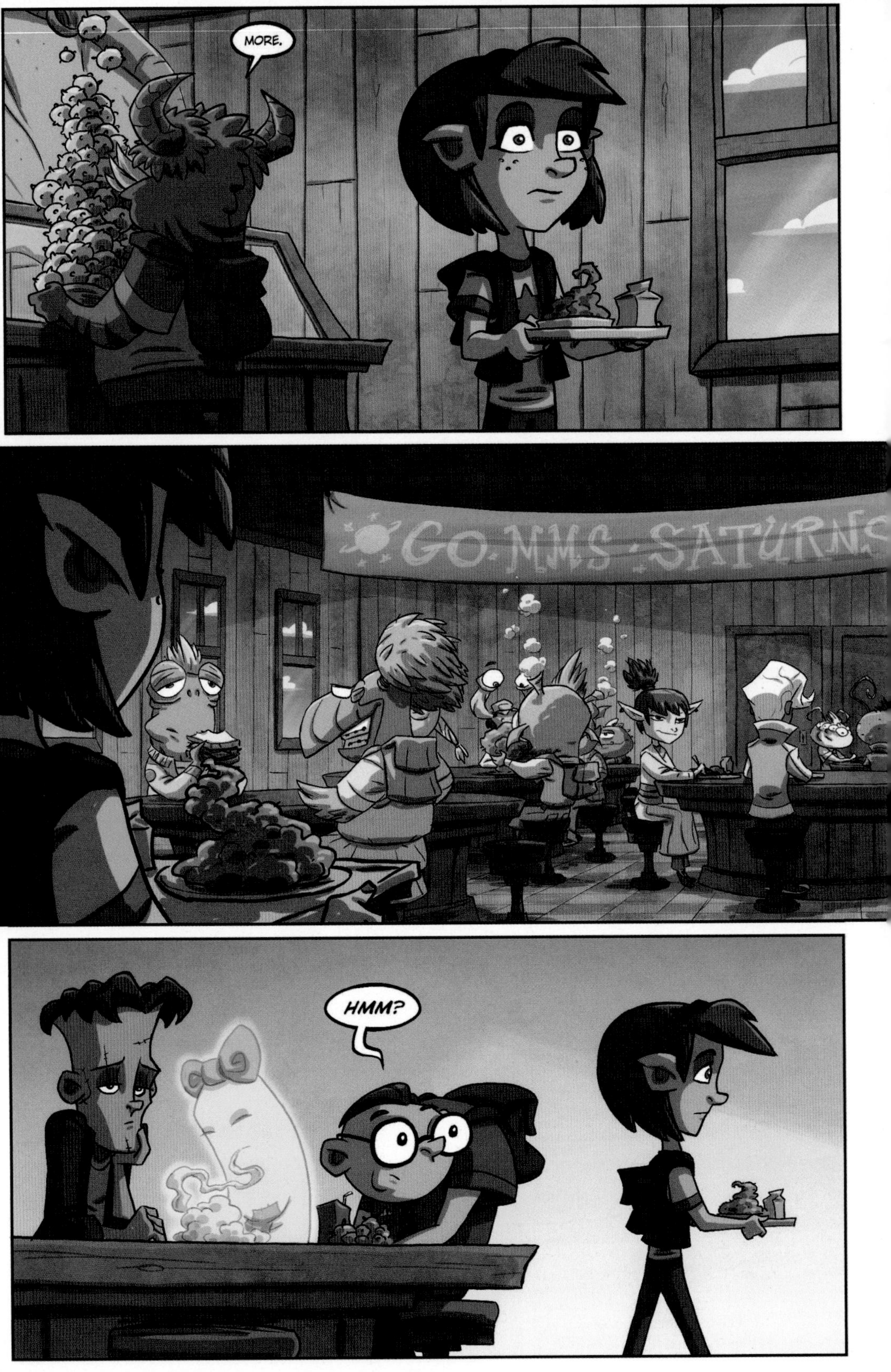
MORE.
GO MMS SATURNS
HMM?

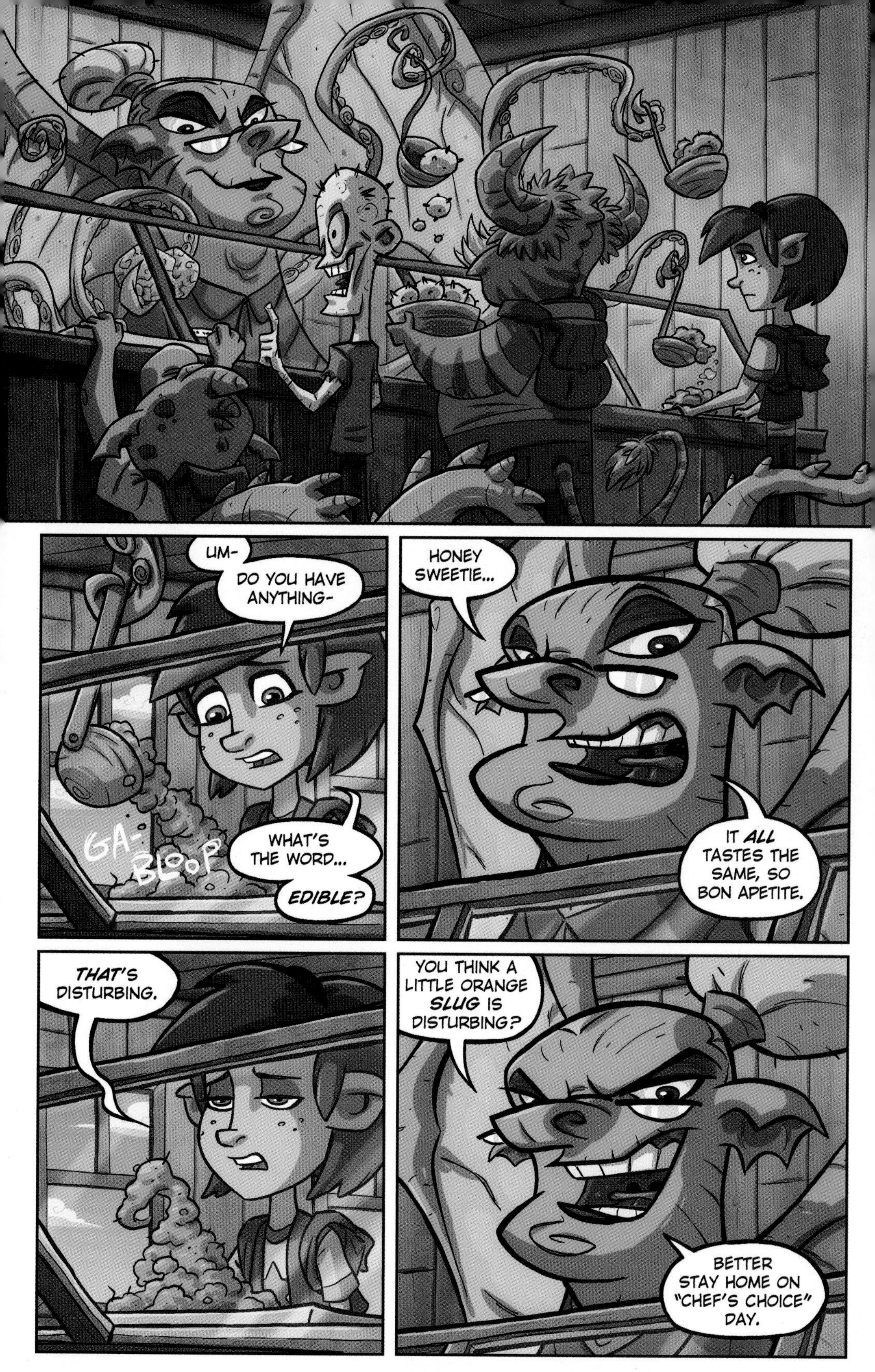
UM-
DO YOU HAVE ANYTHING-
GA-BLOOP
WHAT'S THE WORD... EDIBLE?
HONEY SWEETIE...
IT ALL TASTES THE SAME, SO BON APETITE.
THAT'S DISTURBING.
YOU THINK A LITTLE ORANGE SLUG IS DISTURBING?
BETTER STAY HOME ON "CHEF'S CHOICE" DAY.

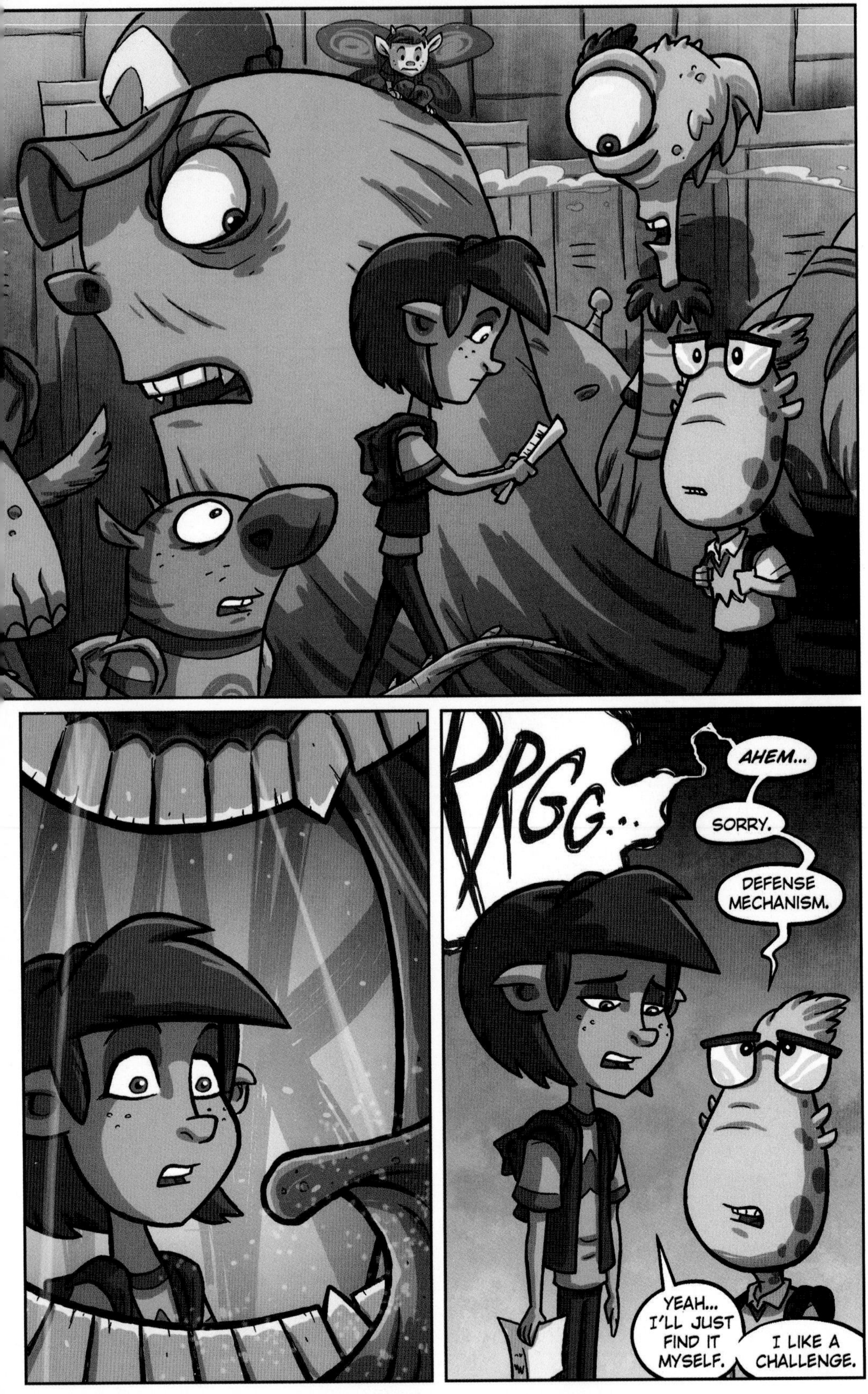
RRGG...
AHEM...
SORRY.
DEFENSE MECHANISM.
YEAH... I'LL JUST FIND IT MYSELF.
I LIKE A CHALLENGE.

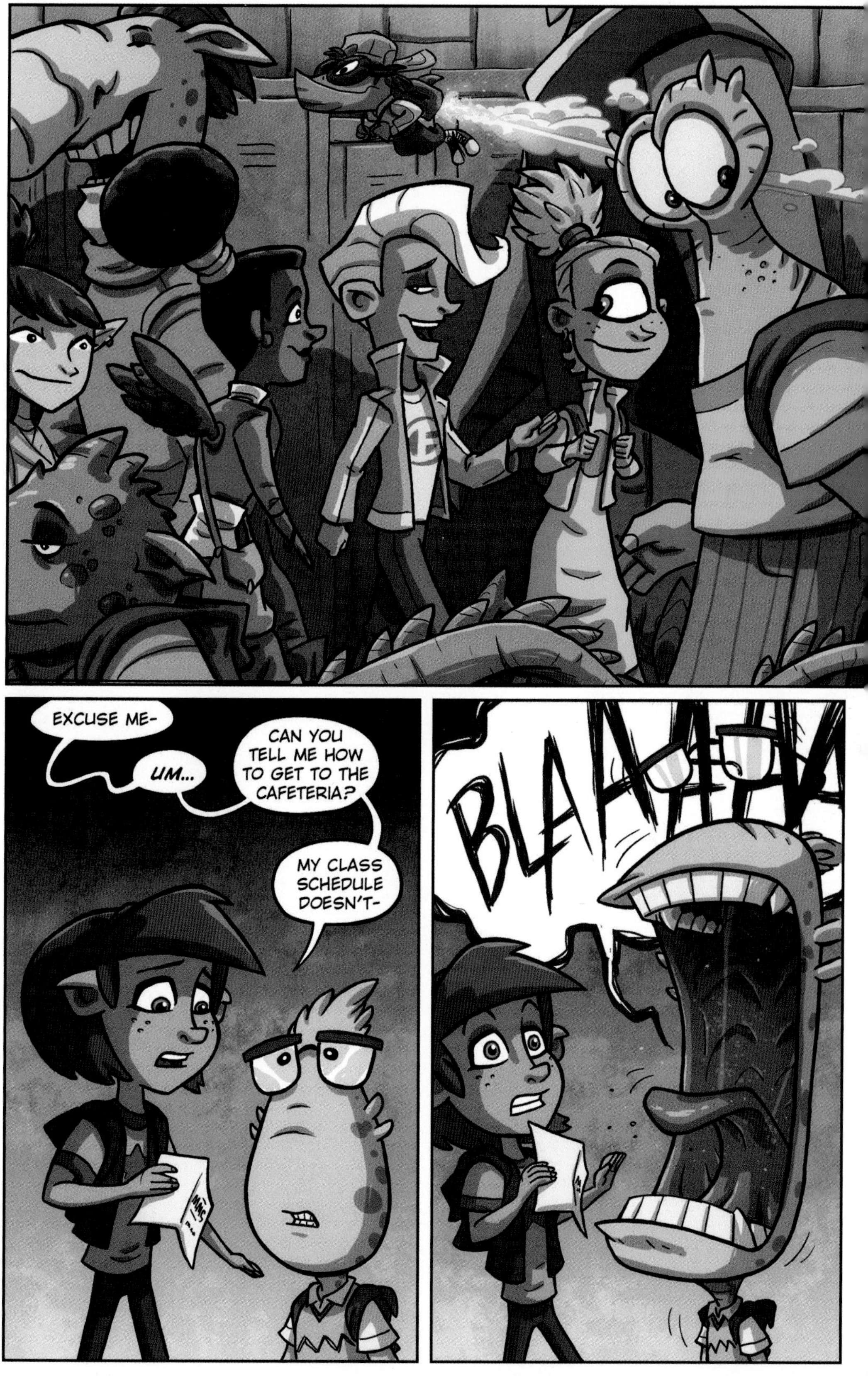
EXCUSE ME-
UM...
CAN YOU TELL ME HOW TO GET TO THE CAFETERIA?
MY CLASS SCHEDULE DOESN'T-
BLAAAA

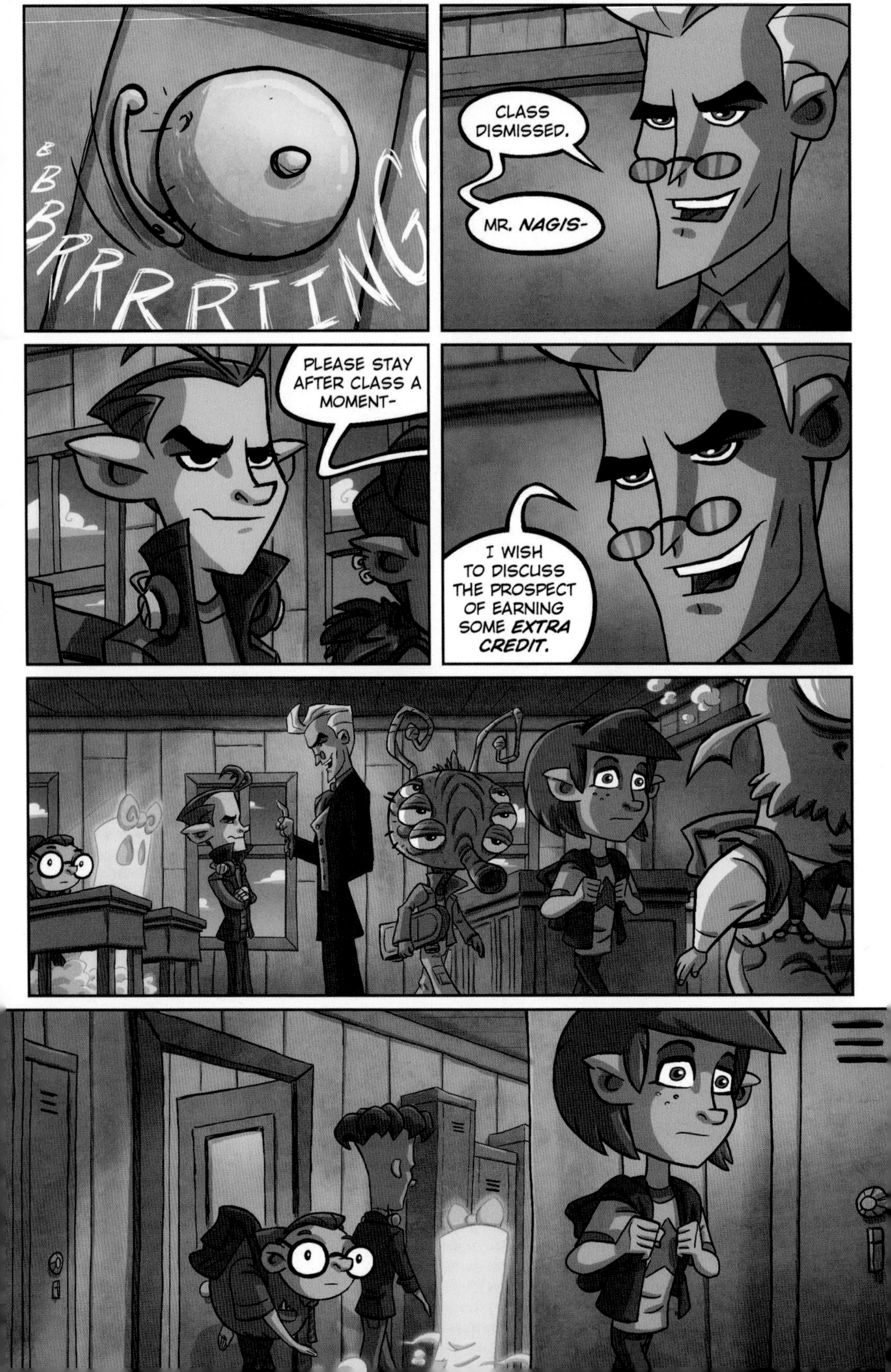
BBBRRRRRTING
CLASS DISMISSED.
MR. NAGIS-
PLEASE STAY AFTER CLASS A MOMENT-
I WISH TO DISCUSS THE PROSPECT OF EARNING SOME EXTRA CREDIT.

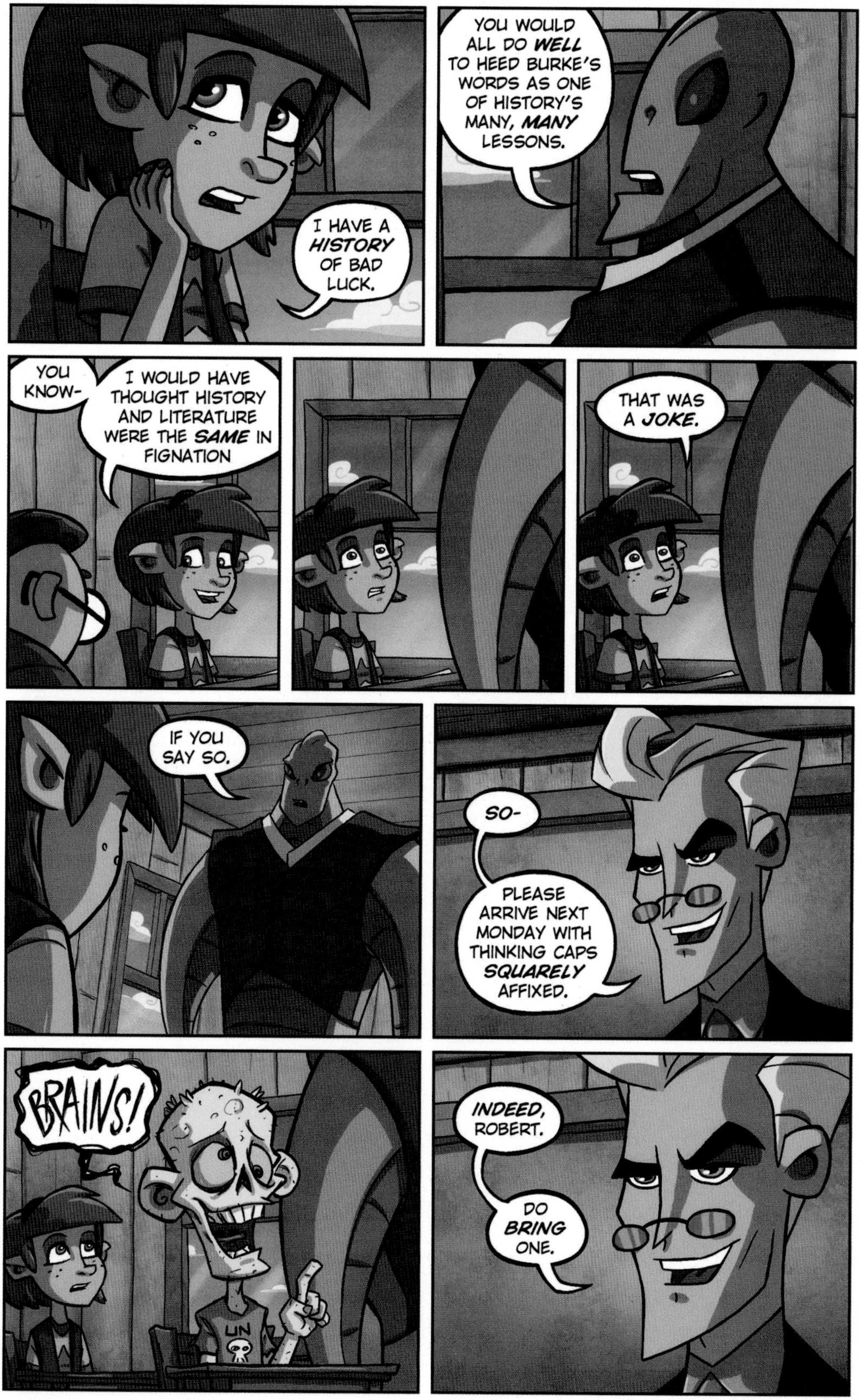
I HAVE A HISTORY OF BAD LUCK.
YOU WOULD ALL DO WELL TO HEED BURKE'S WORDS AS ONE OF HISTORY'S MANY, MANY LESSONS.
YOU KNOW-
I WOULD HAVE THOUGHT HISTORY AND LITERATURE WERE THE SAME IN FIGNATION
THAT WAS A JOKE.
IF YOU SAY SO.
SO-
PLEASE ARRIVE NEXT MONDAY WITH THINKING CAPS SQUARELY AFFIXED.
BRAINS!
INDEED, ROBERT.
DO BRING ONE.
UN

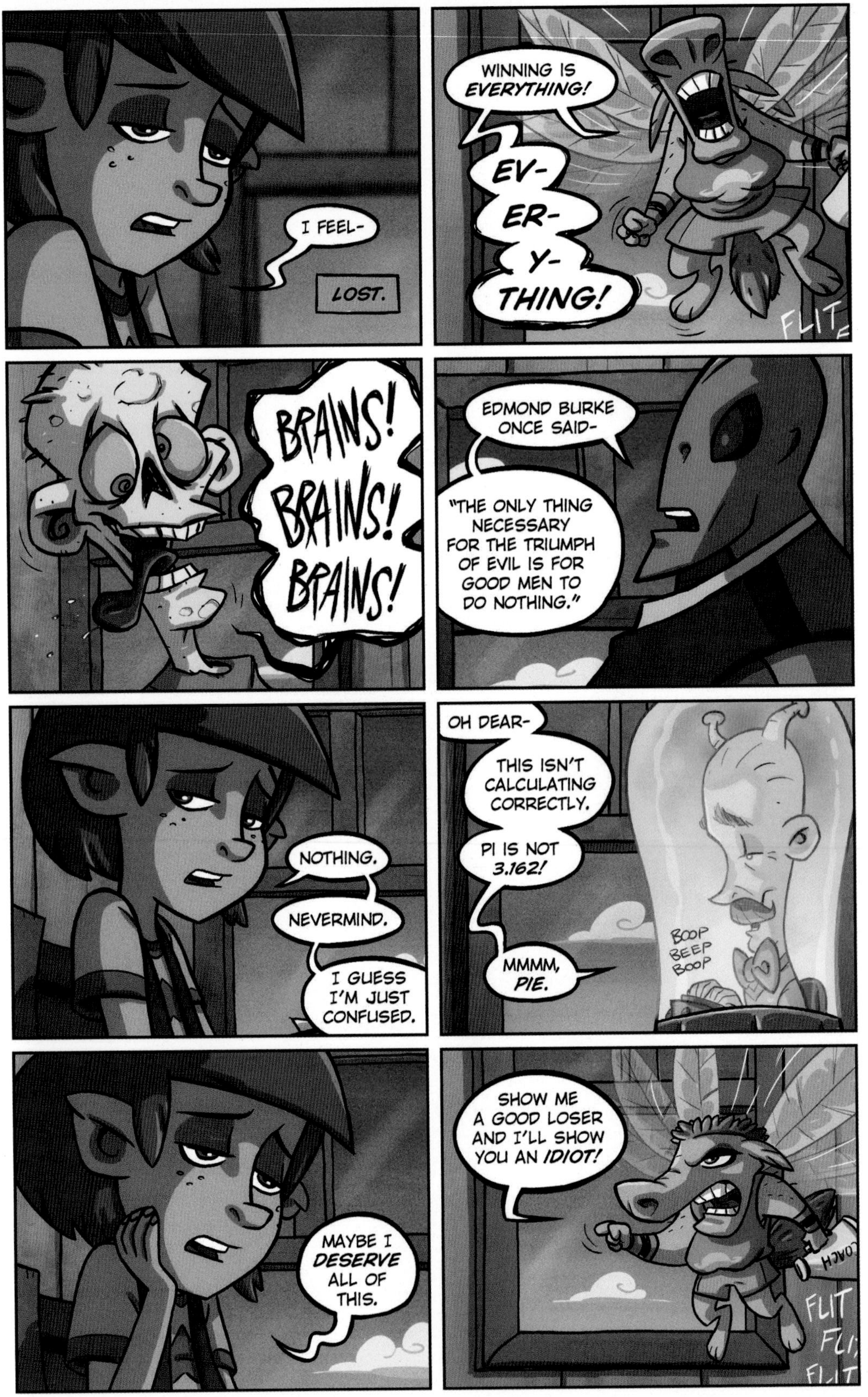
I FEEL-
LOST.
WINNING IS EVERYTHING!
EV- ER- Y- THING!
FLIT
BRAINS! BRAINS! BRAINS!
EDMOND BURKE ONCE SAID-
"THE ONLY THING NECESSARY FOR THE TRIUMPH OF EVIL IS FOR GOOD MEN TO DO NOTHING."
NOTHING.
NEVERMIND.
I GUESS I'M JUST CONFUSED.
OH DEAR-
THIS ISN'T CALCULATING CORRECTLY.
PI IS NOT 3.162!
BOOP BEEP BOOP
MMMM, PIE.
MAYBE I DESERVE ALL OF THIS.
SHOW ME A GOOD LOSER AND I'LL SHOW YOU AN IDIOT!
COACH
FLIT
FLIT
FLIT

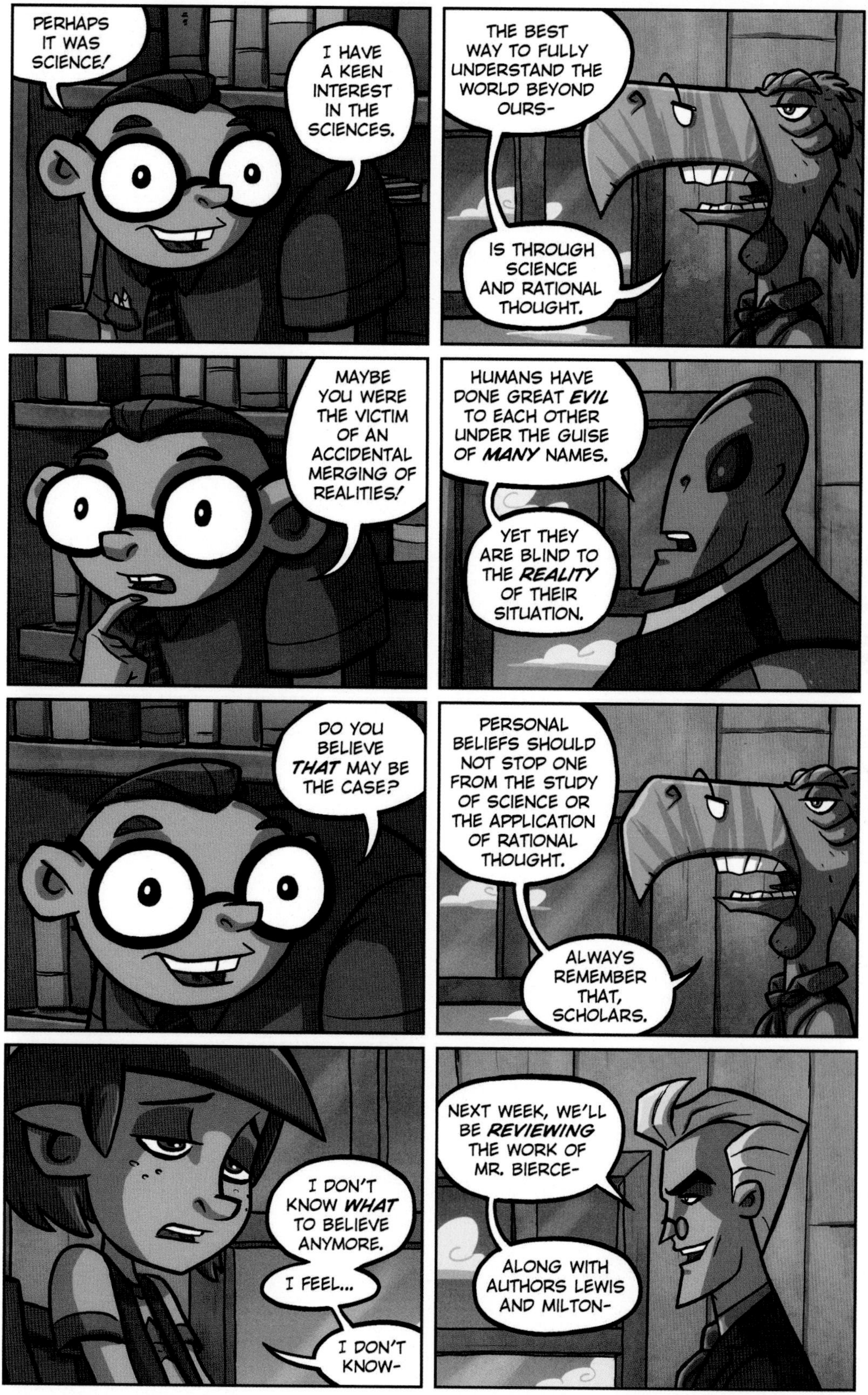
PERHAPS IT WAS SCIENCE!
I HAVE A KEEN INTEREST IN THE SCIENCES.
THE BEST WAY TO FULLY UNDERSTAND THE WORLD BEYOND OURS-
IS THROUGH SCIENCE AND RATIONAL THOUGHT.
MAYBE YOU WERE THE VICTIM OF AN ACCIDENTAL MERGING OF REALITIES!
HUMANS HAVE DONE GREAT EVIL TO EACH OTHER UNDER THE GUISE OF MANY NAMES.
YET THEY ARE BLIND TO THE REALITY OF THEIR SITUATION.
DO YOU BELIEVE THAT MAY BE THE CASE?
PERSONAL BELIEFS SHOULD NOT STOP ONE FROM THE STUDY OF SCIENCE OR THE APPLICATION OF RATIONAL THOUGHT.
ALWAYS REMEMBER THAT, SCHOLARS.
I DON'T KNOW WHAT TO BELIEVE ANYMORE.
I FEEL...
I DON'T KNOW-
NEXT WEEK, WE'LL BE REVIEWING THE WORK OF MR. BIERCE-
ALONG WITH AUTHORS LEWIS AND MILTON-

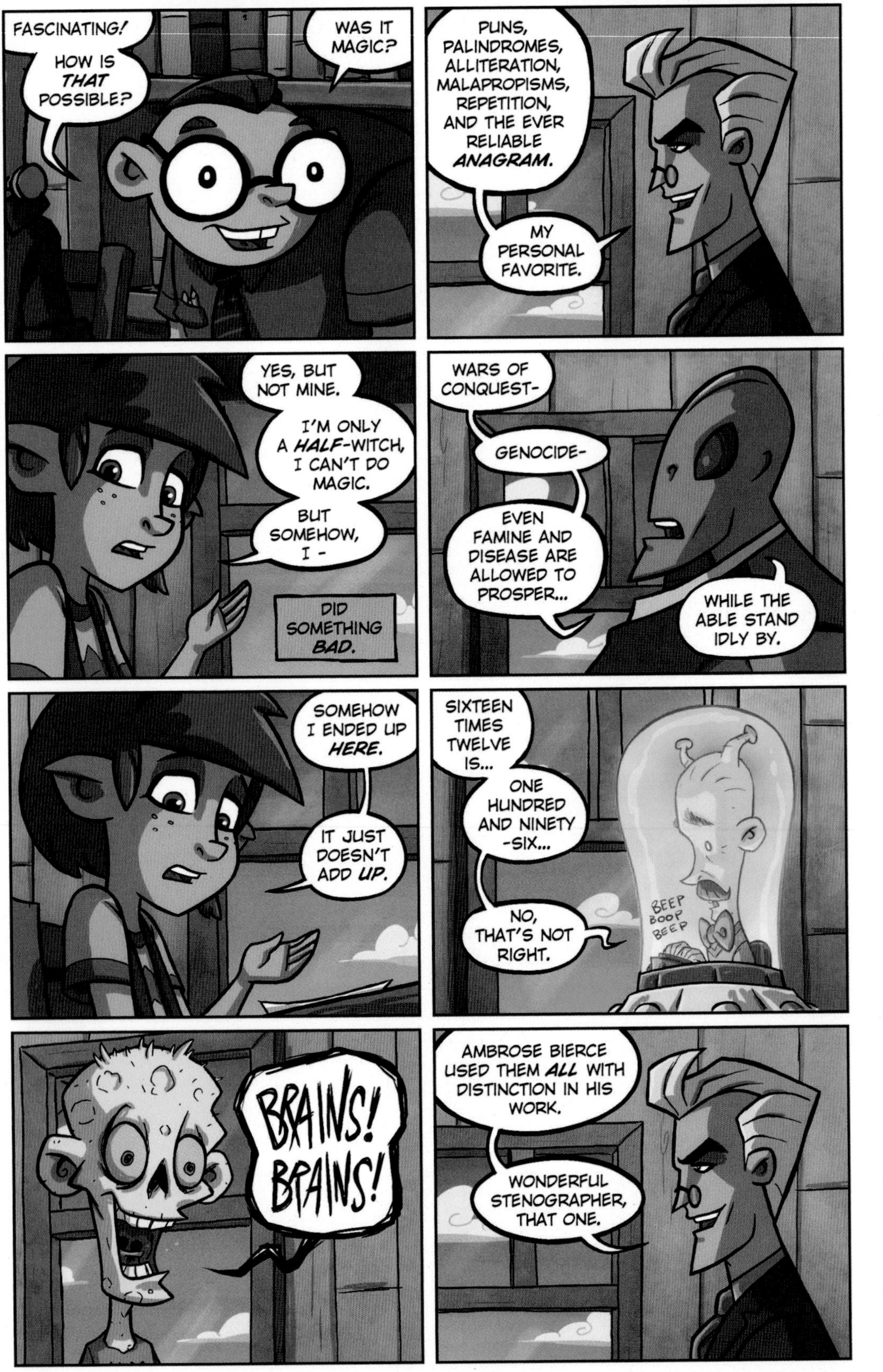
FASCINATING!
HOW IS THAT POSSIBLE?
WAS IT MAGIC?
PUNS, PALINDROMES, ALLITERATION, MALAPROPISMS, REPETITION, AND THE EVER RELIABLE ANAGRAM.
MY PERSONAL FAVORITE.
YES, BUT NOT MINE.
I'M ONLY A HALF-WITCH, I CAN'T DO MAGIC.
BUT SOMEHOW, I -
DID SOMETHING BAD.
WARS OF CONQUEST-
GENOCIDE-
EVEN FAMINE AND DISEASE ARE ALLOWED TO PROSPER...
WHILE THE ABLE STAND IDLY BY.
SOMEHOW I ENDED UP HERE.
IT JUST DOESN'T ADD UP.
SIXTEEN TIMES TWELVE IS...
ONE HUNDRED AND NINETY -SIX...
NO, THAT'S NOT RIGHT.
BEEP BOOP BEEP
BRAINS! BRAINS!
AMBROSE BIERCE USED THEM ALL WITH DISTINCTION IN HIS WORK.
WONDERFUL STENOGRAPHER, THAT ONE.

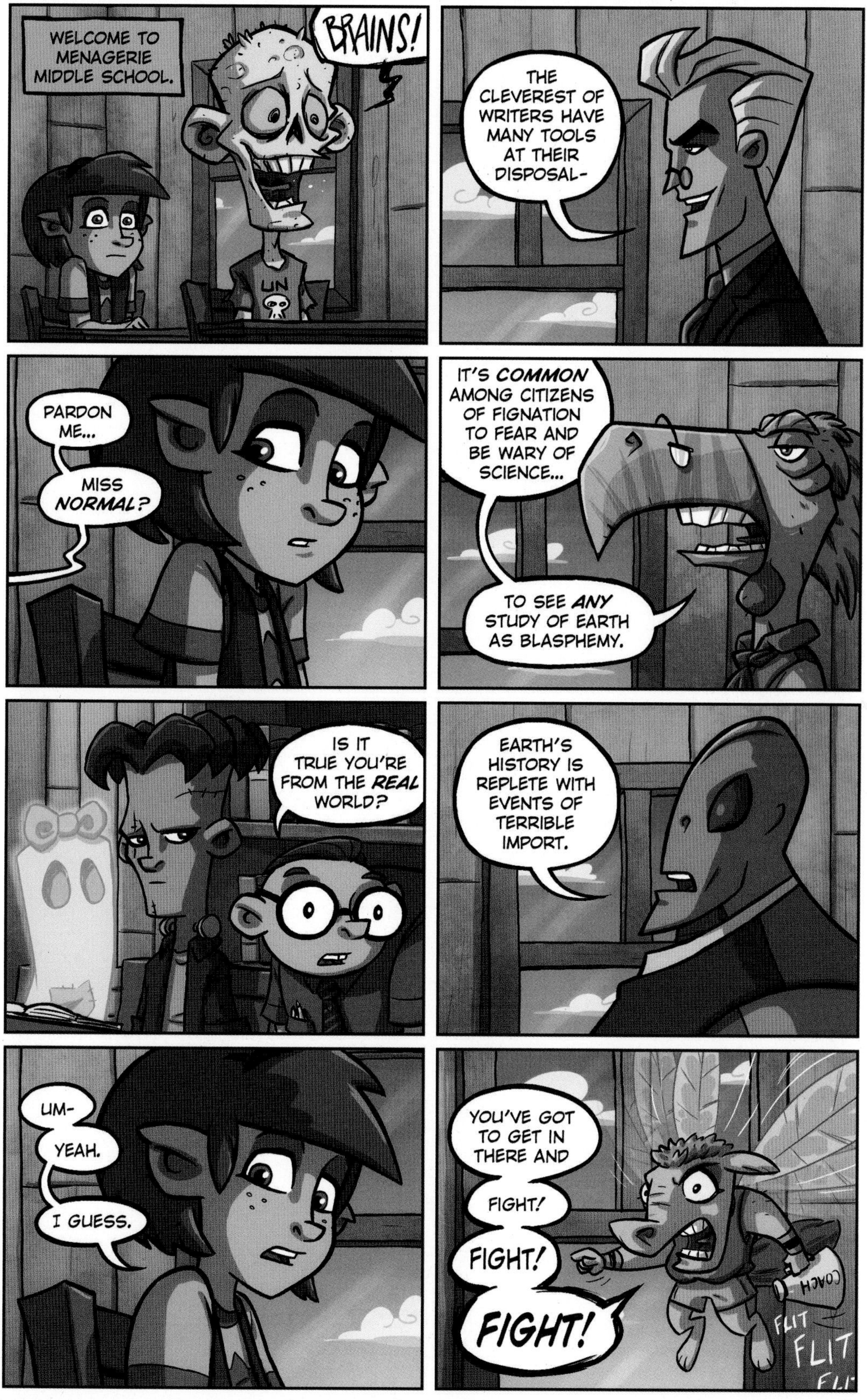
WELCOME TO MENAGERIE MIDDLE SCHOOL.
BRAINS!
THE CLEVEREST OF WRITERS HAVE MANY TOOLS AT THEIR DISPOSAL-
PARDON ME...
MISS NORMAL?
IT'S COMMON AMONG CITIZENS OF FIGNATION TO FEAR AND BE WARY OF SCIENCE...
TO SEE ANY STUDY OF EARTH AS BLASPHEMY.
UN
IS IT TRUE YOU'RE FROM THE REAL WORLD?
EARTH'S HISTORY IS REPLETE WITH EVENTS OF TERRIBLE IMPORT.
UM-
YEAH.
I GUESS.
YOU'VE GOT TO GET IN THERE AND
FIGHT!
FIGHT!
FIGHT!
COACH
FLIT
FLIT

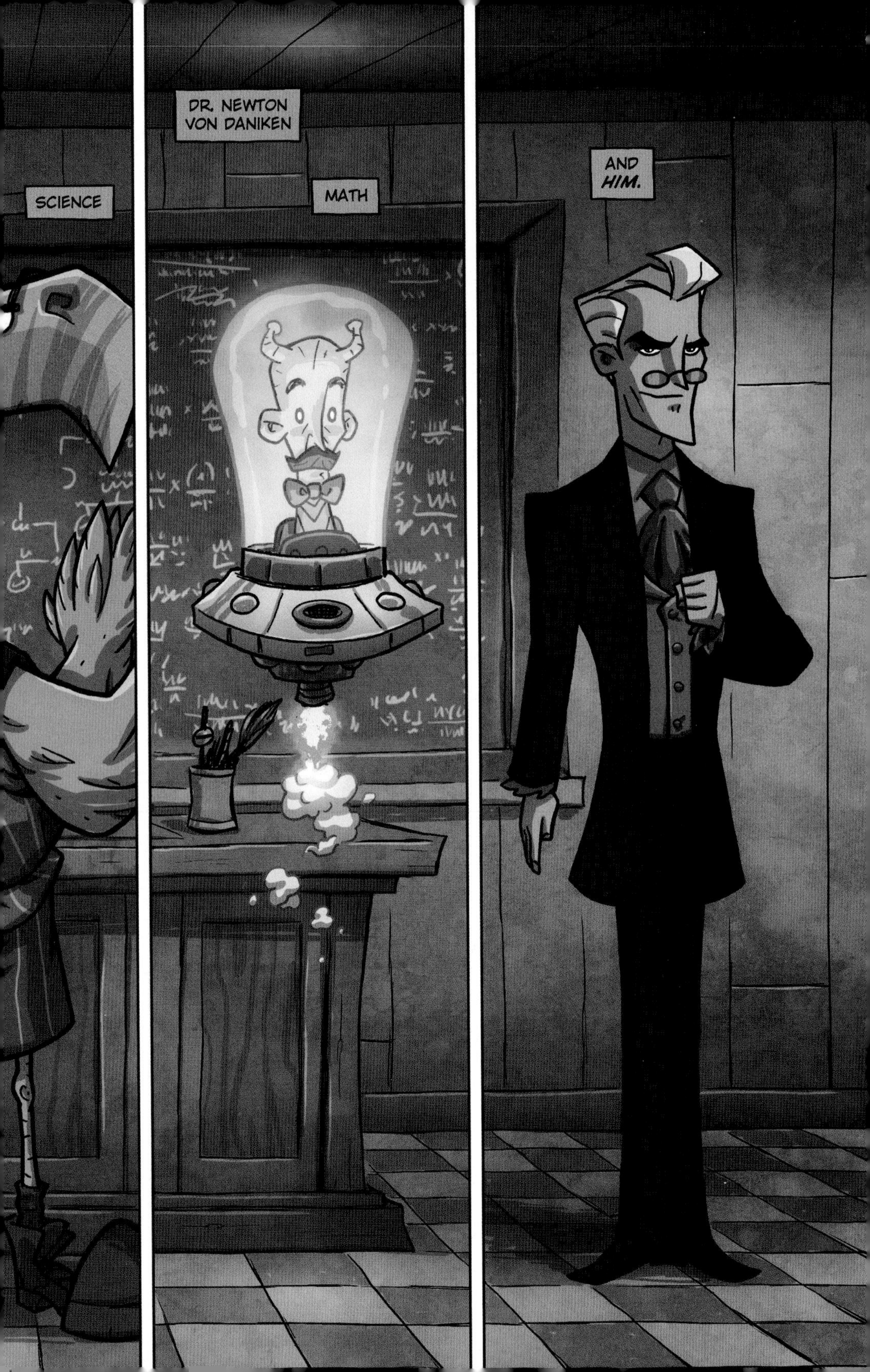
SCIENCE
DR. NEWTON VON DANIKEN
MATH
AND *HIM.*

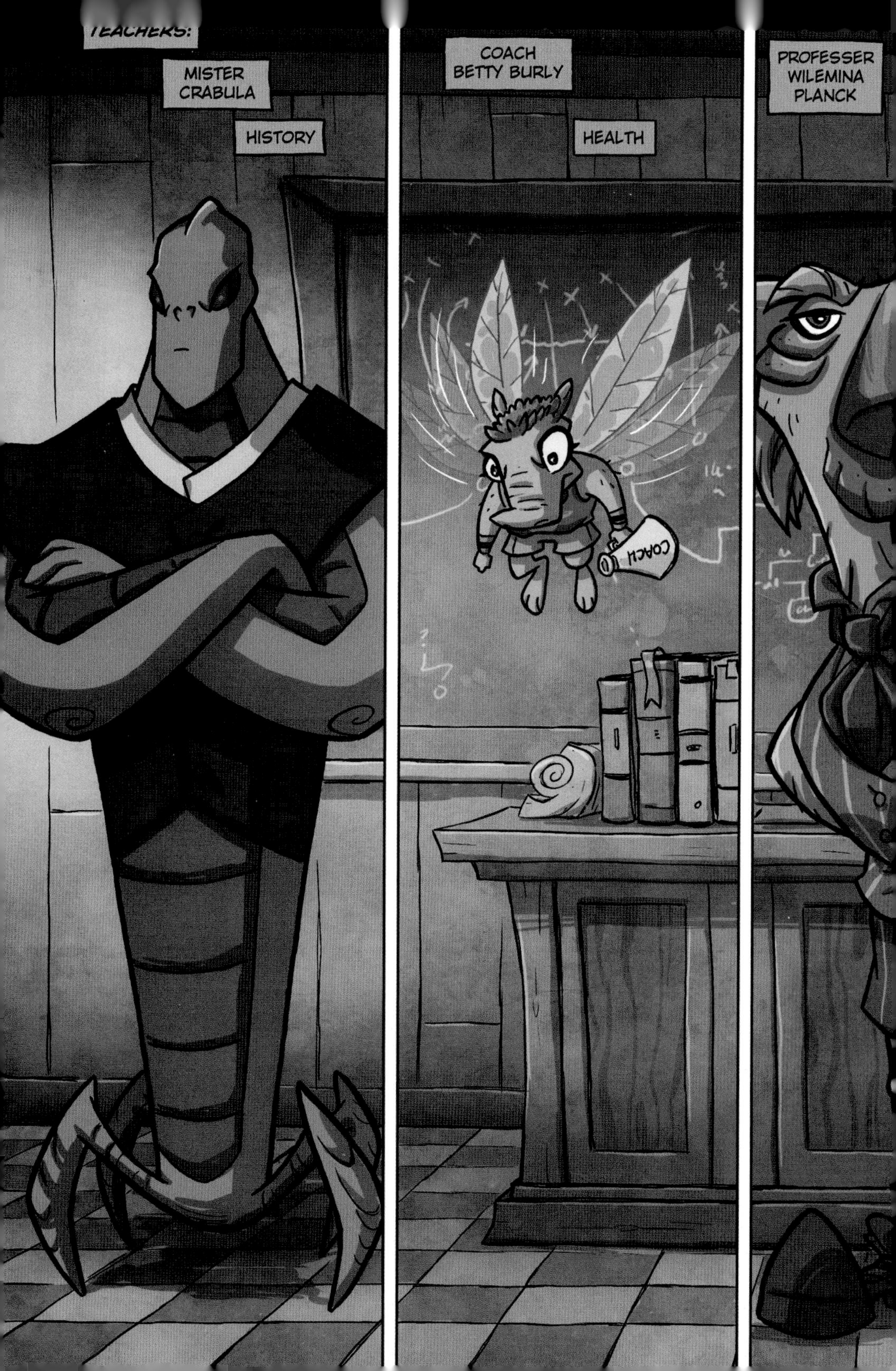
TEACHERS:
MISTER CRABULA
HISTORY
COACH BETTY BURLY
HEALTH
COACH
PROFESSER WILEMINA PLANCK

Chapter 4

The Class ★ Menagerie

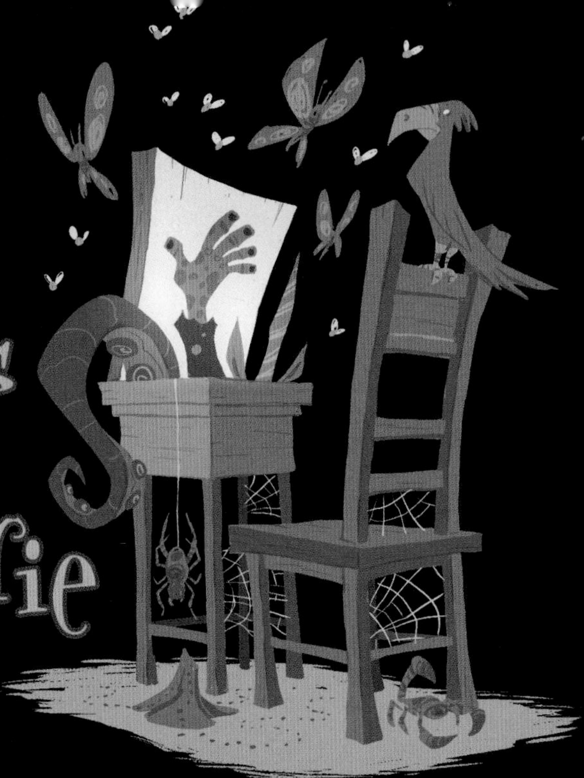

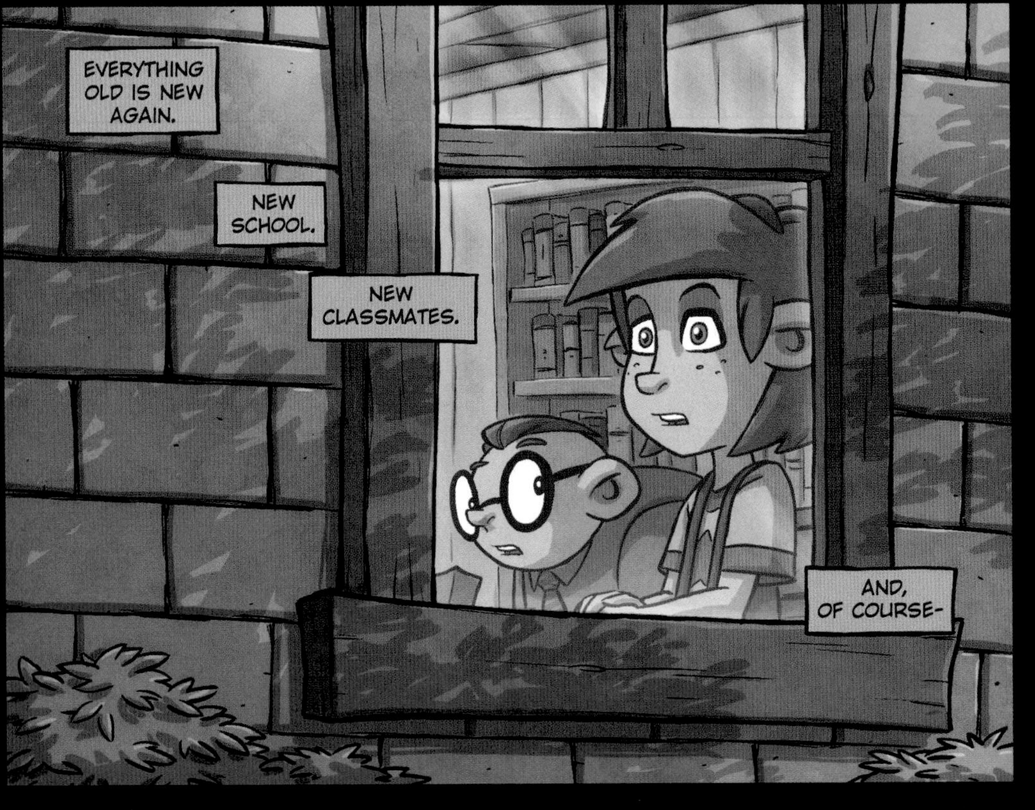
EVERYTHING OLD IS NEW AGAIN.
NEW SCHOOL.
NEW CLASSMATES.
AND, OF COURSE-

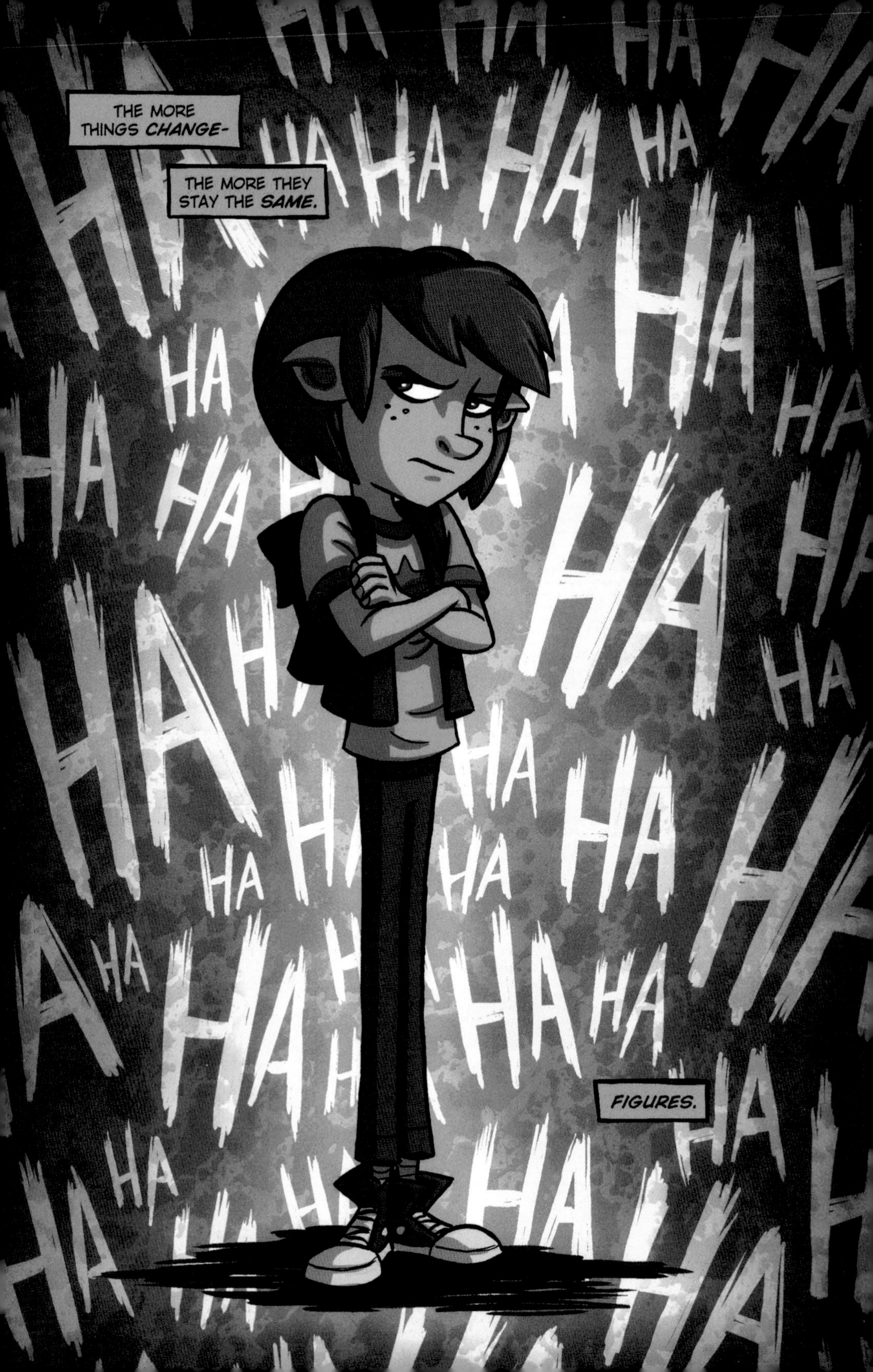
THE MORE THINGS CHANGE-
THE MORE THEY STAY THE SAME.
FIGURES.

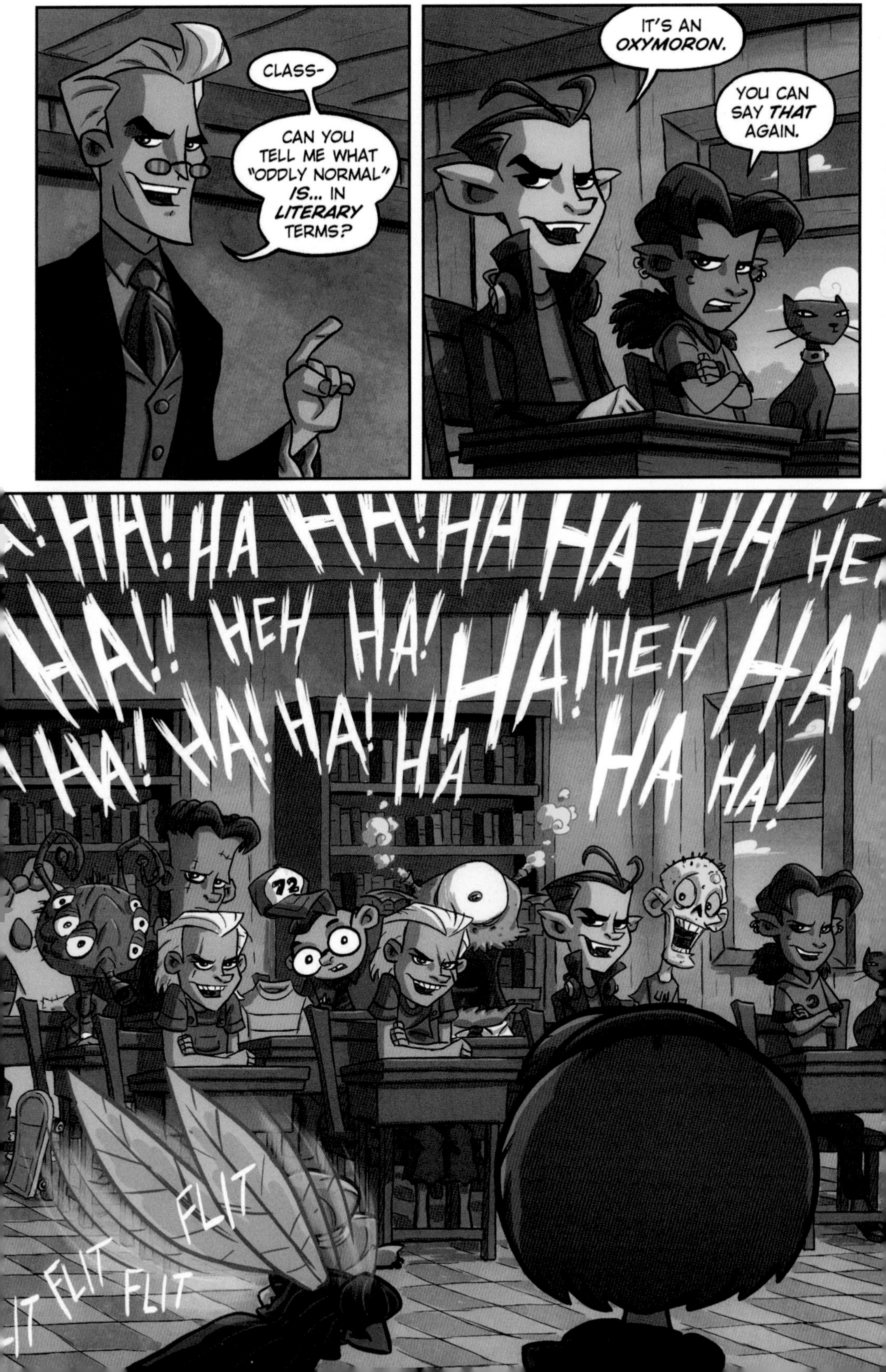

CLASS-
CAN YOU TELL ME WHAT "ODDLY NORMAL" *IS*... IN *LITERARY* TERMS?
IT'S AN *OXYMORON.*
YOU CAN SAY *THAT* AGAIN.
HA! HA HA! HA HA HH
HA!! HEH HA! HA! HEH HA!
HA! HA! HA! HA HA HA HA!
FLIT FLIT FLIT

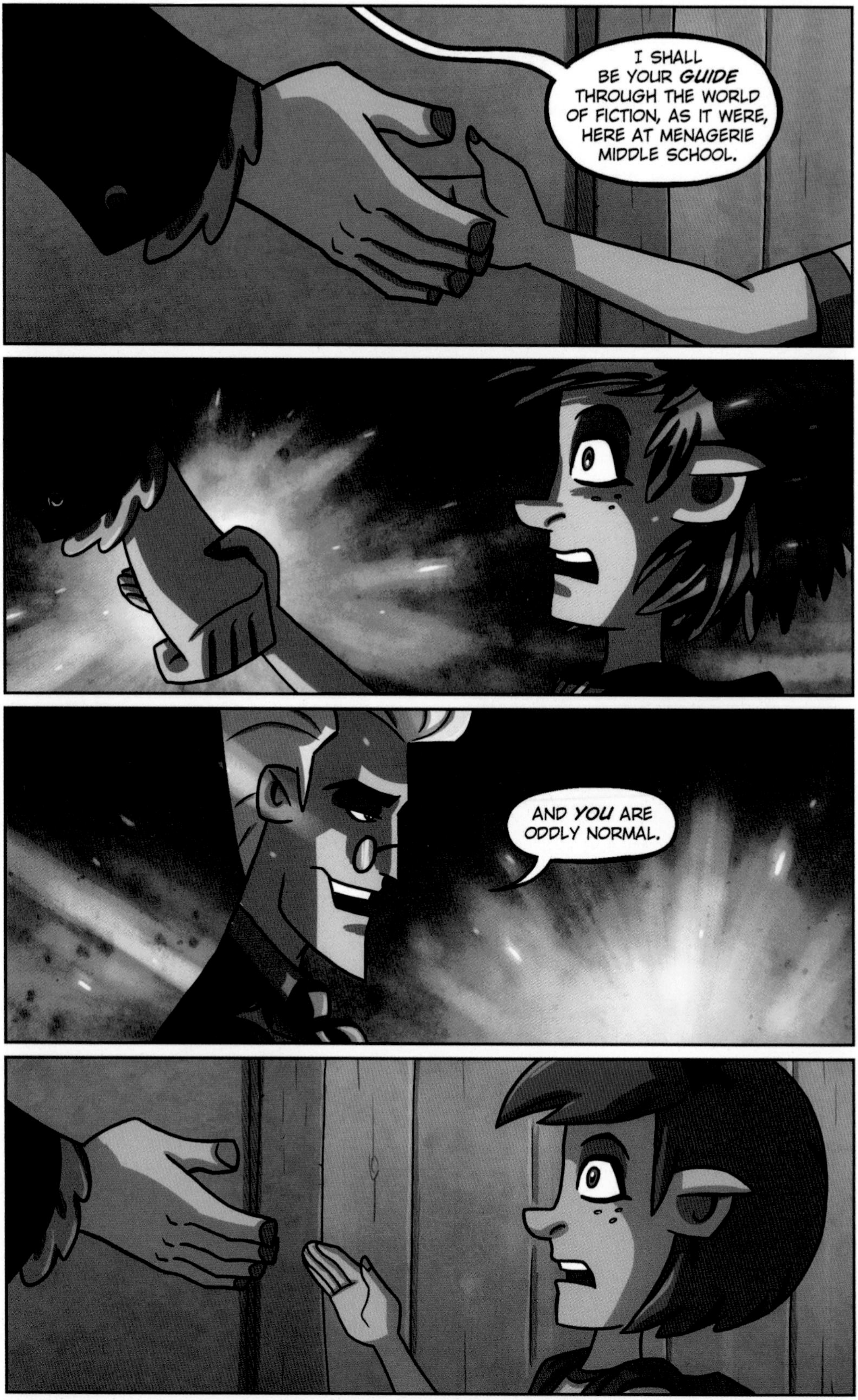
I SHALL BE YOUR GUIDE THROUGH THE WORLD OF FICTION, AS IT WERE, HERE AT MENAGERIE MIDDLE SCHOOL.
AND YOU ARE ODDLY NORMAL.

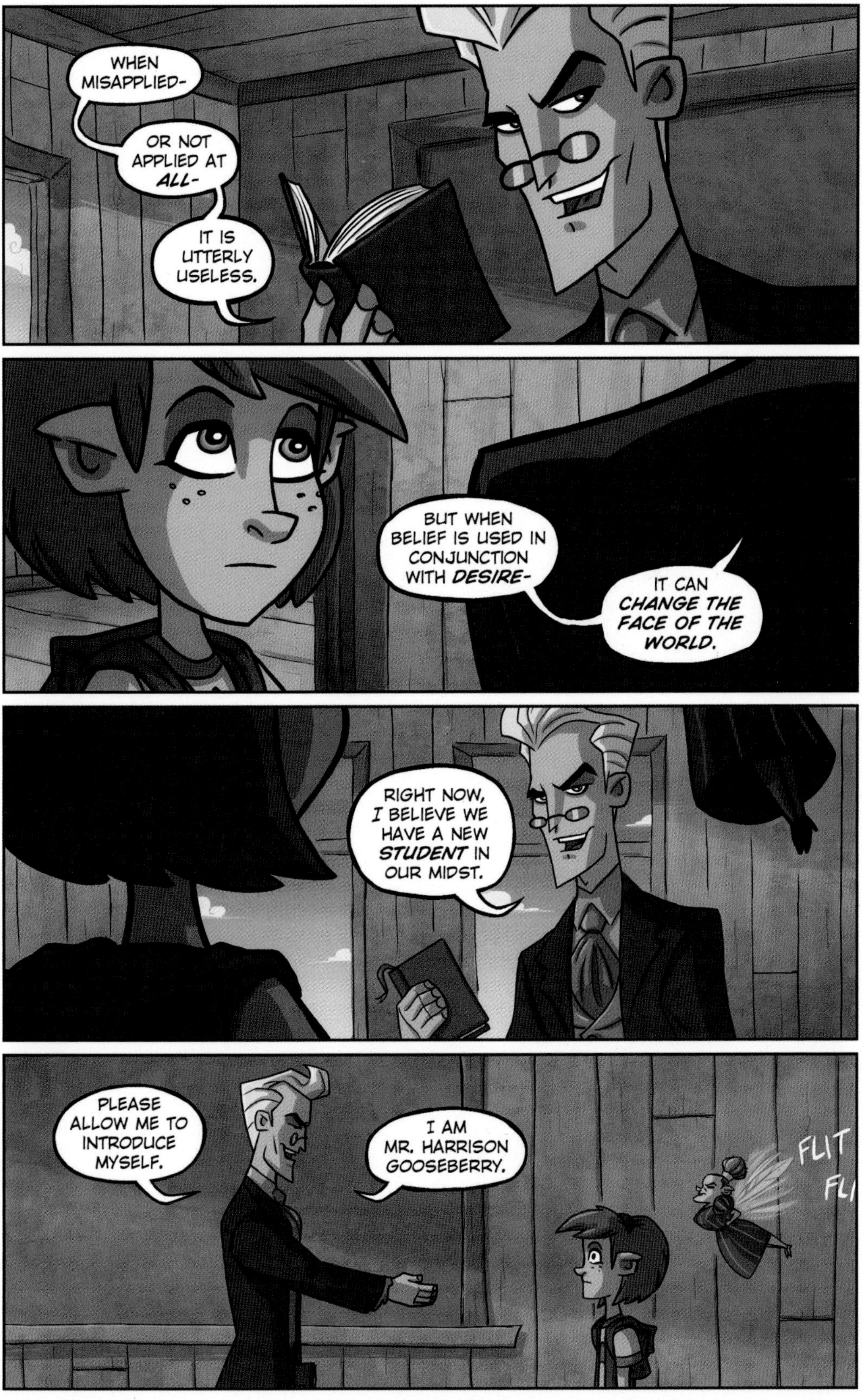
WHEN MISAPPLIED-
OR NOT APPLIED AT ALL-
IT IS UTTERLY USELESS.
BUT WHEN BELIEF IS USED IN CONJUNCTION WITH DESIRE-
IT CAN CHANGE THE FACE OF THE WORLD.
RIGHT NOW, I BELIEVE WE HAVE A NEW STUDENT IN OUR MIDST.
PLEASE ALLOW ME TO INTRODUCE MYSELF.
I AM MR. HARRISON GOOSEBERRY.
FLIT

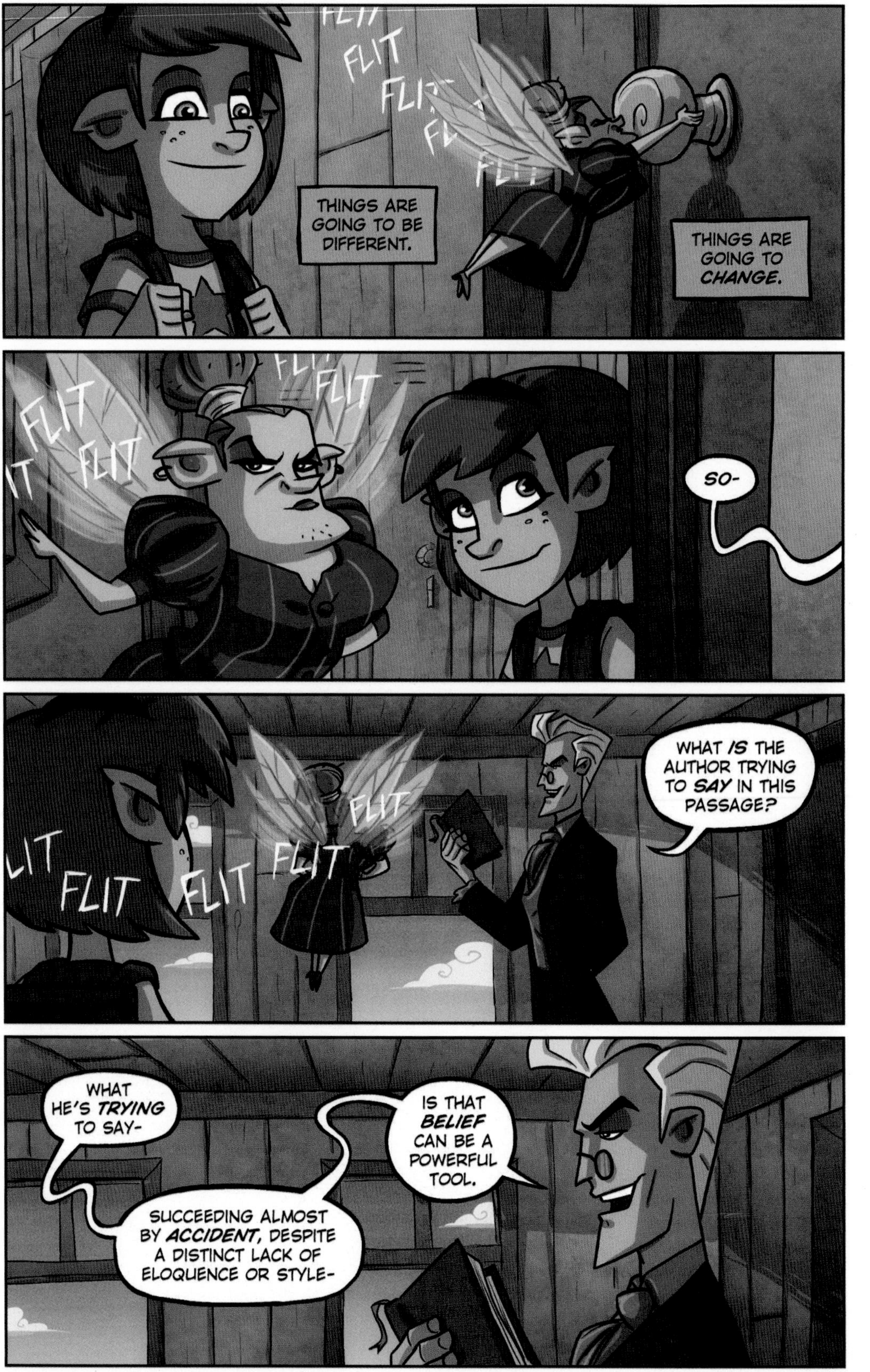
FLIT
FLIT
FLIT
FLIT
FLIT
THINGS ARE GOING TO BE DIFFERENT.
THINGS ARE GOING TO *CHANGE.*
FLIT
FLIT
FLIT
FLIT
FLIT
SO-
WHAT *IS* THE AUTHOR TRYING TO *SAY* IN THIS PASSAGE?
FLIT
FLIT
FLIT
FLIT
FLIT
WHAT HE'S *TRYING* TO SAY-
IS THAT *BELIEF* CAN BE A POWERFUL TOOL.
SUCCEEDING ALMOST BY *ACCIDENT,* DESPITE A DISTINCT LACK OF ELOQUENCE OR STYLE-

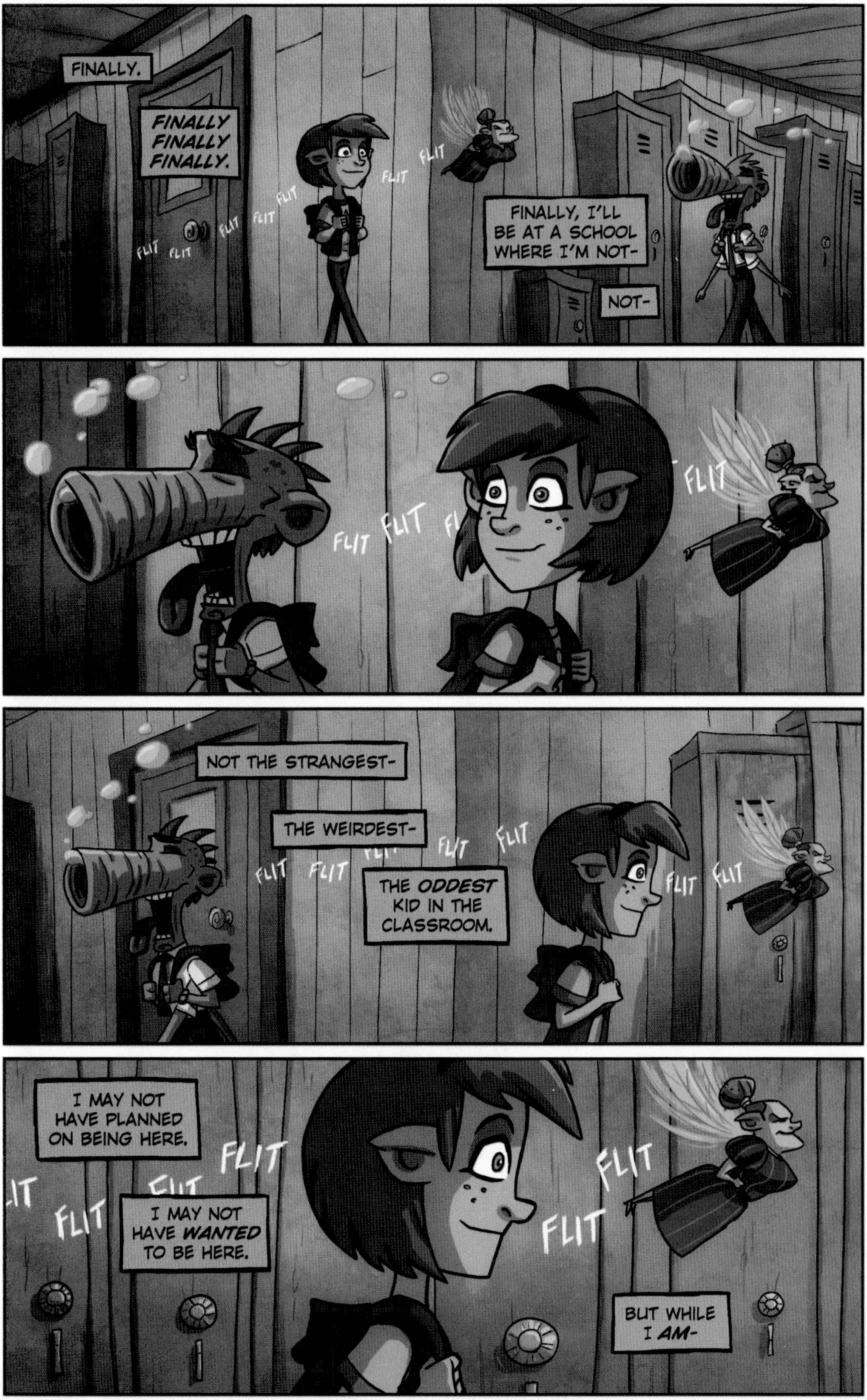

FINALLY.
FINALLY FINALLY FINALLY.
FLIT FLIT FLIT FLIT FLIT FLIT FLIT
FINALLY, I'LL BE AT A SCHOOL WHERE I'M NOT-
NOT-
FLIT FLIT FLIT
NOT THE STRANGEST-
THE WEIRDEST-
FLIT FLIT FLIT FLIT FLIT FLIT
THE ODDEST KID IN THE CLASSROOM.
I MAY NOT HAVE PLANNED ON BEING HERE.
FLIT FLIT
I MAY NOT HAVE WANTED TO BE HERE.
FLIT FLIT
BUT WHILE I AM-

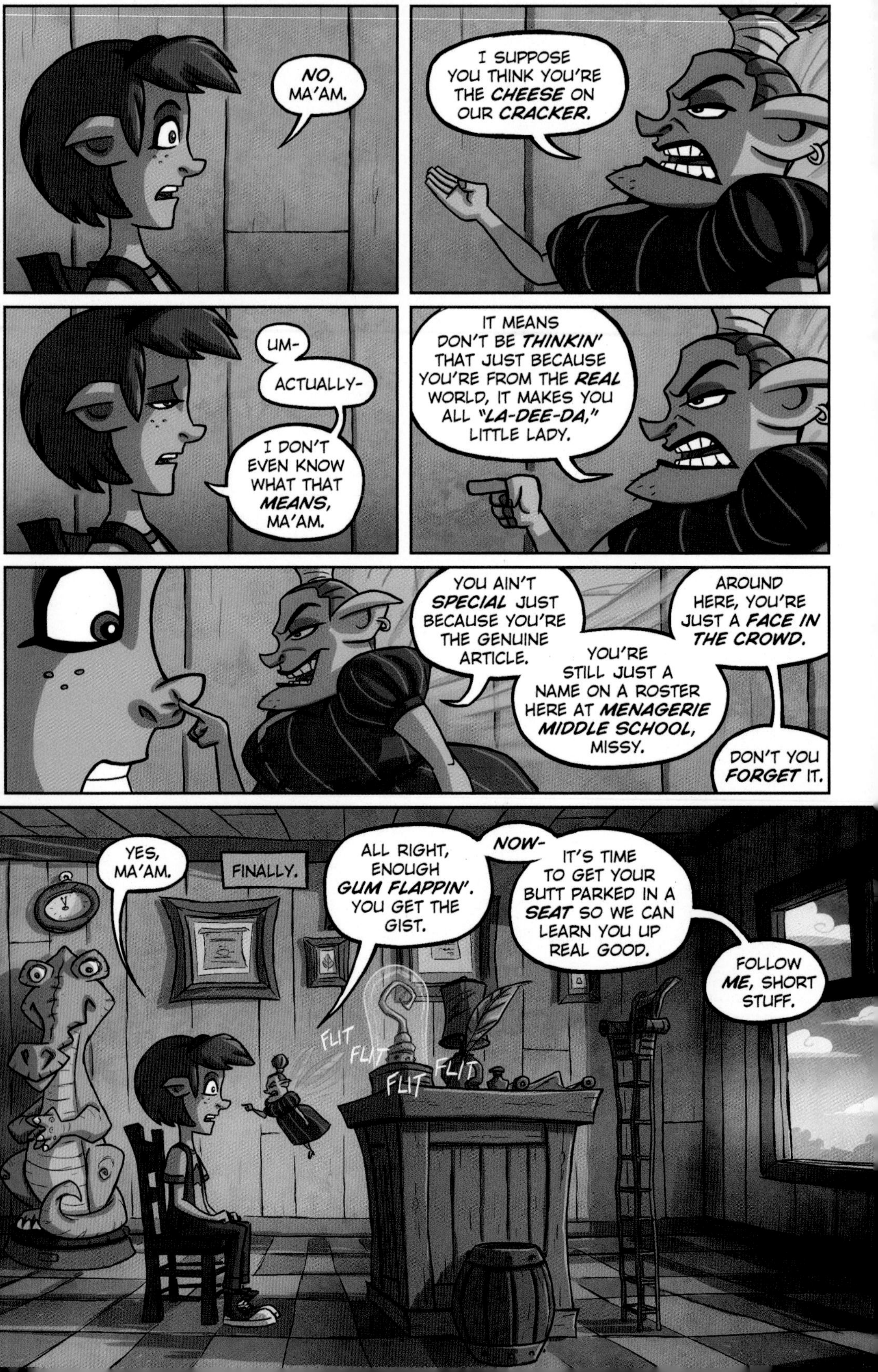
NO, MA'AM.
I SUPPOSE YOU THINK YOU'RE THE CHEESE ON OUR CRACKER.
UM-
ACTUALLY-
I DON'T EVEN KNOW WHAT THAT MEANS, MA'AM.
IT MEANS DON'T BE THINKIN' THAT JUST BECAUSE YOU'RE FROM THE REAL WORLD, IT MAKES YOU ALL "LA-DEE-DA," LITTLE LADY.
YOU AIN'T SPECIAL JUST BECAUSE YOU'RE THE GENUINE ARTICLE.
YOU'RE STILL JUST A NAME ON A ROSTER HERE AT MENAGERIE MIDDLE SCHOOL, MISSY.
AROUND HERE, YOU'RE JUST A FACE IN THE CROWD.
DON'T YOU FORGET IT.
YES, MA'AM.
FINALLY.
ALL RIGHT, ENOUGH GUM FLAPPIN'. YOU GET THE GIST.
NOW-
IT'S TIME TO GET YOUR BUTT PARKED IN A SEAT SO WE CAN LEARN YOU UP REAL GOOD.
FOLLOW ME, SHORT STUFF.
FLIT FLIT FLIT FLIT

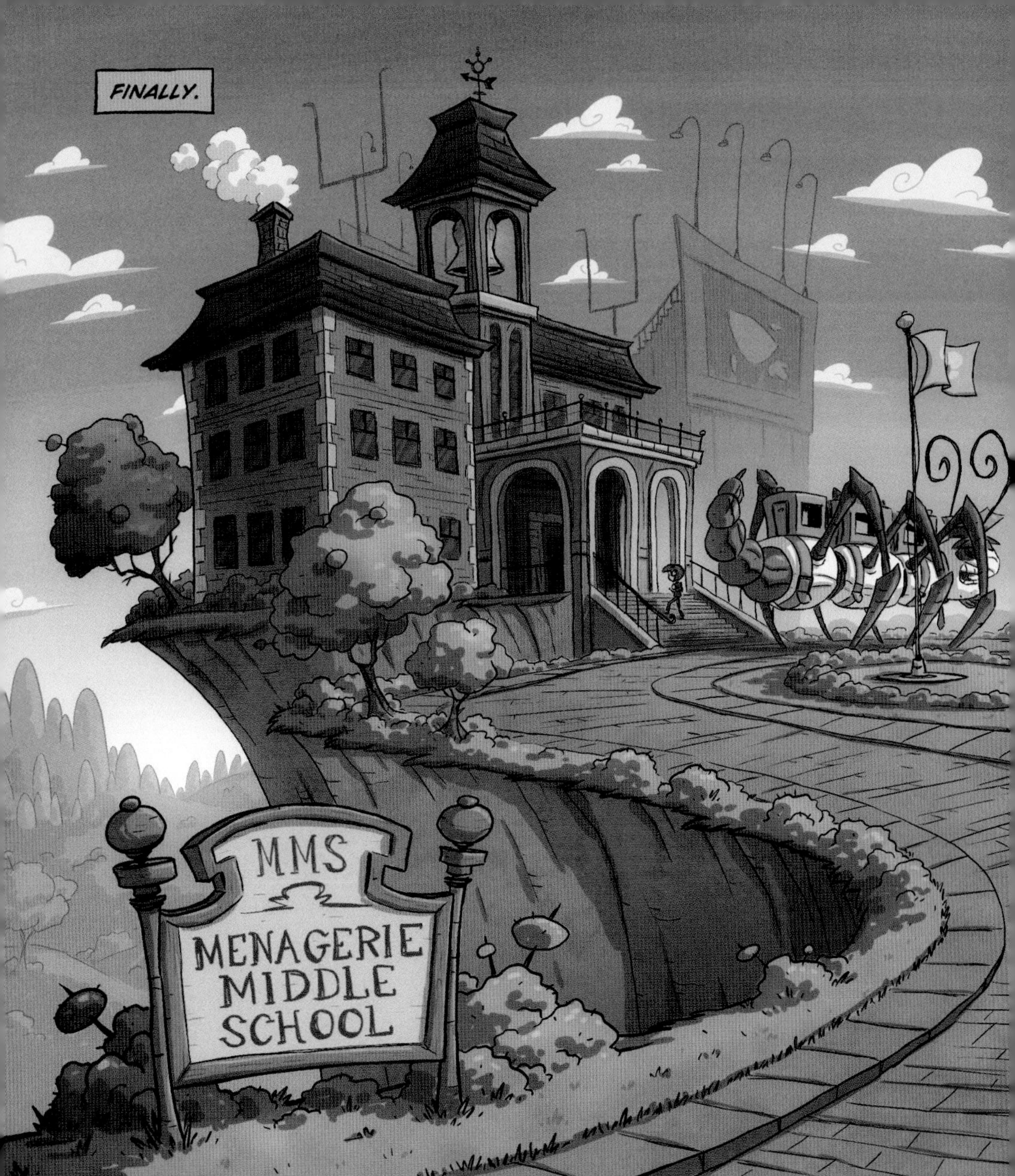
FINALLY.
MMS
MENAGERIE
MIDDLE
SCHOOL

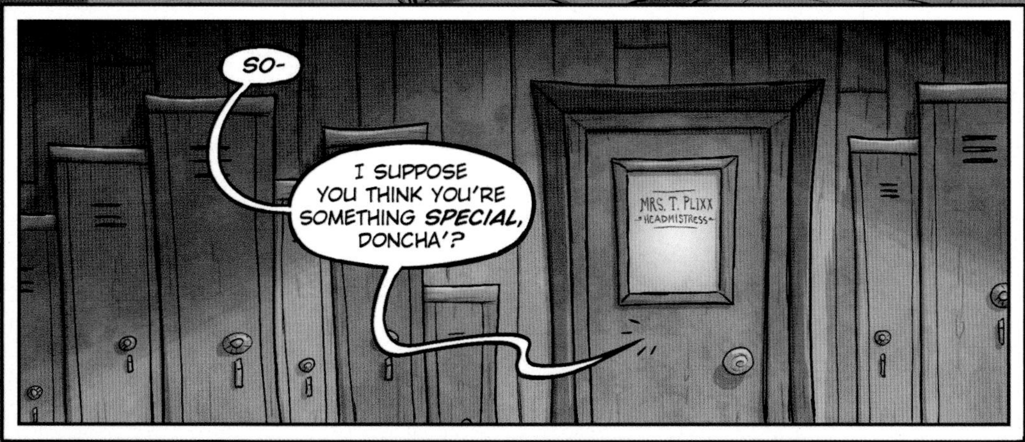
SO-
I SUPPOSE YOU THINK YOU'RE SOMETHING *SPECIAL*, DONCHA'?
MRS. T. PLIXX
HEADMISTRESS

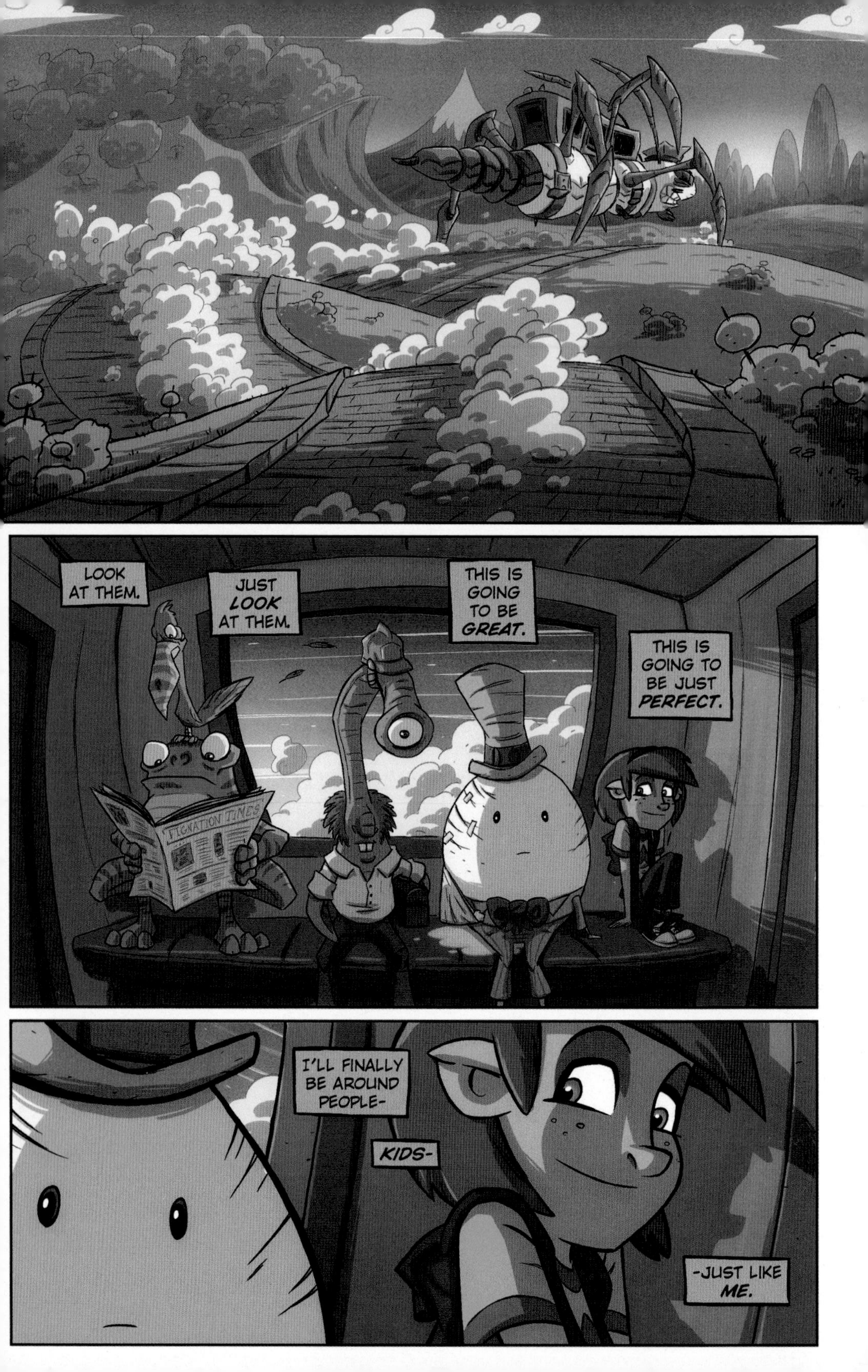
LOOK AT THEM.
JUST *LOOK* AT THEM.
THIS IS GOING TO BE *GREAT*.
THIS IS GOING TO BE JUST *PERFECT*.
I'LL FINALLY BE AROUND PEOPLE-
KIDS-
-JUST LIKE *ME*.

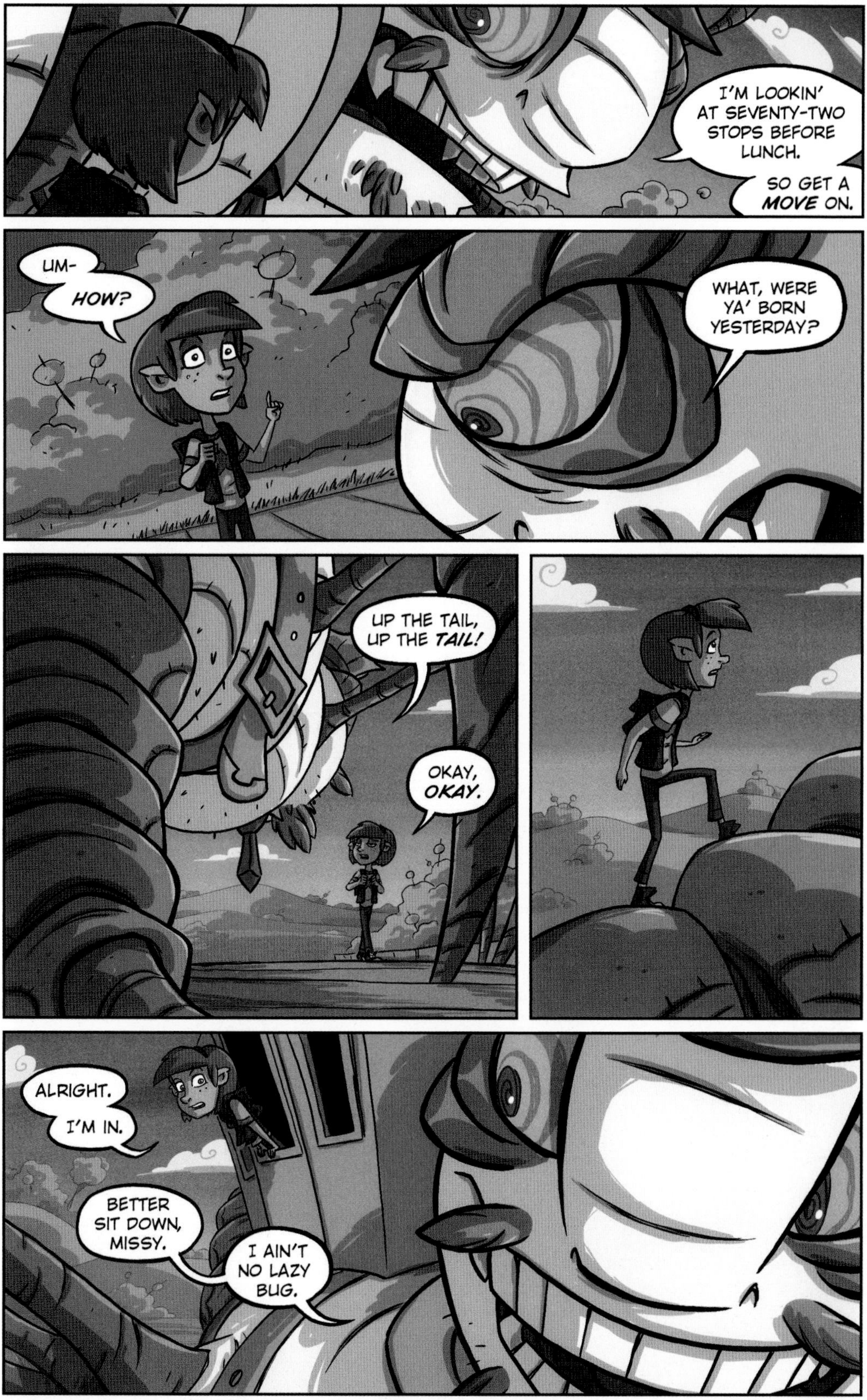
I'M LOOKIN' AT SEVENTY-TWO STOPS BEFORE LUNCH.
SO GET A *MOVE* ON.
UM-
HOW?
WHAT, WERE YA' BORN YESTERDAY?
UP THE TAIL, UP THE *TAIL!*
OKAY, *OKAY.*
ALRIGHT.
I'M IN.
BETTER SIT DOWN, MISSY.
I AIN'T NO LAZY BUG.

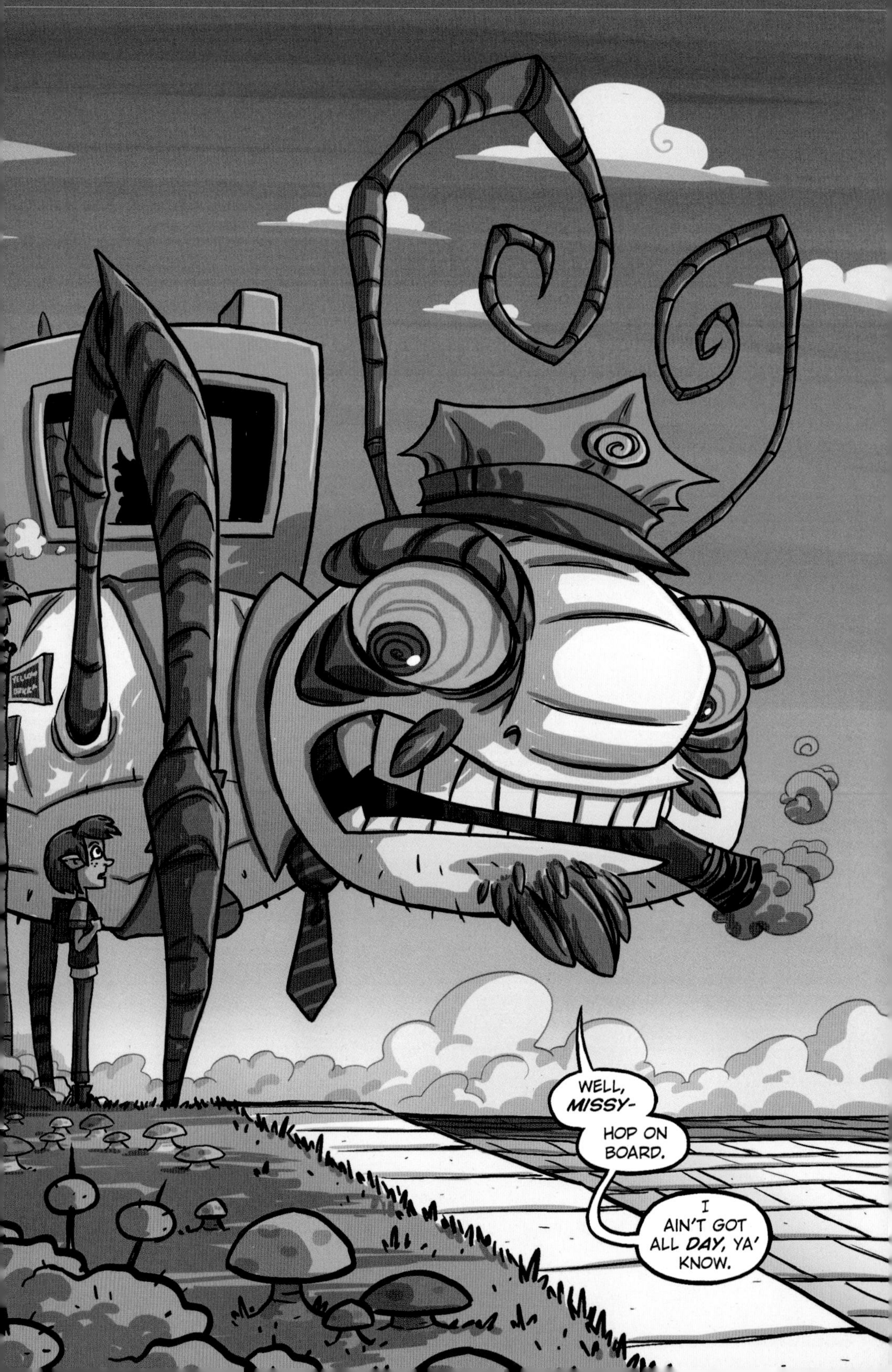
WELL, MISSY-
HOP ON BOARD.
I AIN'T GOT ALL DAY, YA' KNOW.

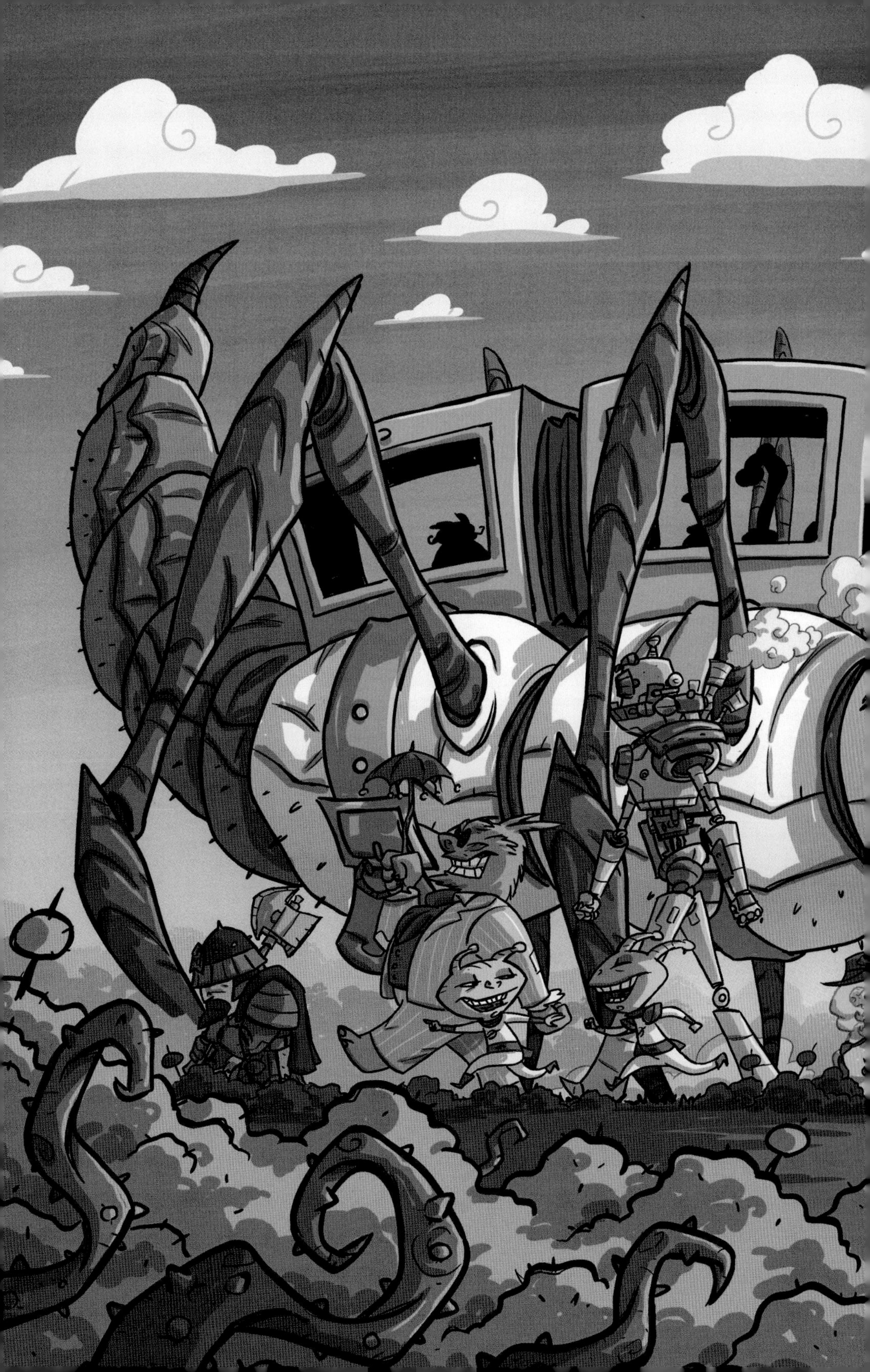

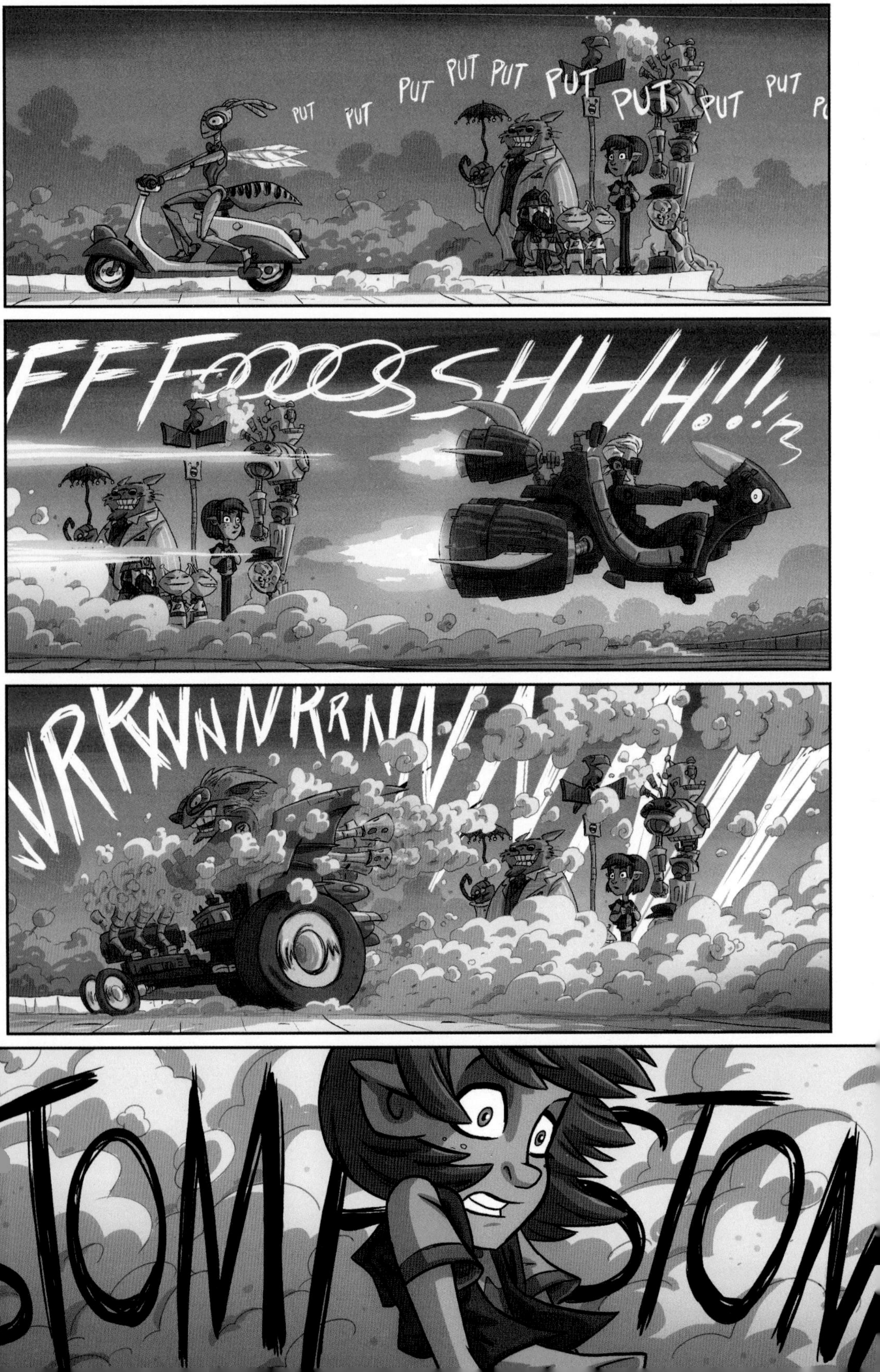
PUT PUT PUT PUT PUT PUT PUT PUT PUT
FFFFOOOOSSHHH!!!
VRKNNNRRNN
STOMP

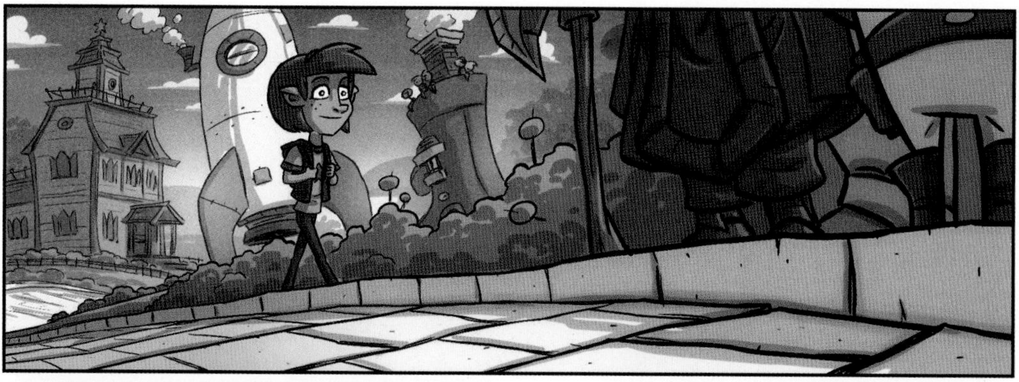

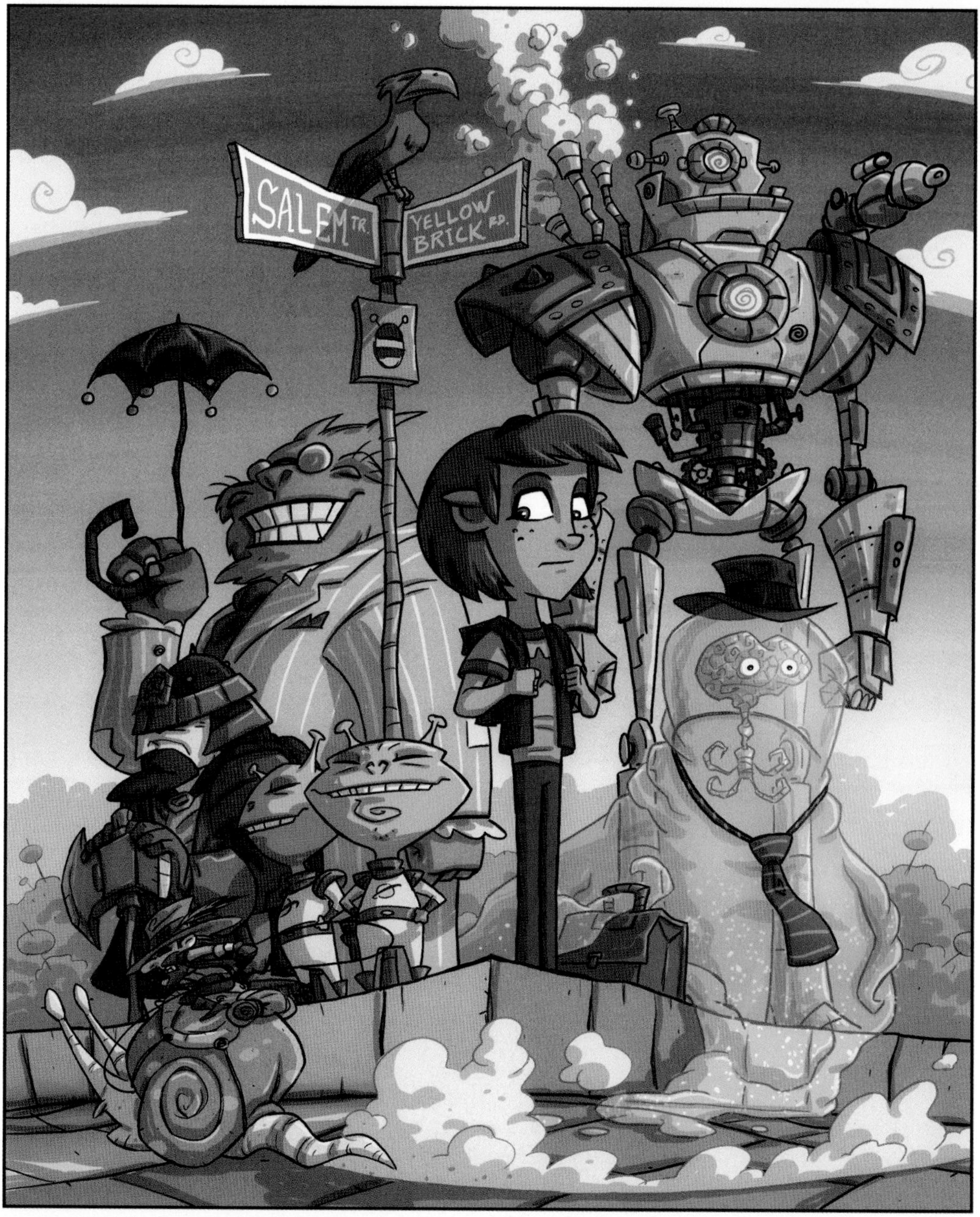
SALEM TR.
YELLOW BRICK RD.

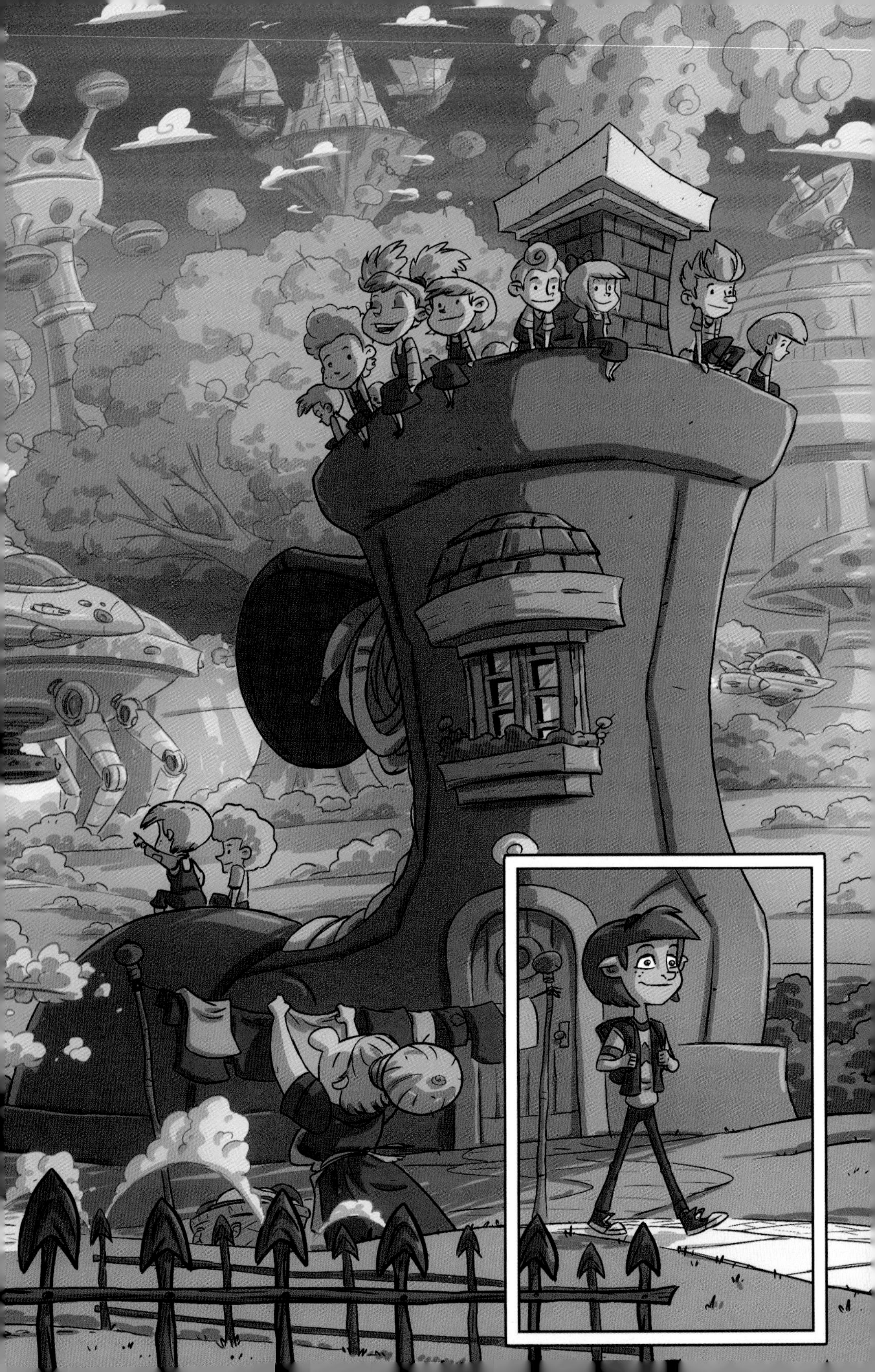

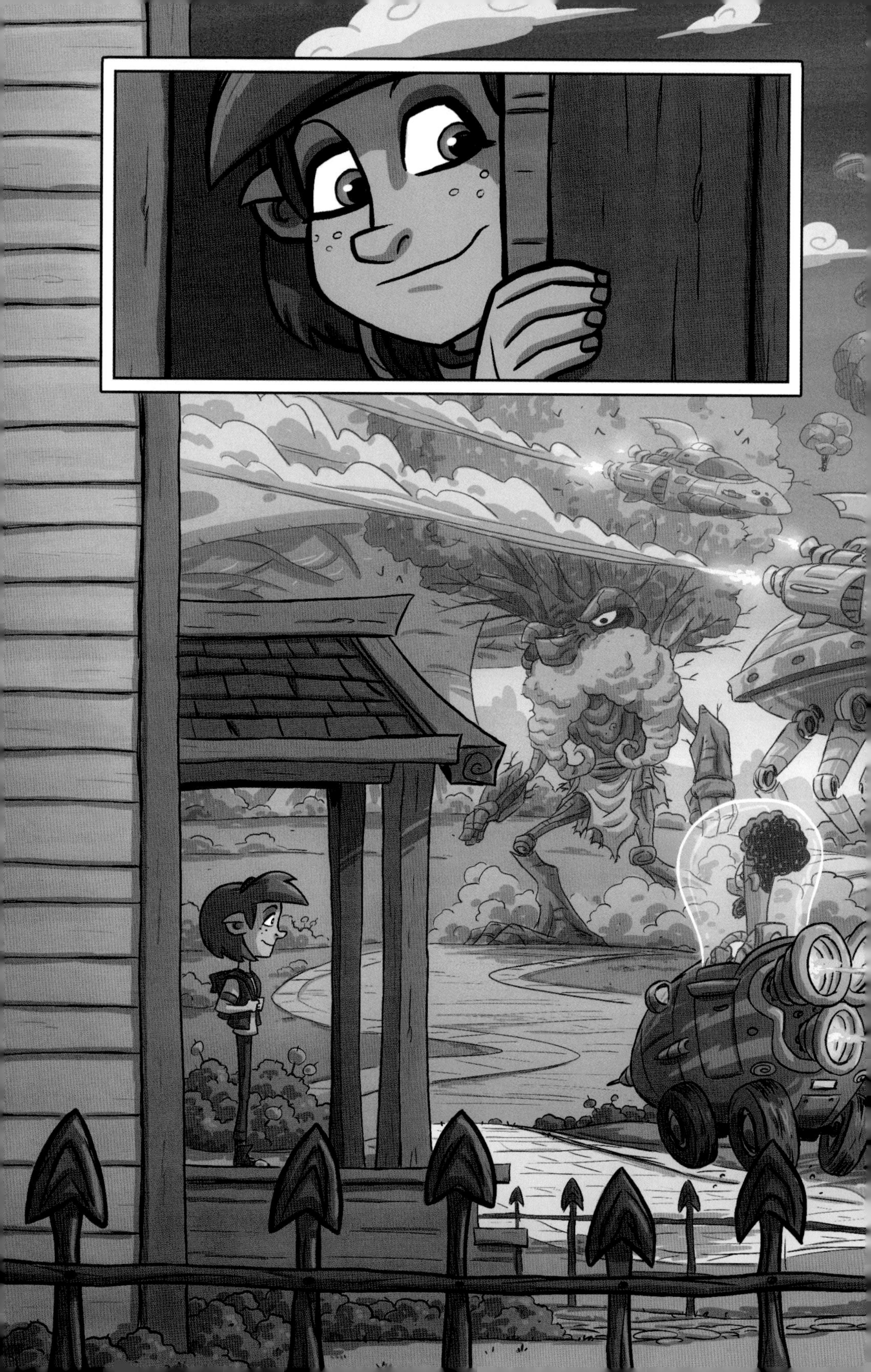

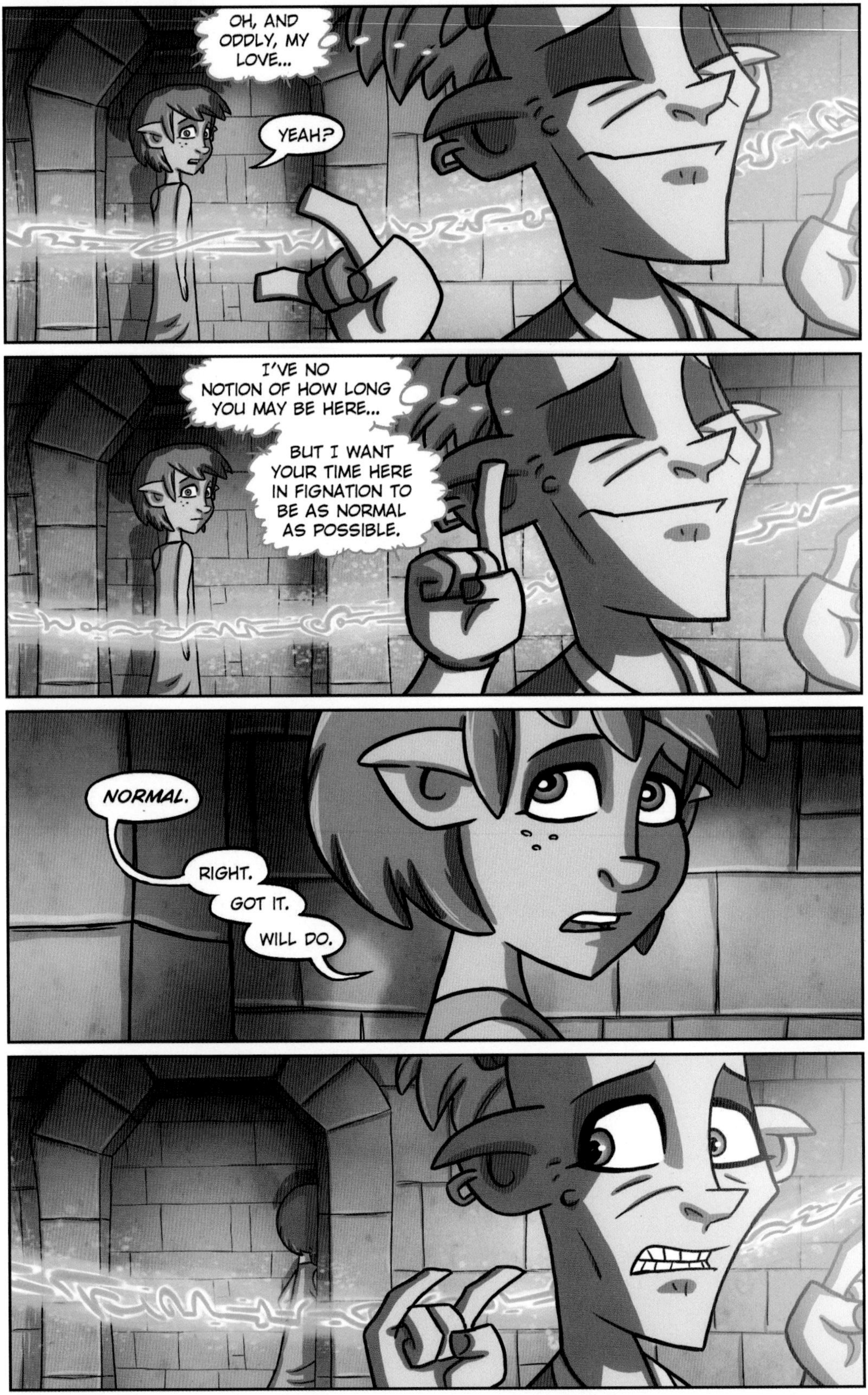

OH, AND ODDLY, MY LOVE...
YEAH?
I'VE NO NOTION OF HOW LONG YOU MAY BE HERE...
BUT I WANT YOUR TIME HERE IN FIGNATION TO BE AS NORMAL AS POSSIBLE.
NORMAL.
RIGHT.
GOT IT.
WILL DO.

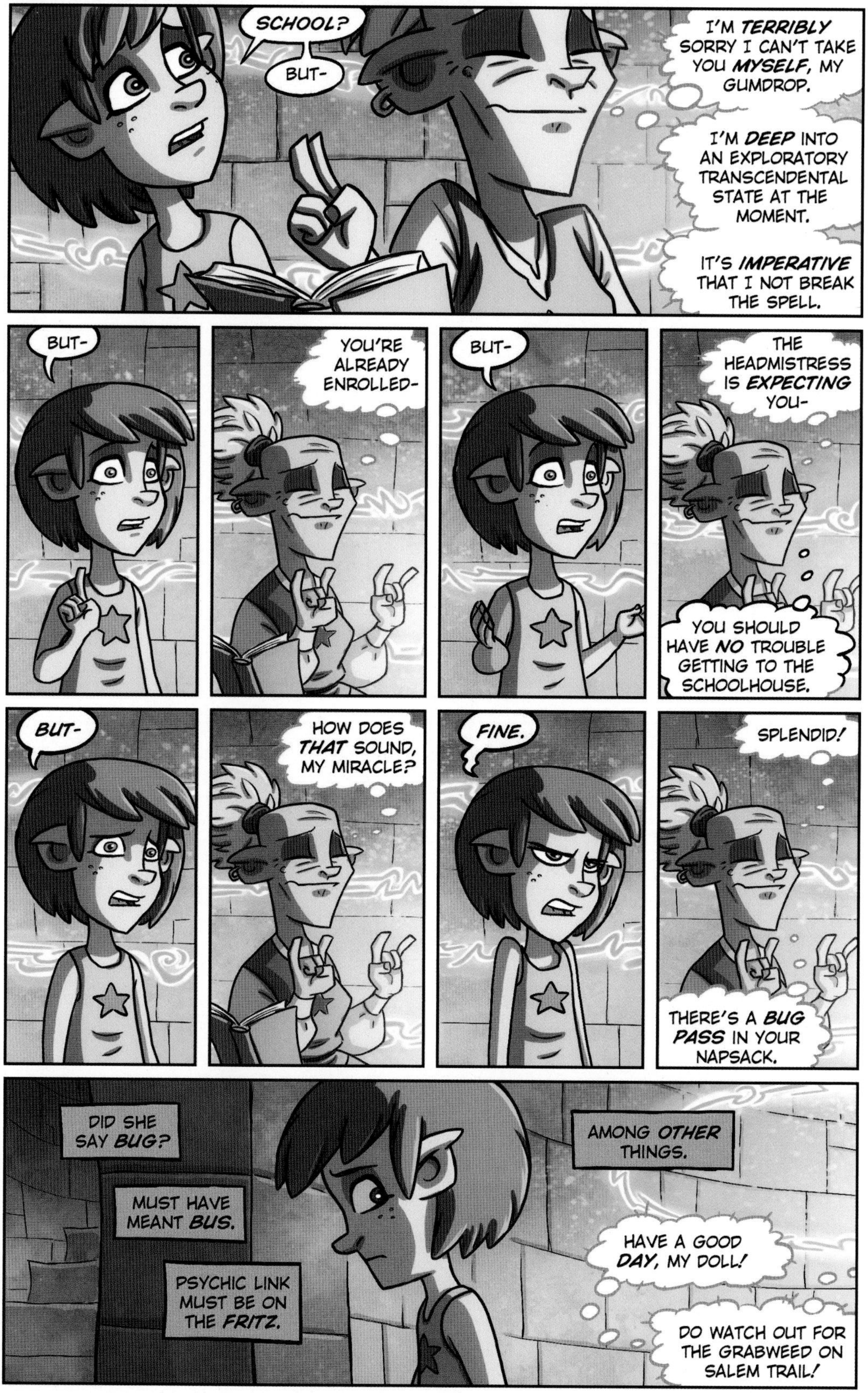
SCHOOL?
BUT-
I'M TERRIBLY SORRY I CAN'T TAKE YOU MYSELF, MY GUMDROP.
I'M DEEP INTO AN EXPLORATORY TRANSCENDENTAL STATE AT THE MOMENT.
IT'S IMPERATIVE THAT I NOT BREAK THE SPELL.
BUT-
YOU'RE ALREADY ENROLLED-
BUT-
THE HEADMISTRESS IS EXPECTING YOU-
YOU SHOULD HAVE NO TROUBLE GETTING TO THE SCHOOLHOUSE.
BUT-
HOW DOES THAT SOUND, MY MIRACLE?
FINE.
SPLENDID!
THERE'S A BUG PASS IN YOUR NAPSACK.
DID SHE SAY BUG?
MUST HAVE MEANT BUS.
PSYCHIC LINK MUST BE ON THE FRITZ.
AMONG OTHER THINGS.
HAVE A GOOD DAY, MY DOLL!
DO WATCH OUT FOR THE GRABWEED ON SALEM TRAIL!

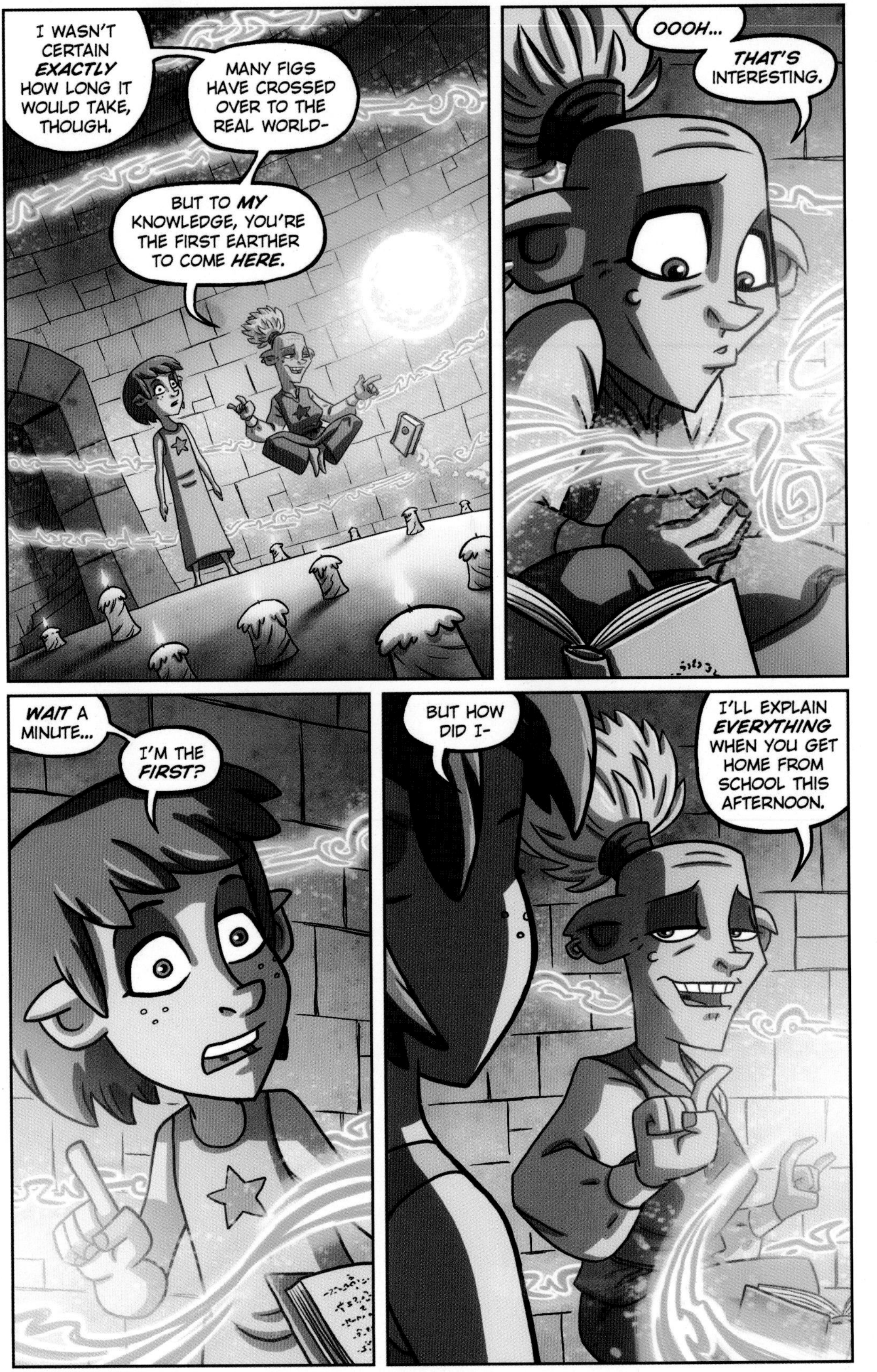
I WASN'T CERTAIN EXACTLY HOW LONG IT WOULD TAKE, THOUGH.
MANY FIGS HAVE CROSSED OVER TO THE REAL WORLD-
BUT TO MY KNOWLEDGE, YOU'RE THE FIRST EARTHER TO COME HERE.
OOOH... THAT'S INTERESTING.
WAIT A MINUTE...
I'M THE FIRST?
BUT HOW DID I-
I'LL EXPLAIN EVERYTHING WHEN YOU GET HOME FROM SCHOOL THIS AFTERNOON.

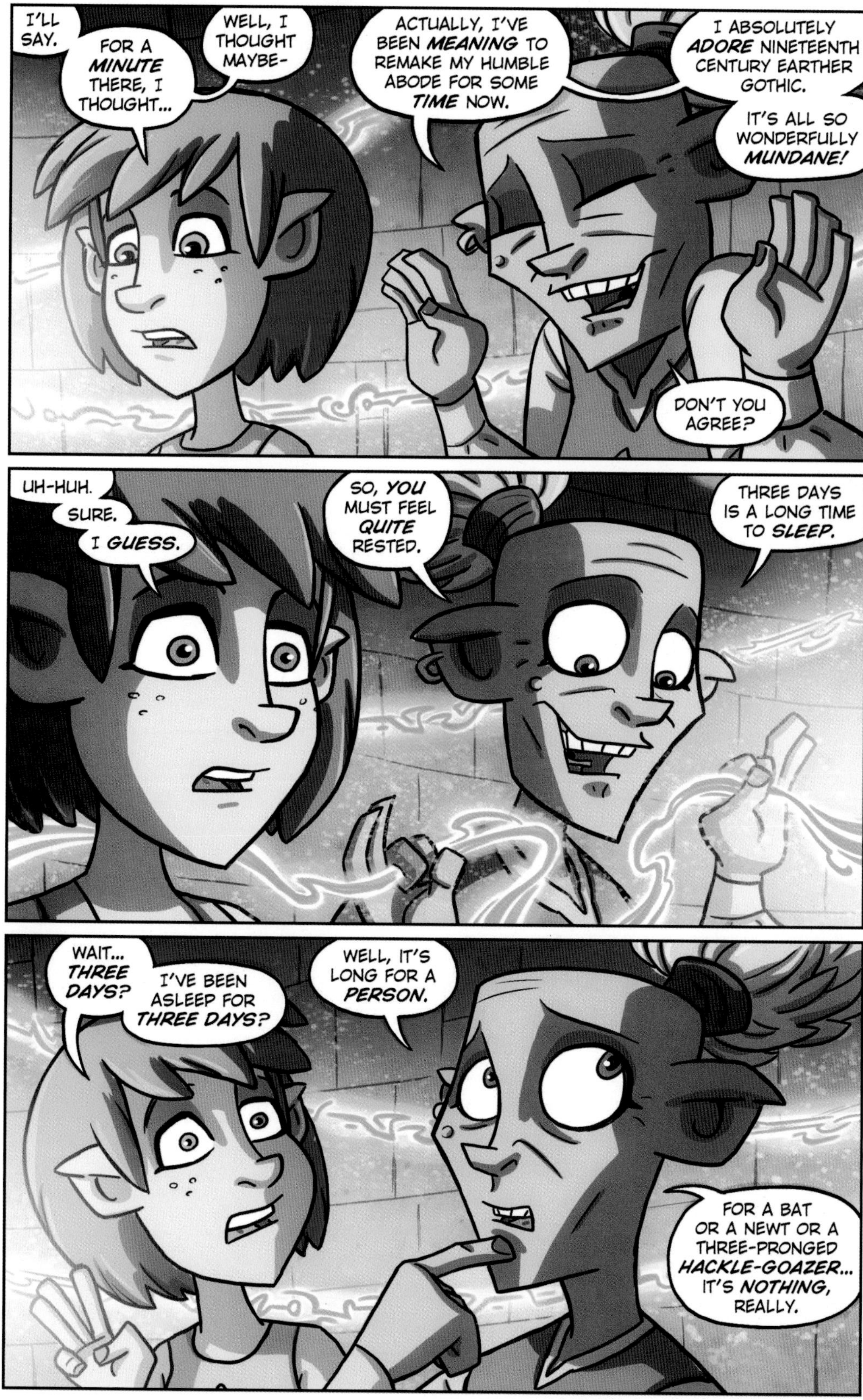
I'LL SAY.
FOR A MINUTE THERE, I THOUGHT...
WELL, I THOUGHT MAYBE-
ACTUALLY, I'VE BEEN MEANING TO REMAKE MY HUMBLE ABODE FOR SOME TIME NOW.
I ABSOLUTELY ADORE NINETEENTH CENTURY EARTHER GOTHIC.
IT'S ALL SO WONDERFULLY MUNDANE!
DON'T YOU AGREE?
UH-HUH.
SURE.
I GUESS.
SO, YOU MUST FEEL QUITE RESTED.
THREE DAYS IS A LONG TIME TO SLEEP.
WAIT... THREE DAYS?
I'VE BEEN ASLEEP FOR THREE DAYS?
WELL, IT'S LONG FOR A PERSON.
FOR A BAT OR A NEWT OR A THREE-PRONGED HACKLE-GOAZER... IT'S NOTHING, REALLY.

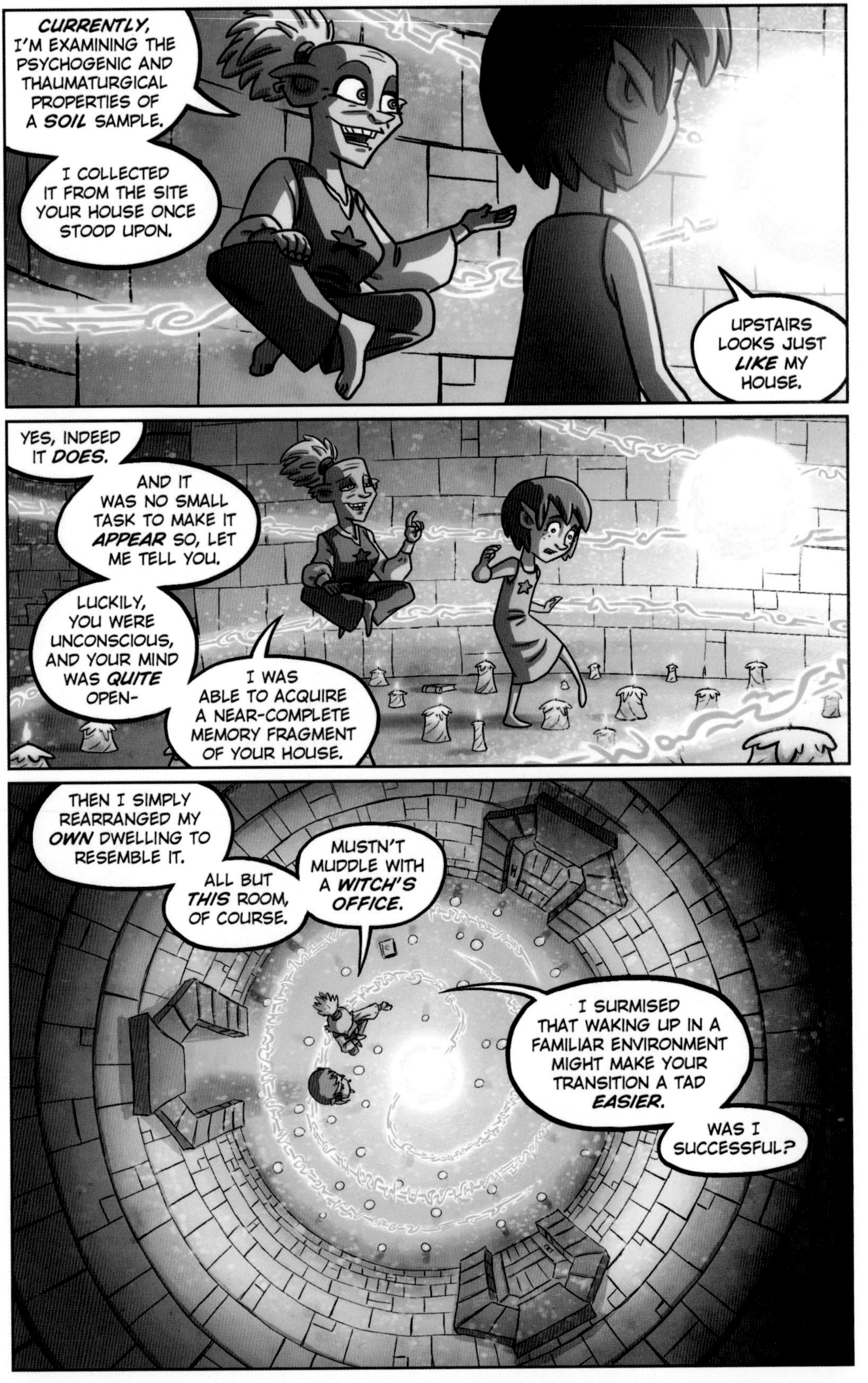
CURRENTLY, I'M EXAMINING THE PSYCHOGENIC AND THAUMATURGICAL PROPERTIES OF A SOIL SAMPLE.
I COLLECTED IT FROM THE SITE YOUR HOUSE ONCE STOOD UPON.
UPSTAIRS LOOKS JUST LIKE MY HOUSE.
YES, INDEED IT DOES.
AND IT WAS NO SMALL TASK TO MAKE IT APPEAR SO, LET ME TELL YOU.
LUCKILY, YOU WERE UNCONSCIOUS, AND YOUR MIND WAS QUITE OPEN-
I WAS ABLE TO ACQUIRE A NEAR-COMPLETE MEMORY FRAGMENT OF YOUR HOUSE.
THEN I SIMPLY REARRANGED MY OWN DWELLING TO RESEMBLE IT.
ALL BUT THIS ROOM, OF COURSE.
MUSTN'T MUDDLE WITH A WITCH'S OFFICE.
I SURMISED THAT WAKING UP IN A FAMILIAR ENVIRONMENT MIGHT MAKE YOUR TRANSITION A TAD EASIER.
WAS I SUCCESSFUL?

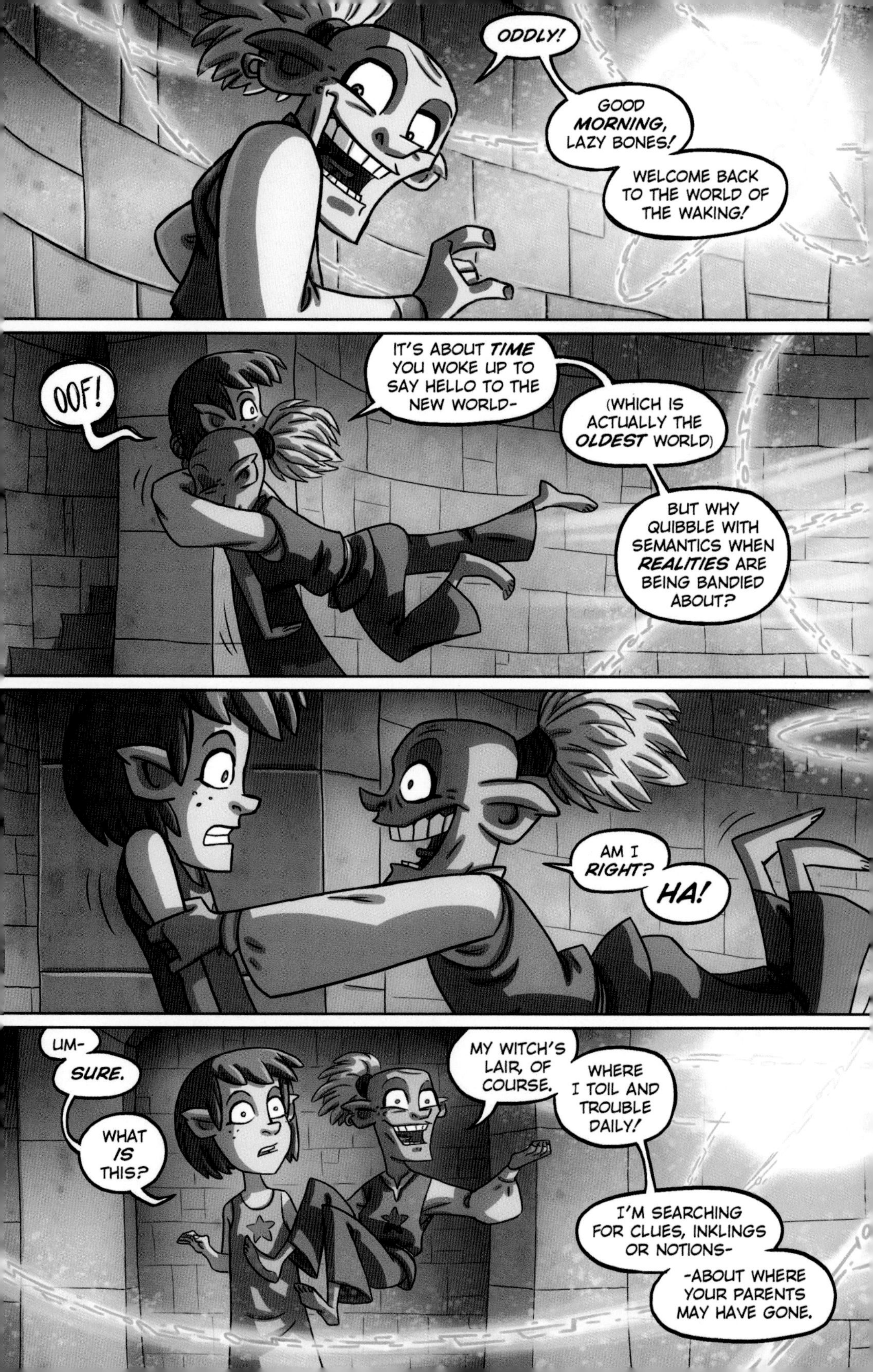
ODDLY!
GOOD MORNING, LAZY BONES!
WELCOME BACK TO THE WORLD OF THE WAKING!
OOF!
IT'S ABOUT TIME YOU WOKE UP TO SAY HELLO TO THE NEW WORLD-
(WHICH IS ACTUALLY THE OLDEST WORLD)
BUT WHY QUIBBLE WITH SEMANTICS WHEN REALITIES ARE BEING BANDIED ABOUT?
AM I RIGHT?
HA!
UM- SURE.
WHAT IS THIS?
MY WITCH'S LAIR, OF COURSE.
WHERE I TOIL AND TROUBLE DAILY!
I'M SEARCHING FOR CLUES, INKLINGS OR NOTIONS-
-ABOUT WHERE YOUR PARENTS MAY HAVE GONE.

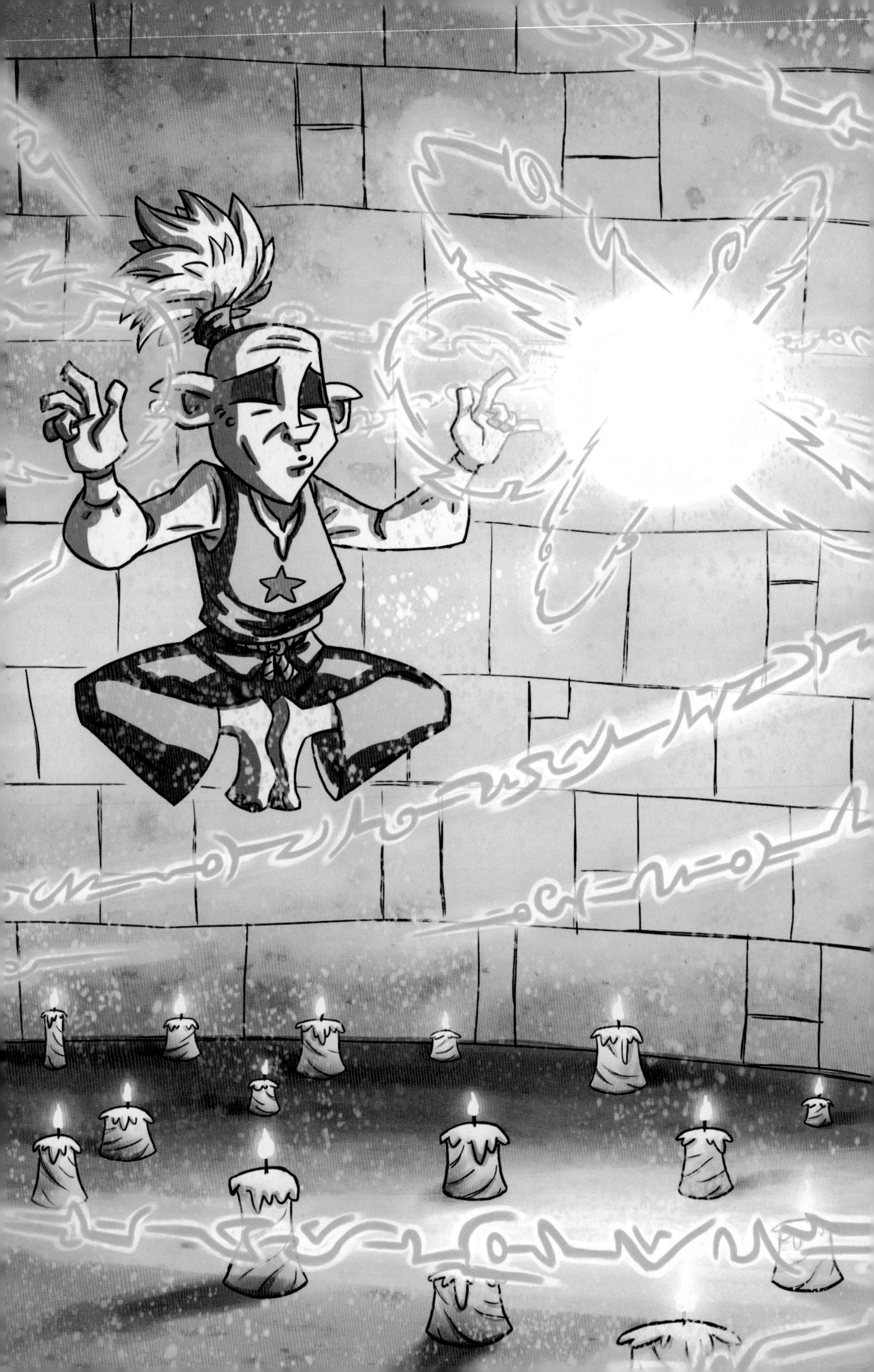

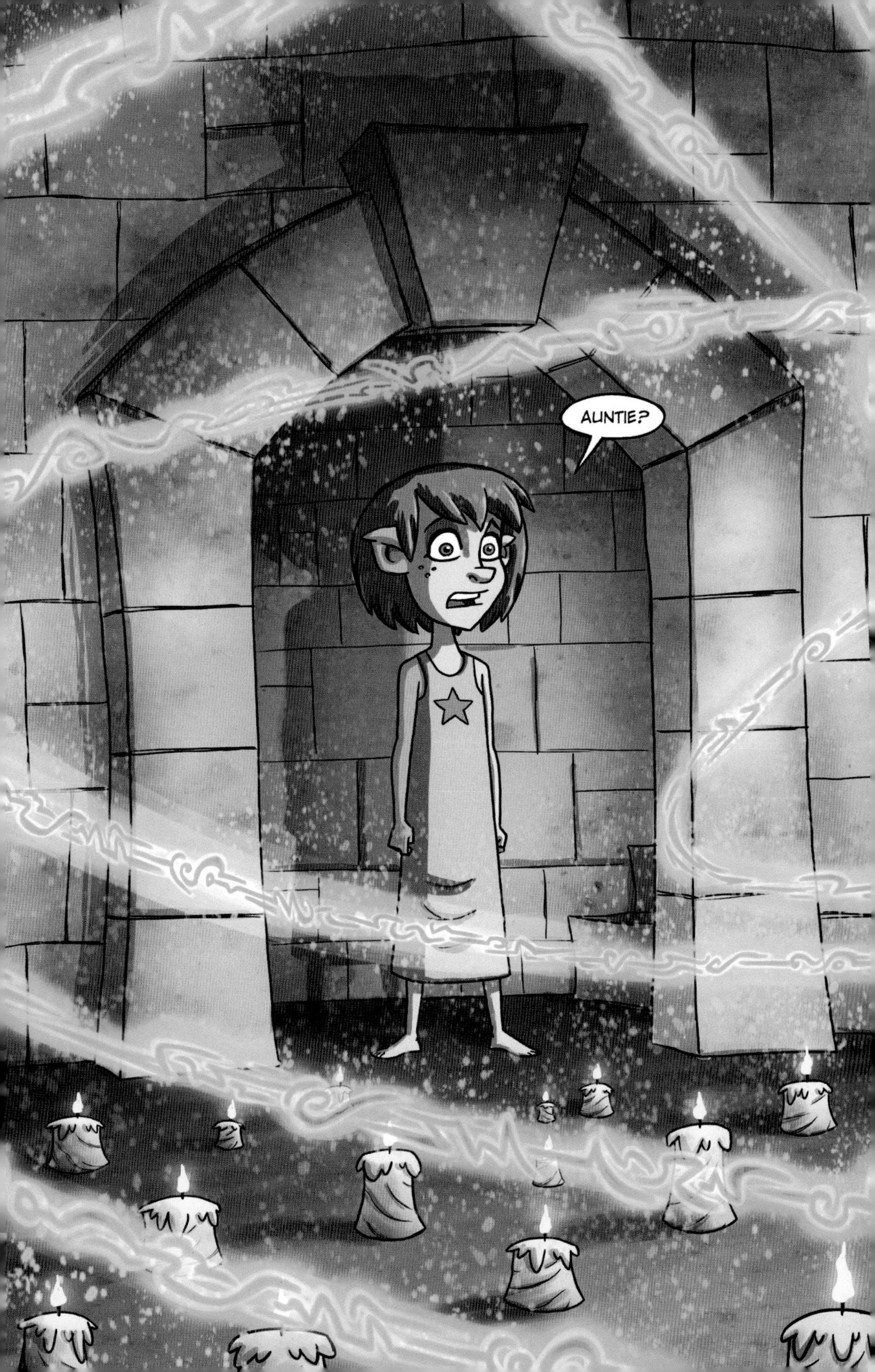
AUNTIE?

Chapter 3
Strange New World

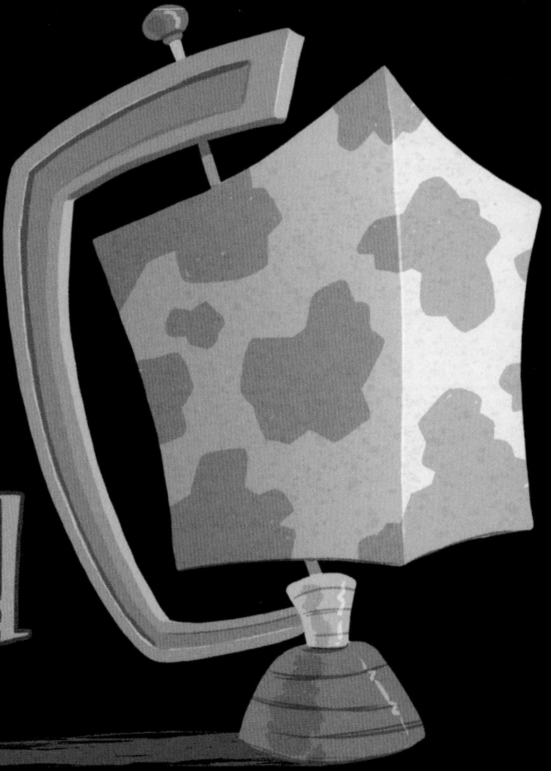

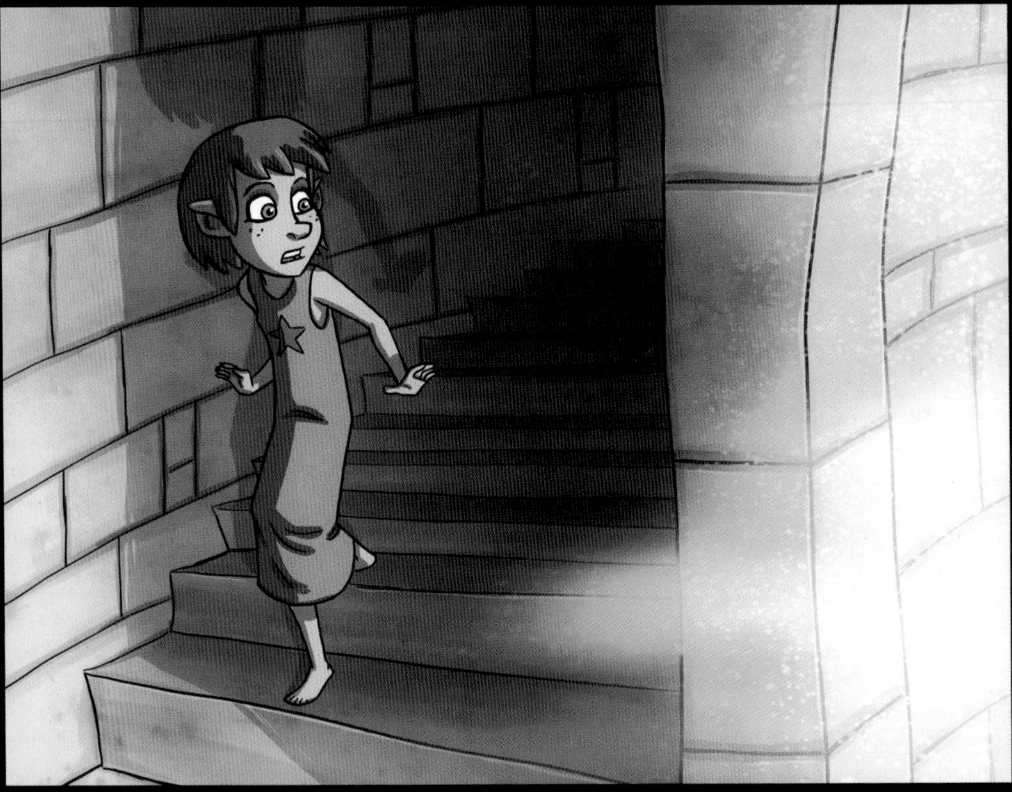

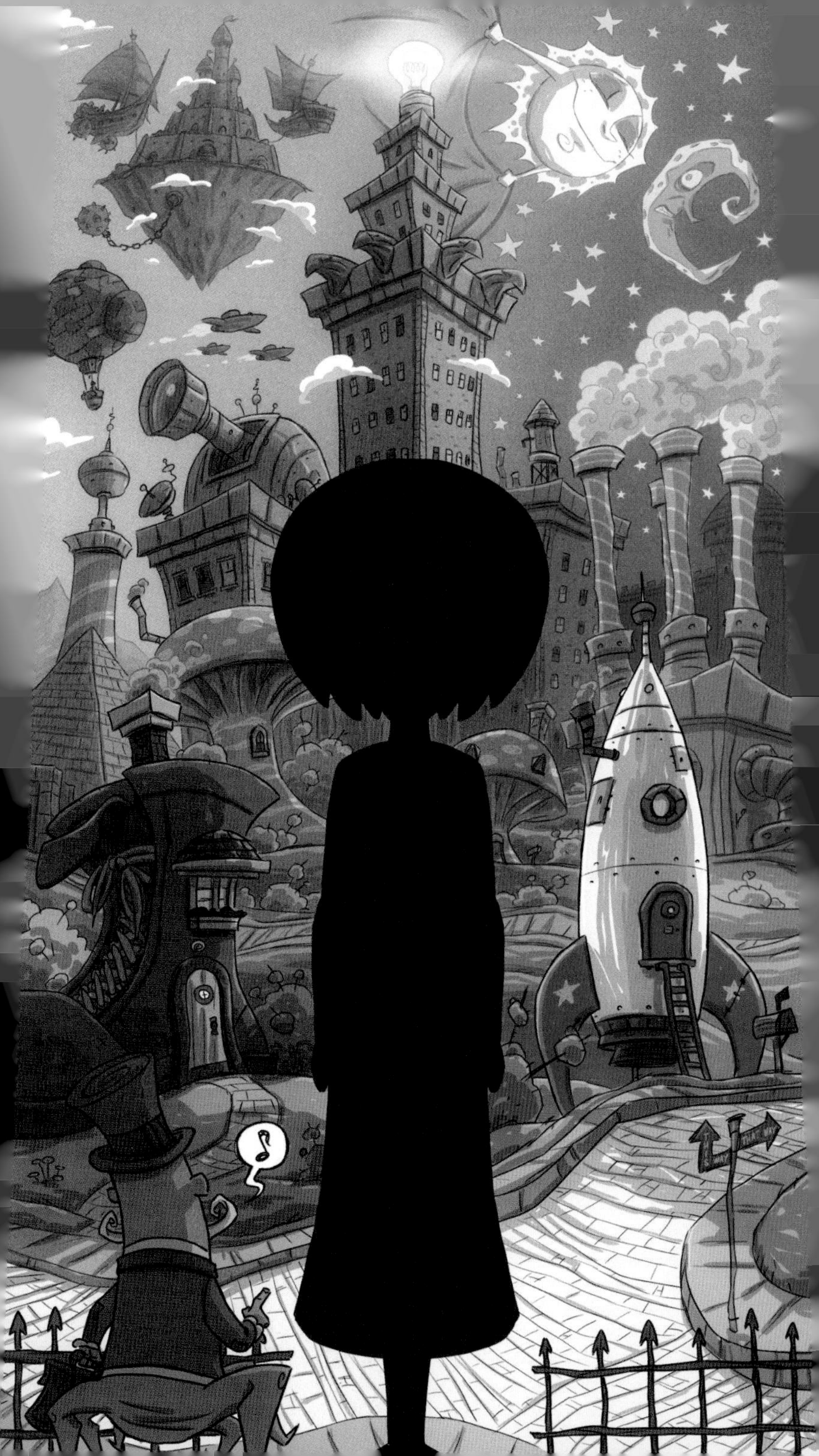

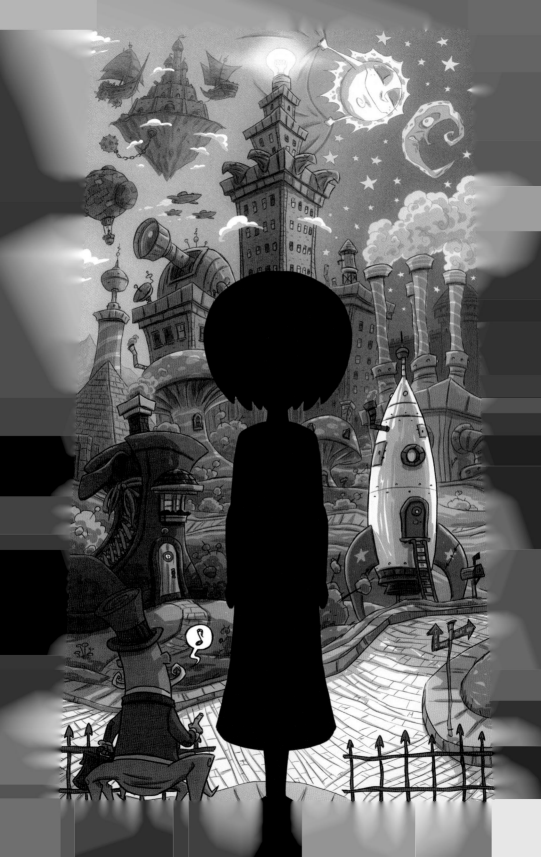

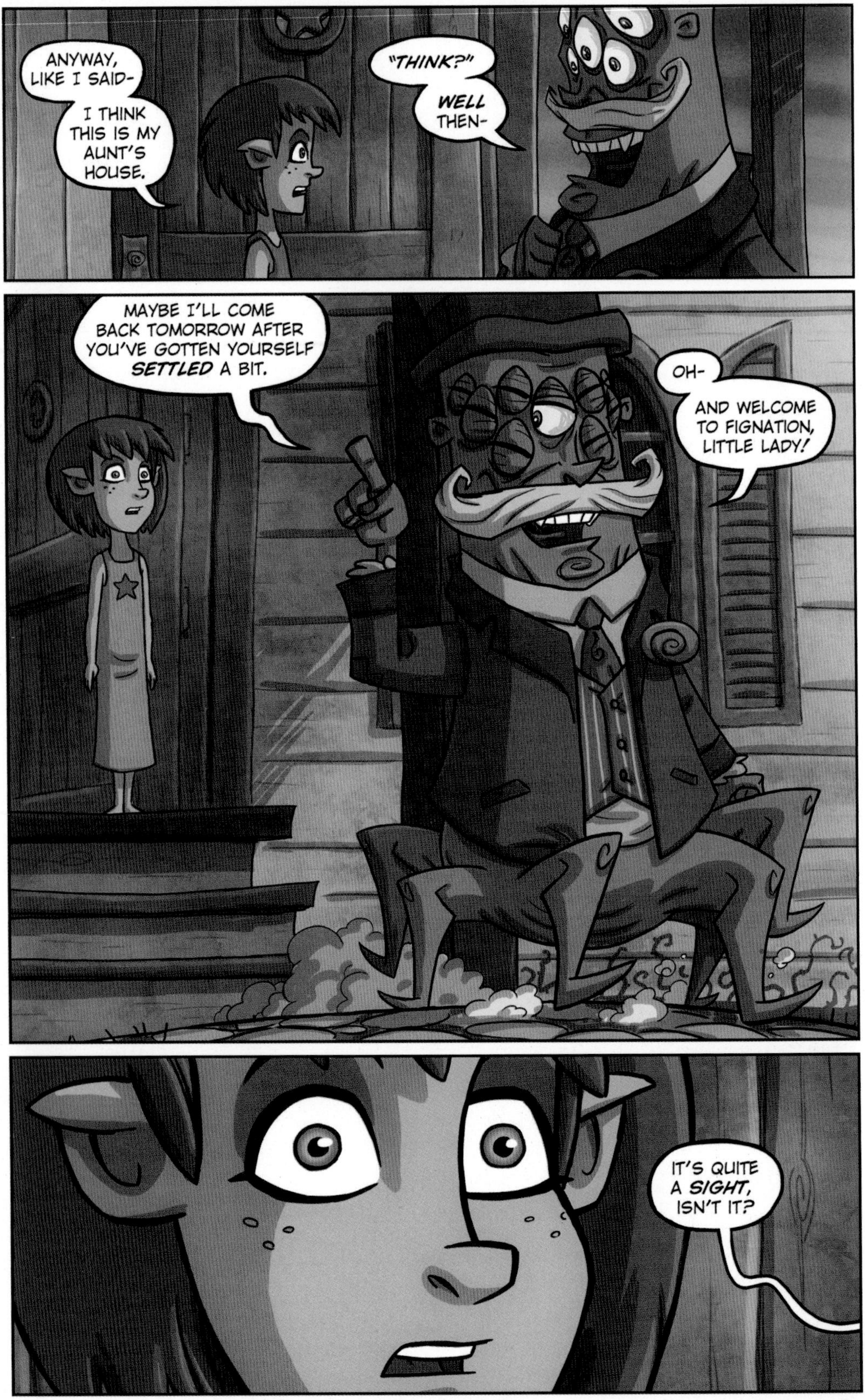

ANYWAY, LIKE I SAID-
I THINK THIS IS MY AUNT'S HOUSE.
"THINK?"
WELL THEN-
MAYBE I'LL COME BACK TOMORROW AFTER YOU'VE GOTTEN YOURSELF SETTLED A BIT.
OH-
AND WELCOME TO FIGNATION, LITTLE LADY!
IT'S QUITE A SIGHT, ISN'T IT?

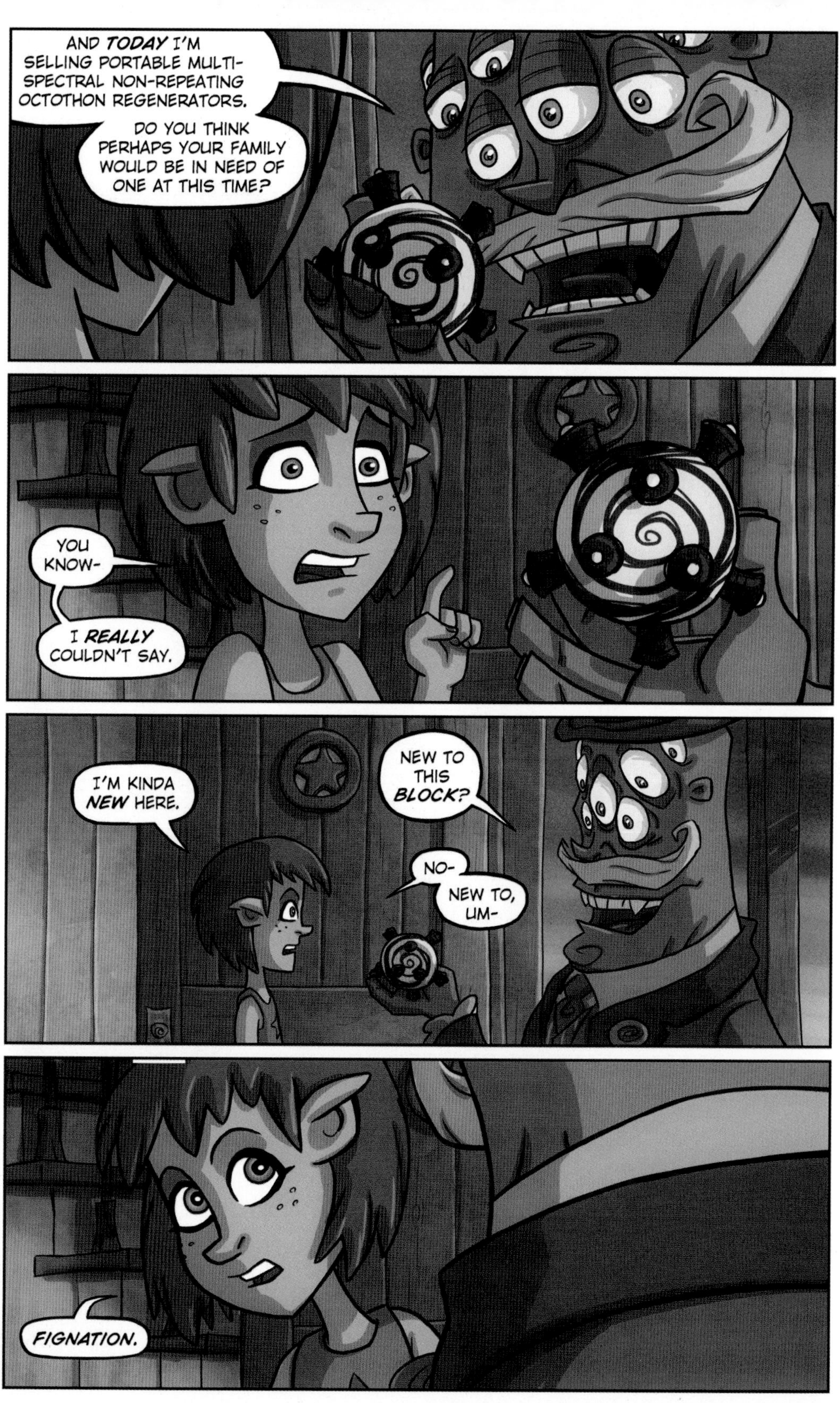
AND *TODAY* I'M SELLING PORTABLE MULTI-SPECTRAL NON-REPEATING OCTOTHON REGENERATORS.
DO YOU THINK PERHAPS YOUR FAMILY WOULD BE IN NEED OF ONE AT THIS TIME?
YOU KNOW-
I *REALLY* COULDN'T SAY.
I'M KINDA *NEW* HERE.
NEW TO THIS *BLOCK?*
NO-
NEW TO, UM-
FIGNATION.

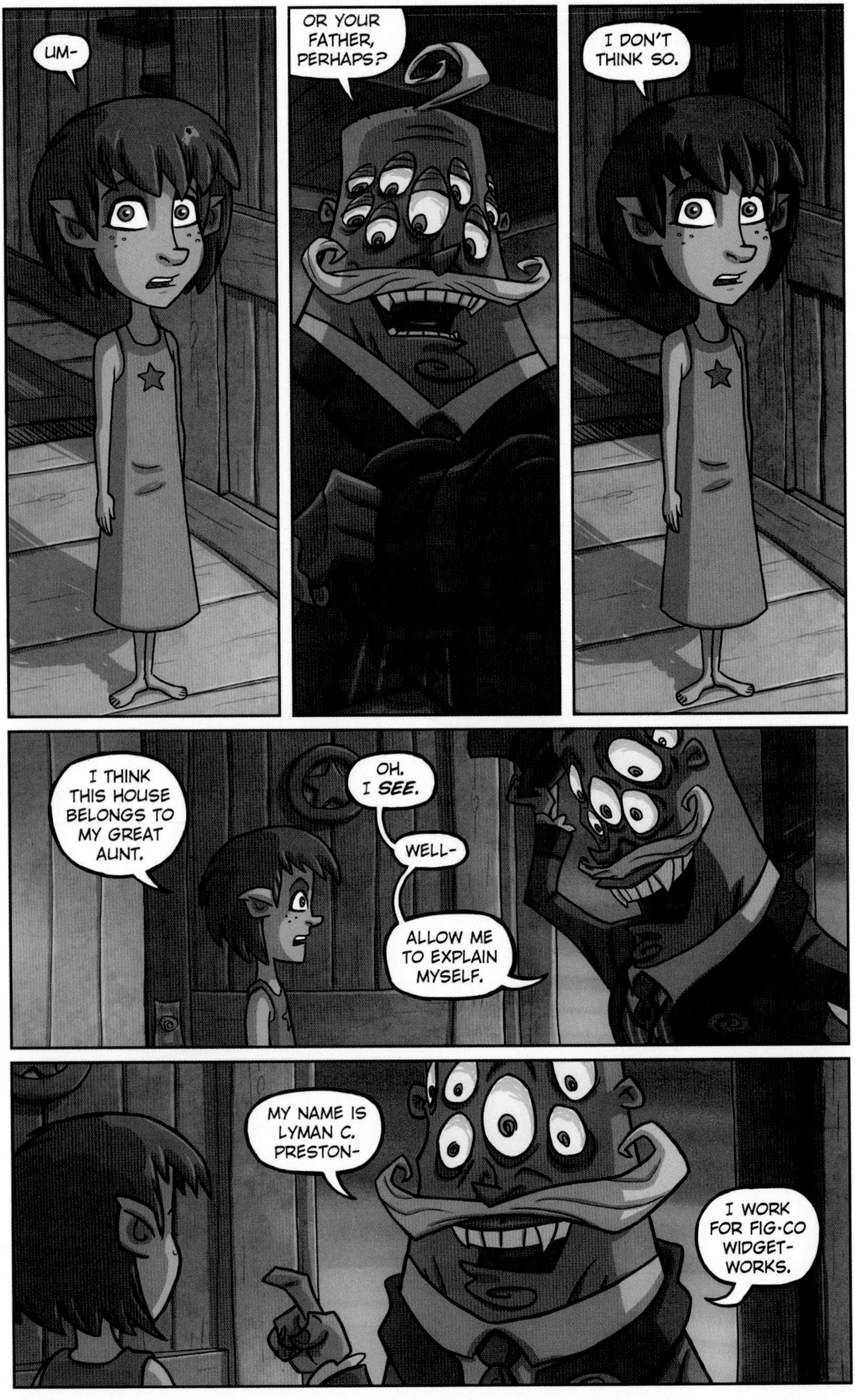
UM-
OR YOUR FATHER, PERHAPS?
I DON'T THINK SO.
I THINK THIS HOUSE BELONGS TO MY GREAT AUNT.
OH. I SEE.
WELL-
ALLOW ME TO EXPLAIN MYSELF.
MY NAME IS LYMAN C. PRESTON-
I WORK FOR FIG•CO WIDGET-WORKS.

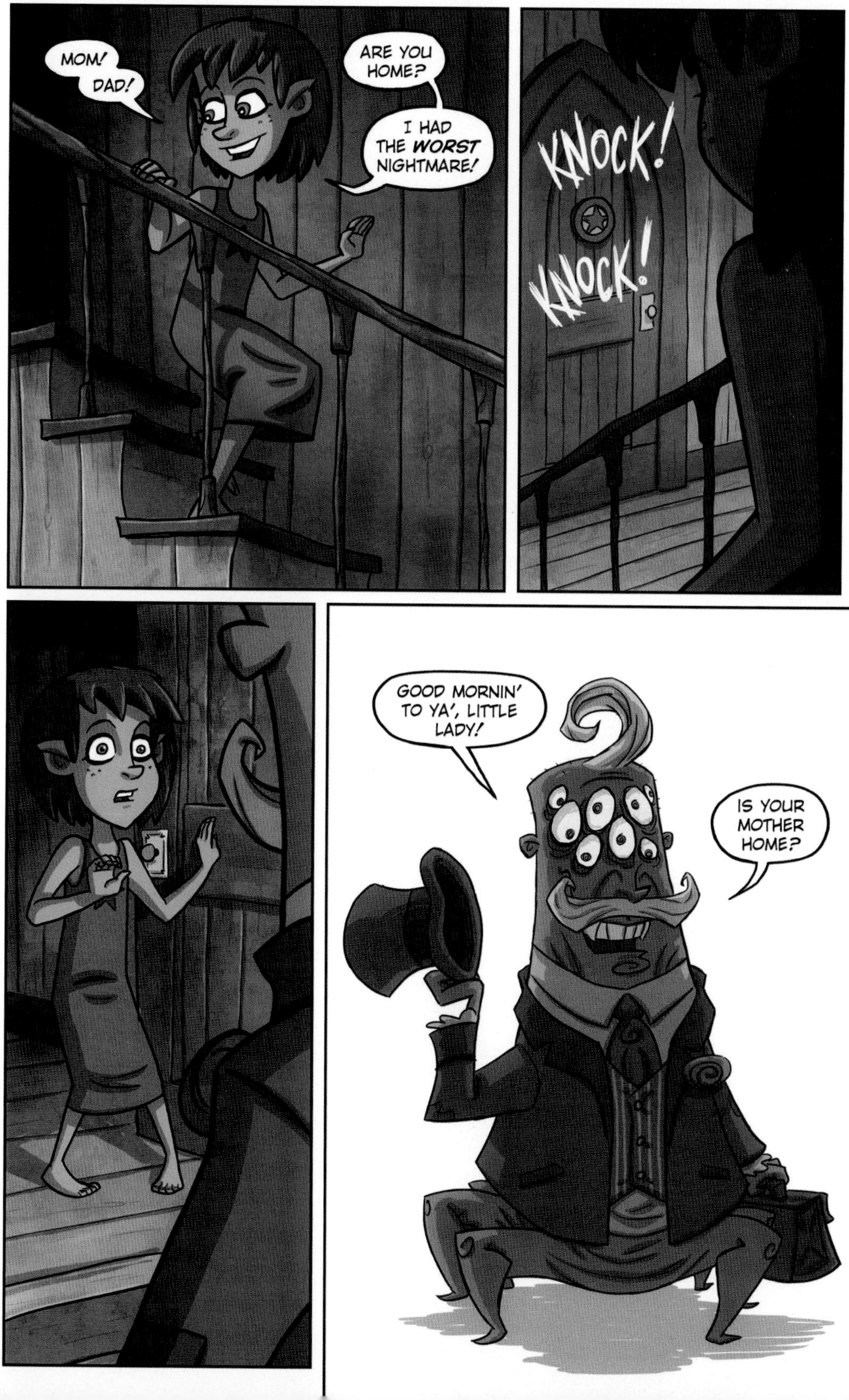
MOM! DAD!
ARE YOU HOME?
I HAD THE WORST NIGHTMARE!
KNOCK! KNOCK!
GOOD MORNIN' TO YA', LITTLE LADY!
IS YOUR MOTHER HOME?

IN *FACT-*

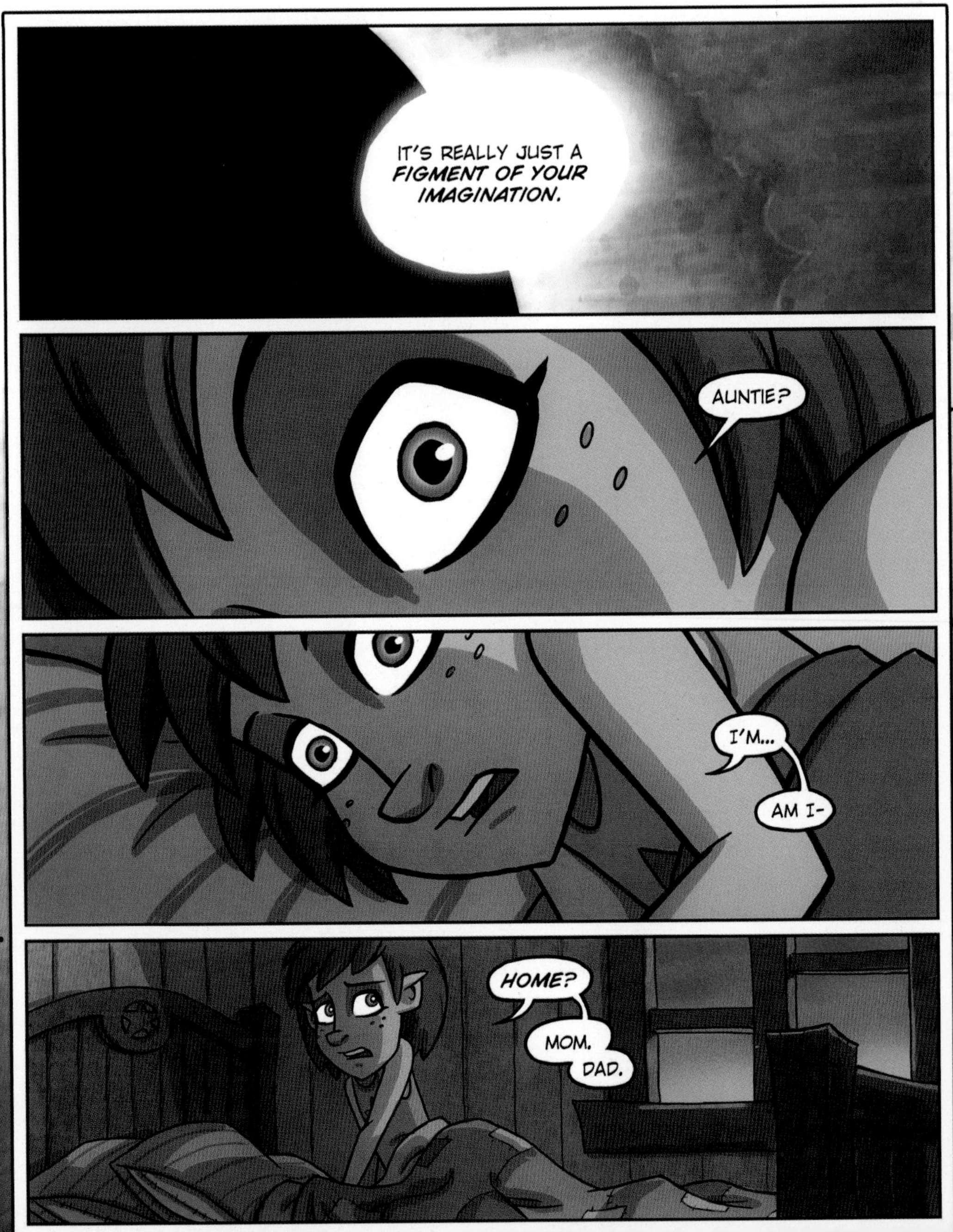
IT'S REALLY JUST A FIGMENT OF YOUR IMAGINATION.
AUNTIE?
I'M...
AM I-
HOME?
MOM.
DAD.

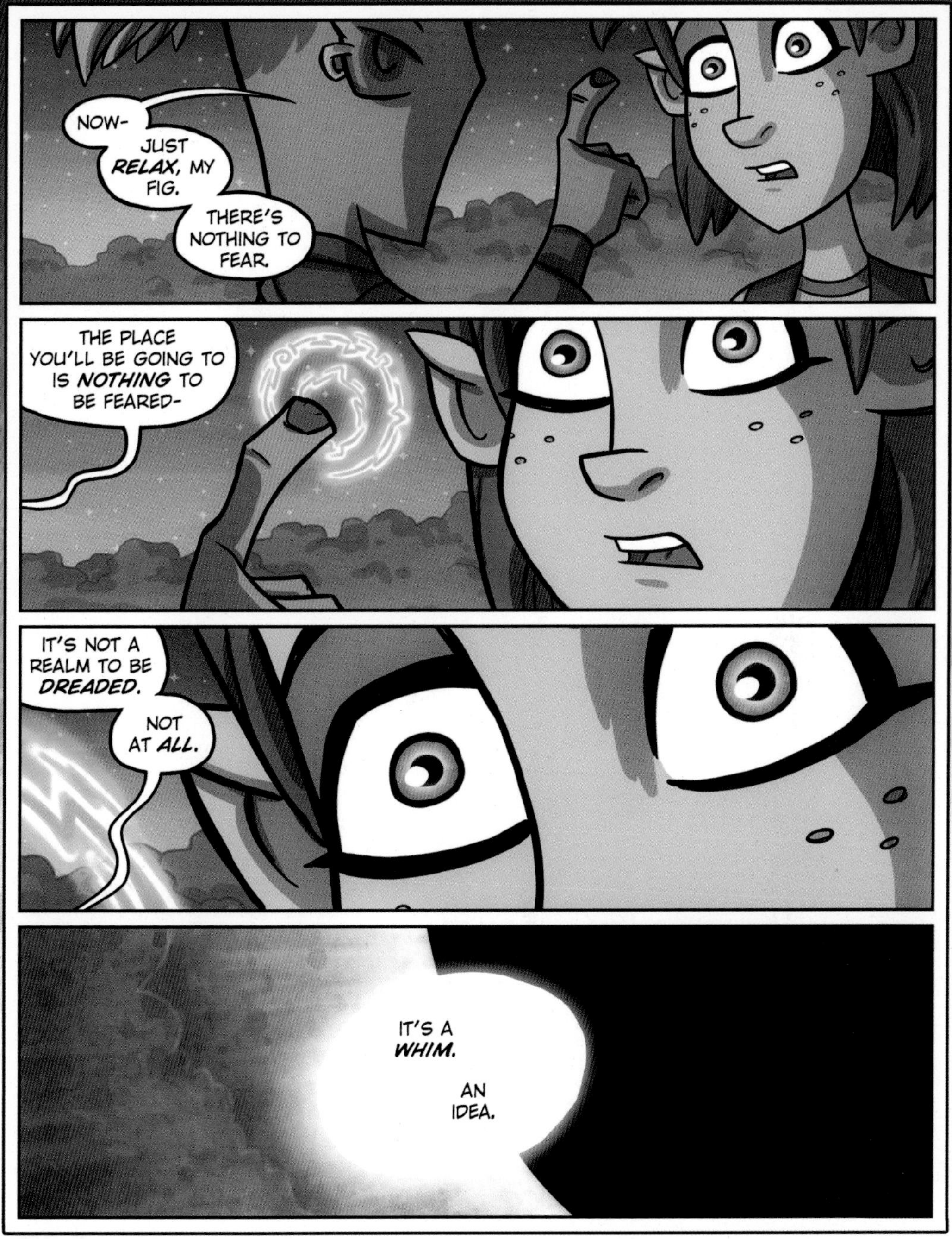
NOW-
JUST RELAX, MY FIG.
THERE'S NOTHING TO FEAR.
THE PLACE YOU'LL BE GOING TO IS NOTHING TO BE FEARED-
IT'S NOT A REALM TO BE DREADED.
NOT AT ALL.
IT'S A WHIM.
AN IDEA.

A SIMPLE *THOUGHT*.

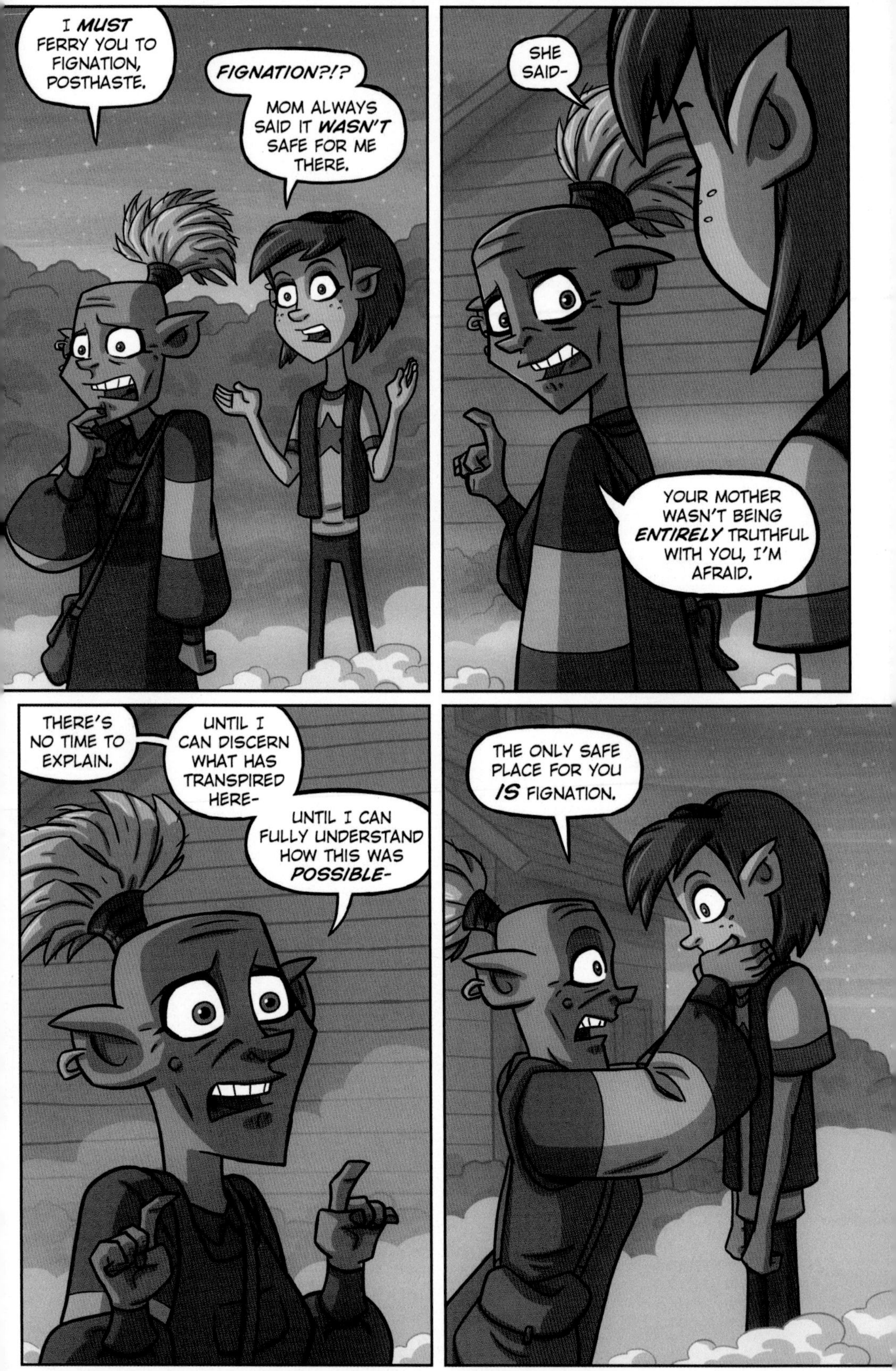
I MUST FERRY YOU TO FIGNATION, POSTHASTE.
FIGNATION?!?
MOM ALWAYS SAID IT WASN'T SAFE FOR ME THERE.
SHE SAID-
YOUR MOTHER WASN'T BEING ENTIRELY TRUTHFUL WITH YOU, I'M AFRAID.
THERE'S NO TIME TO EXPLAIN.
UNTIL I CAN DISCERN WHAT HAS TRANSPIRED HERE-
UNTIL I CAN FULLY UNDERSTAND HOW THIS WAS POSSIBLE-
THE ONLY SAFE PLACE FOR YOU IS FIGNATION.

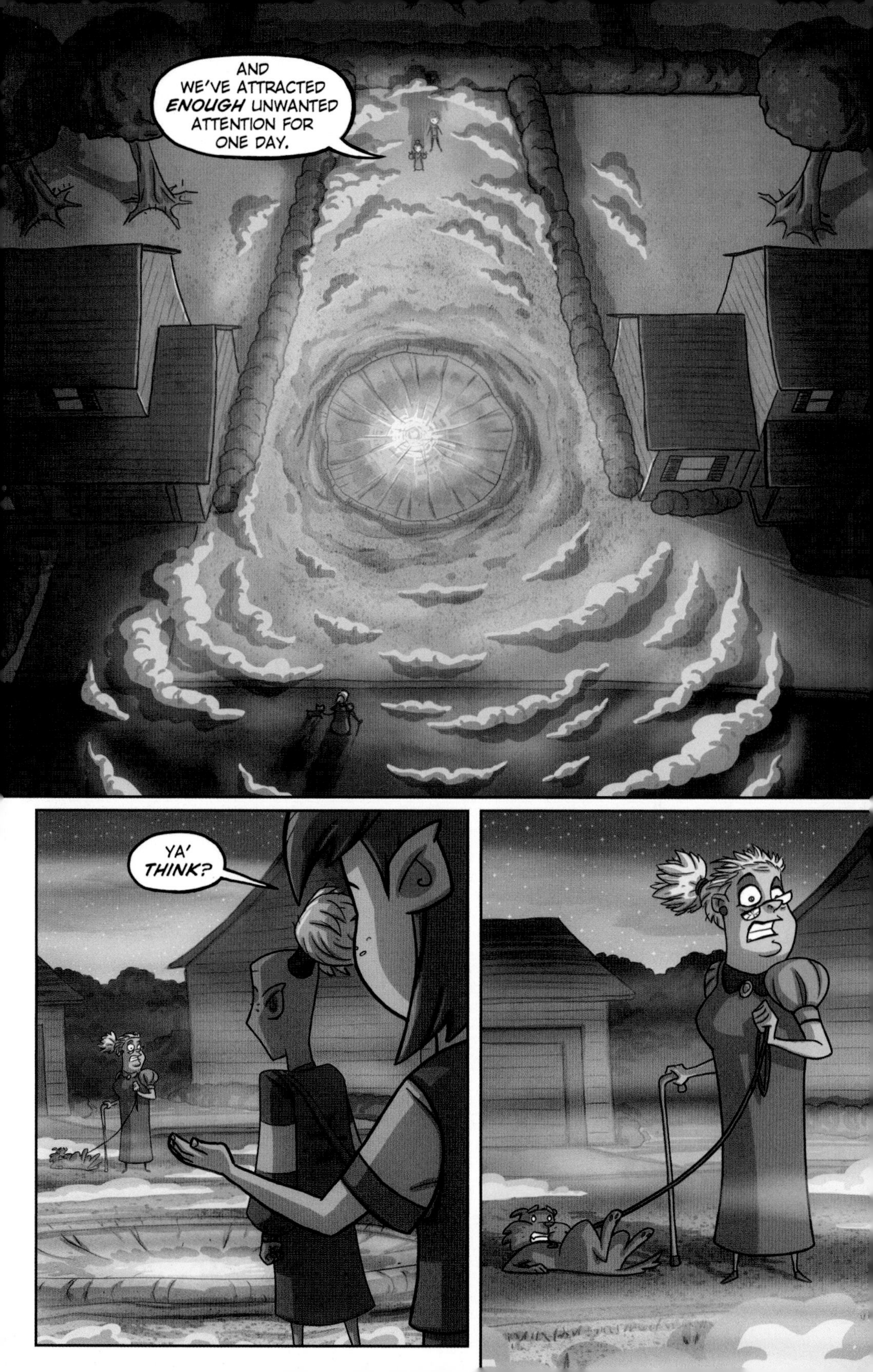
AND WE'VE ATTRACTED ENOUGH UNWANTED ATTENTION FOR ONE DAY.
YA' THINK?

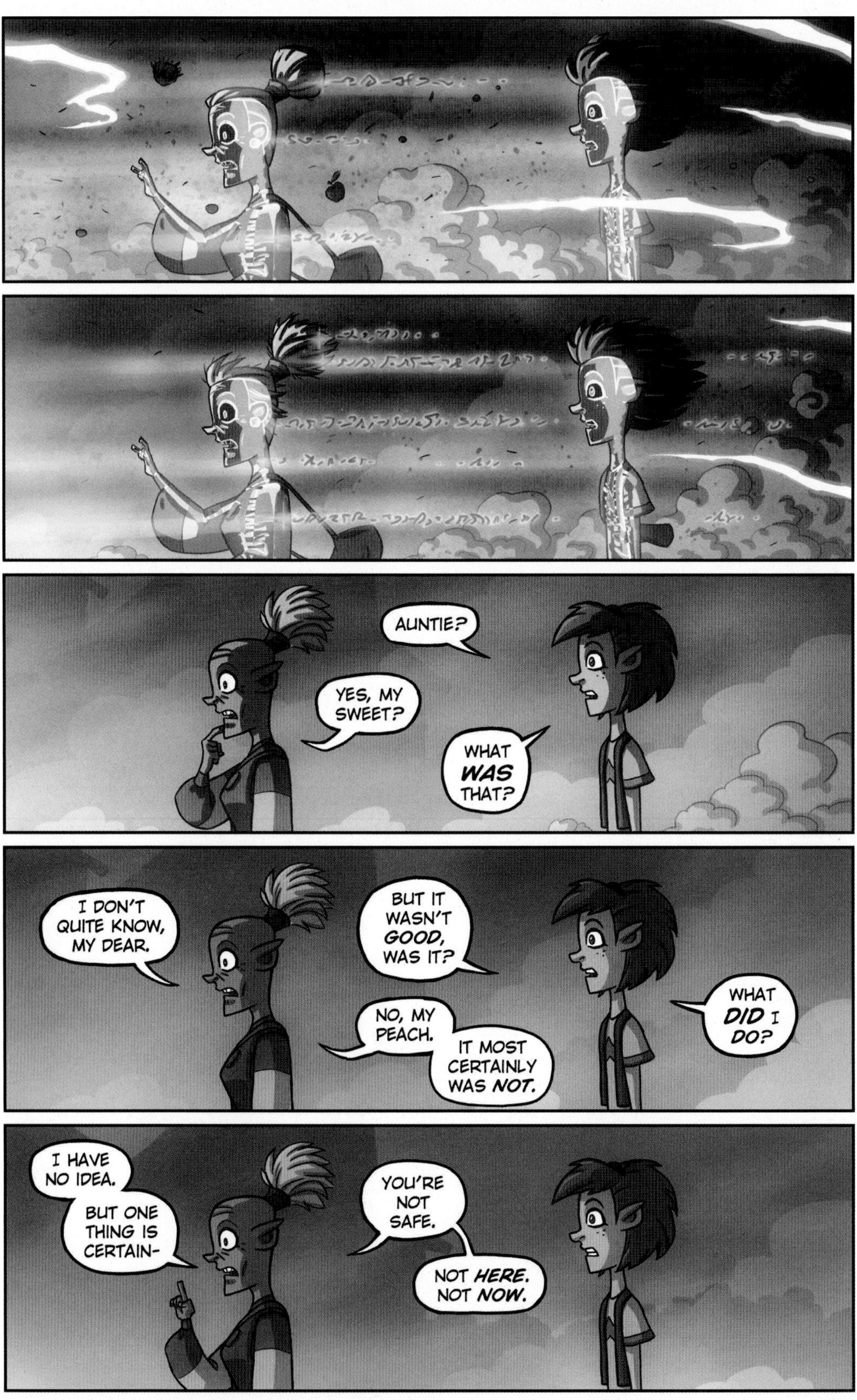
AUNTIE?
YES, MY SWEET?
WHAT *WAS* THAT?
I DON'T QUITE KNOW, MY DEAR.
BUT IT WASN'T *GOOD*, WAS IT?
NO, MY PEACH.
IT MOST CERTAINLY WAS *NOT*.
WHAT *DID* I *DO?*
I HAVE NO IDEA.
BUT ONE THING IS CERTAIN-
YOU'RE NOT SAFE.
NOT *HERE*. NOT *NOW*.

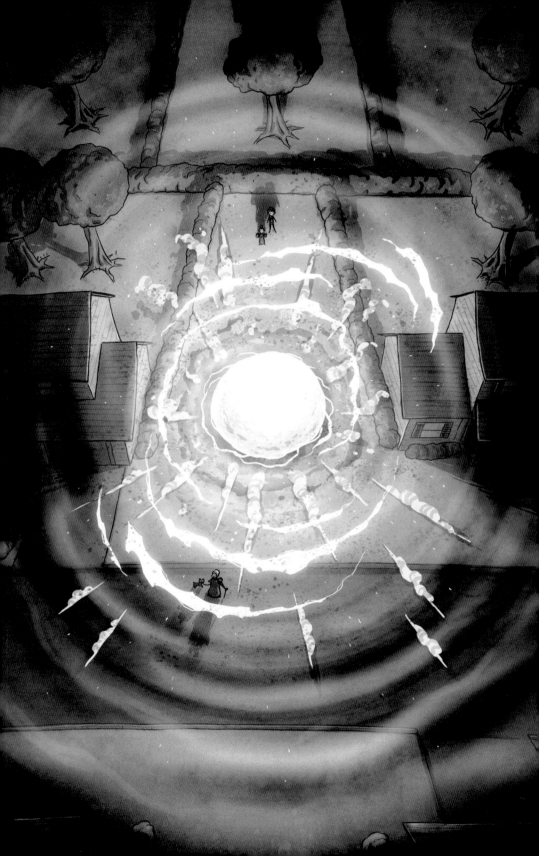

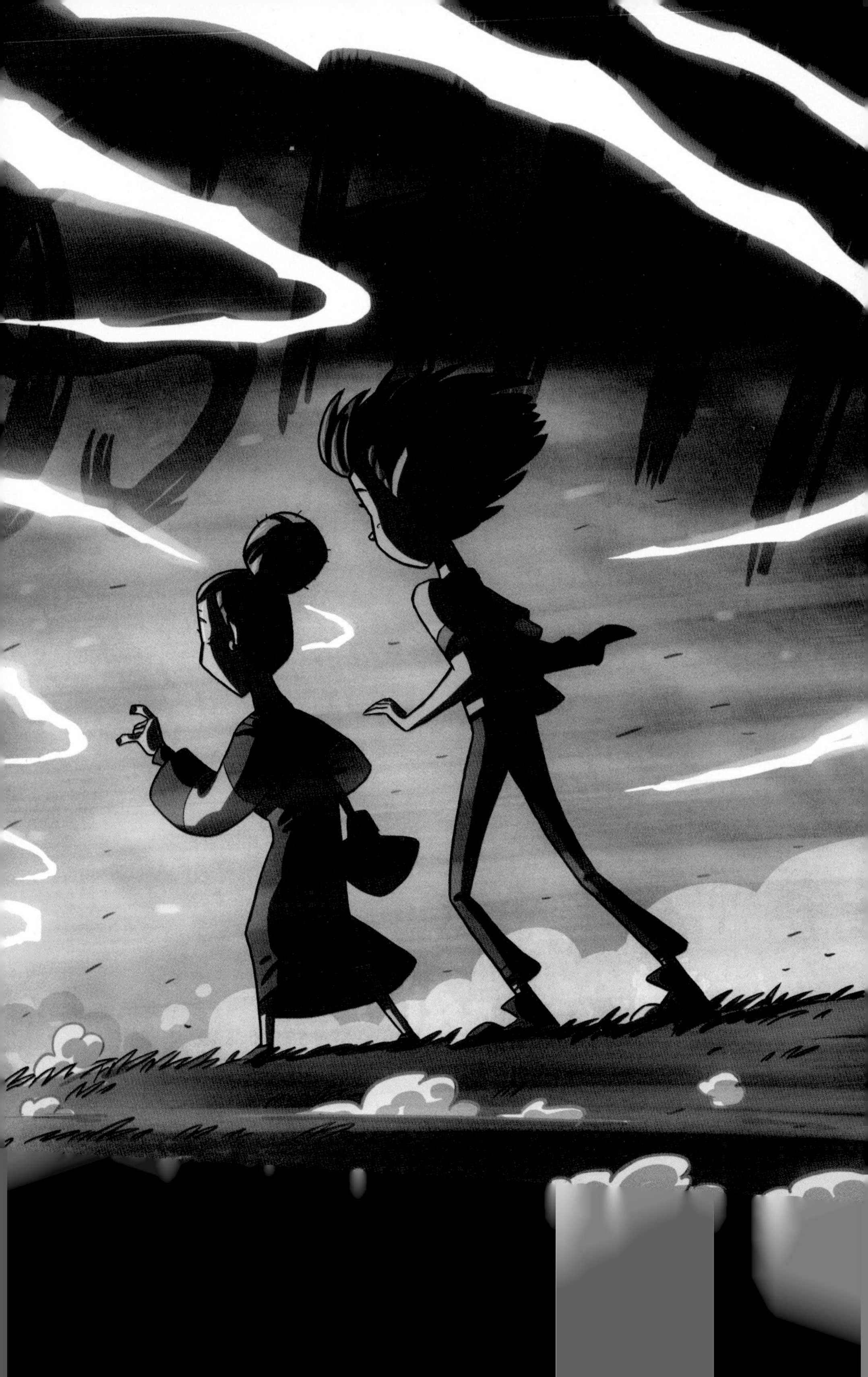

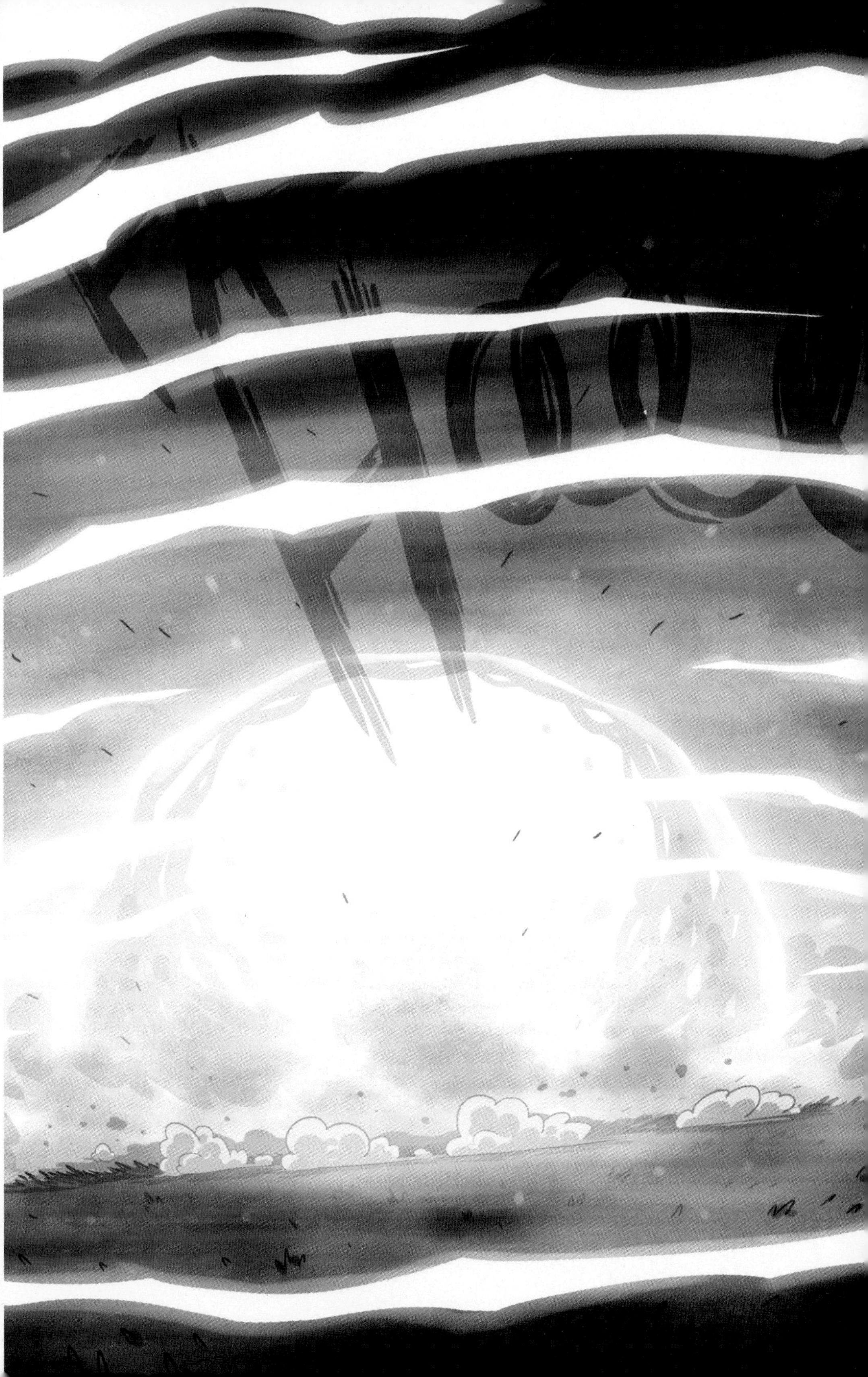

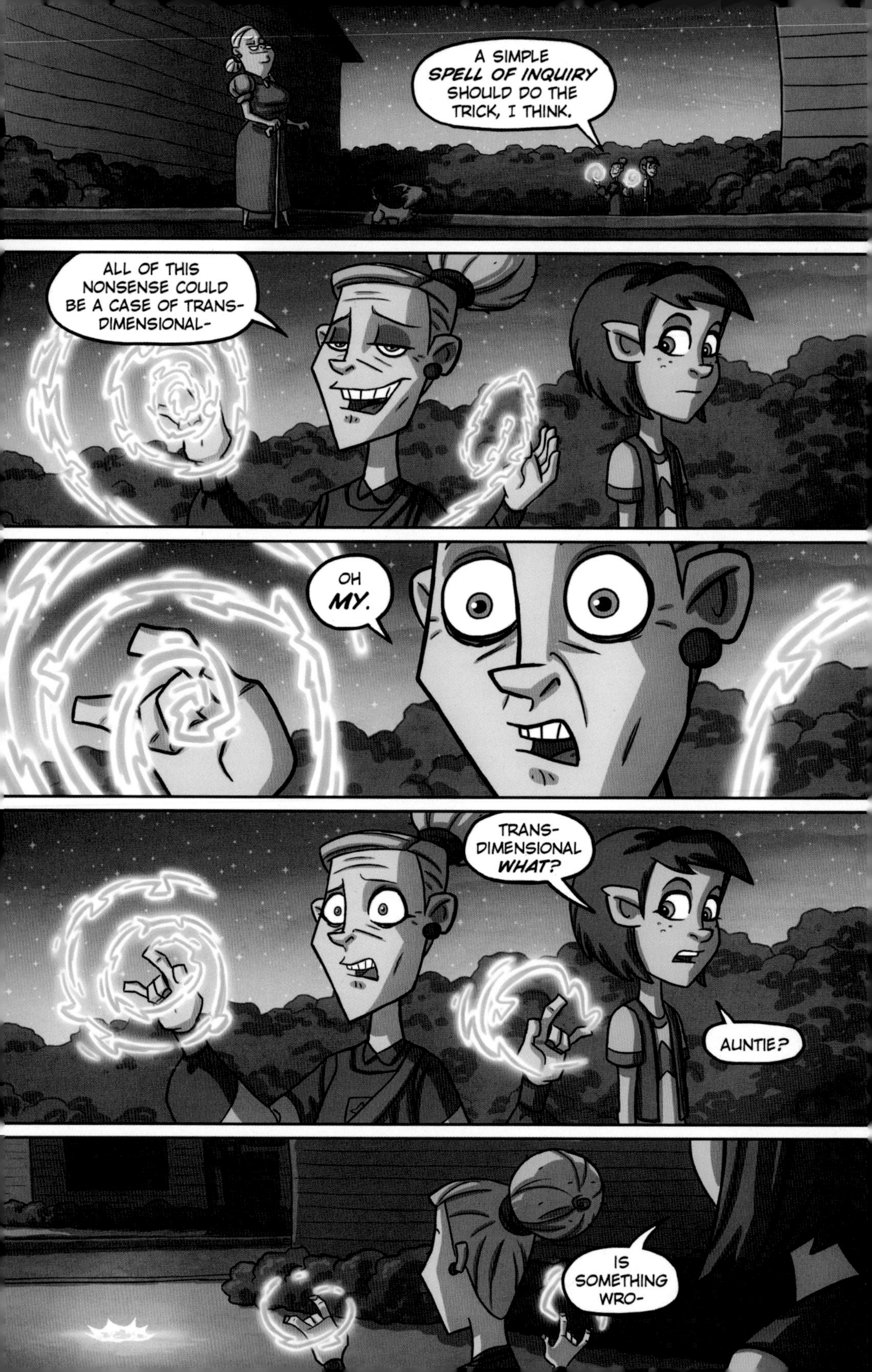
A SIMPLE SPELL OF INQUIRY SHOULD DO THE TRICK, I THINK.
ALL OF THIS NONSENSE COULD BE A CASE OF TRANS-DIMENSIONAL-
OH MY.
TRANS-DIMENSIONAL WHAT?
AUNTIE?
IS SOMETHING WRO-

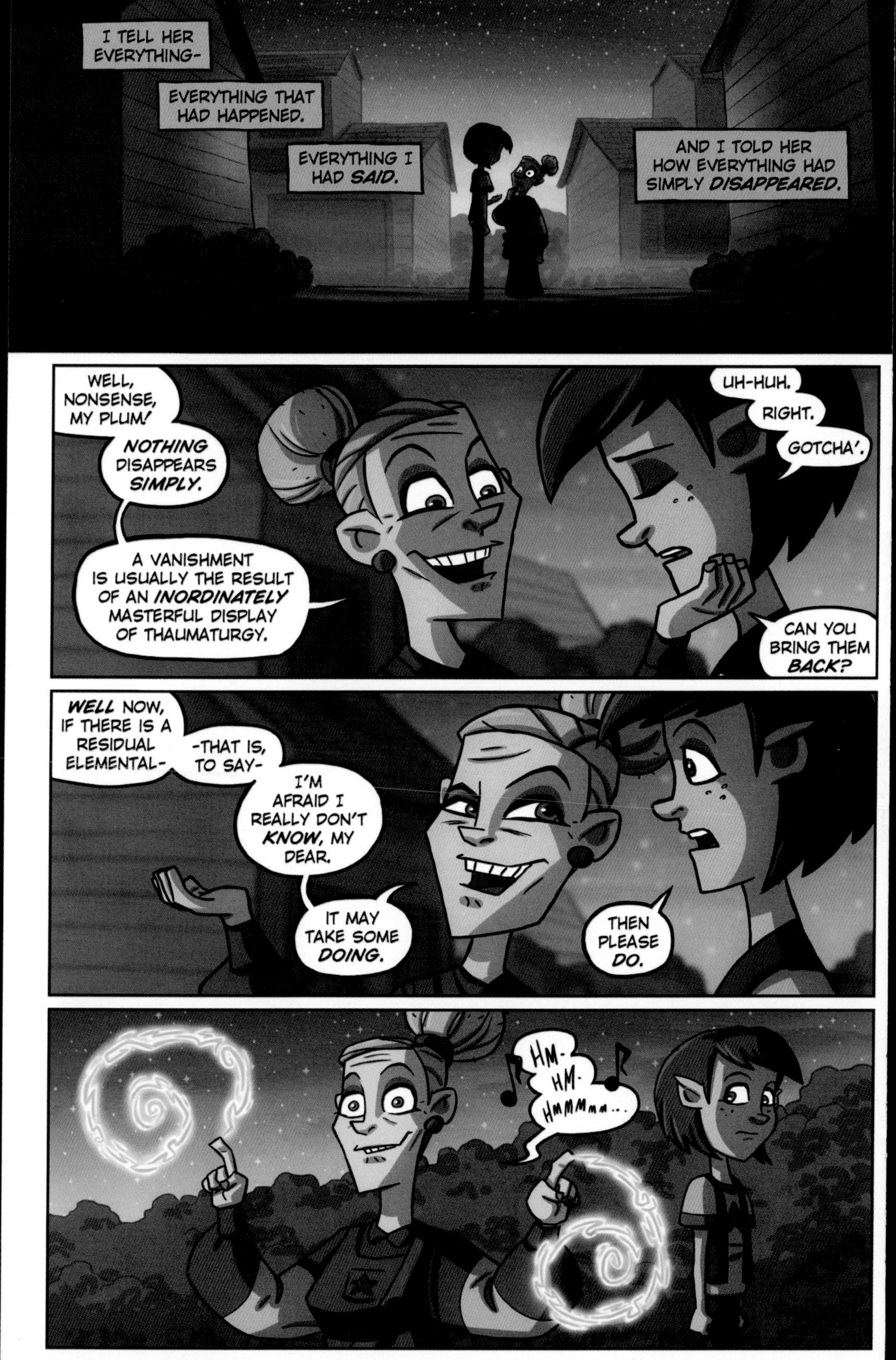
I TELL HER EVERYTHING-
EVERYTHING THAT HAD HAPPENED.
EVERYTHING I HAD SAID.
AND I TOLD HER HOW EVERYTHING HAD SIMPLY DISAPPEARED.
WELL, NONSENSE, MY PLUM!
NOTHING DISAPPEARS SIMPLY.
A VANISHMENT IS USUALLY THE RESULT OF AN INORDINATELY MASTERFUL DISPLAY OF THAUMATURGY.
UH-HUH.
RIGHT.
GOTCHA'.
CAN YOU BRING THEM BACK?
WELL NOW, IF THERE IS A RESIDUAL ELEMENTAL-
-THAT IS, TO SAY-
I'M AFRAID I REALLY DON'T KNOW, MY DEAR.
IT MAY TAKE SOME DOING.
THEN PLEASE DO.
HM-HM-HMMMMM...

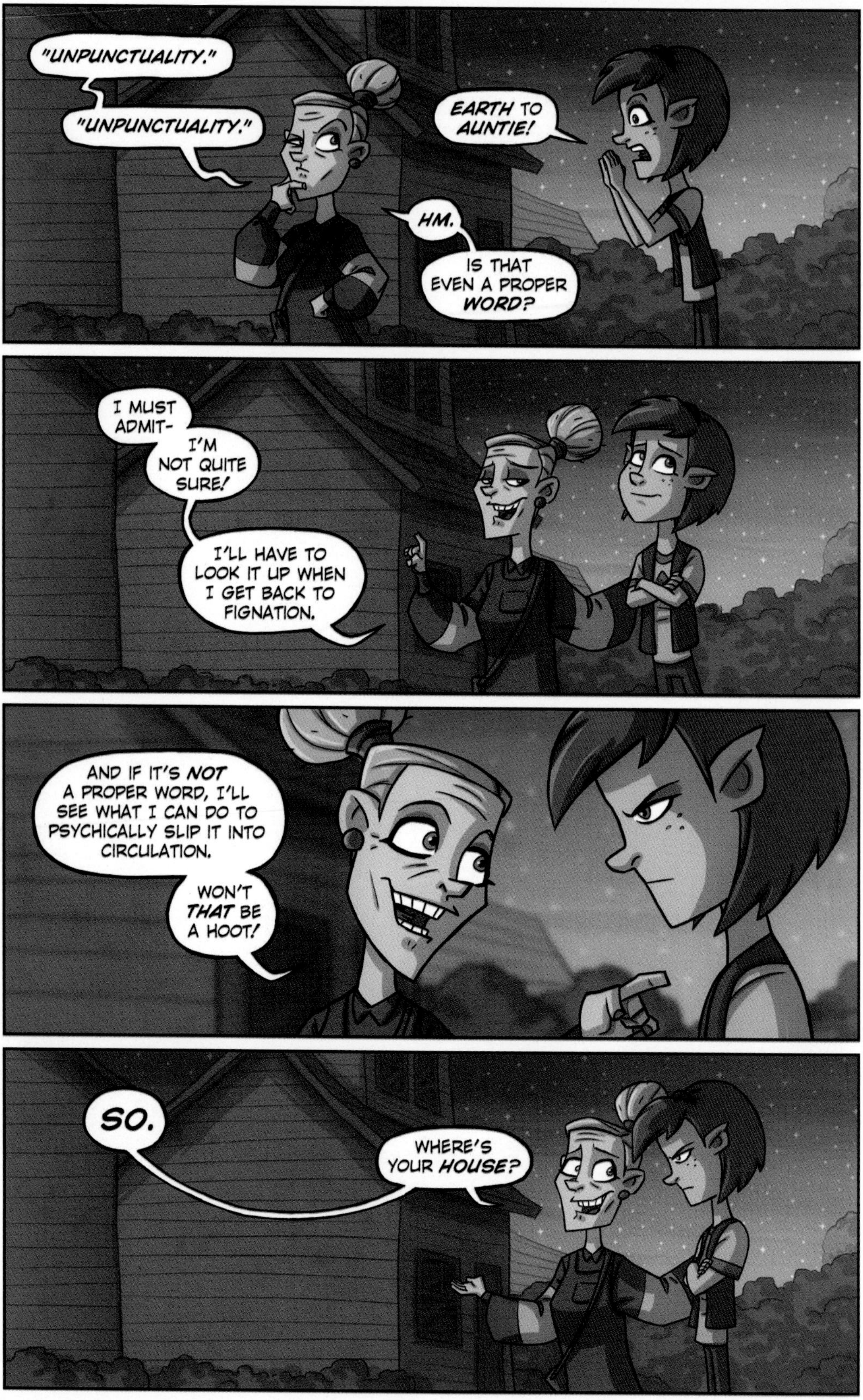
"UNPUNCTUALITY."
"UNPUNCTUALITY."
EARTH TO AUNTIE!
HM.
IS THAT EVEN A PROPER WORD?
I MUST ADMIT-
I'M NOT QUITE SURE!
I'LL HAVE TO LOOK IT UP WHEN I GET BACK TO FIGNATION.
AND IF IT'S NOT A PROPER WORD, I'LL SEE WHAT I CAN DO TO PSYCHICALLY SLIP IT INTO CIRCULATION.
WON'T THAT BE A HOOT!
SO.
WHERE'S YOUR HOUSE?

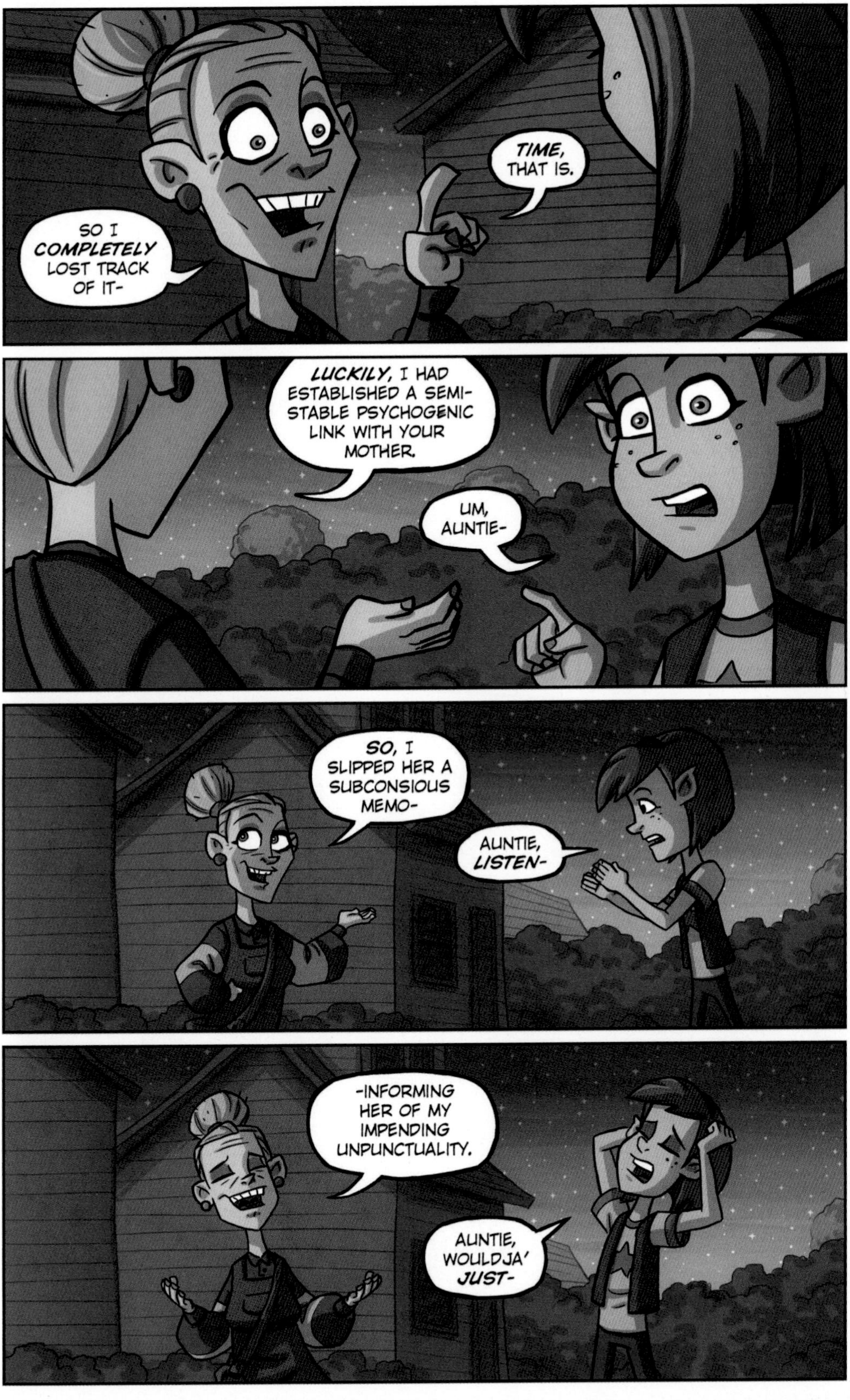
SO I COMPLETELY LOST TRACK OF IT-
TIME, THAT IS.
LUCKILY, I HAD ESTABLISHED A SEMI-STABLE PSYCHOGENIC LINK WITH YOUR MOTHER.
UM, AUNTIE-
SO, I SLIPPED HER A SUBCONSIOUS MEMO-
AUNTIE, LISTEN-
-INFORMING HER OF MY IMPENDING UNPUNCTUALITY.
AUNTIE, WOULDJA' JUST-

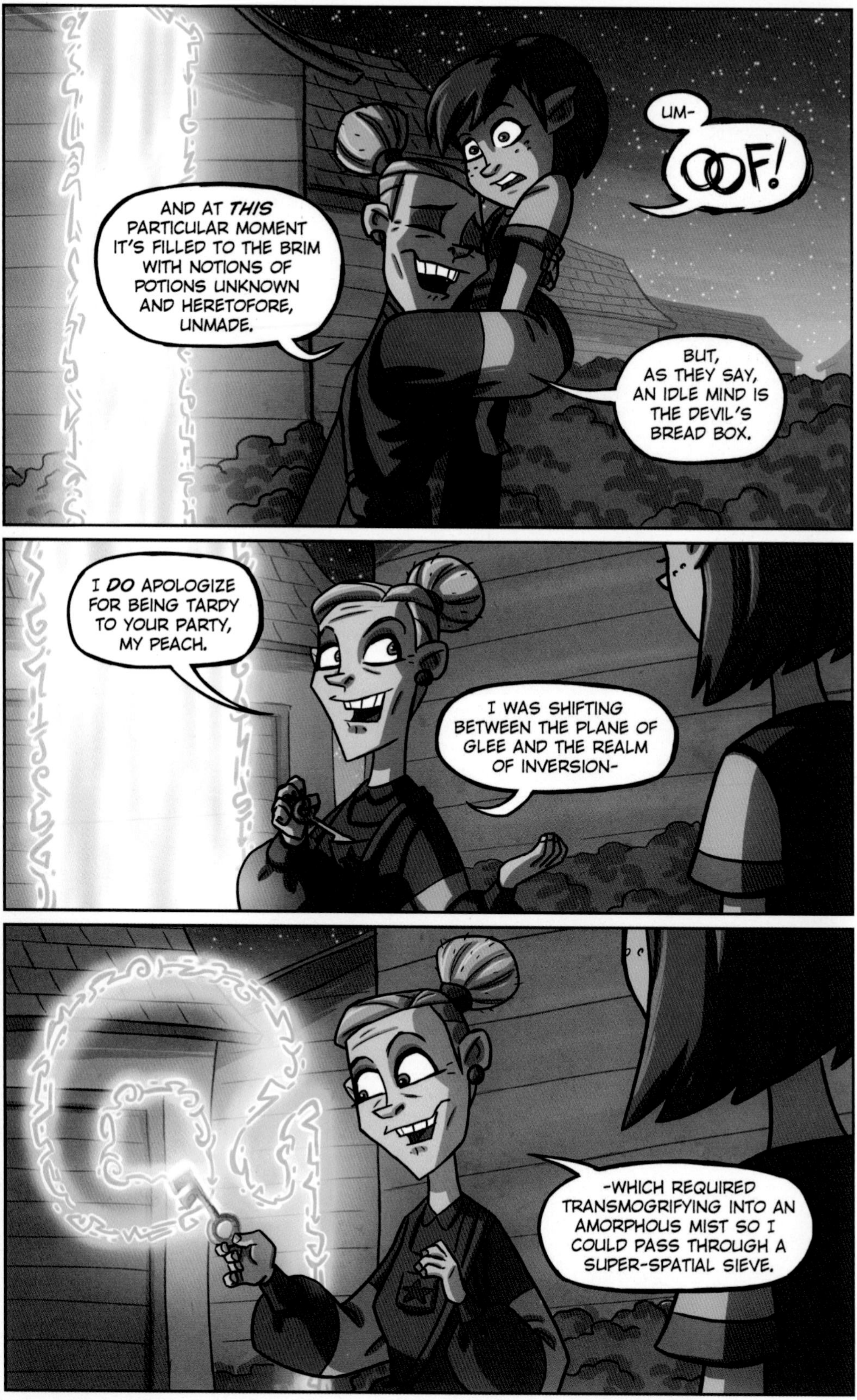
UM-
OOF!
AND AT THIS PARTICULAR MOMENT IT'S FILLED TO THE BRIM WITH NOTIONS OF POTIONS UNKNOWN AND HERETOFORE, UNMADE.
BUT, AS THEY SAY, AN IDLE MIND IS THE DEVIL'S BREAD BOX.
I DO APOLOGIZE FOR BEING TARDY TO YOUR PARTY, MY PEACH.
I WAS SHIFTING BETWEEN THE PLANE OF GLEE AND THE REALM OF INVERSION-
-WHICH REQUIRED TRANSMOGRIFYING INTO AN AMORPHOUS MIST SO I COULD PASS THROUGH A SUPER-SPATIAL SIEVE.

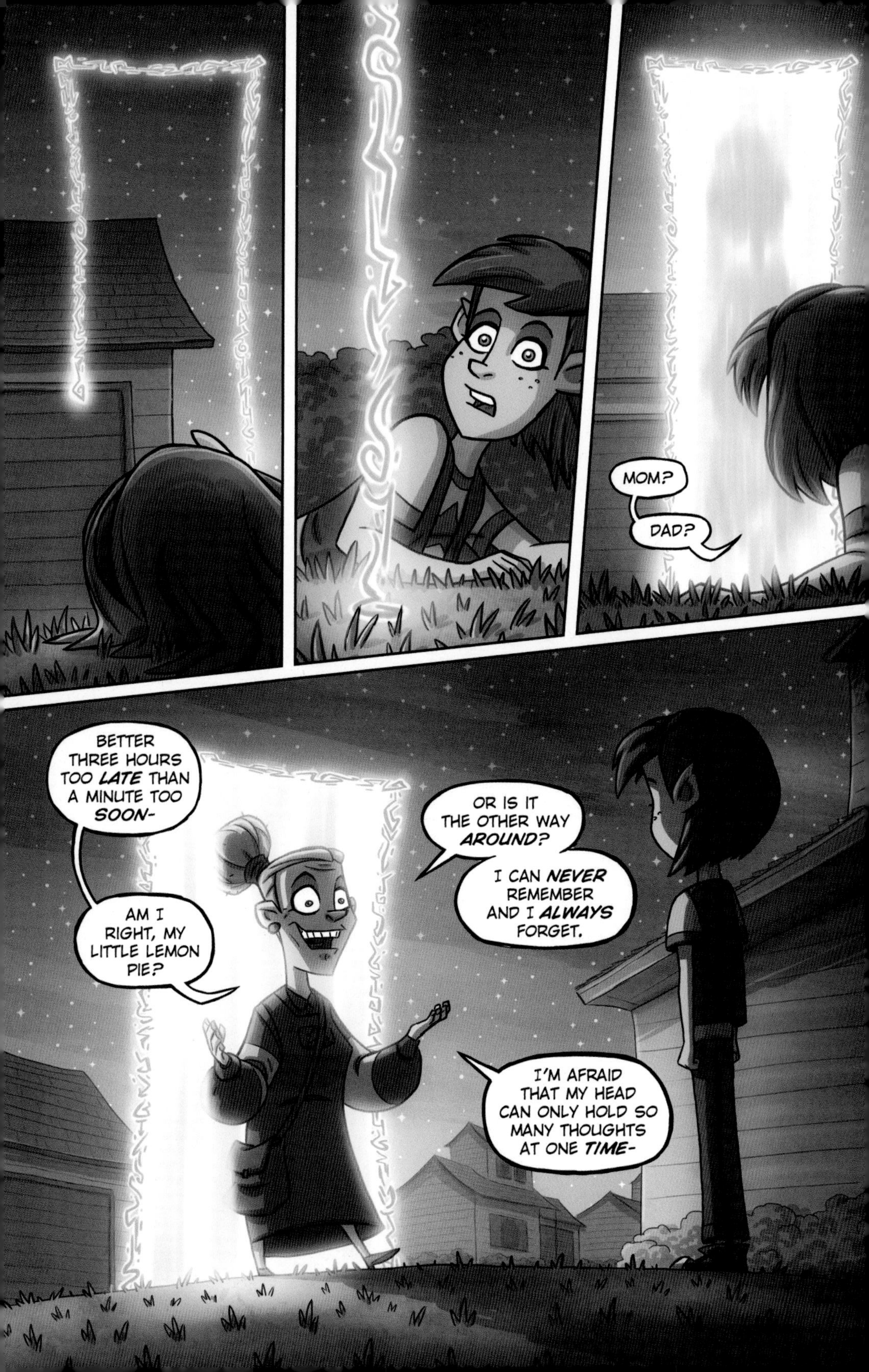
MOM?
DAD?
BETTER THREE HOURS TOO LATE THAN A MINUTE TOO SOON-
AM I RIGHT, MY LITTLE LEMON PIE?
OR IS IT THE OTHER WAY AROUND?
I CAN NEVER REMEMBER AND I ALWAYS FORGET.
I'M AFRAID THAT MY HEAD CAN ONLY HOLD SO MANY THOUGHTS AT ONE TIME-

Chapter 2

A Figment Of Your Imagination

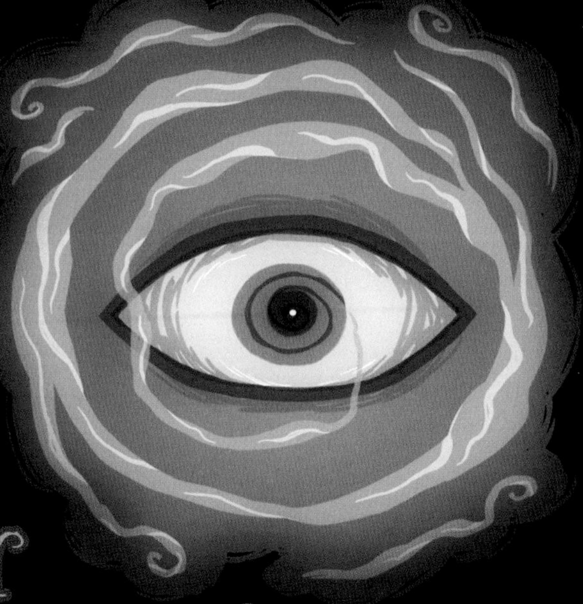

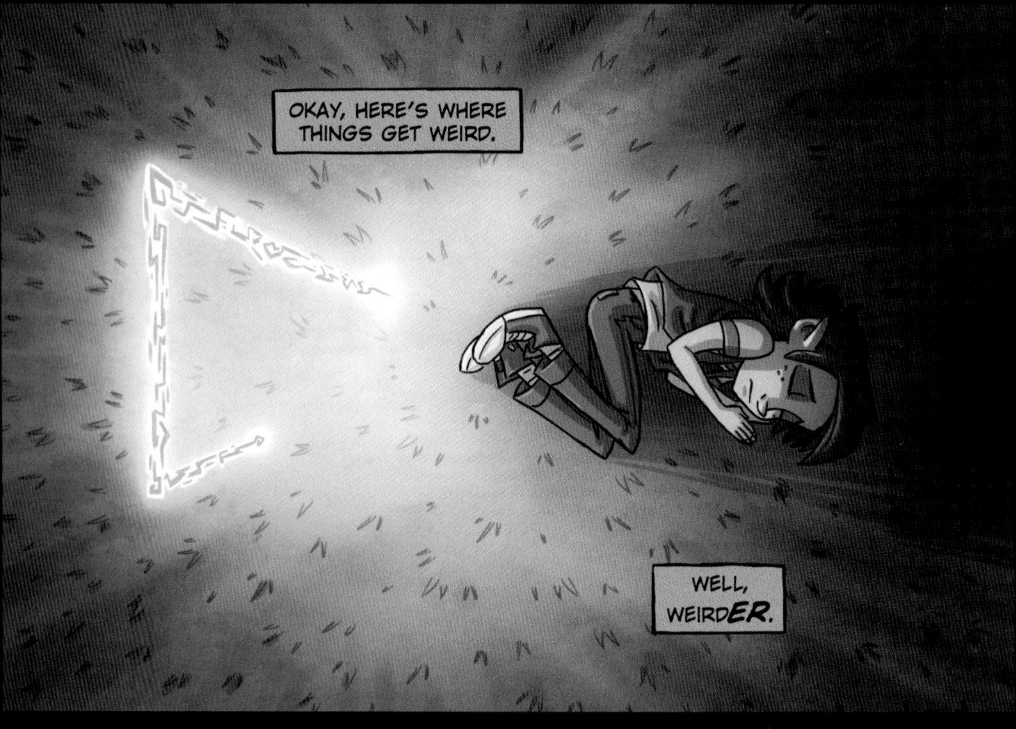

OKAY, HERE'S WHERE THINGS GET WEIRD.
WELL, WEIRDER.

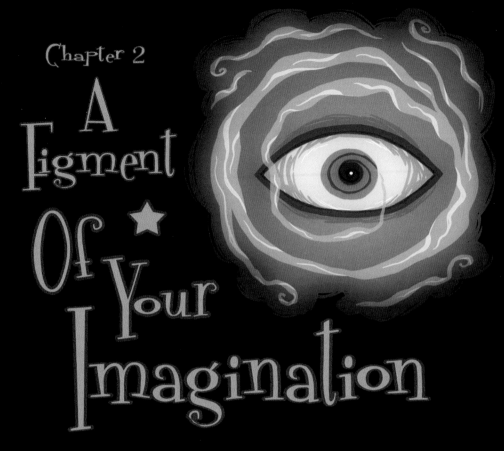

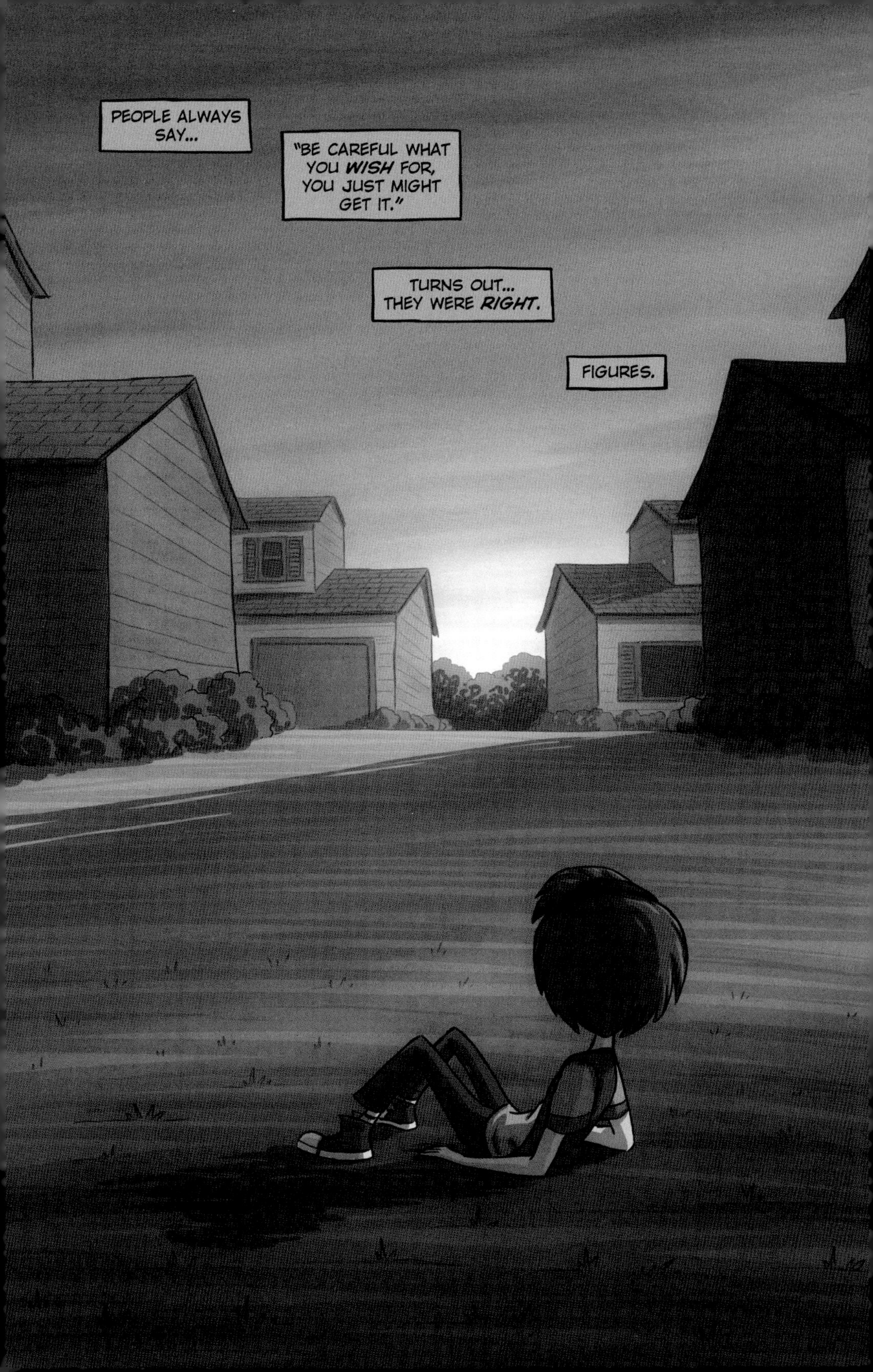
PEOPLE ALWAYS SAY...
"BE CAREFUL WHAT YOU WISH FOR, YOU JUST MIGHT GET IT."
TURNS OUT... THEY WERE RIGHT.
FIGURES.

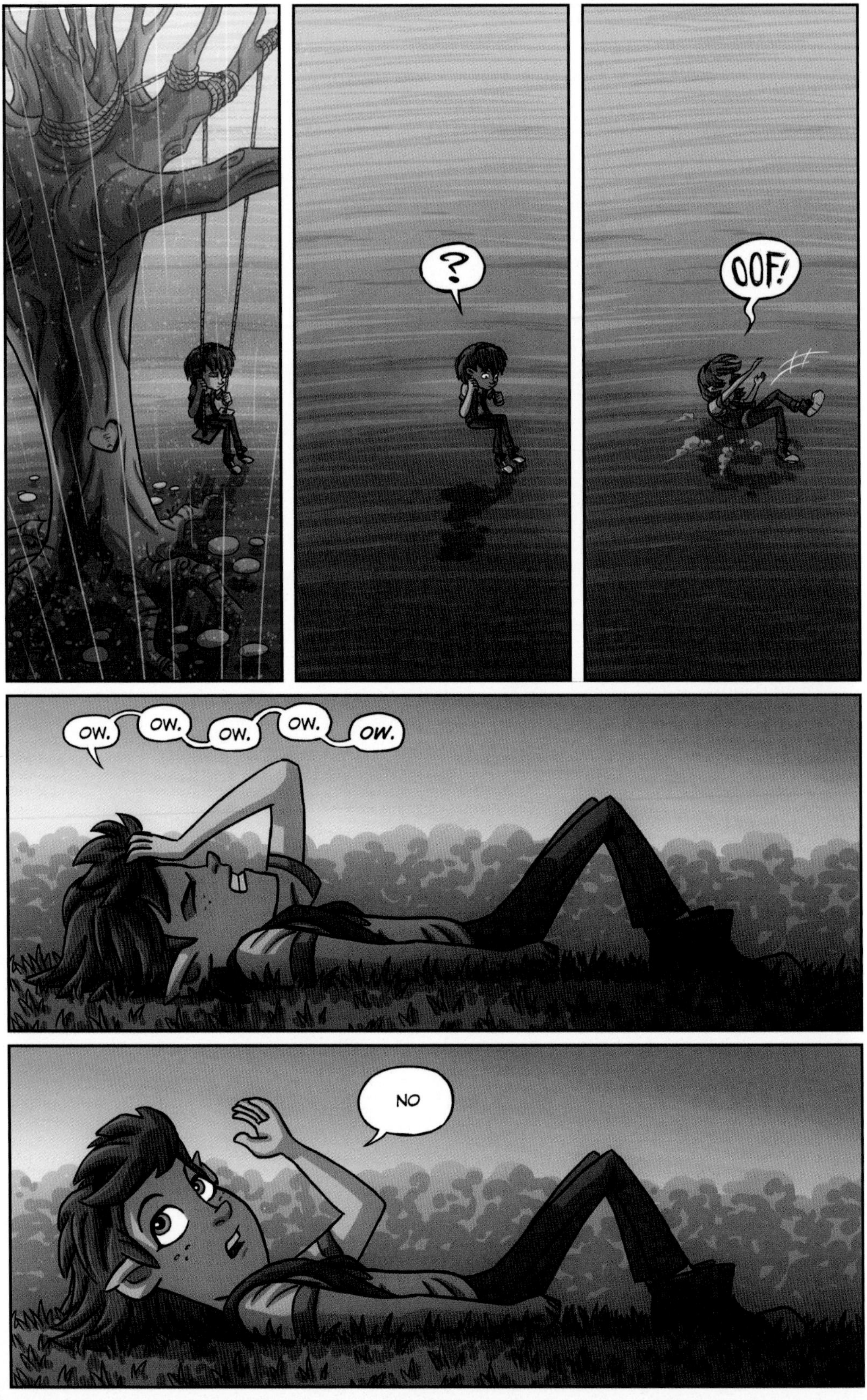
?
OOF!
OW.
OW.
OW.
OW.
OW.
NO

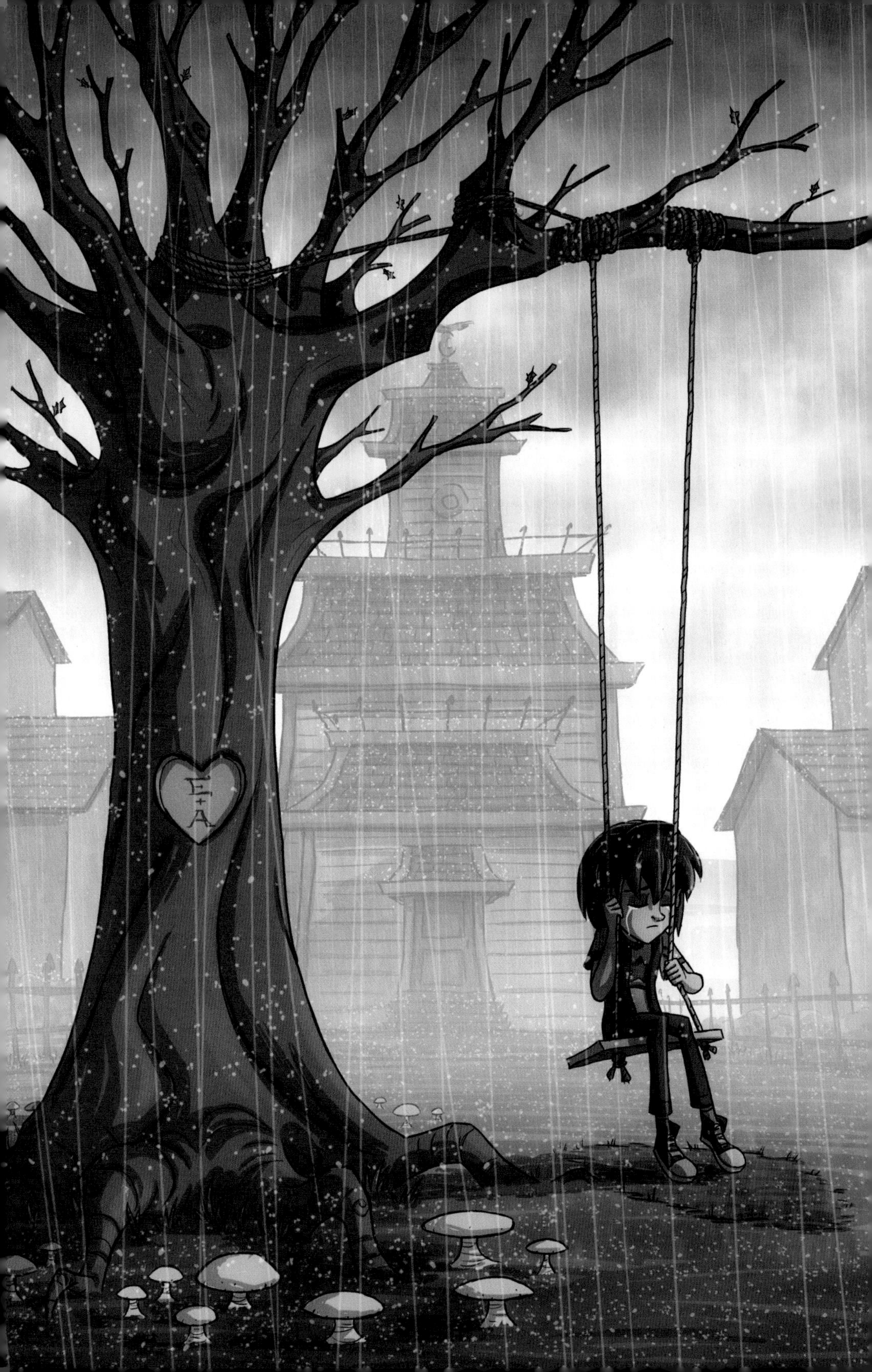
E+A

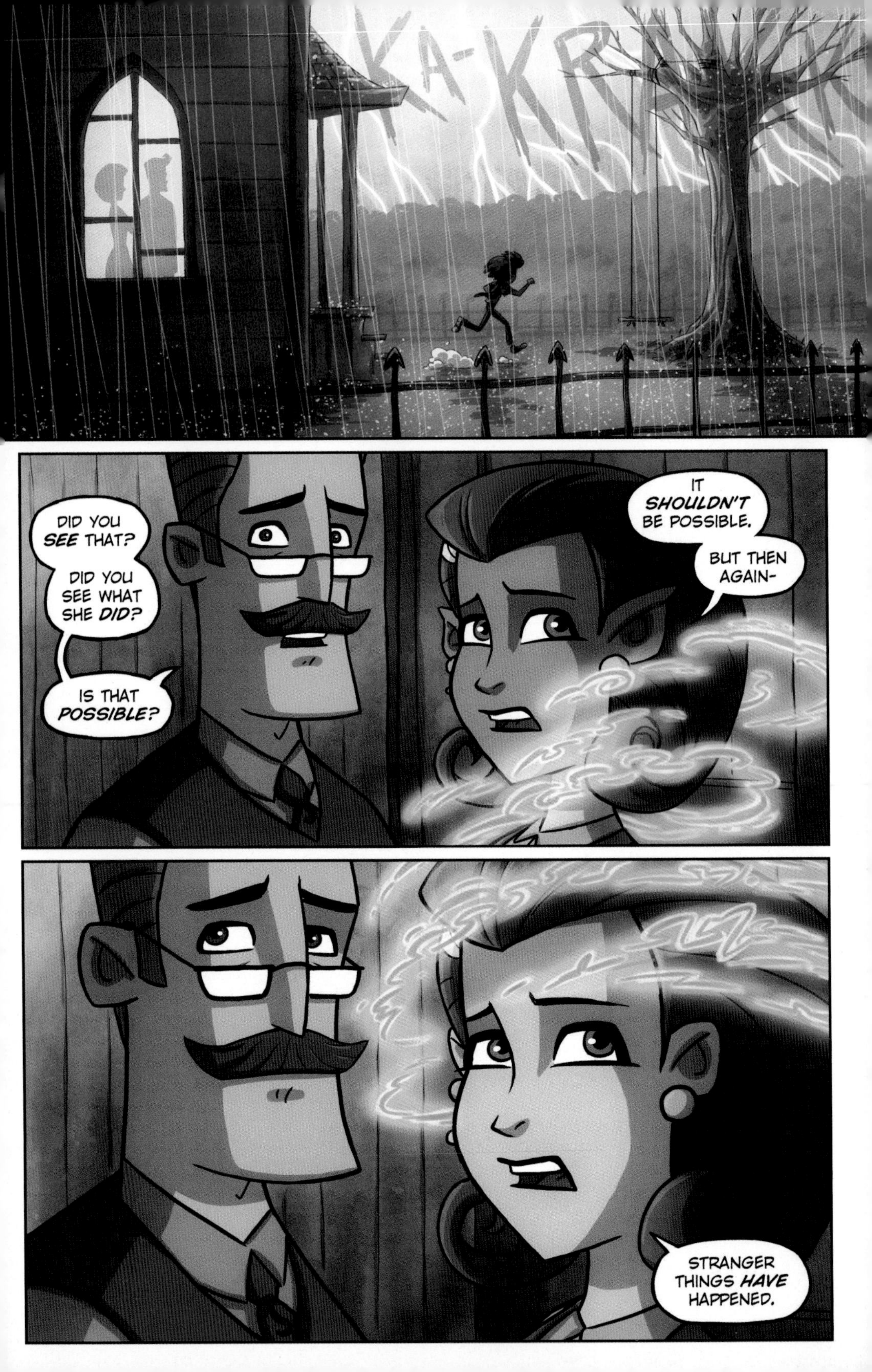
KA-KR
DID YOU *SEE* THAT?
DID YOU SEE WHAT SHE *DID?*
IS THAT *POSSIBLE?*
IT *SHOULDN'T* BE POSSIBLE.
BUT THEN AGAIN-
STRANGER THINGS *HAVE* HAPPENED.

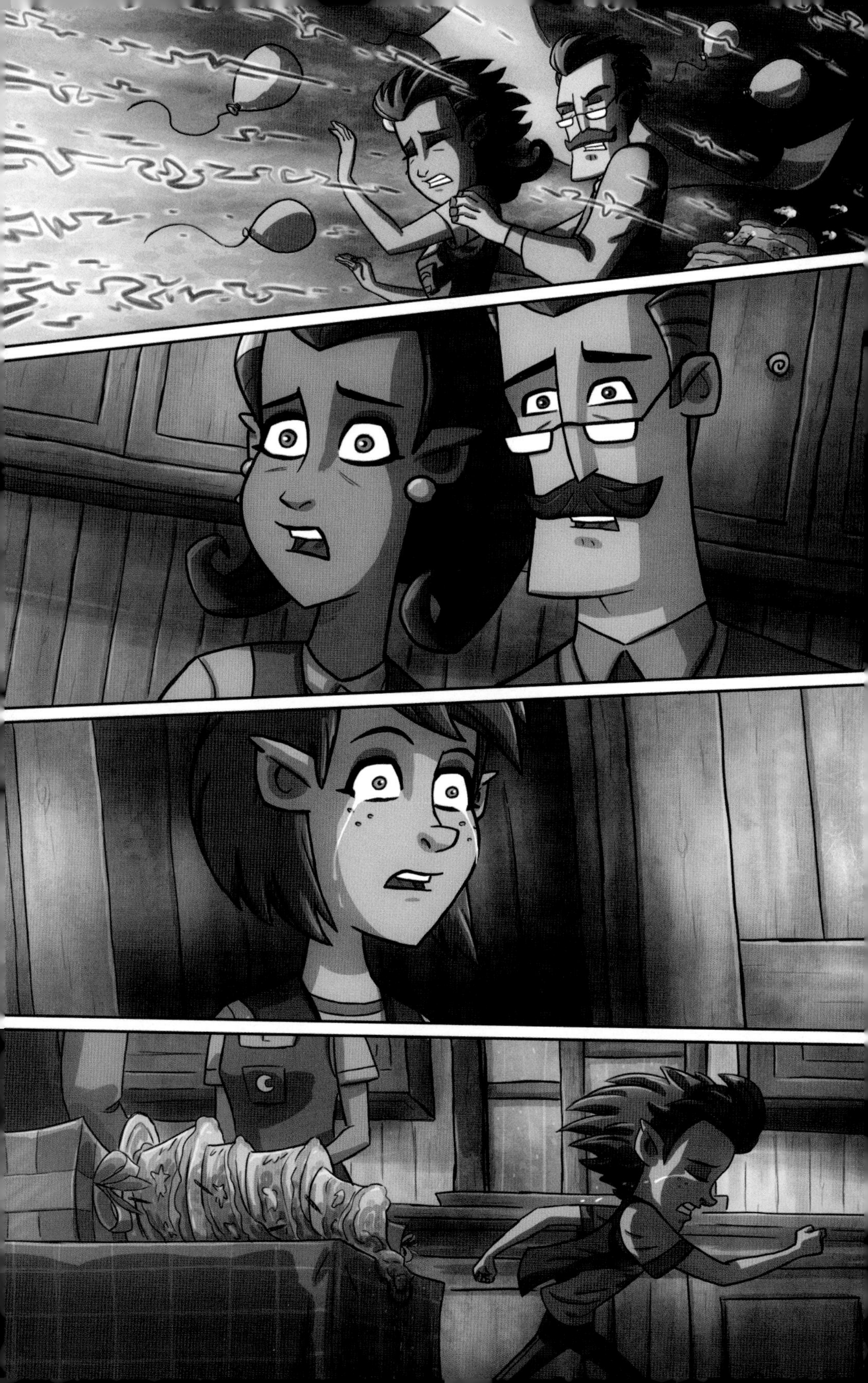

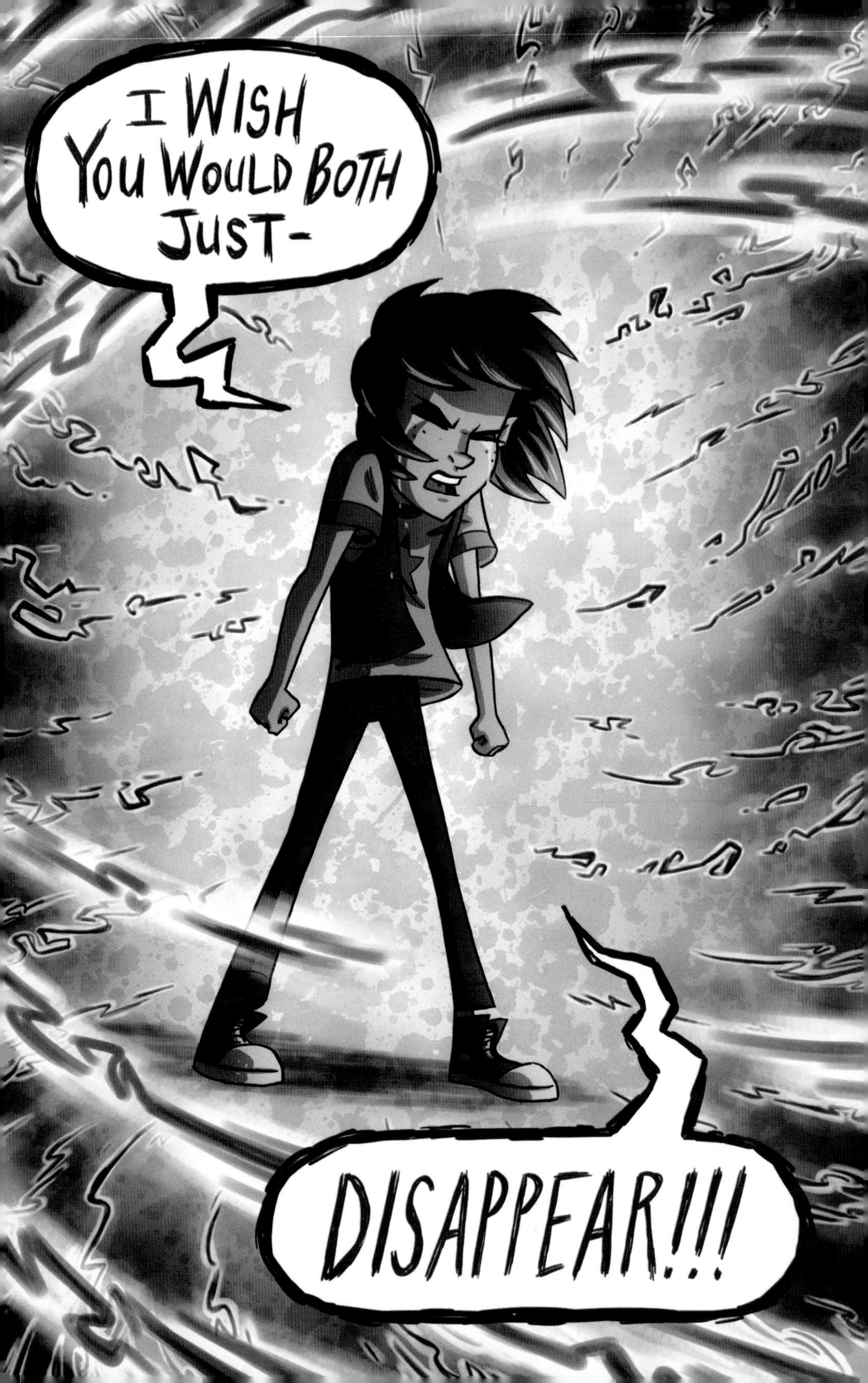
I WISH YOU WOULD BOTH JUST-
DISAPPEAR!!!

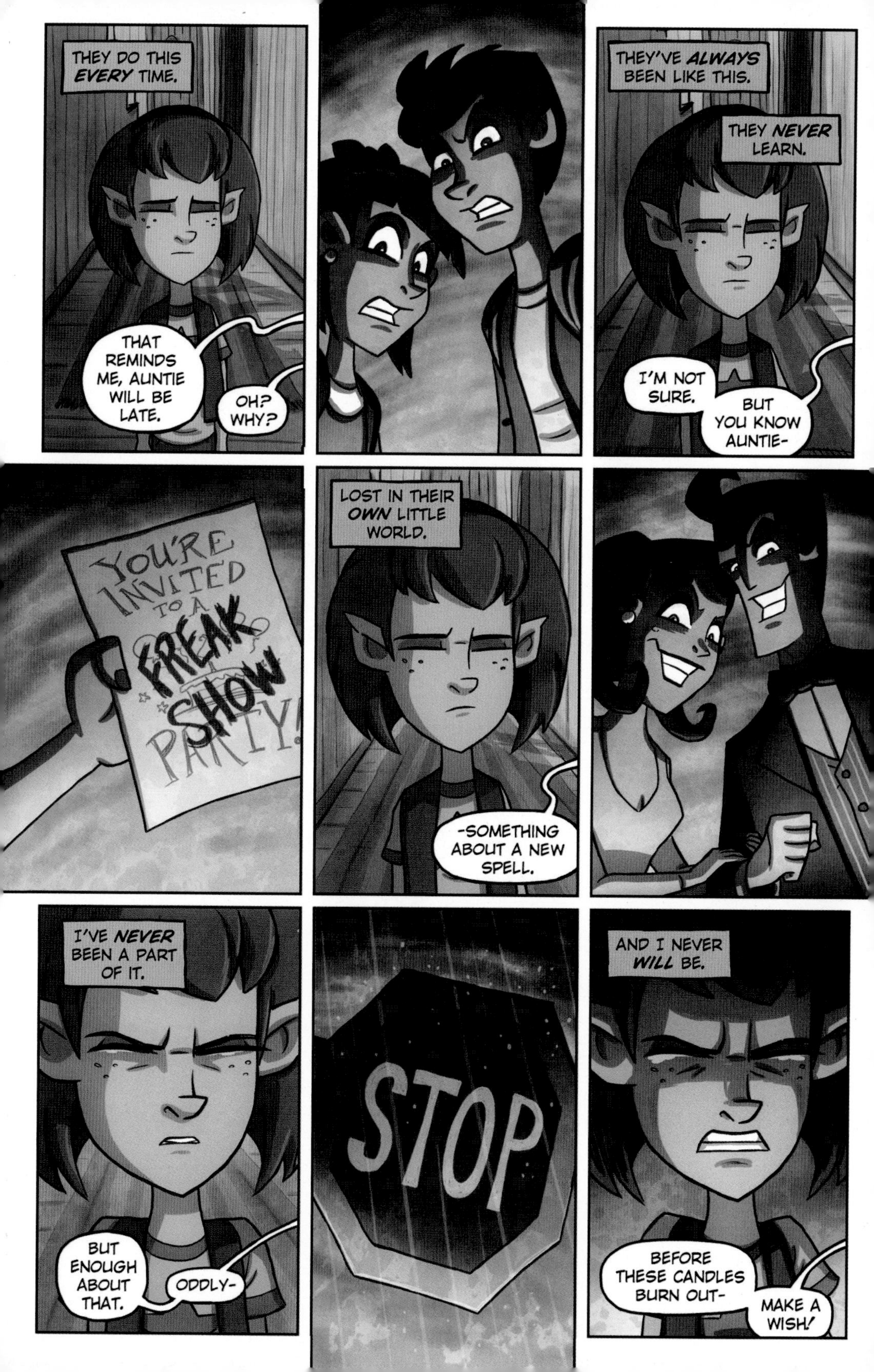
THEY DO THIS EVERY TIME.
THAT REMINDS ME, AUNTIE WILL BE LATE.
OH? WHY?
THEY'VE ALWAYS BEEN LIKE THIS.
THEY NEVER LEARN.
I'M NOT SURE.
BUT YOU KNOW AUNTIE-
YOU'RE INVITED TO A FREAK SHOW PARTY!
LOST IN THEIR OWN LITTLE WORLD.
-SOMETHING ABOUT A NEW SPELL.
I'VE NEVER BEEN A PART OF IT.
BUT ENOUGH ABOUT THAT.
ODDLY-
STOP
AND I NEVER WILL BE.
BEFORE THESE CANDLES BURN OUT-
MAKE A WISH!

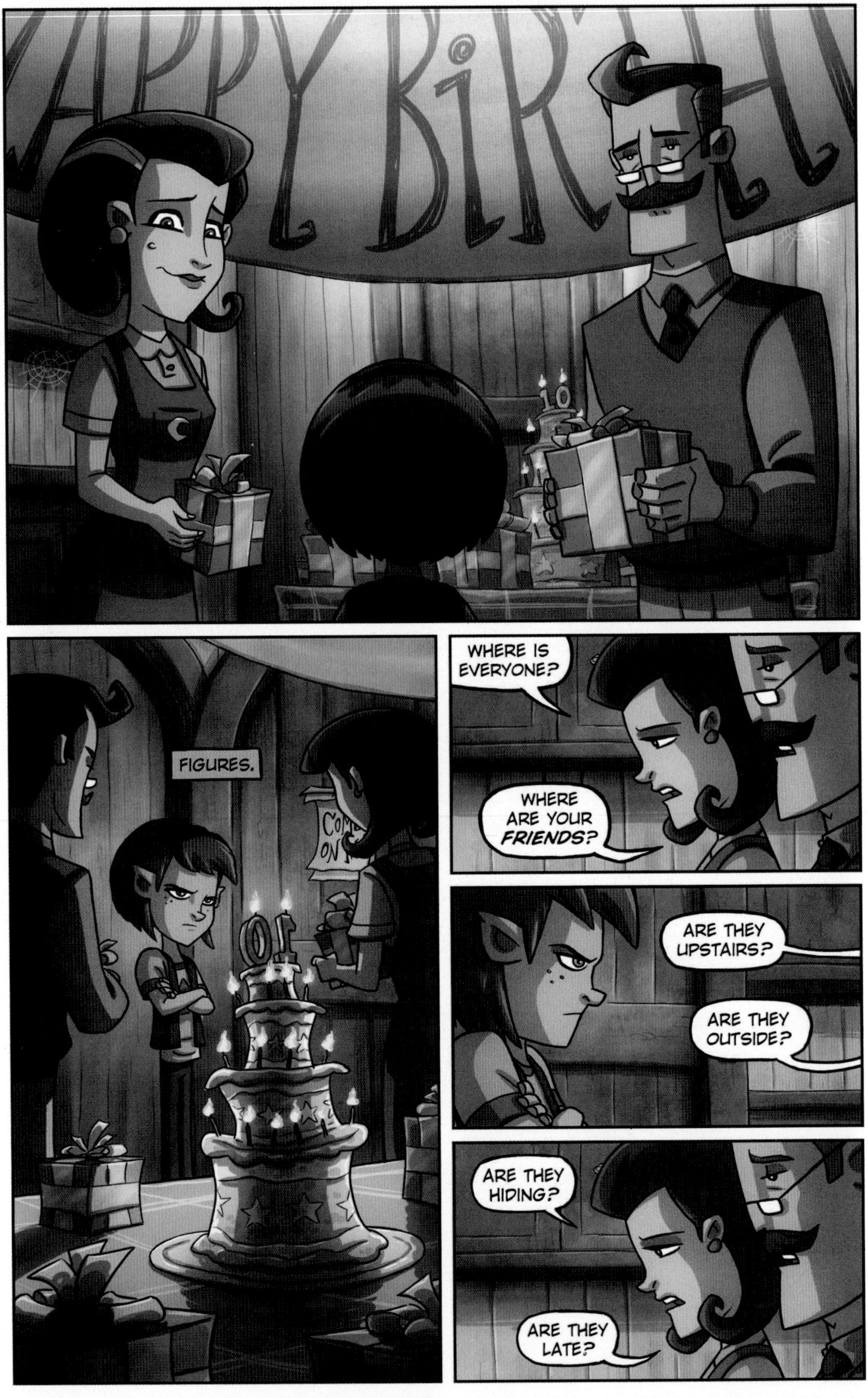
FIGURES.
WHERE IS EVERYONE?
WHERE ARE YOUR *FRIENDS*?
ARE THEY UPSTAIRS?
ARE THEY OUTSIDE?
ARE THEY HIDING?
ARE THEY LATE?

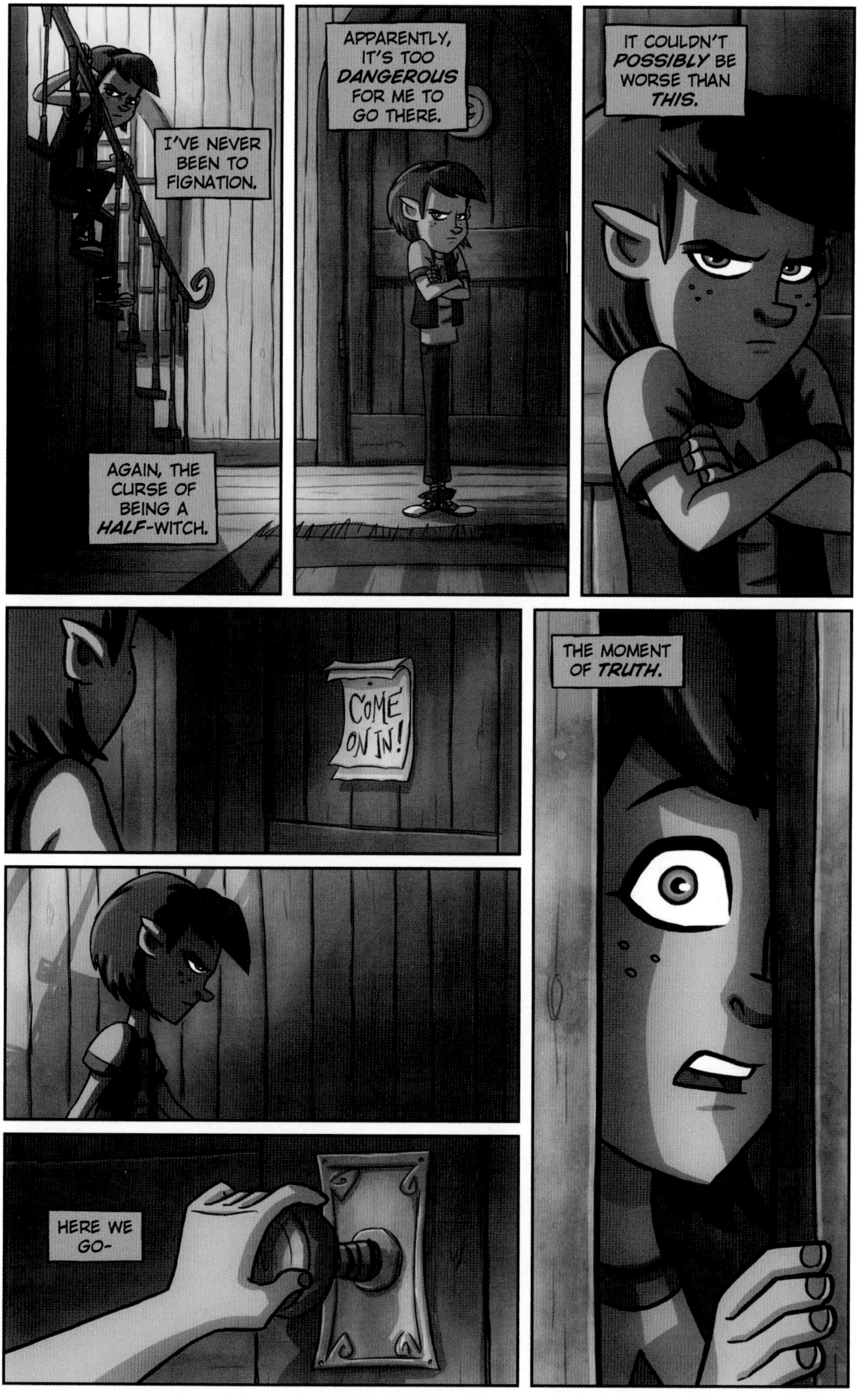
I'VE NEVER BEEN TO FIGNATION.
AGAIN, THE CURSE OF BEING A *HALF*-WITCH.
APPARENTLY, IT'S TOO *DANGEROUS* FOR ME TO GO THERE.
IT COULDN'T *POSSIBLY* BE WORSE THAN *THIS*.
COME ON IN!
HERE WE GO-
THE MOMENT OF *TRUTH*.

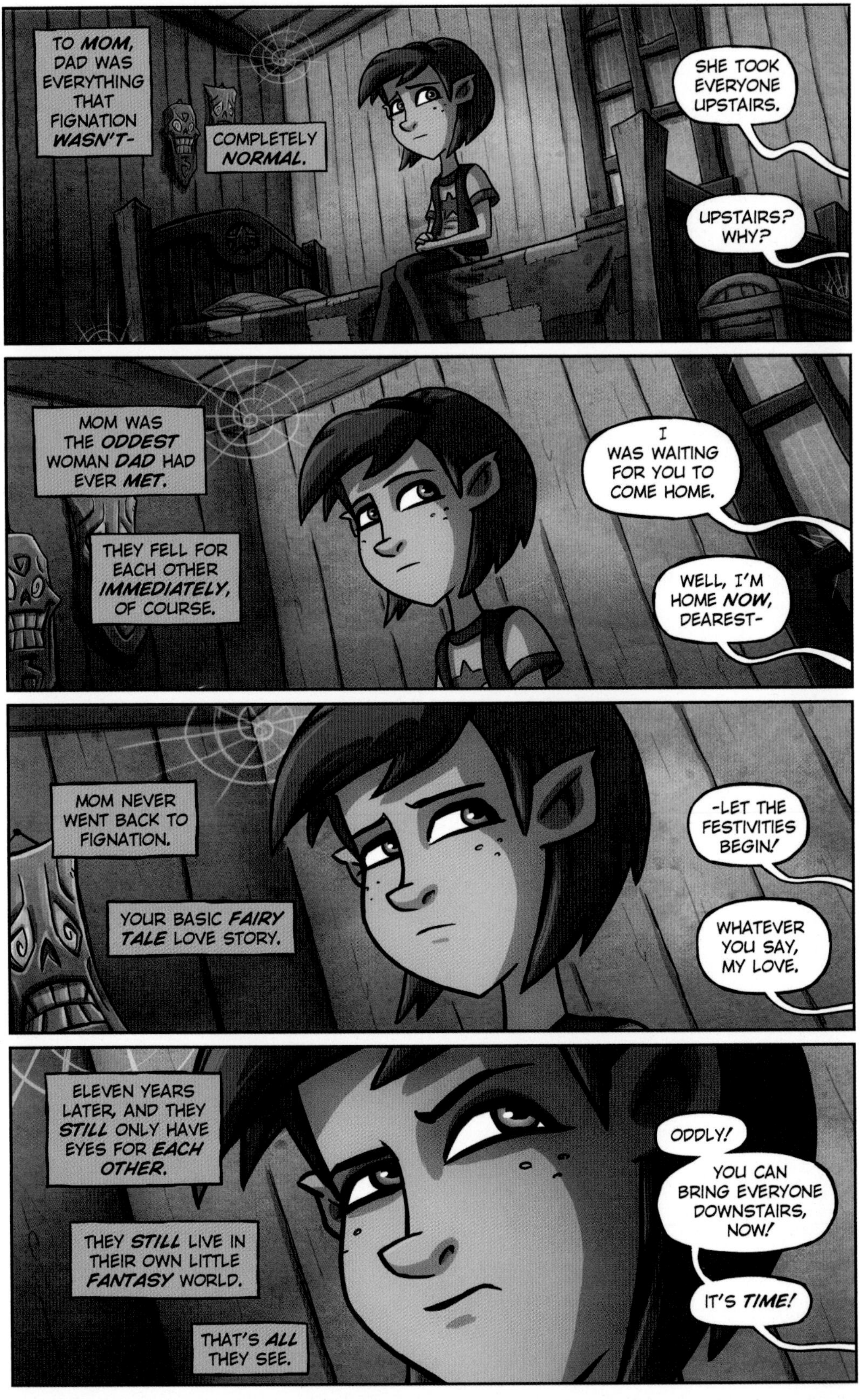
TO MOM, DAD WAS EVERYTHING THAT FIGNATION WASN'T-
COMPLETELY NORMAL.
SHE TOOK EVERYONE UPSTAIRS.
UPSTAIRS? WHY?
MOM WAS THE ODDEST WOMAN DAD HAD EVER MET.
THEY FELL FOR EACH OTHER IMMEDIATELY, OF COURSE.
I WAS WAITING FOR YOU TO COME HOME.
WELL, I'M HOME NOW, DEAREST-
MOM NEVER WENT BACK TO FIGNATION.
YOUR BASIC FAIRY TALE LOVE STORY.
-LET THE FESTIVITIES BEGIN!
WHATEVER YOU SAY, MY LOVE.
ELEVEN YEARS LATER, AND THEY STILL ONLY HAVE EYES FOR EACH OTHER.
THEY STILL LIVE IN THEIR OWN LITTLE FANTASY WORLD.
THAT'S ALL THEY SEE.
ODDLY!
YOU CAN BRING EVERYONE DOWNSTAIRS, NOW!
IT'S TIME!

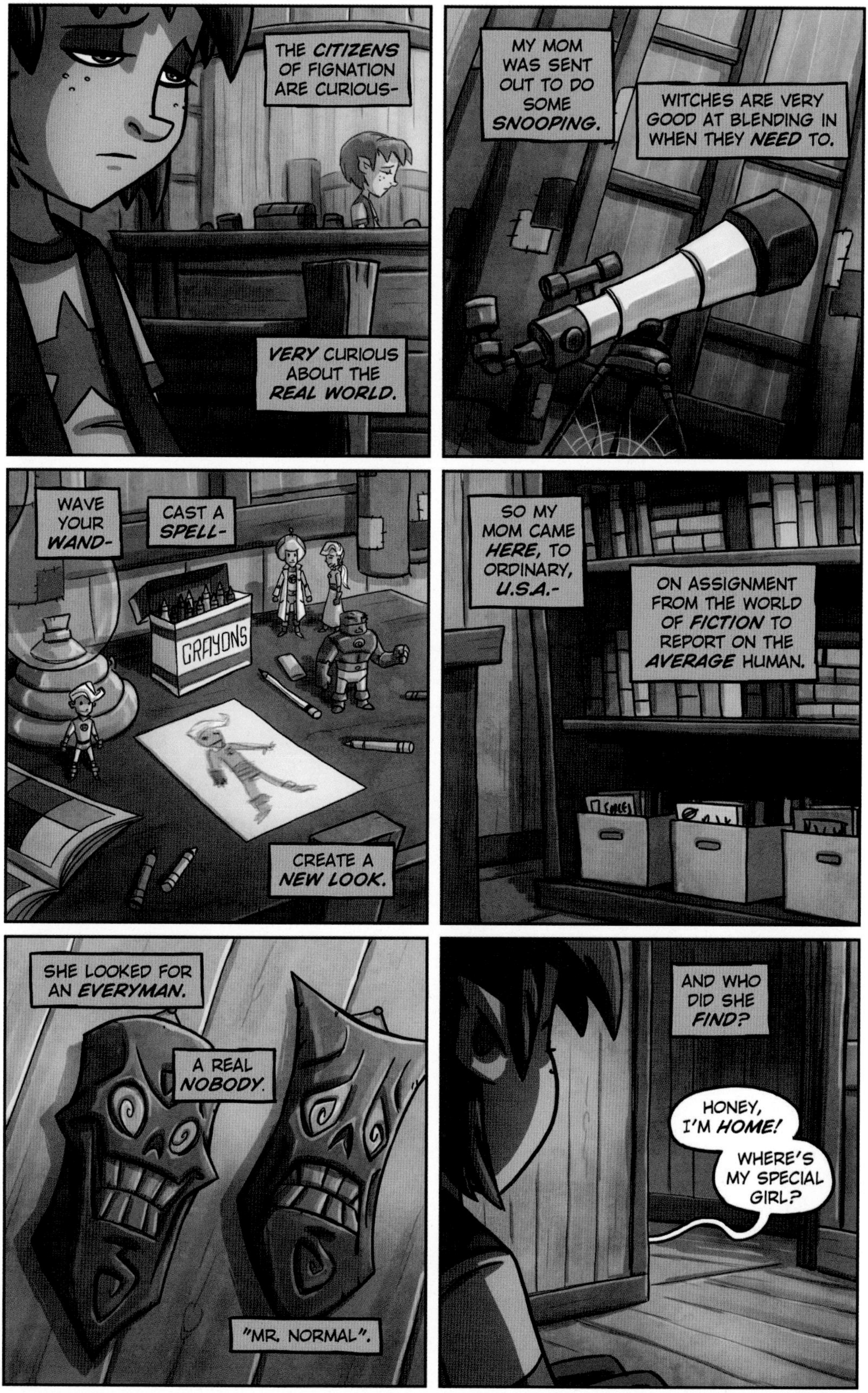
THE CITIZENS OF FIGNATION ARE CURIOUS-
VERY CURIOUS ABOUT THE REAL WORLD.
MY MOM WAS SENT OUT TO DO SOME SNOOPING.
WITCHES ARE VERY GOOD AT BLENDING IN WHEN THEY NEED TO.
WAVE YOUR WAND-
CAST A SPELL-
CRAYONS
CREATE A NEW LOOK.
SO MY MOM CAME HERE, TO ORDINARY, U.S.A.-
ON ASSIGNMENT FROM THE WORLD OF FICTION TO REPORT ON THE AVERAGE HUMAN.
SHE LOOKED FOR AN EVERYMAN.
A REAL NOBODY.
"MR. NORMAL".
AND WHO DID SHE FIND?
HONEY, I'M HOME!
WHERE'S MY SPECIAL GIRL?

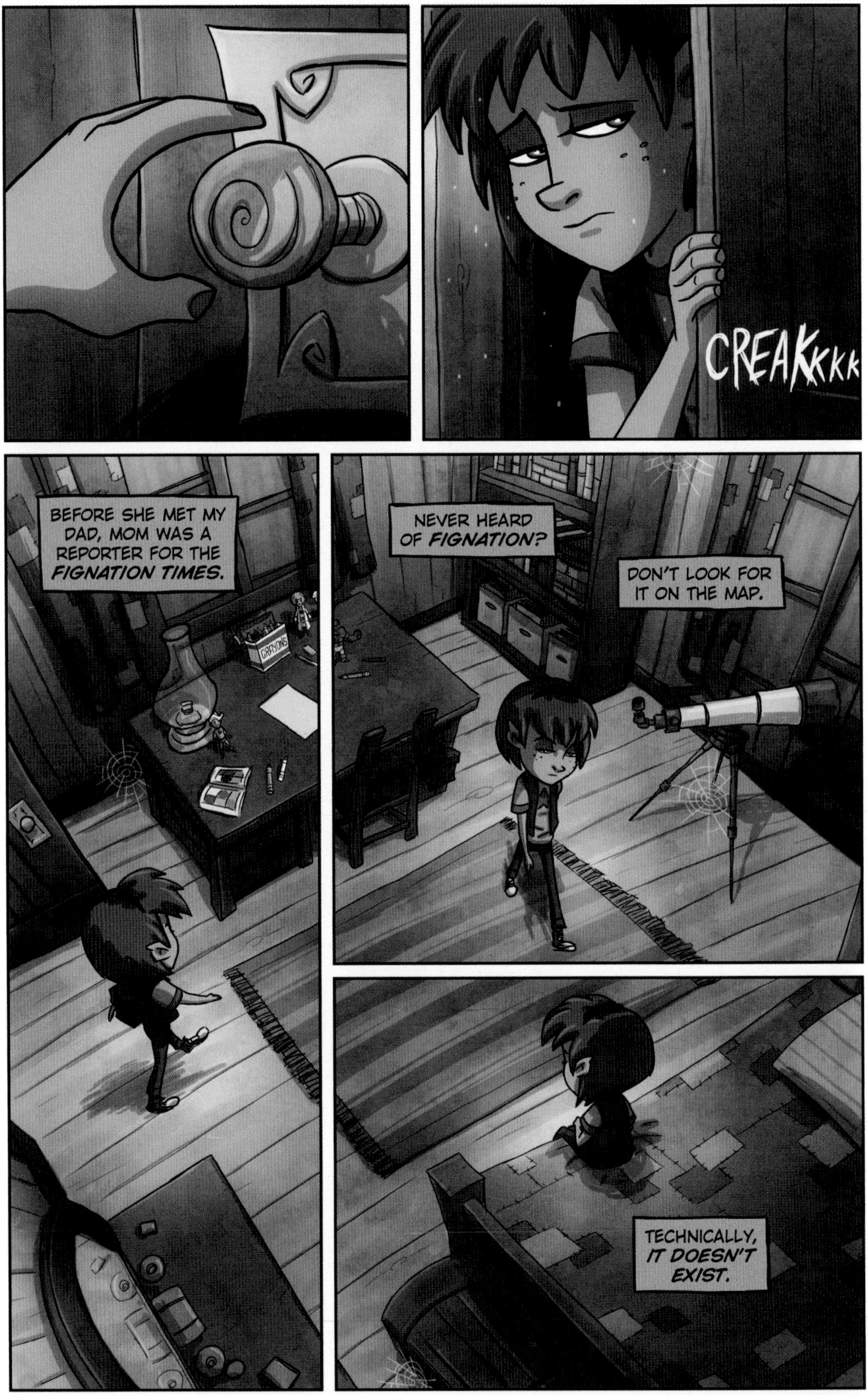
CREAKKKK
BEFORE SHE MET MY DAD, MOM WAS A REPORTER FOR THE *FIGNATION TIMES*.
NEVER HEARD OF *FIGNATION?*
DON'T LOOK FOR IT ON THE MAP.
TECHNICALLY, *IT DOESN'T EXIST*.

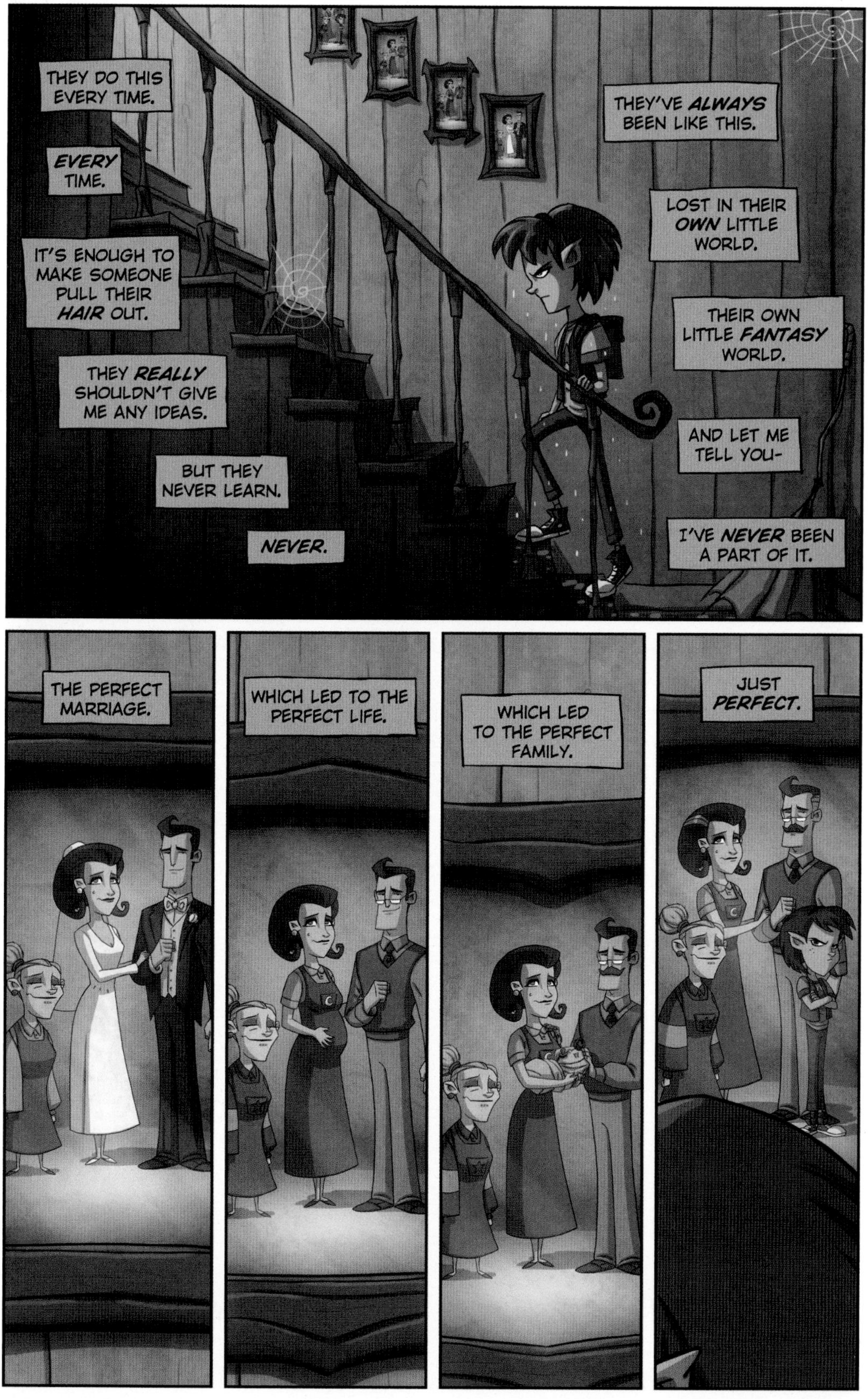
THEY DO THIS EVERY TIME.
EVERY TIME.
IT'S ENOUGH TO MAKE SOMEONE PULL THEIR *HAIR* OUT.
THEY *REALLY* SHOULDN'T GIVE ME ANY IDEAS.
BUT THEY NEVER LEARN.
NEVER.
THEY'VE *ALWAYS* BEEN LIKE THIS.
LOST IN THEIR *OWN* LITTLE WORLD.
THEIR OWN LITTLE *FANTASY* WORLD.
AND LET ME TELL YOU-
I'VE *NEVER* BEEN A PART OF IT.
THE PERFECT MARRIAGE.
WHICH LED TO THE PERFECT LIFE.
WHICH LED TO THE PERFECT FAMILY.
JUST *PERFECT.*

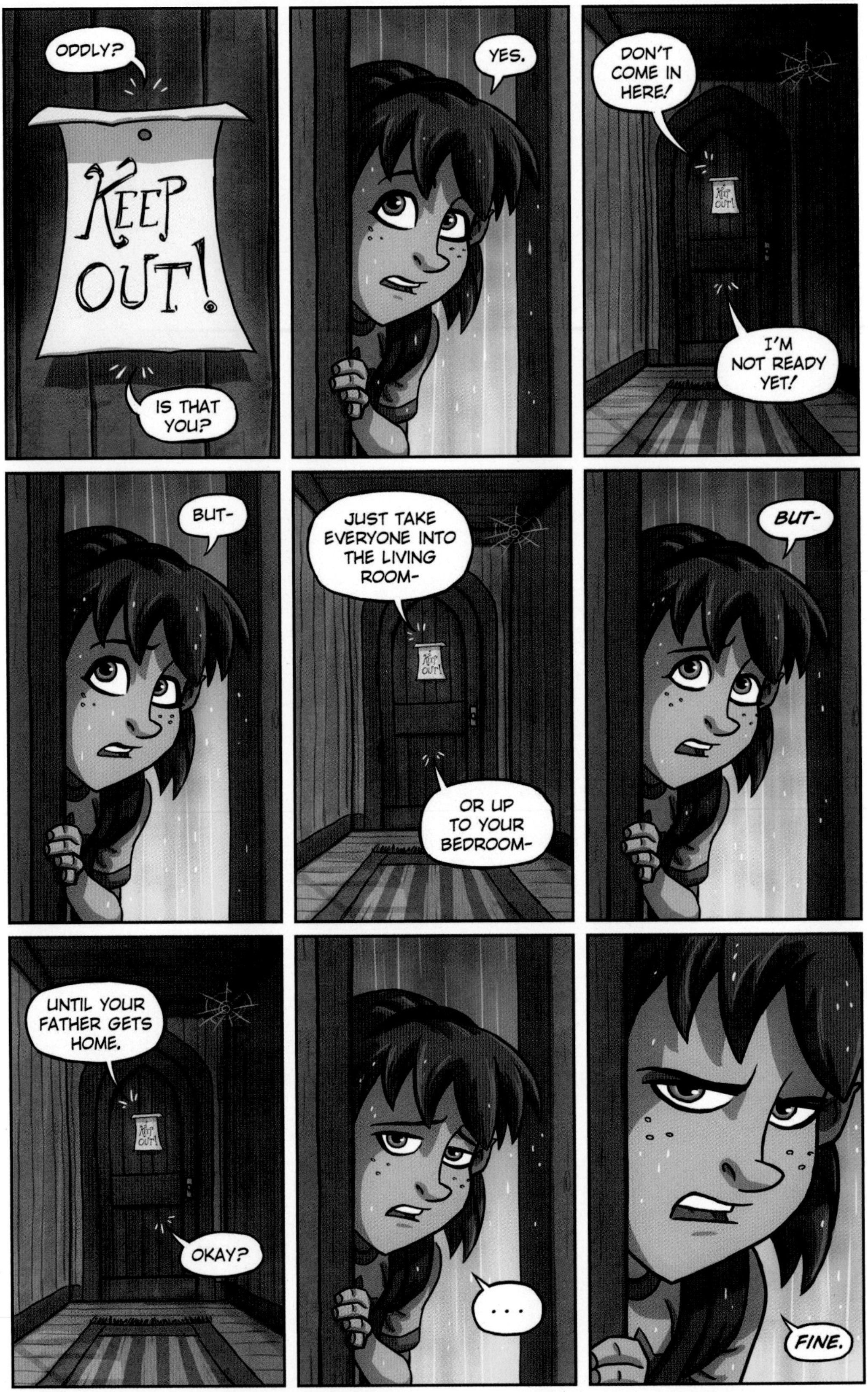
ODDLY?
KEEP OUT!
IS THAT YOU?
YES.
DON'T COME IN HERE!
KEEP OUT!
I'M NOT READY YET!
BUT-
JUST TAKE EVERYONE INTO THE LIVING ROOM-
KEEP OUT!
OR UP TO YOUR BEDROOM-
BUT-
UNTIL YOUR FATHER GETS HOME.
KEEP OUT!
OKAY?
. . .
FINE.

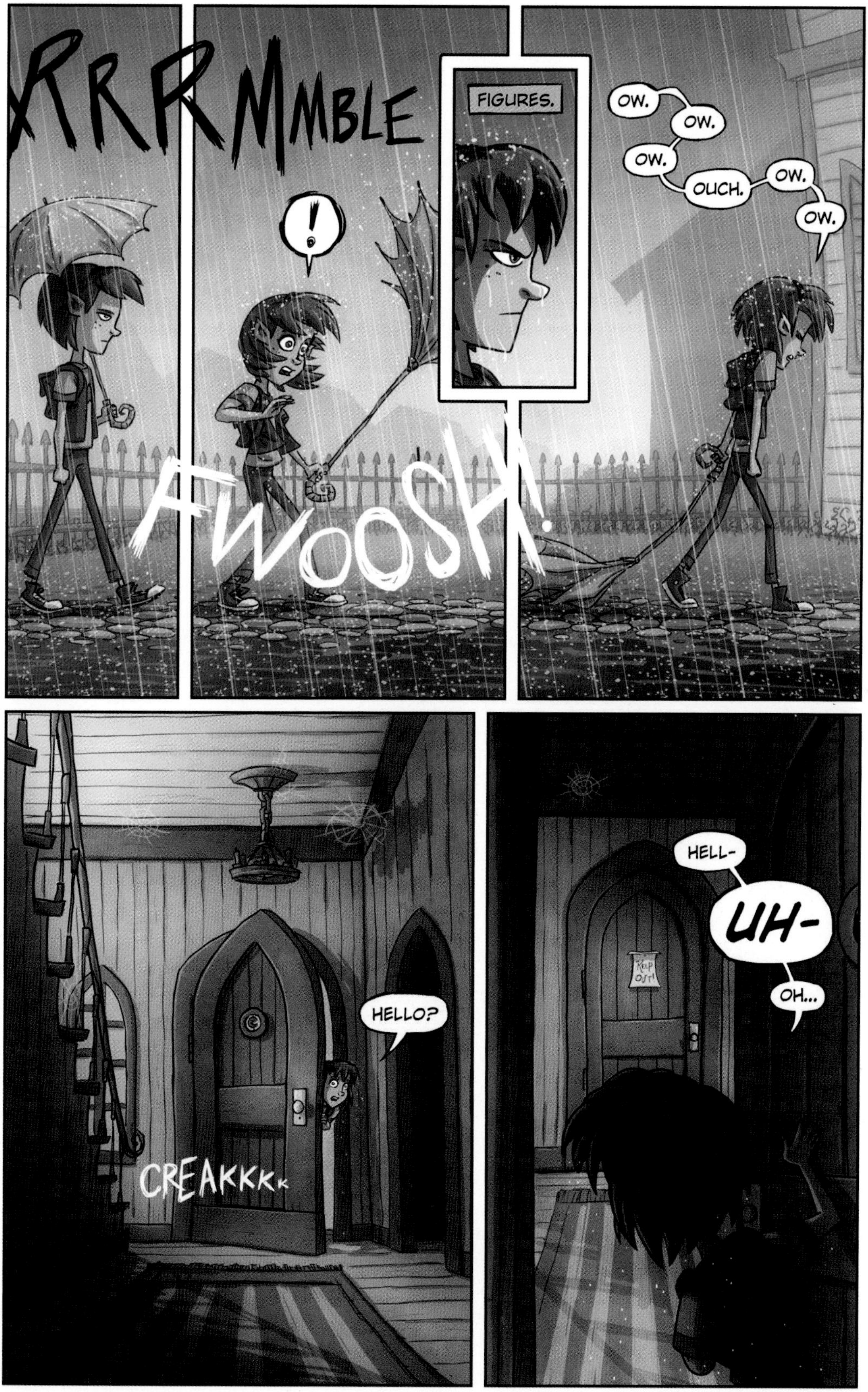

RRRRMMBLE
!
FIGURES.
FWOOSH!
OW.
OW.
OW.
OUCH.
OW.
OW.
HELLO?
CREAKKKK
HELL-
UH-
OH...

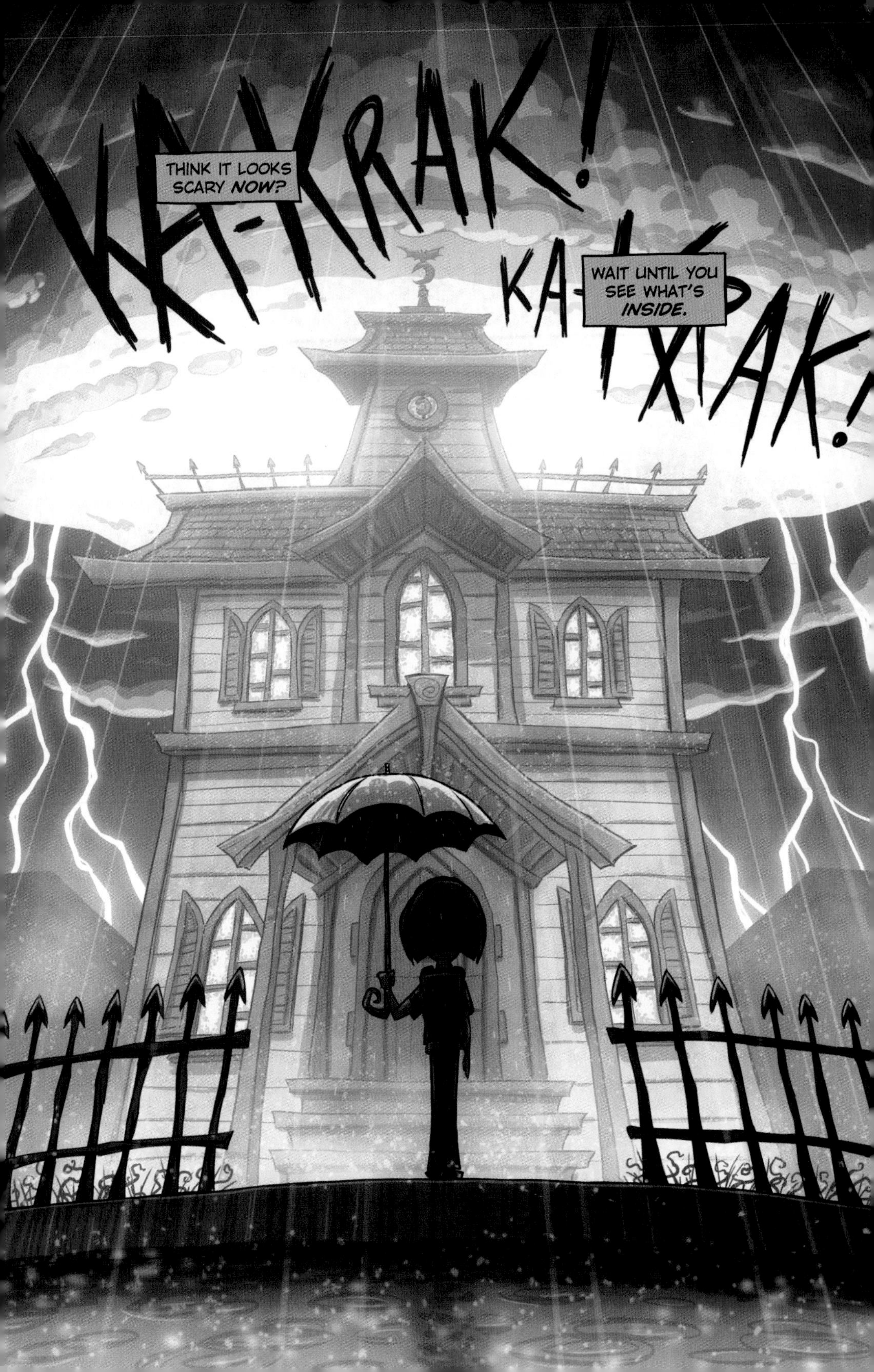
KA-KRAK!
THINK IT LOOKS SCARY NOW?
KA-KRAK!
WAIT UNTIL YOU SEE WHAT'S INSIDE.

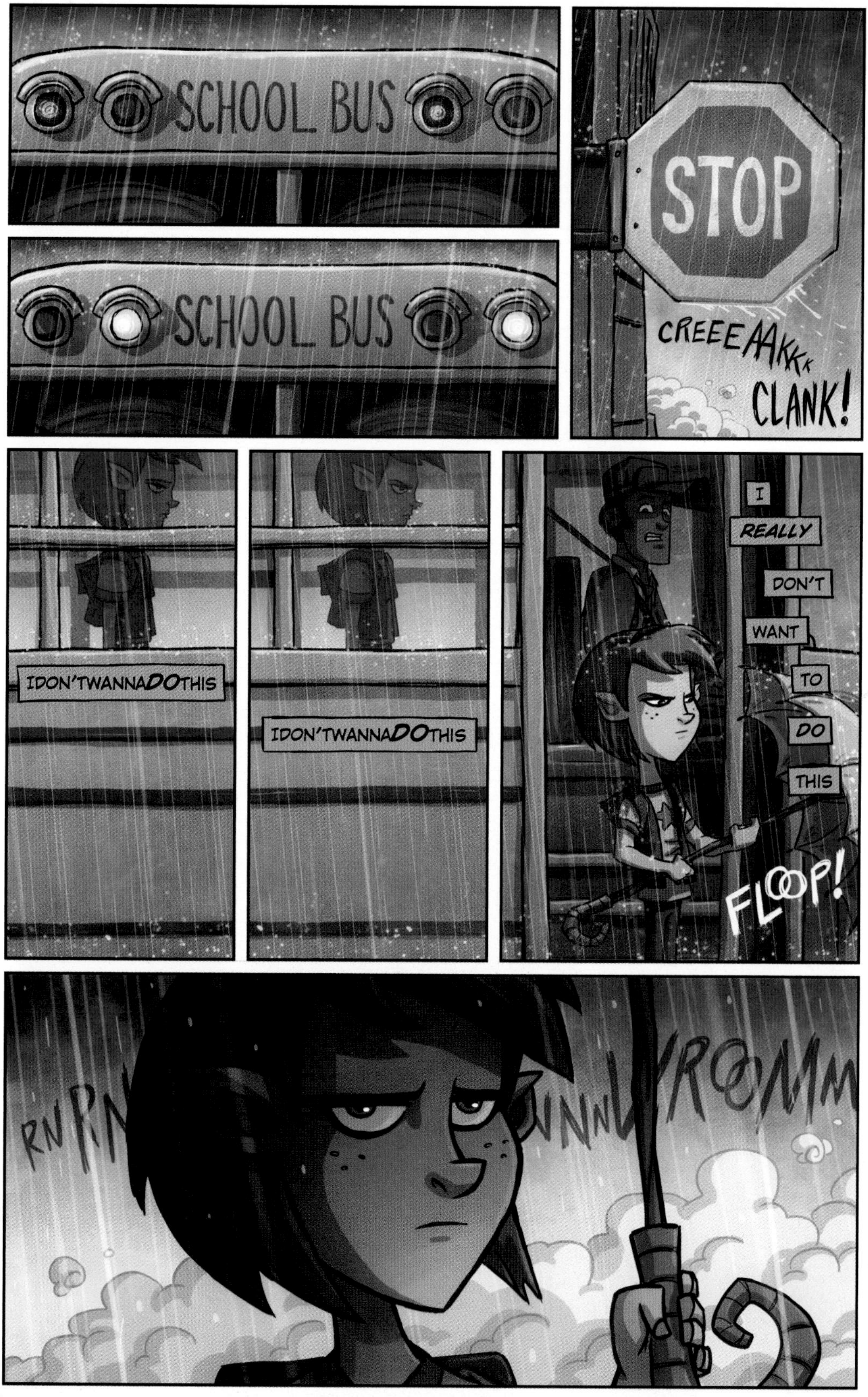

SCHOOL BUS
SCHOOL BUS
STOP
CREEEAAKKK
CLANK!
IDON'TWANNADOTHIS
IDON'TWANNADOTHIS
I
REALLY
DON'T
WANT
TO
DO
THIS
FLOOP!
RNRNNNNVROOMM

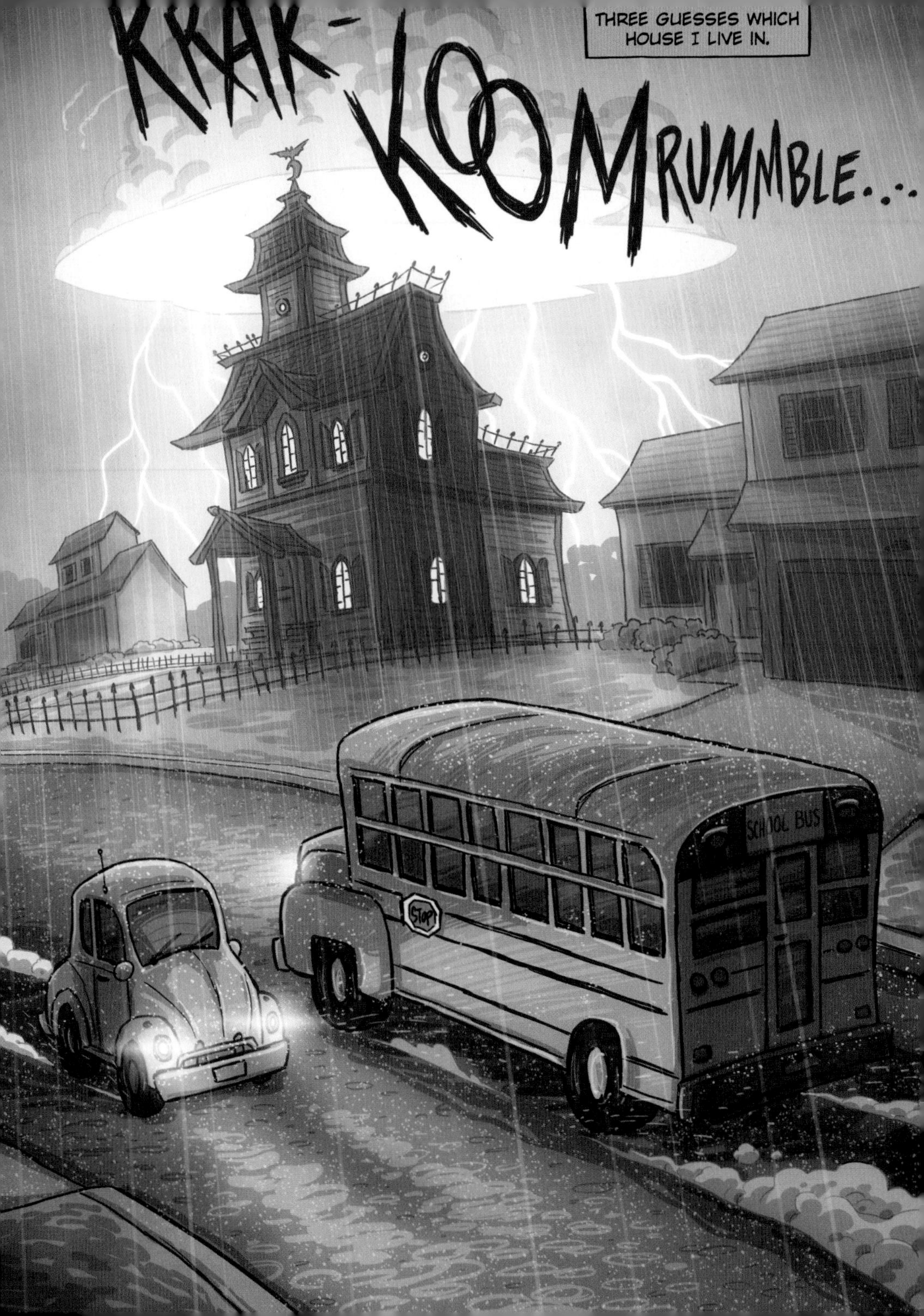
THREE GUESSES WHICH HOUSE I LIVE IN.
KRAK-KOOMRUMMBLE...
SCHOOL BUS
STOP

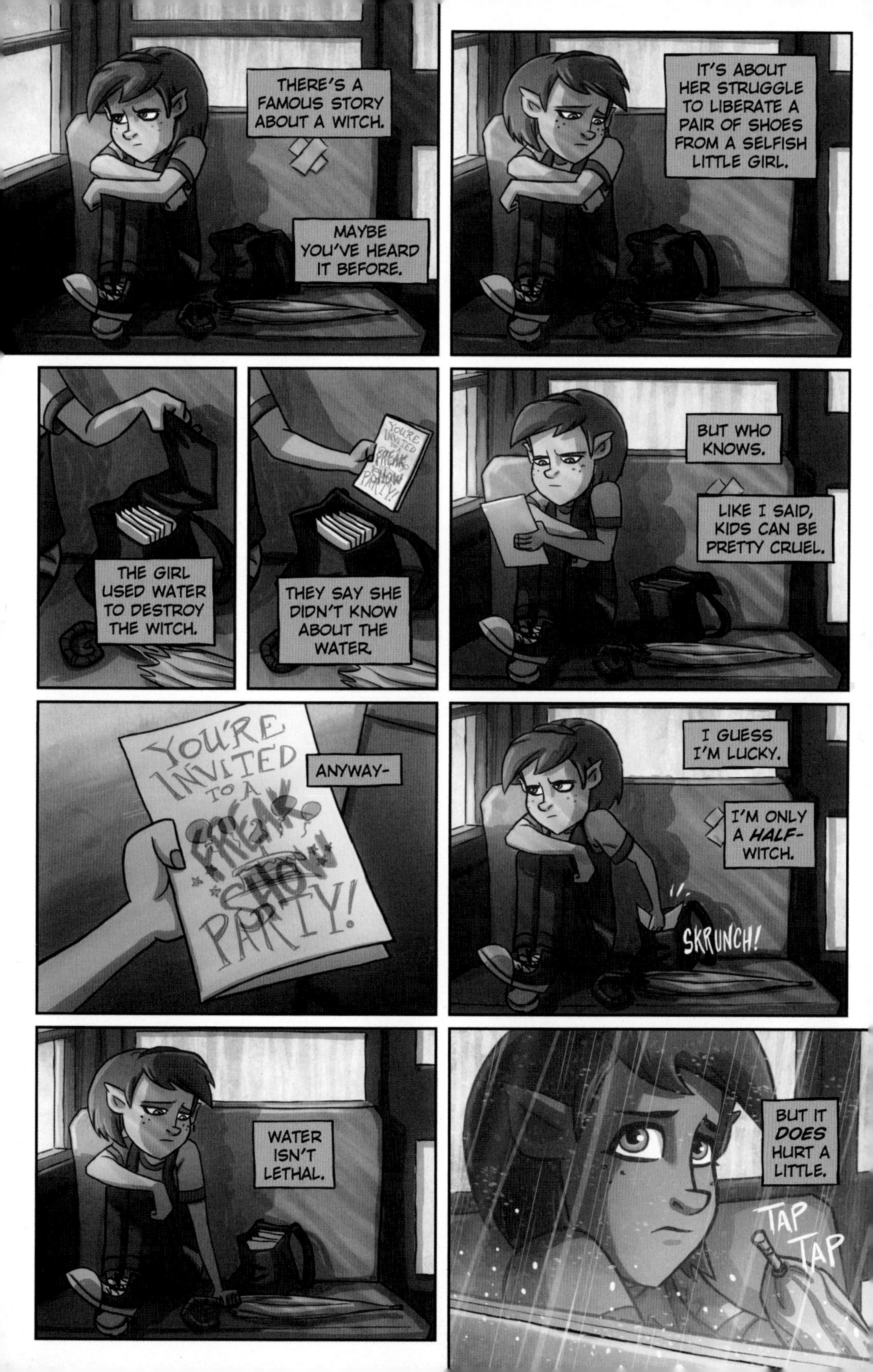
THERE'S A FAMOUS STORY ABOUT A WITCH.
MAYBE YOU'VE HEARD IT BEFORE.
IT'S ABOUT HER STRUGGLE TO LIBERATE A PAIR OF SHOES FROM A SELFISH LITTLE GIRL.
THE GIRL USED WATER TO DESTROY THE WITCH.
YOU'RE INVITED TO A FREAK SHOW PARTY!
THEY SAY SHE DIDN'T KNOW ABOUT THE WATER.
BUT WHO KNOWS.
LIKE I SAID, KIDS CAN BE PRETTY CRUEL.
YOU'RE INVITED TO A FREAK SHOW PARTY!
ANYWAY-
I GUESS I'M LUCKY.
I'M ONLY A *HALF*-WITCH.
SKRUNCH!
WATER ISN'T LETHAL.
BUT IT *DOES* HURT A LITTLE.
TAP TAP

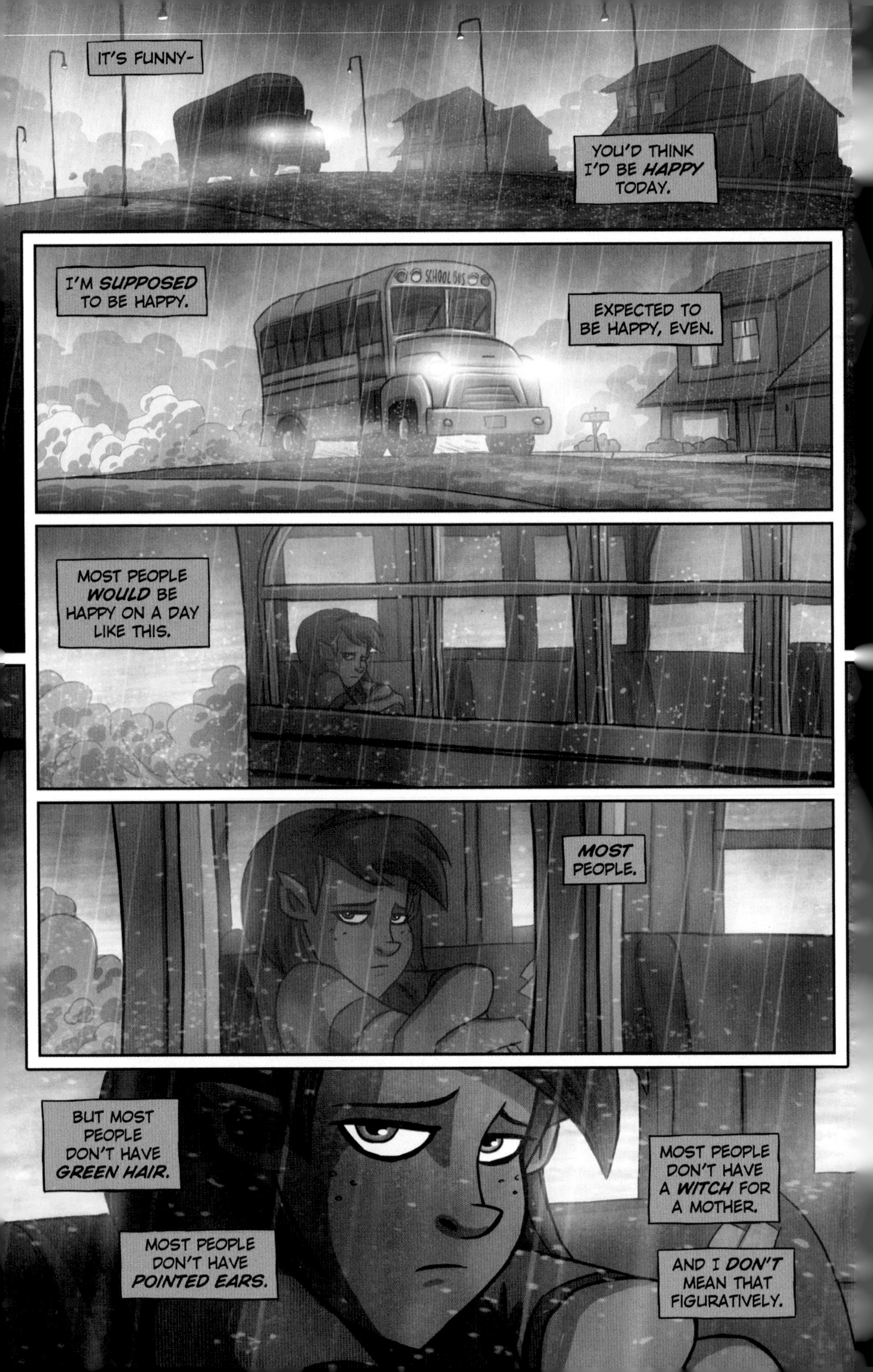
IT'S FUNNY-
YOU'D THINK I'D BE HAPPY TODAY.
I'M SUPPOSED TO BE HAPPY.
SCHOOL BUS
EXPECTED TO BE HAPPY, EVEN.
MOST PEOPLE WOULD BE HAPPY ON A DAY LIKE THIS.
MOST PEOPLE.
BUT MOST PEOPLE DON'T HAVE GREEN HAIR.
MOST PEOPLE DON'T HAVE POINTED EARS.
MOST PEOPLE DON'T HAVE A WITCH FOR A MOTHER.
AND I DON'T MEAN THAT FIGURATIVELY.

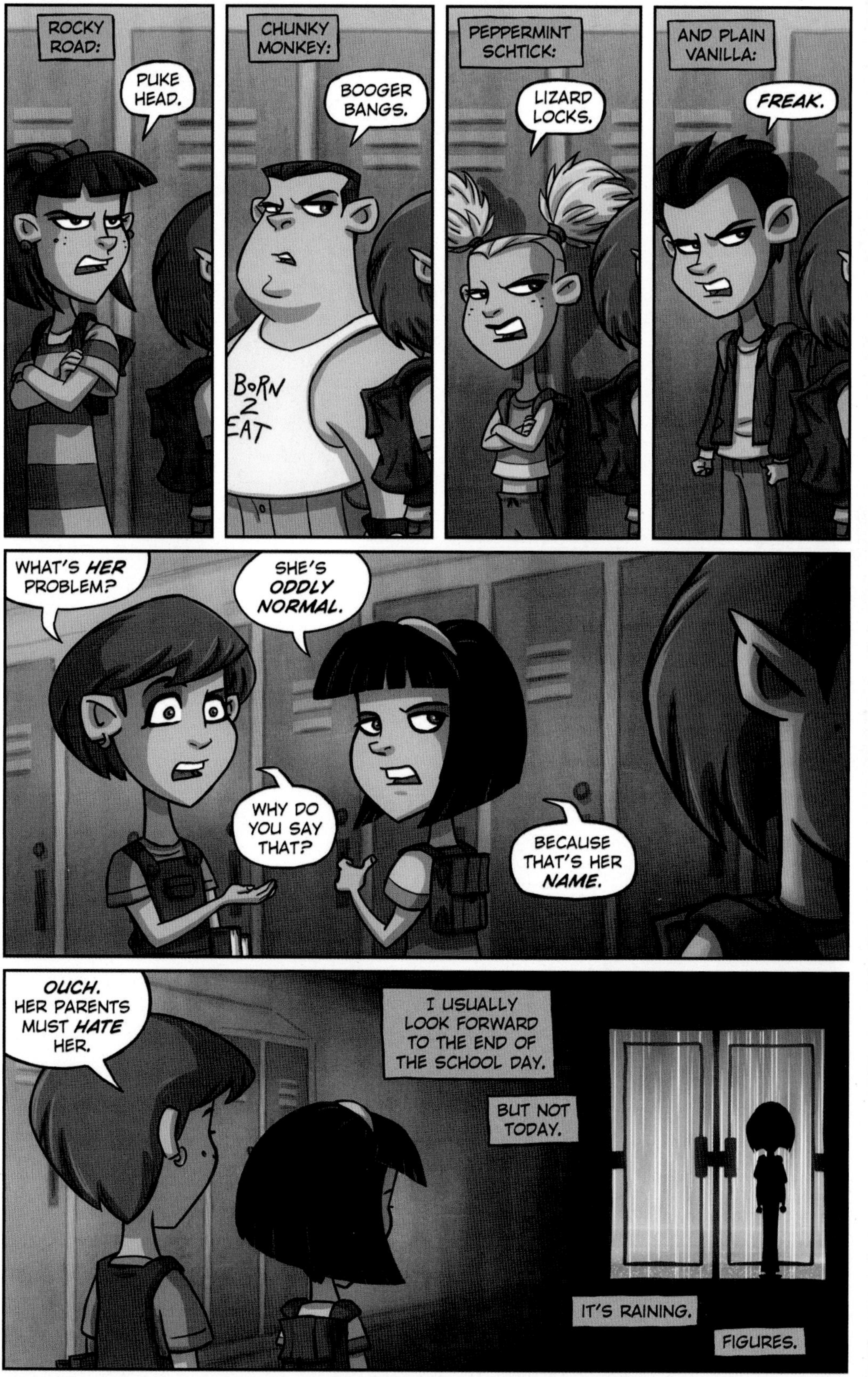
ROCKY ROAD:
PUKE HEAD.
CHUNKY MONKEY:
BOOGER BANGS.
BORN 2 EAT
PEPPERMINT SCHTICK:
LIZARD LOCKS.
AND PLAIN VANILLA:
FREAK.
WHAT'S HER PROBLEM?
SHE'S ODDLY NORMAL.
WHY DO YOU SAY THAT?
BECAUSE THAT'S HER NAME.
OUCH. HER PARENTS MUST HATE HER.
I USUALLY LOOK FORWARD TO THE END OF THE SCHOOL DAY.
BUT NOT TODAY.
IT'S RAINING.
FIGURES.

Chapter 1

Be Careful What You Wish For

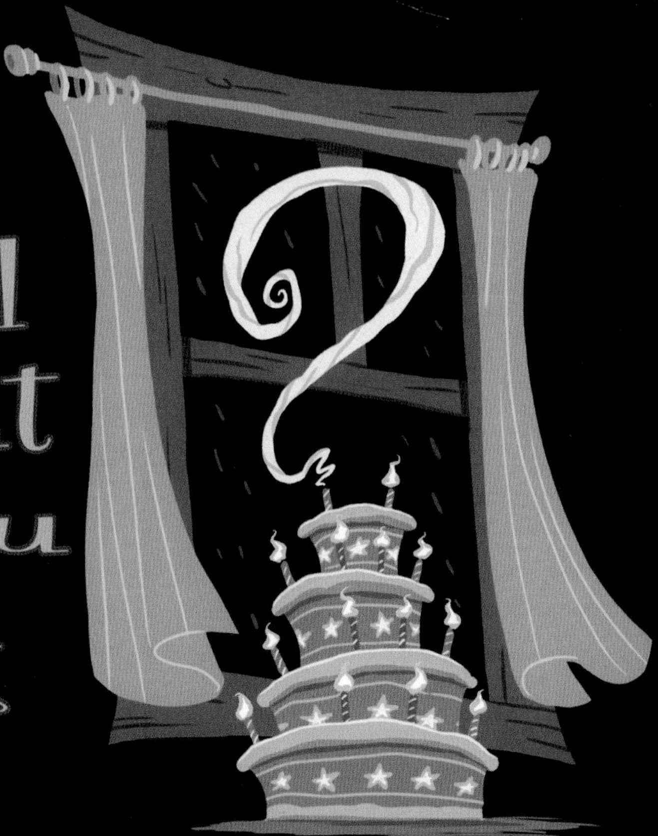

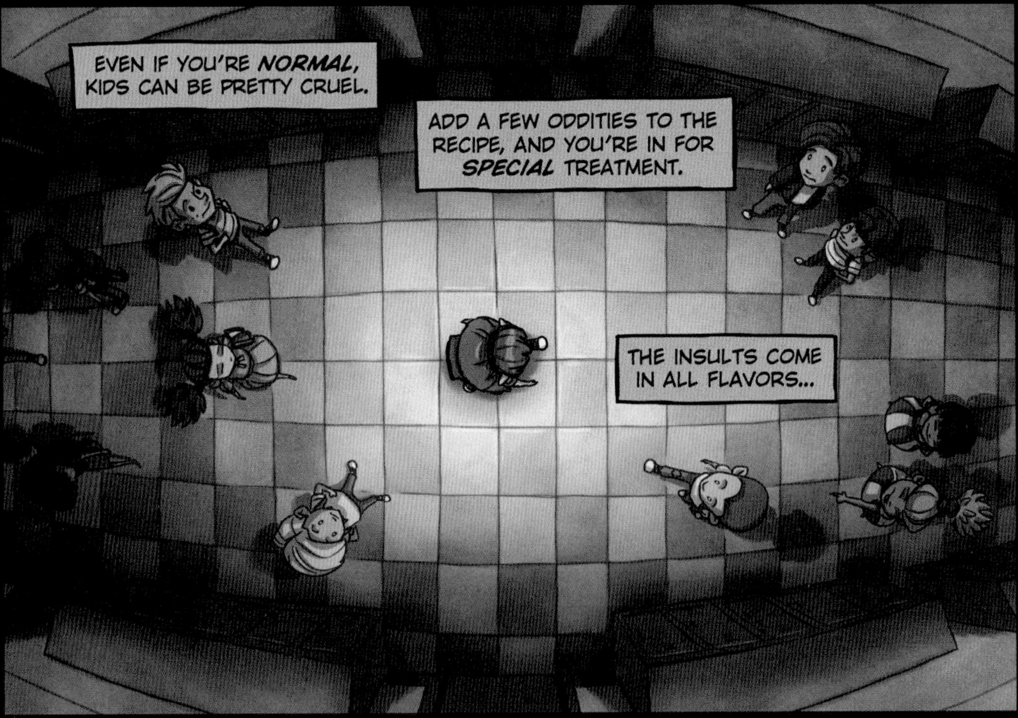

EVEN IF YOU'RE NORMAL, KIDS CAN BE PRETTY CRUEL.
ADD A FEW ODDITIES TO THE RECIPE, AND YOU'RE IN FOR SPECIAL TREATMENT.
THE INSULTS COME IN ALL FLAVORS...

ACKNOWLEDGMENTS

Thank you to everyone who helped make "Oddly Normal" a reality!

To Mom and Dad... your support for me and my work has been invaluable.

To Eric Stephenson and everyone at Image Comics. Having the Image "i" on my creator-owned comic is a dream come true.

To my awesome colorist team: Tracy Bailey, Daniel Mead and Thomas Boatwright.

To the amazing and generous artists who contributed variant covers to issues 2-4: Rob Guillory, Katie Cook, Robb Mommaerts and Dani Jones.

To the many friends and colleagues who have been there for me over the years, including... Leigh Boone, Pat Bussey, Ronn Dech, Tracy Edmunds, Adam Fellows, Brian Fies, Jessie Garza, Grant Gould, Judy Hansen, Gisela Hernandez-Rosa, Josh Howard, John J. Walsh IV and Kate Youngdahl.

And last but not least... many thanks to my "Oddly Normal 2.0" Kickstarter supporters:

Janel A, Regi Aaron, Kathryn Alice, Charles Alvis, John Anthony, Matthew Ashcraft, Ray B., David Barnett, Hudson On Bass, Bchan84, Jessie Beck, Alison Benowitz, Jennifer Berk, Daniel Blackburn, Daniel J. Blomberg IV, Leigh Boone, Brian Braatz, Sacha Brady, Michael Branham, Dominic Brennan, Mark Brenner, John Brown, Darren Calvert, Jeffrey Chandler, Michael Chapman, Chris, Chooi, Chouck, Cody Christopher, Justin Chung, Coffinail, Christopher Cole, CoolB, Cathy Cooper, Corrodias, Aaron Cullers, Julian Damy, Brad Dancer, Lara Dann, Joséantonio W. Danner, Daniel & Kanako, Ted Dastick Jr., DebraS, Ronn Dech, James DeMarco, Harald Demler, Arik Devens, Vic DiGital, Brandon Eaker, Tracy Edmunds, Jamas Enright, Susan Eisner, Leandro Garcia Estevam, Evilgeniuslady, Harry Ewasiuk, Dan Eyer, Adam Fellows, Brian Fies, Fletcher, Phil Flickinger, Thomas Forsythe, Mary Frampton, Tracey Frampton, Corey Funt, Andrea Futrelle, Gdm_online, George, Tim Goldenburg, Sara Gordon, Stuart Gorman, Ingrid K. V. Hardy, Michael Hawk, Helena S. M., Jessica Hightower, Stephen Hill, David Hopkins, Michael Hunter, Chris Inoue, Arul Isai Imran, Jayvs1, Delores Jeffrey, Jimi, JMShelledy, Wendy Johnson-Diedrich, Dani Jones, Anne K, Peter Karmanos III, Kathryn, Kelso, Thanun Khowdee, Kirsten, André Kishimoto, Veronika Knurenko, Matthew Koelbl, Laura Kokaisel, Axel 'dervideospieler' Kothe, Karen Krajenbrink, Zeus & Hera Kramer, Manuel Kroeber, Tom Kurzanski, Amber Lanagan, Patrick Larcada, Jeremie Lariviere, Linda LeClair, Matt Leitzen, Yoni Limor, Lulu Lin, Tim Lindvall, Rick Long, Lisa M. Lorelli, MageAkyla, Dan Manson, Marina, Miles Matton, Fergus Maximus, Jamie McIntyre, Tim McKnight, Jeff McRorie, Daniel Mead, Jeff Metzner, Michael and Liz, Mika, Miroatme, Riaz Skrenes Missaghi, Casey Moeller, Björn Morén, Rich Moulton, Movet, Matthew Munk, Molly Murphy, Jussi Myllyluoma, John Nacinovich, Cynthia Narcisi, Bruce Nelson, Sian Nelson, Niels, Michael "Waffles" Nguyen, Rhonda Parker, James Parris, Merrisa Patel, Shane & Marjan Patrick, C. Raymond Pechonick, Tawnly Pranger, David Recor, Rhel, Ben Rosenthal, Harrison Sayre, Ryan Schrodt, Patrick Scullin, Nick Seal, Jenny Seay, Senatorhung, Sgllama, Shervyn, Todd Shipman, Andy Shuping, Ashtara Silunar, Skraldesovs, Chazen Smith, Stephen Smoogen, Ryan Snow, Daniel Snyder, Stormy, Stu, Stephen Stutesman, Erik Taylor, Bruce Thompson, Tialessa, Kevin Tian, Tom Tinneny, Rachel Tougas, PJ Trauger, TriOmegaZero, Mai Tzimaka, Tim The Unlucky, Frankie Vanity, Martha Wald, James P. Walker, John J. Walsh IV, Shannon Wendlick, Paul Westover, A. M. White, Heath White, Kiwi Wiltshire, Daniel Winterhalter, Stephen "Switt!" Wittmaak, Christoph Wolf, Emiko Wong, Ryan Worrell, Samuel Young, Zabuni, and Matt Zollmann.

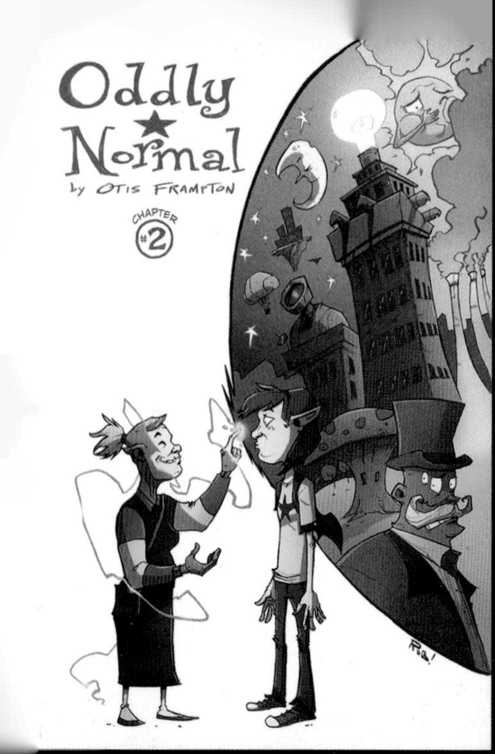
Oddly Normal
by Otis Frampton
Chapter #2

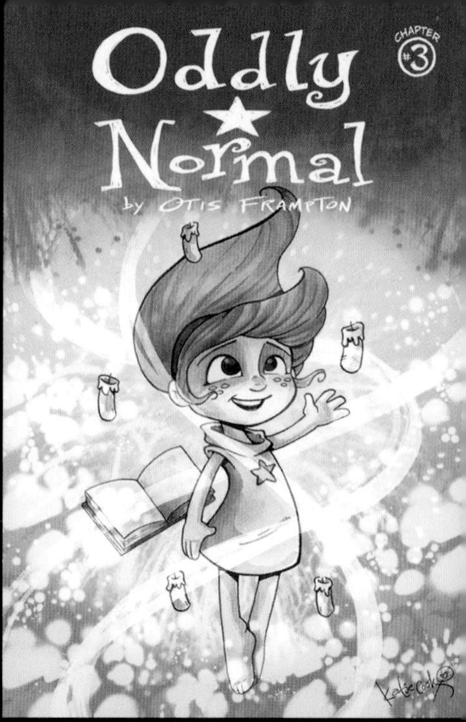
Oddly Normal
Chapter #3
by Otis Frampton

ISSUE #2 VARIANT COVER BY
ROB GUILLORY

ISSUE #3 VARIANT COVER BY
KATIE COOK

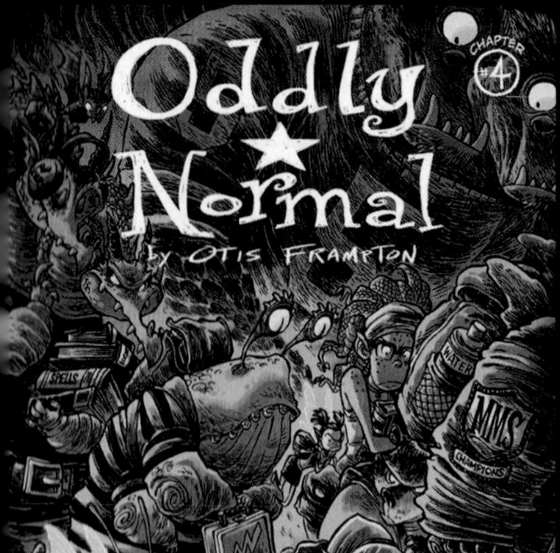
Oddly Normal
Chapter #4
by Otis Frampton

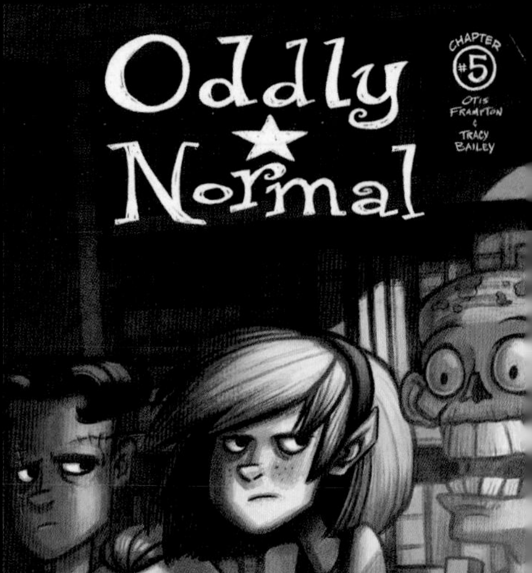
Oddly Normal
Chapter #5
Otis Frampton & Tracy Bailey
Literature

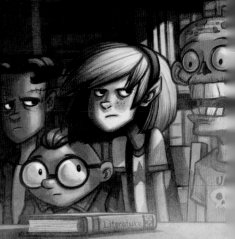